# An Orphan's Song

**H. M. R. Dueck**

# *An Orphan's Song*

## H. M. R. Dueck

*Windflower*
*Communications*

Winnipeg, Manitoba, Canada

*An Orphan's Song* Copyright ©1993 Hilda Dueck

Published by Windflower Communications
Winnipeg, Manitoba, Canada

Canadian Cataloguing in Publication Data

Dueck, H. M. R. (Hilda M. Riediger)
  An orphan's song
  ISBN 1-895308-16-X
I. Title.
PS8557.U3507 1993  C813'.54  C93-098199-5
PR9199.3.D8307 1993

Windflower Communications gratefully acknowledges the assistance of the Manitoba Arts Council for the publication of this book.

Cover design by Kathyrn Dahl, Winnipeg, Manitoba
Printed in Canada by Derksen Printers, Steinbach, Manitoba

International Standard Book Number: 1-895308-16-X

# ACKNOWLEDGEMENTS

My sincere thanks to Henry and Katie for sharing this story, and for their patience and trust during the years that it took for this book to take shape.

To my husband Ernie and daughter Karla, for their encouragement and faith in me, a heartfelt thank-you.

. . . . .

The characters and events in this novel are based on real people and actual events as told to the author by Henry and Katie Huebert. In some instances, where details were sketchy, events have been reconstructed in keeping with what most likely took place. Some of the dates are approximate and several names have been changed.

In spite of careful attention to the factual account, this is a work of fiction.

# CONTENTS

# 1

# A ROCKING HORSE
# FOR MATHEW

The garage is cool in spite of the blast of hot air from the heater hanging in the corner of the room, but Henry does not notice as he runs the tips of his fingers over the wooden surface of the rocking horse he is making. Just now it is little more than a lifeless, wooden shape with stiff, immovable legs, hardly the galloping "horsey" his three-year-old grandson's dreams are made of.

But in his mind it is there—Moschka—small and graceful, with a proud, aristocratic head and warm, intelligent eyes—a reincarnation from another lifetime—little more than a fragment of a dream of a past that still haunts him, sometimes filling him with pain so intense that he struggles to escape the nightmare, but at other times, like when he remembers *Moschka*, filling him with comfort and warmth, even after all these years.

Mathew's horse will have a mane and a tail, a leather saddle and stirrups, and the motionless legs will spring to life as soon as the rockers are attached.

There is quiet satisfaction in Henry's face, in spite of its grey pallor. It is really such a little thing to do for his grandson. Until now, the only horse the little boy has known is an imaginary one as he bounces merrily on his grandfather's knee and they both sing in German, *"Hop, hop, hop, hop, hop, Pferdchen lauf gallop."*

A rasping cough catches Henry, violently shaking his tall, slightly bent frame as he takes up the sand paper and resumes his work. There is an urgency about his movements, like those

1

of a wood carver intent on releasing his work of art from its wooden prison.

A phantom emerges in his memory like an apparition in a prairie snowstorm. It beckons and he follows, carried by the steady swish, swish of the sandpaper in his hand, away from the security of the Alberta town he calls home, away from the Huebert name he has adopted, back to some forgotten road he must have travelled once outside a long forgotten Russian village when he was still Heinz Rempel.

He does not remember his age, only that it is winter and bitterly cold. He hears the sound of horse's hooves beating a quick staccato against the snow-covered road behind him. A horse and rider pass, the horse groaning sharply with each hoof beat. Its brown coat glistens wet and frothy from the exertion. The rider spurs it on, shouting for it to go faster.

By the time Henry arrives in the village there is no sign of the rider, but the brave little horse stands alone outside, its head tied high, engulfed in a cloud of steaming breath, its heaving body wrapped in the hoary blanket of its own frozen lather.

It still stands . . . an eerie, white phantom . . . fixed in Henry's memory like the thousands of other memories from his past. Why, he can not tell. . . . Maybe someday he will tell Mathew about the brave little nameless horse.

Another angry cough rips through Henry's lungs, doubling him over with pain just as Katie comes through the breezeway door into the garage with a cup of tea and a plate of crackers.

With him having to eat so often, she usually brings his snacks out to him. It saves him having to fuss with taking off and putting on the dusty coveralls which she simply won't have in the house.

"Gee whiz, Henry!" she explodes, "You gotta go see the doctor. I don't like the way your lungs are actin' up." She pronounces the "th's" like "d's" and her "r's" roll gently as she speaks, betraying a German accent that has not worn off even after almost sixty years of living in Canada. Everything about her, from the simple threadbare housedress hanging over her strong frame, with the print bib apron pinned to it, to the salt and pepper *Schups* knotted at the nape of her neck, reflect a

Mennonite tradition alien to the easy slang she uses. Apparently something has rubbed off from the "English neighbours" as she refers to the town's people, regardless of their nationalities.

Henry does not look at her, but continues sanding.

"I don't like that cough, Henry," she says, setting the snack on the arm of an unpainted lawn chair. "I can hear you chokin' and coughin' all the way from the kitchen! You gotta' go see the doctor!" She has been after him for the past few days to make an appointment. Lately the cough has been getting much worse and it scares her. At night he is awake coughing, walking the floor. During the day, working in the cold garage in the sawdust, he can hardly breathe. She can tell he is in pain, even though he won't admit it. He is a stubborn man.

"Henry, are you listening?" Impatience colours her voice. "I said you gotta go see a doctor!"

"I hear ya' loud and clear," Henry retorts tersely.

"Well?" she needles.

"Well," he says firmly, "I'm better off stayin' right here. All the doctor will do is put me back into the hospital again."

"You don't know that for sure," she replies, "anyway, they might be able to help you get better."

"Or kill me," he says with conviction.

"Now Henry!" Katie exclaims.

"You forgot what happened last time?"

"I know, I know, they cut back on your insulin too much . . . "

"And I went into coma and just about died," he interrupts. There is a bitter edge to Henry's voice. These people are all the same. He has learned that long ago. . . . "I told them, but they knew better, and look what happened." He pauses. "I can take better care of myself at home!"

"I know Henry, you're real good with the diabetes," Katie soothes, "real good, but your lungs . . . "

"They'll mess with the insulin Katie. They always do when they put me on other medication."

She knows there is no use arguing. He will have to make up his own mind. Hopefully it won't be too late.

She turns abruptly towards the breezeway door. "Mathew would be just as happy with the red barn," she says pointedly, without looking at him.

The door closes resolutely behind her while Henry sits down in the lawn chair to eat his mid-morning snack. His eyes take in his cluttered surrounding. The garage is piled high with his handiwork and contains any number of things he could give Mathew. Katie is right, the little hip-roofed barn would make a fine present, or even the red, wooden wagon, but it would not be the same. Mathew is wishing for a rocking horse. . . .

He gets up slowly, panting from the effort, moves back to the rocking horse and painstakingly continues his sanding. He works with determination, his jaw set against the pain licking like hot flames in his chest. His grandson will discover soon enough that life is full of disappointments and broken promises. For now his Grandpa will see to it that the boy has his horse!

A vision of another little boy floats before Henry's eyes. His tear-stained face nuzzles into the soft dapple-grey coat of a little horse. . . . Ah yes, Henry sighs inwardly—Moschka.

Memories surge into view, threatening to take him where he does not wish to go. Henry's jaw tightens as he fights to rein in his racing emotions. Some things are better left alone . . . no need to dig up the past. . . .

Katie's words echo menacingly through his mind—"Mathew would be just as happy with the red barn"—she makes it sound so simple, but what does she know? No, he chides himself, he shouldn't blame her. Can't expect her to know what a little horse can mean to a boy, even to one who isn't an orphan.

The soft swish, swish of Henry's sandpaper continues purposefully, like the plaintive accompaniment to some ancient song, while outside the town of Tofield lies snow covered and silent, snuggled against its twin life-sources, the highway and the railroad, like a child secure against its mother's breast. It is a healthy growing Alberta town, almost an oddity among its many prairie siblings who have died or are in the process of dying, having been abandoned or neglected for one reason or another.

Still, if Tofield is aware of its tenuous privilege, it does not speak of it. Only in its compulsive work ethic, its stubborn resistance to change, its gossipy self-awareness, and its almost

4

fanatic loyalty, does it communicate most eloquently its awareness that life and death are never far apart. For even in Tofield, the struggle for survival has never stopped.

At first the people are indistinguishable from each other, painted in a drabness that blurs one face into the next, erasing distinctions. There is an uncanny sameness, like the sameness of a man and a woman who have lived together for many years. Or is it a mask they have chosen to wear to protect themselves from prying eyes, or perhaps even from themselves?

Henry is part of this town, has been for the past forty-three years, ever since he moved off the farm in the Lindbrook district ten kilometers west to build a feed mill in the town. It is gone now, only an empty lot where it once stood. The years in the mill, working in the grain dust, have not been kind to his "bad lung."

It is twelve years since the doctor told him he would have to give up his work. Twelve years since he tore down the mill with his own hands. But he is not bitter. He has already made it past his seventy-second birthday, and "that's not bad when you're living on borrowed time like I am," he tells people. Besides, how can he blame the mill? The doctor tells him that his troubles go back a long, long time, long before the mill.

Maybe he has known it all along, except it has been easier to blame the dust on the mill. But he knows the "bad lung" is just one more of the wounds from the Russian Revolution. It is as though all the pain of those early years of his life has buried itself deep in his chest, embedded in a bad lung that will, like the memories, not be appeased.

Perhaps it is because he is retired now that the past haunts him more. He tells himself that, but even then he knows the truth. He has been going back all his life, retreating behind the silent walls of the past, searching for the broken fragments of that other lifetime to piece together what might remain, to recapture the wholeness that must have belonged to that time too distant to be remembered. Somewhere in that hazy past is a part of himself . . . lost . . . a part he needs to recover somehow.

There is often a wistfulness in his face as he stands at the kitchen window, looking out at that empty lot. Somehow, he has always thought that time would heal some of the old wounds and help him recapture the distant dreams of what must have been home.

Not that he hasn't had a home. He has lived in Alberta for most of his seventy-two years. Fifty-one of those years have been spent with his Katie, making a home for their three sons and one daughter. It is what he has lived for.

The children, Wilmer, Rudy, Dennis, and Brenda are all grown now and married, with children and homes of their own. Not a day passes that he does not give thanks for them and each one who is added to his family.

But even after all these years, his childhood dream of somehow going back to his own home and family, the one he never really had, has not faded. Over the years he has carefully gathered up pieces of his forgotten past any way he can: from the few distant relatives he has found, from asking around, from reading—trying to recreate the home, the family to which he, Heinz Rempel, really belonged. Details don't always fit, and in the end he has to decide what to believe and what to discard.

His jaw tightens. Dreams . . . that's all he's had to hang on to . . . and the fragile hope that time won't run out before he finds what he has been looking for all these years.

The shabby, grey, two-storey house where he and Katie raised their children hovers like a shadow behind the new, white bungalow that his sons helped him build, constantly reminding him that time is slipping by. Maybe it's too late already. The thought torments him. But he does not speak of it, even when he and Katie stand next to each other doing dishes together at the kitchen sink, as they do every day now. It is easier to talk of other things, or not to talk at all.

Their new home, with its quiet, almost solemn dignity is not unlike the others in this town. Its white awnings are edged in black, and there is an ornate black grille railing around the cement front porch and down the stairs.

In the summer, the yard is an orderly pattern of trees and flowers. A wooden wishing well which he has made stands boldly on the lawn. The bird house, hangs in the branches of the spruce tree, awash with a wren's song whenever she takes a rest from feeding her noisy family.

But now in January the bird house hangs empty in the branches, and the house blends into the bleakness of the snowy yard. Beyond the attached garage that serves as Henry's workshop and hidden from view behind a high white board fence is a patio where he and Katie often sit in the evening, near a huge garden plot that Katie lovingly tends from early spring to late fall. It too is buried beneath the mounds of snow, like much of his past, awaiting the return of the warm promise of the summer sun.

"Henry!" Katie's voice jolts him from his reverie. She is standing in the doorway and impatience edges her voice. "You're not lookin' at your watch again. It's after twelve o'clock already. You gotta eat somet'in'!"

A glance at the empty plate standing on the arm rest of the lawn chair reassures her that at least he has eaten the mid-morning snack she brought him a few hours ago. Good thing too, she muses. Ever since they found out he has sugar diabetes on top of his bad lungs, she has to watch him like a hawk. Without her, he forgets to eat when he's supposed to.

Even when she brings his snacks out to him, if she doesn't stay and make sure he eats, he sometimes forgets and goes into a coma. It's happened a few times already. She shudders, remembering. She goes to the cupboard where they have the recipe for the sugary drink and the straws that bend. Her hands are shaking so much she can hardly hold the glass, but she holds it close to his mouth, pushing the end of the straw between his teeth.

"Suck on the straw, Henry. Come on! Drink!" She drags him out of the fog, nagging and badgering him, all the while praying that he won't die. . . . Not her Henry. . . . Not this time. She can't bear to think of being without him.

She has even gone with him to the city hospital for a special course so that she can help him look after his diabetes—she, a simple Mennonite housewife who didn't get beyond grade five before she had to quit school and work out to earn money to help feed and clothe her brothers and sisters. She, taking a course. Imagine!

7

The coldness in the garage abruptly brings Katie back to her present concern with Henry. "My gosh," she says in exasperation to no one in particular, "he's going to be the death of me yet!" Then her eyes fix accusingly on Henry.

"Seven times a day I gotta feed you! Seven times! At least you could get yourself inside on time for *Meddach* so I can keep you alive!" She is barely aware that she has slipped from English to Low German as she speaks, so agitated has she become.

Henry straightens slowly, brushing at the wood dust on his coveralls. His face is expressionless as he says drolly, "Haven't ever heard of nobody dying from waiting a few seconds."

He throws Katie a sidelong glance. "Guess there's always the first time."

There is hardly a trace of an accent in his speech, evidence of years of business dealings in the community and his dogged determination to speak his adopted language properly in spite of his lack of education.

Katie catches the mocking note in Henry's voice, but before she can reply another coughing spell seizes him. She waits a few minutes until he regains his composure and then she is gone.

Henry steps back to inspect the little horse, grimacing as he straightens. Then he peels off his coveralls and goes through the chilly hallway connecting the garage and the house, leaving his shoes just inside the kitchen door.

Katie has the fried potatoes and farmer sausage on the table by the time Henry takes his place at the head of the table. She hurries back to the kitchen counter and brings the tea pot to the table, sitting down with a tired sigh. Instinctively they bow and Henry gives thanks for the food. It is not just a ritual. Henry remembers too well how it feels to be hungry.

He eats in silence, the past luring him, dragging him back, mocking him with its own stubborn silence. How desperately he has tried for as long as he can remember to find his family, patiently, endlessly sifting through the rubble to salvage any scraps of memory of his real family, searching and asking, gathering together what little others can add. And always hoping. Hoping that one day a letter will come, or a phone call, so that finally they will all be together again. Or at least those who are still left of the six of them.

"No use getting your hopes up," he admonishes himself sternly. He is the youngest. The others would be in their mid seventies or eighties, as far as he can figure out. Long dead probably, killed in the Revolution or starved to death in the famine. That can be the only explanation, he tells himself, otherwise they would surely have found him. Unless—he can hardly bear to entertain the thought, but it will not be denied— "What if they were alive all this time and just didn't care about finding me?" The thought torments him.

"No!" He takes himself firmly in hand. "They would have tried." He is sure of it.

# 2

# A SIBERIAN HOME

Two cold little hands insistently patted Maria Rempel's face, pulling her out of a restless sleep. It was October 25, 1917 and still dark at five o'clock in the Siberian village, but Maria did not need any light to know that it was her two-and-a-half-year-old Heinz, her perennial early riser, at her bedside.

"*Ach, mien Kjint*, you're getting cold," she said in Low German. She reached out and lifted her youngest child into the bed beside her, cupping his cold little feet in her hands as he snuggled against her plump body. Her heart pounded from the slight exertion.

Maria stroked the tousled, dark head beside her. "Today we're going home, Heinza," she whispered. Her own excitement added to the rapid rat-a-tat of her heart under her warm flannel nightgown.

She could feel her small son's head turn questioningly towards her. "You never saw it, my boy," whispered Maria into the darkness. "It was before you were born. But today we're going back."

A heavy sigh escaped her lips. Three and a half years they had worked and lived here, torn away from family and friends, but today they would begin the week-long journey back to the Ukraine, the place she still called home. How she had dreamed and prayed for this day.

"Heinza," she said, pulling back the feather quilt, "go wake the other children. Today we start out for *Onkel* Bernard's in Osterwick."

It was still an hour before they had planned to get up, but Maria was restless to begin the day.

The boy needed no prodding. He was out of bed before she could finish her sentence, eagerly calling out in Low German to his five-year-old brother sleeping in the cot across the room, "Petie, get up, get up. Today we go on the train to Oswik!"

His brother rolled over sleepily. "Not Oswik, Heinza, Os-ter-wick." But Heinz was already padding his way through the darkness to the other bedrooms to wake up Lisa, Tina, Jasch, and Anna.

Maria reached over and lit the lamp on the little table beside the bed she shared with her husband Jacob. He yawned noisily beside her as the clock in the *Grootestov* chimed five times.

"What is it with this household?" Jacob grumbled. "It's the middle of the night and everyone is wide awake."

"I'm sorry Jacob," apologized Maria. "You know how early our little Heinz likes to get up, and I didn't sleep well either, so I thought . . ."

"You should have sent the boy back to bed for another hour so we could all get a proper night's sleep," he continued firmly. "You're already overtired from all the packing and getting ready, and this is going to be a long day."

Jacob Rempel pulled his muscular, six-foot frame to a sitting position, shuddered in the sharp, late fall chill in the room, and swung his legs out from under the warm covers. He leaned over and grabbed the pair of wool trousers folded neatly over the back of a wooden chair, and stepped in, pulling them up as he stood. He buttoned only the bottom two buttons. Then he took the shirt Maria had laid out on the table for him, and put it on, tucking it into his pants before meticulously doing up the rest of the buttons. The suspenders, already buttoned to the pants, snapped into place over his shoulders, and with two easy moves he slid one arm at a time into his elastic arm bands and let them snap into place above his elbows. Jacob slid into the vest of his Sunday suit as he stepped into a pair of *Schlorre* standing beside the bed.

Maria sat up in bed, but Jacob motioned for her to lie down.

"I'll go stoke up the fire for breakfast," he said. "It will warm

11

up the house a bit too. You stay in bed and rest a few minutes yet. There's lots of time. Reimer isn't coming with the wagon until nine anyway." It was an order.

"I'm not sick," said Maria with exasperation, lying down obediently. "You make me feel like an invalid."

"You know what I mean," he replied.

"No I don't," she said abruptly. "I can take care of my household as well as any other woman in the village. I don't need a *Kjinjamäakje*."

Jacob patted her arm. "You do very well with your bad heart, Maria," he said.

"With your bad heart," she mimicked, her eyes threatening to spill over with tears. "Just once I would like to be strong and healthy like the other women, so you could just say, 'You do very well'."

Jacob's face registered surprise at the unusual outburst. "I only meant—" he struggled for words.

"I know, Jacob," Maria replied, feeling ashamed. "Just go stoke up the fire; I'll rest."

He was right, of course, she thought as he left the room. She wasn't healthy like a Mennonite wife was supposed to be. She knew what some people said about her in the village. . . . "She's just lazy. She'd feel a lot better if she just got off her fat behind and did some work."

Remarks like that cut deep, but the looks of pity, especially those directed towards her husband for being saddled with a "sickly wife" cut deeper. She could still feel the sting of one man's loud-mouthed observation,"Next time he'll be more careful who he takes."

It wasn't fair to take out her frustration on Jacob, but oh, just once, to be strong and healthy like the other women. . . .

Maria closed her eyes sighing heavily, willing away her sense of inadequacy and the crushing pressure in her chest. Even the smallest task, like lifting up little Heinz, left her gasping for air.

The more she tried to ignore her bad heart, the more it clamored in her breast like an angry, raging beast, leaving her gasping and weak. Jacob understood, giving her the easier farm tasks and chores, and making sure the children helped in the house.

But the conscription letter two weeks ago had changed everything. Jacob would have to go away for nearly three years, and she and the children couldn't possibly look after things on the farm alone. So now they were going back to the Ukraine, where she and the children would stay with Jacob's brother Bernard and his family until Jacob came home.

Maria sighed. For three years she had dreamed of going back home, but not like this.

Three years. . . . The thought agitated Maria. Why should there be a need for any of it anyway? Why should there have to be men carrying guns at all, and her Jacob, just because he wouldn't fight, having to go away to work in a government forestry camp? She did not understand how people could think of killing each other's sons and husbands. Three years of fighting already, and so many dead—not just soldiers either—so many innocent people. And where had it gotten them?

Jacob said the war was using up the country's supplies, and now people in the cities were cold and starving. Sometimes, said Jacob, they even gathered in the streets of Petrograd and in other cities, shouting angrily for bread and coal. It all frightened her.

Bernard had written that there was still food and fuel in the Mennonite village of Osterwick, just like here. He said that evil men had stirred up the people to revolt. A Bolshevik called Lenin was thought to be behind it all. And now everything was in a turmoil and no one seemed to know what would happen next. The czar was gone, deposed and arrested, Bernard said, and the country would never be the same again.

Maria shivered involuntarily. All the talk of war and revolution terrified her. And now, on top of everything, more uncertainty lay ahead. Why, Lisa would be fourteen before she saw her father again, and Heinza, five and a half, as old as Peter was now. Why did the thing she had so hoped and prayed for have to cause so much pain? Maria took a deep breath, trying to quiet her uneasiness.

*So nimm denn meine Hände und führe mich . . .*

The comforting words of a song she had learned at her father's knee flowed unbidden through her troubled mind.

Take Thou my hands oh Father and lead Thou me,
Until my journey endeth, eternally.
Alone I will not wander one single day;
Be Thou my true companion and with me stay.

She was only vaguely aware of the sounds in the rest of the house, sounds of a family making last minute preparations for a long journey.

Outside, the night lay cold and silent over the sleeping village, while in a city three time zones away, far across the Ural Mountains, events that would change the course of Russia's history, and affect the future of the Rempel family were already unfolding.

A short, stocky, forty-seven-year-old man, dressed in shabby clothes, with pants much too long, huddled in his secret headquarters in Petrograd with his friend Leon Trotsky. The man's name was Vladimir Ilyich Ulyanov, known for the past sixteen years as Lenin. He was a man with a dream. It was a dream for a new Russia. A country with a government run by the people instead of the rich, and a country owned by the people. Already, for many months, the people's cries for bread, for fuel, and for change had been heard in the streets of every major city across Russia.

Some of those voices urged gradual reform, but Lenin's voice, and the voice of the other Bolsheviks that rallied around him, cried out for change now. They had already tried once and failed. But four months in hiding in Finland had been time enough to understand what had gone wrong the first time, and time enough, too, for planning an attack that would not fail. If all went as planned, Kerensky and his provisional government would come toppling down before this day was over.

From their headquarters Lenin and Trotsky issued orders, keeping out of public view.

Meanwhile, groups of Bolshevik revolutionaries waited outside strategic targets in the city of Petrograd, guns aimed and ready for the order to advance. The clock in a church tower chimed two a.m.

. . . . .

Henry sits at the kitchen table, eating in silence, aware of Katie's comforting presence around the corner from him. Somewhere in his past, childhood lessons of death and separation have burned so indelibly into his mind that he has lived all his adult life braced, expecting to lose everything he treasures and everyone he loves, never trusting tomorrow, holding on tightly to today, and even yesterday.

It comes to him now as a profound revelation that it hasn't happened. Is it really fifty-one years that he and Katie have been together and she hasn't been snatched away from him and not one of his children or grandchildren has died? Henry sips his tea, savouring its warmth.

Maybe he has held on too tightly. Some people in his church seem to think so.

Still, there are some things that are his, like his family and his church, and he will fight to the death to keep them.

Thankfully, no one has tried to take any of his family from him—but the church, that's another story. He's been made to feel like a stranger there. Even the name has been changed. Well, some people might not like being called Mennonites anymore, but that's who he is, and he's not ashamed of it either.

Like the faded Kroeger clock downstairs—it's his inheritance, passed on to him from Henry Rempel Huebert. He won't give it up without a fight either, not the clock which Katie makes him hang out of sight in the basement, or his Mennonite Brethren beliefs, which some people tell him are outdated.

He holds the people at the top responsible for trampling on the things he holds dear. It rankles and hurts him. It's his church! He helped establish it before most of those who attend there were even born, and he won't allow them to push him out, even if they don't appreciate him and his old-fashioned beliefs.

He tells Katie there's nothing they can do about all the changes, and there isn't. But not one cheque has he written to the church with the new name, and he never will! Instead, he sends his donations directly to the Mennonite Brethren offices in

Winnipeg. It is a silent protest, but it is something he has to do, even if nobody else cares about the battle of one lone man in a little Alberta town.

A heavy sigh escapes his lips. In spite of all his protests, he feels his Mennonite identity being forcefully taken away, like all the other elusive links to his Rempel past, and there seems to be nothing he can do to stop it.

# 3

# PREPARATIONS FOR
# A JOURNEY

Maria became aware of sounds of dishes clattering in the kitchen. Now I am getting up, she told herself resolutely. She got out of bed, slipped her warm flannel nightgown over her head, and reached for the Sunday garments which she had laid out the night before. She would wear the loose-fitting under-vest, a long, white cotton petticoat, bloomers, dark woolen stockings, her high-top Sunday shoes, and finally, her best, brown, ankle-length dress. She wanted to look her best for travelling.

She glanced briefly around the small room in the gently flickering lamplight. The furniture would be left behind. Everything had been sold with the house, including the cot which Heinz and Peter shared, a crude table and dresser, the wooden bed, and the furniture from the rest of the house. Everything, that is, except the wicker trunk.

Maria remembered how neatly all her earthly possessions had fit into that trunk when she, Maria Janzen, had become the wife of Jacob Rempel. In it, she had brought the warm feather quilt and feather pillows made from goose down from her mother's flock, the pillow cases she had embroidered herself, the tablecloth that mother Janzen had made for her, and the lace doilies that were given to her from her mother's mother, *toom aundenkje*.

That trunk would accompany them back, along with one other crate and several suitcases, a sack of dishes and utensils for the trip, and of course the sacks of food she had prepared. All that needed to be done yet, was to secure the bedding into tight rolls, and pack the tea kettle and the remaining dishes and utensils after a quick breakfast of *Prips* and brown bread.

Jacob came back into the room and began rolling up the bedding as Maria opened the long brown braid at the back of her neck and began brushing her hair with long, deft strokes. Their eyes met in the mirror as he came to stand behind her. He was a big handsome man, much taller than she. Concern softened his strong angular features.

"You're panting already Maria, and the day hasn't even begun."

"It's nothing, Jacob," she said, picking up the hairbrush. Jacob gathered up the bedroll and took it into the living room.

"I don't want you overdoing it, Maria," he said firmly as he left the room.

. . . . .

In Petrograd, the command was given. Men brandishing guns burst into the two railway stations. Unsuspecting gendarmes guarding the stations were swiftly overpowered, and in minutes the revolutionaries had commandeered the telegraph rooms, the ticket counters, and the trains waiting in the stations. So swift and bloodless was the take-over, that people, dozing or waiting on the station platform, were hardly aware of what was taking place.

. . . . .

Maria brushed her long dark hair, humming snatches of one of the many melodies she loved to sing. Her thoughts were back in the Ukraine. It seemed only yesterday that they had said good-bye to Mother and Father Rempel and a host of other relatives. It was 1913, and she and Jacob had been the ones staying then. How often Maria had wished that they could have gone to Canada with the others. But Jacob had a good job as secretary in a large flour mill and she and Jacob had just moved into their own house.

Jacob had not thought much of the doom-sayers who were instilling fear in the hearts of his people, forecasting unrest and revolt, and the withdrawal of the religious and economic freedoms which Czarina Catherine the Great had promised the

Mennonites in the first place. So they had decided to stay in the Ukraine: their home.

The very next year the war had broken out, and Jacob had received his first notice to serve in the forestry service. It had been while he was at a village meeting, discussing their future, that he had heard the cry "Fire!" echoing through the village. It had been their home. Maria shuddered, remembering. Fortunately, she and the children had escaped unharmed, but their new home had burned to the ground. All they had been able to save was the trunk and its contents.

What a difficult decision it had been. Their home was gone, and Jacob faced two years and eight months away in the forestry service. Where were Maria and the children to live, and how were they to manage?

Then they had heard of a way out. The government was offering incentives for people to settle in Siberia: low railway fares, a government subsidy of 160 *rubljei*, tax exemptions, farming inventory on credit, and, best of all, a three-year exemption from state service. Many had already accepted, and there was still room in the settlements.

And so it had been decided. They would move to Siberia. At the time it had seemed the perfect answer. The generous money gift that Jacob's relatives had sent from Canada, and the help they had received from their village and the surrounding ones, had softened their terrible loss, and had helped them have a strong beginning in their Siberian village.

Coaxing crops from the virgin prairie soil had been hard work. With their own hands, they had built this house with its attached barn, smaller, but just like the ones back home. Crops had been good, and they had added to their livestock.

Maria looked fondly at the home-made cot in the corner. Anna had been just a year old when they came, and not a year later little Heinz, their sixth child, had been born. And now, they were going back. She lowered her arms and sat on the edge of the bed to catch her breath, and to quiet the pounding of her heart from the exertion of brushing her hair. Who would have expected that after the three-year exemption that had been promised, Jacob would be called up again.

Maria stood up resolutely, twisting her long brown hair into a tight knot at the back of her head.

A sharp pain exploded in her chest. Her breath caught in a moan. She leaned heavily against the dresser, steadying herself.

She tried to straighten, glad for the privacy of her room. No need to alarm the family. She groped for the edge of the bed and sank gratefully onto the straw-filled mattress. She was breathing more easily now in great hungry gulps. She could feel the wild rat-a-tat of her heart gradually subsiding.

"Thank God," she breathed; this was no time for being sick. She sat for a few minutes longer, then slowly she stood, picking up her bib apron and slipping it over her head before going into the kitchen to help with the breakfast.

The kitchen was buzzing with excitement when Maria stepped into the room. Nine-year-old Tina, the second oldest, had already set out the few utensils needed for breakfast. Maria could always count on her to get things going when she wasn't feeling well. Heinz and Peter were charging about like bear cubs, climbing over boxes and rolling on the floor, while Jascha helped his father with the bed rolls.

Anna squirmed in a chair as Lisa braided her hair.

"I can't hardly wait," Anna's eyes shone. "It will be my first ever train ride!" she said in Low German.

"Can hardly," corrected eleven-year-old Lisa. Her face was grim and her voice impatient. "Hold still now," she ordered, giving Anna's braid a sharp yank.

"I'm going on my very first train ride," sang out Anna, undaunted.

"That's not so," snapped Lisa, "we all rode the train when we first came here. Just Heinz wasn't born yet."

"Well, I don't remember it," retorted Anna, "so this will still be like my very first train ride all the same, right Jascha?" She turned to her brother Jacob who had just plopped himself on a bedroll nearby. Anna, being four, and the youngest girl often looked to her seven-year-old brother as a trustworthy ally and teacher in the fine art of holding one's own against their two "big sisters."

"Right," echoed Jascha. "You were just a baby when we came,

so of course you can't remember." He sat up importantly, gesturing as he continued. "It takes ages and ages, and we go right through the Ural mountains and Petrograd, and . . ."

"No we don't," interrupted Lisa. "We don't go through Petrograd. We go through Moscow."

"Well . . ." he began.

"Breakfast," Maria's voice interrupted. The children scurried to their places on the wooden benches alongside the table.

Father opened the family Bible as Maria, panting hard, sat down at her place. Not a morning passed without the reading of the Scriptures and prayers.

"We are reading from Matthew, chapter 10," said Jacob in High German, the language reserved for church and family devotions.

Lisa could still remember when they had finished the whole Bible. After that they had started over again. "In the beginning God created heaven and earth," it said. She didn't like beginnings. Nothing ever turned out right anyway—Cain killing his brother Abel, the Flood killing everybody except Noah's family, and everybody killing everybody else all through the Old Testament. Well, some of the stories had been rather nice, she grudgingly admitted to herself—baby Moses found in the bullrushes by the Egyptian princess, the ravens bringing food to Elijah. But now they were reading in the New Testament again. That was happier, somehow, even if she couldn't understand a lot of it.

"Are not two sparrows sold for a farthing? And one of them shall not fall on the ground without your Father. But the very hairs of your head are all numbered. Fear ye not therefore, ye are of more value than many sparrows. . . ."

They were gone now, the little sparrows. How funny they had looked at first, beaks gaping, waiting to be fed, and then the first wobbly attempts to fly. It had been early one morning that she had found one of them at the foot of the tree, dead. It had seemed cruel and unfair—such a tiny, helpless creature—dead. Maybe God didn't really care what happened to sparrows after all. Why should He anyway? They were a nuisance. That's what Papa said.

21

The prayer was over before Lisa realized that it had begun. She ate sullenly. She hated moving. Just when she had made some new friends in this Siberian village, they were going back to Osterwick. It wouldn't be the same as when they used to live there. Her friend Sarah would not be there, nor cousin Katherina, or Opa and Oma, and worst of all, Mama said that Papa would have to go away for a very long time.

A lump caught in her throat. Why couldn't they have gone to Canada with the others in the first place. Then Papa wouldn't have had to bring them to Siberia and she wouldn't have had to leave all her friends behind.

"So gloomy, Lischen?" Mama's voice interrupted her thoughts.

She could not answer. She was choking back the angry lump that threatened to spill over. She was a big girl now. That's what Papa said. Too big to cry.

Across the table Heinz's quizzical gaze caught her attention.

"Lischen cry?" he asked wide-eyed.

"Of course not, you silly boy," she said, blinking vigorously, "what's to cry about? We're going for a long train ride." The back of her hand swiped purposefully across her eyes. "Right?"

"Right!" the little boy echoed, a smile spreading over his chubby face.

Outside, the night sky was beginning to give way to a new day as breakfast ended in the humble Siberian home. It was not long before the last of the utensils were packed, and promptly at nine o'clock, Onkel Reimer was at the door with his horsedrawn wagon to take them to the train station.

# 4

# THE JOURNEY BEGINS

"You're so quiet today, Henry." Katie's inquiring voice breaks into his thoughts. It is a part she knows best, the wall of silence that shuts her out, troubling her, making her want to reach out to him, to ease whatever the silence reflects.

"You're feelin' sick, ain't ya' Henry? Why don't you let me make you an appointment with the doctor?" It is easier to deal with the tangibles: a fever, a cough, even the insulin shots.

Her voice probes Henry's reverie, and he is reluctant and irritable as he drags himself back to the present.

"I don't need no doctor!" he snaps.

Katie angrily pushes her chair away from the table, and without another word goes to the kitchen counter and begins energetically kneading down the fluffy mound of white dough in the large metal bowl.

Henry's eyes have been following her heated reaction.

"Oh all right," he says impatiently. "If it will make you feel so much better."

Katie looks at him suspiciously, trying to understand his sudden change of heart. She has been badgering him for weeks to go see a doctor, always to be met with the same stubborn refusal.

"I know already what he's going to say," says Henry, draining his teacup and setting it down with finality.

"What's that Henry?" Katie's face registers alarm.

"Nothin' much," he replies with measured calmness, "just that this old wind bag's out of wind."

She sighs in exasperation, turning back to her dough. After all these years of being married to the man, she still can't tell when he's teasing her and when he's serious. Katie is as annoyed with herself as she is with him.

"Well, you can't be too sick if you're still makin' jokes," she says grudgingly. Briskly she begins pinching off small blobs of satiny dough, setting them in neat, double decker rows in the pans on the counter. The dough whistles gently as she pinches and pummels it into shape.

Henry reaches for the magazine under the big German family Bible on the small table in the corner beside his chair, his thoughts already far away from any visit to the doctor.

Large curly letters announce *Die Mennonitische Rundschau*. He thumbs through its pages, squinting at the small print through his dark-rimmed glasses, as Katie continues putting her *Tweeback* on the pans.

She watches warily. "You already checked the obituaries for any sign of your *Geschwister*," she says testily. "What're you lookin' for now?"

"Just an address," he replies casually. "Get me the writing paper, will you Katie?"

A lump of dough is poised in her hand. "You're not thinkin' of writin' there again, are you Henry?" There is reproach in her voice. "I thought you gave up on that."

"Can't hurt trying just once more, can it?" he says.

But she knows it won't be just once more. It's what he used to say all the time when they were first married. Always it was "Just once more." After all those letters to magazines, the phone calls and packing up the family for another wild goose chase to track down Henry's family. She can't bear to see it any longer. The terrible disappointments. He doesn't say much, but she can tell that each time he dies a little more. It isn't fair! Why should strangers, people she has never known, and people whose faces Henry can't even remember, have such a hold on him, the one more dear to her than anyone else in the world?

There was a time when the children were growing up that she thought he had finally let it be. At least the frantic trips and the anxious letters stopped. Instead, he threw himself into his work. Up before dawn, and not home until bedtime, with brief snatches at home for meals, driven by some invisible need for hard work. She and the children hardly saw him. "Maybe it's his way of trying to forget," she would tell herself. She tried in her own way to make it up to the children, but they needed their Dad and he wasn't listening.

But the past few years, with things finally slowing down, he's been at it again, and for what? Just to get on the merry-go-round of hoping and being disappointed again? She can't stand it!

"My gosh, Henry," she explodes, "can't you just leave it alone for once?"

"You're a fine one to talk," he says, still paging through the paper. "You've got your real family."

There is a moment of stunned silence. "Real family?" Katie's face reddens with anger. "Real family? You've got a real family too! What are you talkin' about, your 'real' family?"

He looks up, taken aback by her anger. "You know what I mean," he says quietly but firmly, turning his attention back to the *Rundschau*.

"No Henry, I don't!" Her words tumble out bitterly. "Four kids I give you. But is that enough? No! Not for Henry. He's still lookin' for his 'real family'. Real!"

He looks at her in shock and disbelief, but she is not through. "I guess your Huebert parents weren't 'real' either. Never mind that they loved you like their own son." She takes a deep breath. Her voice quivers and drops almost to a whisper. "And you loved them too, Henry. Look how you worked for them, took care of them. Your father, here in your own house after your mother died. . . ." She turns her back abruptly, but not before he has caught sight of the tears springing up in her eyes.

"Katie . . ." he gropes for words. Hasn't she always wanted him to find his real family as much as he? Can't he still see her counting the worn bills they had managed to save, getting on the train with him and the children to go to Vancouver when he thought he had found a brother? Hasn't she even encouraged the trips, the phone calls, the letters, in the hope that one day he would find them . . . his 'real' family? She has used those very words too. He remembers it clearly.

He gets up heavily.

"Just stay there, Henry. Sit down." Katie waves him back impatiently, brushing floury hands against her print apron. "I'm gettin' your paper. I'm gettin' it." She knows he needs to keep trying for some reason she cannot understand. It is a part of him she can not share. A part hidden away behind a high fence. She can only imagine what it might be like behind that fence, and imagining, weep for the boy who has never come home.

. . . . .

The morning air was cold as Maria and the children, Lisa, Tina, Jasch, Peter, Anna, and Heinz snuggled down under blankets between the suitcases, the trunk, one crate, and several bags of supplies. Jacob and *Onkel* Reimer rode on the seat at the front of the *Ladawoage* for the thirty *verscht* trip to the train station. Maria watched the retreating village and sighed, as much from relief as from the chest-crushing exhaustion she felt. They were going home.

In her mind's eye she could see the neatly laid out farming village of Osterwick with its well-kept buildings and its orderly orchards, gardens and flower gardens. She could smell the rich, fertile fields, and the grass of the communal pastures outside the village. She could see the huge stands of trees, with leaves awash in the red and gold of late autumn, where firewood was even now being cut in preparation for winter. She could almost imagine sinking her teeth into a wedge of a sweet, juicy watermelon, the like of which she hadn't tasted in all their time in Siberia.

Maria's face glowed in anticipation as much as from the cold of the icy Siberian wind against her face. It wasn't that long ago that the Mennonite forefathers had come to make their homes in the untamed steppes of mother Russia, and it was not by being feeble-hearted that they had made good.

Maria took a deep breath, the freezing air tingling her nostrils. She would have courage too, like her ancestors before her, trusting the God who had cared for them to take care of her and her little ones too. She must remember to think of that through the three years apart from Jacob so the time would not seem so long.

Her mind travelled to her relatives in Canada—pioneers,

much like she and Jacob had been here in this Siberian village. It was more than four months since they had gotten a letter from Jacob's mother. She wrote of being hungry for watermelon too, of missing the fruit orchards, and of finding wild berries called Saskatoons, with which they made *Platz*. They were doing without many things too, making many adjustments in their new land. Maria could tell that they were homesick too. She hugged her body to herself, trying to keep warm.

"Let's sing." Anna's voice broke into her thoughts. No matter what the occasion, there was always a song in the Rempel household. Maria smiled. The children knew many of the songs from the *Glaubensschtimme*, each child having picked a favorite which would be sung as often as possible. And of course there were all the little nursery rhymes and singing games that Maria had taught them, songs she had learned at her father's knee.

"Mama, let's all sing," repeated Anna.

"You children sing without me," said Maria. "I'm just going to rest for a while."

"*Sinje*," echoed Heinz in Low German.

"What do you want to sing, Heinza?" asked Tina.

"*Hop, hop, hop*," he said emphatically, jumping up and down. It was the little rhyme Papa sang while bouncing him on his foot.

"Oh Heinza," said Jascha disapprovingly, "that's for babies."

"No it's not," said Tina.

"I wanted to sing *Mariechen Saß Auf Einem Stein*," pouted Anna.

"Okay," said Tina, "we'll sing that one after we sing the one Heinza wants. Now do stop bouncing, Heinza. You're letting the cold air get under the blanket."

The carefree voices of the children rose over the treetops as the winding road took them farther and farther away from the Siberian village which was Heinz's birthplace and their home for the past three years.

| | |
|---|---|
| *"Hop, hop, hop, hop, hop,"* | Hop, hop, hop, hop, hop, |
| *Pferdchen lauf galopp,* | Horsey go gallop, |
| *Über stock und über Steine,* | Over sticks and over stones |
| *Pferdchen brich nicht deine Beine* | Horsey do not break |

*Hop, hop, hop, hop, hop*
*Pferdchen lauf galopp."*

your bones
Hop, hop, hop, hop, hop,
Horsey go gallop."

Maria closed her eyes, content finally to be able to rest, the children's happy voices lulling her to sleep.

. . . . .

It was six o'clock in Petrograd, the city just beginning to rouse itself for the day's work. Armed Bolsheviks surrounded the State Bank, and forced their way into the building. There was little resistance as they occupied it. Swiftly, they moved through the streets towards the Phone Exchange building, right on schedule and according to plan.

Kerensky, asleep in the Winter Palace, was roused by a phone call, one of the last he would receive before the lines were cut. "There is an insurrection in progress. The Bolsheviks are trying to take over," the agitated voice said.

Hastily he called together his ministers for an emergency conference at the Palace. His position was precarious. Only a month ago he had freed the imprisoned Bolsheviks who had staged an unsuccessful revolt earlier in the year and let them arm the workers in order to defeat General Kornilov, who was trying to seize power.

Now, it was not only the guns of the revolutionary Bolsheviks, but the workers as well, pointing at him and his government, ready to overthrow him. He had thought that as the only socialist member of the provisional government, his position was secure, but now he had neither the support of the non-socialists nor the revolutionaries. There was no one left to defend him and the Winter Palace, save an inexperienced group of students from a military school.

At seven a.m. the phones in the Winter Palace went dead as revolutionaries took over the Phone Exchange. Wires to the seat of Karensky's government had been cut.

Life in the rest of Petrograd went on much as it always did, with most of the population being unaware that there was a revolt in progress. But some of the armed workers, who just last February had been on strike demonstrating for higher wages and greater representation in the government, joined the Bolshevik-supporting government troops and naval crews. Others joined in the revolt; soldiers sick of war, and peasants hungry for land, women, who the day before had stood all day in line-ups outside empty bread shops trying in vain to buy bread with meagre ration tickets. Unrest had escalated into revolt, and there was no turning back.

Lenin got up, pacing restlessly in his headquarters. No more would the country's *burzhuazii* ride roughshod over the backs of the working class to fatten their own estates. Let the peasants take back the land, and the workers take over the factories. Give them back their dignity, by whatever means. Today a socialist revolt would reclaim Petrograd, tomorrow Moscow, then all of Russia, and yes, eventually the whole world!

. . . . .

The day slipped by as the horsedrawn *Ladawoage* rolled towards the Siberian city of Omsk. The Rempel family, tired from the excitement and the singing with which they had begun the trip, sat wrapped in blankets watching the passing scenery or dozing comfortably as they made their way to the train station.

. . . . .

It was late afternoon, before the Trans-Siberian Express lurched into motion car by car, shuddering and hissing with its effort. It was crowded, but Jacob and Maria had managed to settle their family, along with the bedding and supplies, into the small compartment that would be their home for the next five or six days, depending how many delays there would be on the way. In Moscow, there would be a change of trains for the remaining part of the trip to the Ukraine.

There was room for all six of them to sit comfortably, facing each other, on the two wooden benches extending about three-quarter of the way across the car. They had discovered that the backs of the seats could be raised and used for beds, and a narrower third shelf overhead on both sides, which during the day served as storage for baggage, could also be used for beds later on.

For now, there was too much to see and to explore to think of sleeping. Jacob and Maria were trying to calm the children's excitement.

"Not so loud, children," cautioned Jacob, speaking in Russian. "We do not want to disturb the other passengers." He glanced at the two soldiers who occupied the small compartment across from them.

He had noted that his was the only Mennonite family in this train car, and was well aware of the unfriendly stares they had received as they had made their way to their compartment. He was not unused to this attitude. Russia and Germany had been at war for three years, and super-patriotic propaganda labelled those with any ties to Germany as "agents of the enemy."

"We must remember to speak Russian," he had cautioned his family before they had gotten on the train, but he knew full well that only Lisa and Tina, who had been studying Russian in school, could speak it properly. The younger children and even Maria were not comfortable with it, although they could understand well enough.

Jacob caught the eye of one of the Russian soldiers. "I guess we'll be neighbours for a while." He spoke Russian with schooled accuracy. "How far are you going?"

The man's eyes narrowed, "*K chortu van* you German spies." He spat on the floor. His companion snickered.

Jacob's face colored, but he did not reply.

"What did you expect?" whispered Maria in Low German, her voice tense with humiliation.

"It's nothing," Jacob's voice was low and unruffled. He had met other Russians who did not trust anyone who looked to be German. But in his experience with them, once they got to know you they could be most friendly and hospitable.

Maria was not convinced that it was "nothing." The soldier's vulgarity echoed in her ears. How dare he speak to them like that? They were Russian citizens too, born in Russia just like he. Of course he could not know that, she conceded to herself grudgingly. Everything about them set them apart.

It was fine and good for Jacob to say it was nothing. He was used to dealing with these people. He'd had contact with the Russian school teacher in the village, the Russian officials in

30

charge of administration in the neighbouring villages, and even with the Russian peasants, while she, a simple Mennonite housewife, had not needed to mix very much with the world beyond her village here and in the Ukraine. The remark continued to smart.

She felt Jacob's fingers press reassuringly against her arm.

"Mama, isn't it time to eat yet?" Jascha's question came as a welcome distraction, even though it was not the first time he had asked.

Maria looked at him, letting a smile erase the tense lines in her face. She could imagine how tempting the wonderful assortment of dried *Tweeback*, smoked sausage, dried fish, cheese, cookies, and dried apples that she and the girls had prepared for the trip must be for her energetic seven-year-old. It was all sitting tantalizingly close by on the shelf overhead.

"Now Jascha, you are going to have to do a lot better than this if the food is to last us to the end of the trip," she chided gently in Low German, "or should we eat all of it right away?" Young Jacob pouted good-naturedly. "A growing boy has to eat, doesn't he?"

"Ha," snorted Lisa, "growing boy? You're just a *kjleena Kjnirps* yet."

His face darkened, the mischievous twinkle gone. He might just be seven, but he was definitely not a pip-squeak. He could take down any boy his age in the village school, and even some of the bigger ones too.

"Well it's better than being a big. . . ."

"*Kjinja!*" Jacob said sternly, glancing uncomfortably across the aisle. "We will eat soon enough. Now Jascha, stop pestering your mother about food. Can't you see how tired she is?"

Jasch hung his head.

"Now be a good boy," his father continued, "go and take your two younger brothers here to see the rest of the car."

"Be careful and hold on tight to each other," Maria cautioned.

Four-year-old Anna's head was nodding, and Maria settled her on the bench beside her so she could nap while her brothers were exploring the train. She leaned her head against the back of the hard seat, feeling too exhausted for words, and glad for

31

the relative quiet. Her chest ached with a pressure that threat-ened to suffocate her.

"Dear God," she prayed silently, "Give strength for the days ahead." Suppertime finally came, much to Jascha and the other children's delight. From the mysterious depths of the carefully guarded sacks, materialized a meal fit for a czar. To the children nothing could be more exciting than riding on a train, eating a meal of cheese, dried *Tweeback*, and some of Mama's delicious apple-filled *Perschkji*, and washing it all down with some tea made from the boiling water in the samovar at the front of the car.

Getting the kettle full of boiling water safely past all the boxes and bags strewn in the aisle had been quite a challenge for Lisa. And now, even her dark mood had lifted with the excitement of eating their first meal on the train.

"This is just like a picnic," chirped Anna happily. There was no rush to finish the meal. After a while, when everyone had had enough, the food was cleared away, and the wooden shelves were made ready for sleeping. Each person's bedroll was untied, and the pillows and blankets laid out.

The *provodnik*, looking official in his black blouse worn over wide, dark trousers tucked into high boots and a *pojas* around his waist, popped his head into their compartment to ask if they needed any extra pillows or blankets.

"Bedding for one, just one ruble," he said, smiling.

"*Spasibo*, thank you, we have brought our own," said Jacob courteously. He knew that any services from the attendant would have to be paid for extra. They had come prepared, and the Russian attendant would not get rich on them. Then the provodnik was gone, as quickly as he had come.

Slowly the train chugged westward as the Rempel family settled in for their first night. The Siberian village of Heinz Rempel's birth was already far behind them. It's name, like so many other details of his earliest years, would be lost in the days ahead, in the cacophony of events that were about to take place.

. . . . .

In Petrograd, Kerensky's furious scurrying between con-ferences with ministers at the Winter Palace and with staff officers at the district headquarters on the other side of Palace Square, had come to nothing, and now he could only watch as the Bolshevik revolutionaries advanced.

By 6:30 p.m., Petrograd time, the final capture of the Winter Palace had begun, and before the day was out, the Communist Bolsheviks, led by Lenin, had formed Russia's new government. At 11 p.m., the Second All-Russian Congress of Soviets opened at the Smolny Institute, the headquarters for the Petrograd Soviet, with Lenin in charge.

Before the week was out, slogans proclaiming the Bolshevik coup as an accomplished fact, would be plastered all over Petrograd. For thousands upon thousands who would be crushed under the pounding hooves of change, the Russian Revolution had yet to run its course. It was October 25, 1917, a fateful date which would become November 7 when the old Julian calendar was replaced by the Gregorian.

# 5

# DEATH ON THE
# TRANS-SIBERIAN RAILWAY

Two days had come and gone, the novelty of the train ride having worn thin in the endless hours in the cramped and smelly train car. The flat, lush, farmland, had given way to birch trees and shrubs, and finally, to the graceful rolling Ural Mountains sweeping to the north and the south of the great valley through which the train passed. Stops and delays had been many, as the train waited on sidings for long freights to rumble by. Occasionally, they had had to wait until earth brought down by the freight's rumblings was cleared from the track. At each station more and more passengers crowded onto the already overcrowded train.

Occasionally, to the delight of the Rempel children, Papa would purchase fresh rye bread at three kopecks a loaf, or big jam turnovers for two kopecks each from vendors peddling their wares at the stations. But mostly, they ate from the sacks of dried *Tweeback*, smoked sausage, and other food that Mama and the girls had prepared before the trip began.

Other groups also travelling in third class were getting by in much the same way as the Rempels. With each passing day the smell of sardines, cabbage, stale tobacco, and body odor was becoming more and more stifling.

The Rempel family had established a routine complete with meal times, chores and morning devotions, which were not to be missed in spite of the suspicious stares from across the aisle. The excursions to the lavatory for washing at one end of the car, and to the toilet at the other end, were kept to a minimum because of the cluttered aisle, the unfriendly stares of the other passengers, and the limitations of the facilities.

For the older children, used to an outhouse, the wide, wooden seat, only four inches from the floor proved uncomfortable. There was no plug in the steel basin in the lavatory at the other end of the car, and from the tap came only cold water. For more thorough bathing, a bucket and a hole in the floor provided the facilities. The cold autumn wind, accompanied by the thunder of the wheels, whistled up through this hole. Before the trip was over, thought Maria, they would have to subject themselves to such a bath, but for now she was content to wait.

For Maria the hours dragged by with the wearisome jostle and joggle of the train, as it lurched its way across Russia like some inebriated beast, each motion adding another layer of tiredness to her oxygen-starved body.

She did not complain, but Jacob's alarm at her uncharacteristic listlessness grew with each passing day. Most of the time she sat numb with a tiredness that threatened to suffocate her.

Evenings she was glad to be able to undo her bedroll, and stretch out her tired body on the wooden bench, hoping to escape the discomfort under a welcome blanket of sleep, even though it was fitful and interrupted. The children, in their quarters above her, seemed oblivious to the erratic movements of the train and the sounds that punctuated the night.

But tonight sleep would not come. She threw back the blankets in spite of the chill in the train car. The air was heavy and stale, and there was a steady, heavy tightness in Maria's chest that made breathing difficult. She lay gasping, fighting the claustrophobic shortness of breath, trying not to waken the others.

Slowly she eased herself to a sitting position and lit the candle in the holder on her side of the compartment. Jacob stirred on the bench across from her, and then his own breathing was rhythmic and even again.

If only she could open a window, or go outside for fresh air, she thought. Maybe if she walked back and forth for a bit she would feel better. She tried to get up. A pain exploded in her chest, and a wave of nausea overcame her.

"Jacob!" she gasped, as she slumped onto the bench.

Her husband was at her side in a flash. "What is it Maria?" In the candle light he could see her clutching her chest, her face contorted with pain.

"Maria!" There was alarm in his voice.

"Help . . . me," she gasped.

"You need a doctor." His voice was a hoarse whisper. "I'll go see if I can. . . ."

"No . . . Jacob." She clung to his arm. Her voice was so weak he had to lean forward to make out the words. "Don't . . . leave . . . me."

"I'll call the attendant," he said, fumbling to pull the bell marked *konduktor*.

But Maria did not hear him. The train was closing in on her. Her mouth gulped for air, but there was no air, just the blinding pain crushing her and . . . everything spinning spinning.

"Dear God! Maria!" Jacob's arms circled her as she slumped towards him. Panic knotted his throat. "Maria!"

He was not aware of the children, awakened by the commotion, now huddled nearby, whimpering and afraid.

The attendant hovered in the open doorway to their compartment but refused to step inside, while other passengers, awakened by the disturbance, also shrank back. Not a single person offered to help.

How long he sat there holding her, pleading with God, willing her to breathe again, he did not know. How could it possibly be, that his beloved Maria, just thirty-three years old, was gone? Gone!

. . . . .

Henry sits at the kitchen table, gazing out the window, the *Mennonitsche Rundschau* still in his hand. He does not see the snow curling away in phantom wisps as cars drive by. He is studying a picture so indelibly imprinted on his mind that he does not need to get it from its special place in the dresser drawer.

It is the only photograph he has of his "real" parents, Jacob and Maria Rempel. They are young, in their late twenties, perhaps, or younger. He cannot tell. They sit straight-faced, dignified, and distant. He has searched and searched for a glimmer of recognition. Sometimes it is almost there, like a vague, restless stirring, and then it is gone. Or have the years of dreaming, of trying to remember, woven their own fragile link between him and the photograph?

If only he had even one real childhood recollection of them. But all he has are the pitifully few fragments he has been able to gather up. These he has jealously, painfully guarded, immersing himself in them until they have become uniquely and solely his own. Sometimes he allows himself the luxury of imagining life with his "real" family, but always the memory ends in the shadows of the same nightmare.

"Mama," a little boy's voice cries out, but no one hears in the commotion. Hours go by. Grim, tear-stained, fear-filled hours, before the train finally hisses and snarls to a stop in front of a remote station.

If only someone could tell him the name of it, but no one has thought to look.

Jacob Rempel steps out into the chill of the fall morning air carrying his wife's body in his arms. Six children follow, carrying bags and bedrolls. A trunk and a crate are unloaded from the baggage car and then there is a shrill whistle and steam billows as the train pulls away. They stand lost, wide-eyed and frightened.

Where would they lay her? Henry wonders. A blanket probably—on the ground— while the father digs a shallow grave. The Russian station master does not help. In his tradition, it is bad luck to touch the dead.

The grave is ready. But how does one have a funeral without a casket, a choir, and a minister? They wrap her in the blanket and lay her gently at the bottom of the grave. She wears a warm coat, a kerchief, and boots. The father takes the worn Bible from his ample coat pocket and reads:

Behold, I tell you a mystery: we shall not all sleep, but we shall all be changed, in a moment, in the twinkling of an eye, at the last trumpet (I Cor. 15:51,52 NAS).

Yes . . . perhaps that. Then a prayer, and maybe a song. . . . No! No song! Only the wind in the branches, and the sobbing. That is the only music there is.

The children are told to go and wait in the station, and as they turn to go, their father kneels, covering her with another blanket. He is still kneeling there when they look back from the station, his head bare in the wind, his hands, clawing through the dirt, covering her. He is crying bitterly.

"Henry, you're so quiet. What are you thinking?" Katie stands beside him holding the writing paper and a pen, unable to bear the heavy silence any longer.

He does not answer. There are no words. Only the cavernous vacuum of a two-and-a-half-year-old boy who has just lost his mother. Henry gets up heavily.

"What are you doing now Henry?" Katie asks reproachfully. "You just sent me for paper for the letter. Aren't you writin' the letter now?"

He moves slowly towards the door and begins to put on his shoes. "It's no use Katie." His head is bent. "It's like you said. . . ." He straightens with a weary sigh and without looking at her pauses with his hand on the doorknob.

"Anyway, Mathew's horse isn't going to get finished if I keep sittin' around in here, is it?" Henry steps out into the breezeway and the door closes noiselessly behind him.

# 6

# MILLEROVO
# WINTER 1917-1918

Jacob Rempel, along with his children Tina, Lisa, Jacob, Anna, Peter, and Heinz, sat silently in the *Droschka* as they skimmed by the homes along Millerovo's main street. Mr. Dyck had picked them up at the train station at the edge of the city, and now he was taking them to his home. Their baggage would be picked up later, Mr. Dyck had said. As the horse clip-clopped along the dirt-packed street, Wilhelm Dyck pointed to the homes and businesses of some of the more prominent and wealthy Mennonite citizens. "This," said Dyck, with a wave of his hand, "is the farm machinery factory of Martens, DeFehr and Dyck, and up ahead, is the flour mill I own with several other brethren." Jacob's eyes followed Wilhelm's gestures towards the huge five-storey brick building some distance down the street, and the adjoining building next to a tall chimney. It was one of several large buildings dominating the Millerovo streets. Jacob Rempel nodded. He had heard that Wilhelm Dyck, known far and wide as a devout church leader and a generous man, was also a very successful businessman, but he had not been prepared for all of this.

The two had met during Wilhelm Dyck's preaching trip to Siberia just the year before. Jacob had been impressed with the man's knowledge of the Scriptures, and with his genuine warmth. "You must stop at Millerovo and visit if you are ever out our way," Wilhelm had urged. It was an invitation that Jacob and Maria had hoped to accept, planning to stop and visit the

Dycks in Millerovo before continuing on to Osterwick.

But now, everything was different. Maria was no longer with them, and in his hand was the letter from his sister-in-law in Osterwick, which Wilhelm had handed him at the station. It read:

*I'm sorry to have to send word that much has changed since we last wrote. By now you will be almost here, but you should know that Bernard has also been conscripted to work in the forestry camps. How I will manage without him, with the children so small, and all the farm work to do, I don't know.*

*The situation here is not good. Our own family is struggling to make ends meet, especially since the Bolsheviks took power. Our Russian workers have left us, and people saying they are from the workers' soviet in this district have been here demanding horses and other livestock.*

*I fear for our lives. It is not enough that we have already been labelled as enemies of our own homeland because of our German language and heritage. Now we are cursed and hated because we own factories and land. Imagine! Have they forgotten so soon how eagerly the Russian people came to us in search of jobs? Many a peasant household would have gone hungry if it hadn't been for the generosity of their Mennonite employers. And look at the thanks we get!*

*But enough of our troubles. Yours are greater and sadly we are unable to help. Perhaps, though, you might seek counsel from Ältester Dyck. I am sending this letter to you at his address because I know you plan to stop in Millerovo before you come here. As a Mennonite Brethren church administrator, he will surely find a way out for you and Maria and the children. We have been told that he is a very kind and wise man. He will know what is best.*

Jacob's eyes moistened as he read the letter. Of course his brother and his wife couldn't know about Maria. He must send word immediately.

". . . only God knows what is ahead," Wilhelm was saying. "It is as though the Bolsheviks have given a licence for anarchy."

Jacob folded the letter and tucked it into his breast pocket, trying to rein in his wandering anxious thoughts to focus on the man beside him. What was it Wilhelm had just said? Something about the Russian workers taking over the factories and mills, and peasants looting some of the Mennonite homes. He was ashamed he had not been listening.

Wilhelm mistook Jacob's startled, questioning look as his response to the terrible news he had just shared with him. "I do not wish to alarm you, my friend. You have troubles enough of your own." The *Droschka* was turning into the driveway now, and Jacob's attention was turned towards the massive house surrounded by a huge, well tended yard. To the rear of the property towered the mill which they had seen from a distance.

As they pulled to a stop, a woman somewhat younger than Wilhelm, hurried towards them. "*Willkommen,*"she said in High German, "welcome." She smiled warmly, as her eyes scanned the little group. "You did not bring Maria?"

Her question was cut short as Wilhelm touched her arm. "Our friend's wife died suddenly on the journey from Siberia, Justina. We will talk more of it later."

"*Ach, nein!*" Justina's eyes caught Jacob's for one fleeting instant before he looked away, but not before she had read the intense pain written there.

"Wilhelm also lost his first wife," she said quietly. "Her name also was Maria."

Jacob turned to look inquiringly at Wilhelm, but the man had turned abruptly towards the children still seated in the *Droschka*. "Now, let's see if I can remember all your names." He smiled mischievously at the six Rempel children, little wrinkles gathering at the corners of his eyes as though he were used to smiling. It was as though he had turned on a light in their sad, frightened eyes.

Just then two of his own children came running. "Ah, my dears," he said, "I want you to meet the Rempel family. Come, come, children," he urged, "your legs must be tired from all the sitting. Let me help you down so you can meet our children."

Shyly, the Rempel children began clambering from the *Droschka*. "This is Lisa, the eldest, just about your age Agatha." Wilhelm smiled at his twelve-year old daughter. "And Tina here is nine. Right?" Tina nodded shyly, enjoying the guessing game.

"And this young man is Jascha. Seven, just like our Willie here." The two boys eyed each other with interest, as Wilhelm continued. "And what's your name young man?" he asked, tweaking five-year-old Peter's chubby cheek. "I'm Petie," the boy grinned.

"Ah, such a big boy already." Mr. Dyck patted his shoulder. "And of course, we mustn't forget little Anna. How old did you say you were?" he coaxed, smiling.

"Four," whispered Anna. Justina Dyck stepped forward and took the child's hand in her own, her eyes fighting tears as she looked over the motherless brood.

"And this young man," said Wilhelm, hoisting the two-and-a-half-year-old boy onto his shoulders, "is Heinz." The boy grinned happily from his perch. "Now children," said Wilhelm to Agatha and Willie, "I want you to say hello to the children's papa, *Onkel* Rempel."

The children politely shook Jacob's hands. "*Gutentag, Onkel* Rempel," they said with schooled formality.

"Do come in, brother Rempel," said Wilhelm, turning and walking briskly towards the house with Heinz on his shoulders. "And as for you children, Agatha and Willie will take you into the back yard to play. Good?" He stopped in front of a large verandah, and with one swift motion, he had deposited Heinz on the ground beside Agatha.

Wilhelm's older son, Abram, had come from the back buildings and was about to take the horse and carriage to the barn. "Maybe if you ask Abram," Wilhelm nodded in his direction, "he will show you the rest of the horses. How would you like that?" Heinz nodded vigorously.

Wilhelm turned to Jacob, "The boy's sixteen already. A big help."

Jacob nodded. It was a fortunate man who had a good strong son or two, and some sturdy daughters to help with the farm work. Just a few more years, and he too would know that kind of help. Right now the children were more willing than able.

The letter burned in his pocket. It had all been arranged. Maria and the children would go to stay with Bernard's family until Jacob was released from the service. But now everything had changed. What, dear God, was he to do? The children were much too young to be left alone somewhere, and there were no relatives to help. And he would be shut away in some remote forestry camp for three years with no way of protecting them from the Bolshevik terror already stalking the land. His jaw clenched as he tore his gaze away from his children standing among strangers, looking lost and bewildered.

"Come Heinza," Agatha said, seeing the boy's preoccupation with the departing horse. "Let's go see the horses." The boy reached up eagerly and took her hand. Lisa took his other hand. The other children joined them as they dashed down the lane after the horse and *Droschka*.

"Please, come in," said Justina gently, leading the way up the steps. Jacob drew a long slow breath as he followed his hosts up the front steps and across the expansive verandah of the big, gracious house. The door opened as they approached. "Brother Rempel," said Justina, "this is the rest of our family, anyway those that are still at home. Two sons are married and on their own you know. This one here is Katya," she motioned to the one holding the door. Behind her, in a wheelchair, sat a young woman, likely in her late twenties, her expression vacant and her mouth drooling."

From what Justina had said, it was apparent to Jacob that the older Dyck children, including the one in the wheelchair, must be from Wilhelm's marriage to his first wife Maria. The two standing here, and the other three outside would be from the second marriage.

Wilhelm followed Jacob's glance. "Our poor Martha," he said simply, patting the young woman in the wheelchair tenderly on the cheek, "and this," he motioned to the girl pushing the wheelchair, "is our Esther."

The girl accepted Jacob's outstretched hand with the poise and grace of the cultured eighteen-year-old she was. Her fourteen-year-old sister, Katya, did the same, without shyness or embarrassment. Their impeccable manners and fine clothes seemed to surround them with a superior air, and it was Jacob who suddenly felt ill at ease.

The *Vorhaus* in which they stood was as large as any *Grossestube* Jacob had seen. It was furnished with ornate benches, plants, a small lace covered table, and a carefully crafted shelf with hooks for hats and coats.

"Your coat and hat, please," said Wilhelm cordially.

Jacob felt clumsy as he undid the buttons on his overcoat, suddenly aware of how shabby and worn his clothing must appear. Back in his home in Siberia, sitting across the table from *Ältester* Dyck, he had felt perfectly at ease. But now, seeing the distinguished man in his own setting, Jacob felt uncomfortable.

Whatever had possessed him to accept this man's invitation in the first place? Clearly, the Dycks were in a class of their own. And now, coming here when his situation had suddenly become so desperate, what must the Dycks think? One more person looking for a hand-out, no doubt. Well, it was not charity he wanted! He wanted only the wise counsel of this distinguished man.

"The girls and I will see about *Abendbrot*," Justina Dyck was saying in High German. "We will leave you to yourselves for now." And with a nod of the head, she excused herself and disappeared through one of the doorways.

"Come, brother Rempel," said Wilhelm, when they were alone, "we will talk in the *Grossestube*."

Jacob looked into the face of the man his sister had mentioned in the letter. He was in his early sixties. The eyes were kindly, and he was tugging thoughtfully at his grey, wispy beard as he led the way into a room much more spacious than the first.

The formal sitting room, or *Grossestube*, was resplendent with its polished hardwood floor, its imported furniture and ornate lamps. Jacob's eyes took in the fine china in the cabinet against one wall, the *Hammerklavier* against another wall, and the fine crochetwork in the tablecloth and doilies gracing the furniture. In one corner stood the traditional fancy bed, piled high with feather-filled quilts, and draped on top with a rich display of hand-embroidered pillowcases and hand-sewn quilts, edged in the finest, hand-made lace. Every Mennonite home had such a bed, which was used not for sleeping, but for displaying the handwork of the lady of the house and for storing extra bedding; but Jacob had never seen such a beautiful one before.

Rich drapes adorned the large windows, and on the wall hung exquisite tapestries. Jacob sat gingerly at the edge of the chair which Wilhelm Dyck offered him.

"The letter from your brother's wife," said Wilhelm, seating himself across from Jacob, "the news was not good?"

Hesitantly Jacob explained the contents of the letter, and his present plight.

As Jacob spoke, Wilhelm Dyck's mind was running through the list of options. Because of his position in the church, he was often asked to deal with difficult situations. God always provided the necessary solutions if one just asked and searched for them. Now he was examining the possibilities. To ask another family to take in all six children for such a long period of time did not seem feasible, but to separate them seemed cruel and unfair.

His own home, with its twenty-eight rooms, was certainly large enough, but he had his own family to consider. Justina was already caring for his invalid daughter, and with five children of their own he could not ask her to look after another six.

Perhaps if the servants were still with them, he mused, but only last week when the Bolsheviks had taken control proclaiming equality for all and denouncing the wealthy *Burzhuazija* for exploiting the Russian peasants by hiring them as servants, he and Justina had decided to let all their help go.

Besides, his two married sons, along with their families, would be looking to him for help, as would the other families he had brought here to Millerovo to work in the businesses he and his associates had established. How could he possibly ask his family to take on the care of six children under these conditions.

Jacob seemed to be reading his mind. "I have a little money," said Jacob. "If I could find a suitable place for my children to live, perhaps I could hire a reliable girl to look after them." He hesitated. "At least for a time."

A smile wrinkled the corners of Wilhelm Dyck's eyes. "Well, I believe I can help you with that," he said standing up abruptly. "I don't know why I didn't think of it myself. Come with me."

He led the way through the house and out the back door. There was a sharp chill in the late autumn air, but as yet no snow.

"We have a rather spacious *Sommerstube* out back," Wilhelm Dyck was saying. "You may take a look and see if it would meet your needs."

He led the way to a white, brick building not far from the main house. It looked to Jacob at least as large as their modest home in Siberia.

Wilhelm opened the wooden door and they stepped into a large kitchen fully equipped with a stove, cooking utensils, table and chairs, a wash stand with a basin and pitcher, and even dishes.

Jacob was familiar with summer kitchens. Almost every home in the Mennonite villages in southern Russia had one, either as a room in the house, or as a separate building nearby. In the summer when it was hot outside, the cooking and canning could be done there and the main house would stay relatively cool.

"There is another room over there," said Wilhelm, gesturing to a door in the far wall. "It could be used as a bedroom." He walked over and opened the door to a good-sized room. It was being used for storage, Jacob observed, but would be ample as a bedroom.

"I think I may know someone who would be willing to come and look after the children too," continued Wilhelm. He looked inquiringly at Jacob, not knowing what to make of his silence.

"Do you think it would do, *Bruder* Rempel?" He could not shake the feeling that he should be offering his own home. "Of course, we will be right next door, so we will see that they are well cared for."

Jacob could not meet Wilhelm's gaze. He was not used to accepting charity, and he was overcome with both humiliation and gratitude.

"What can I say," he said, his eyes still lowered. " You are very kind. May God reward you for it." He extended his right hand.

"You would do the same for me if I were needing help," Wilhelm replied, accepting the outstretched hand. "Now, let's get your belongings so we can get the children settled in right away. I will just go and tell Justina what we have decided."

And so, after supper, with the help of the Dycks, the children were settled into the summer house along with their middle-aged housekeeper, Herta. The next day Jacob Rempel said good-bye to his little brood and was gone. Such were the times.

# 7

# MILLEROVO UNDER SIEGE

All that winter Lenin's scheme of maximum encouragement of peasant violence in carrying out the abolition of private landownership and the nationalization of industry and private business, sent shockwaves through the land.

The Rempel children clung together in their tranquil little nest, secure under the watchful eye of Herta and the Dyck family and oblivious to the drastic changes taking place in the lives of their wealthy hosts.

During the daytime, Lisa, Tina, and Jasch went to school with the Dyck children, making friends with the other children in Millerovo. It was not long before twelve-year-old Agatha Dyck and eleven-year old Lisa were best friends, sometimes walking in the crisp winter air, talking eagerly of many things.

"Of course there are schools in Siberia, silly. And yes, there are Russian teachers too, ever since the start of the war with Germany," said Lisa importantly, enjoying Agatha's endlessly inquisitive questions.

"And do they also say that there is no God, and that 'religion is the opiate of the masses'?" Agatha continued dramatically, echoing the forbidden words she had been hearing from her older cousin, Karl, who was going to the *Zentralschule* where a new Russian teacher had replaced *Onkel* Fast.

"They didn't used to," said Lisa, sobering. She was both shocked and a little intimidated by her friend's daring. She was used to keeping her questions to herself. Whatever would Papa or Mr. Dyck say if they heard them talking like this?

Lisa's reserve only urged Agatha on as she continued expansively, "And did you know that God didn't create the world?" Her face was set in mock seriousness as she parodied Karl's teacher. "No indeed He didn't. Once upon a time there was a big bang!" She clapped her hands together. "And gradually things evolved, changing, changing, . . ." She moved her fingers in front of Lisa's dumbfounded face as though stirring up a magic spell as she continued eerily, "fishes changed into birds, and birds changed into monkeys." She paused, spun around and stopped dead in her tracks. "And one of those monkeys, my dear Lisa, turned into you!" She laughed uproariously as her finger shot out and jabbed Lisa's nose.

"Is that so?" countered Lisa. "Well you're still a monkey, and a very naughty one too." Their peals of laughter echoed along the village street as they headed for home.

But underneath all the bravado was an uneasiness that the secure and simple world they had known was rapidly changing. Who could prepare for the great unknowns that lay ahead?

For Lisa and her brothers and sisters, it seemed there could be nothing worse in store than what they had already experienced. Mama dead and Papa gone away for two years and eight months. Lisa did not mind living in the Dycks' summer house, or even talking High German like the Dycks instead of Low German, as they had always talked with Mama and Papa but it was hard to have to take orders from *Tante* Herta, a total stranger, and not at all as nice as Mama. Even the little ones seemed to resent the intrusion, clinging rather to Lisa or Tina when their tears needed drying.

*Tante* Dyck kept saying that they must be good and do as *Tante* Herta said, or Papa would be upset. And so they tried to be good, and not say too often, "But *Tante* Herta, Mama didn't do it that way." After all, Papa would soon be home, and they did not want to disappoint him.

Sometimes at night shooting could be heard in the streets, and in the morning Mrs. Dyck and her two eldest daughters could be seen going to the neighbours to offer help and consolation to anyone who had been hurt. "Bandits," is all Mrs. Dyck would say, shaking her head disapprovingly.

Most often the bandits were simple Russian peasants, their

bodies reeking of filth, their beards unkempt, and their hair crawling with lice. They demanded food, money, jewelry, livestock, anything they desired, giddy with their newly acquired power, and brandishing weapons which they had also stolen, sometimes from the fallen bodies of soldiers. They did not much care whose weapons they stole, whether from the opposing czarist, or "White" army, or from the "Red" army that Lenin and Trotsky had formed in January to squelch any resistance to his new policies.

The Dyck household also had these unwelcome visitors, and Agatha was learning to follow her mother and elder sister's example in trying to outwit the would-be plunderers.Much of their wealth had already been hidden away, where the lusting eyes of the thieves could not find it. Sometimes Agatha, Lisa, and Susie, Agatha's twelve-year-old niece, unaware of their own real danger, even made a game of helping with the packing and hiding, and were always delighted when the nasty thieves hadn't been able to find their hidden treasures.

. . . . .

On a dull March day in 1918, the girls again heard the approaching riders. Mama Dyck and the older sisters had taken the younger ones to the station to meet the train, as they often did, taking with them freshly baked bread and sausage for the poor, hungry travellers who inevitably were there.

"It is as though all of Russia is on the move and without bread," Justina Dyck would often say.

On this particular day no one was at home except the three girls and their invalid sister, whom they were looking after. Father Dyck had gone to a hastily called meeting of Mennonite church leaders in the Donskoi district to discuss the growing oppression upon the villages. The ominous sound of hoof beats, and the belligerent shouts were coming closer and closer.

"*Jetzt kommen sie!*" shouted Susie in High German, hearing the riders turn into their lane. "*Wollen wir schnell alles weg schaffen.*"

And with that the girls dashed through the bedrooms, grabbing armsful of their finest clothes and hiding them. Especially treasured and now the most urgent objects of their efforts, were the beautiful satin dresses that Papa had brought from his

49

most recent trip to Moscow.

"Here," he had said, his face glowing with pleasure as he handed them the dresses, "Everything is changing so quickly. You may never have nice things again."

He knew from experience what it was like to be an orphan and hungry. And now that he had a family and ample means to support them, nothing was withheld or denied. Seeing their pleasure soothed the pain of his own past deprivations. His generosity knew no bounds, and his love for fine clothing expressed itself as he lavished the finest upon his sons and daughters, in-laws and grandchildren.

Not only his own family benefited from his generosity, however. Anyone who asked for his help received it. One widow whom he had met on his preaching trip to Siberia had told him that her cow had died, making it very difficult for her to support her family. So he had given her enough rubles for another cow.

It was not long before others had written to him telling him of the demise of their cows, and before long, he laughingly told people, he had seventy cows in Siberia.

Now the girls were frantically stuffing the beautiful clothes into their secret hiding place, while outside the banging and shouting intensified.

"Open the door," one of the rogues shouted in Russian. "Open up, or we'll set a match to you and roast you alive." Other voices chimed in, cursing and shouting threats.

"Susie, Lisa, hurry," whispered Agatha, "before they break down the door or burn down the house."

The girls ran to open the front door, the invalid sister forgotten in their haste. Trembling visibly, Agatha slid back the bolt.

"What took you so long?" demanded the leader, roughly pushing the girls aside with his rifle.

Before the intruders could stop them, Agatha, with the other two girls in hot pursuit, had slipped past their legs, and were running for the safety of a thicket of currant bushes.

From there they watched, still panting with fright. They could hear a great deal of clattering and crashing coming from inside the house, and then there was the sound of gunshots.

"Oh no," gasped Agatha, "we forgot Martha! Now they've

shot her!" She covered her face, and began weeping uncontrollably.

"Sh-sh," cautioned Susie, "they'll hear you and come after us too."

Agatha's muffled sobs continued as they waited, shivering with fright and imagining the worst. This was not a game any more.

Finally, after what seemed like hours, they saw the bandits plunge out of the front door carrying pillow cases full of things they had taken from the house. With triumphant shouts, they jumped onto their horses and galloped away.

As soon as the coast was clear the girls ran back to the house, dreading the awful scene that would meet their eyes. But there, God be praised, in the kitchen where they had left her, was Martha, still sitting in her wheelchair, wide-eyed but unharmed.

"Oh Martha," Agatha threw her arms around the young woman's neck, "you're alive!"

In their relief, the girls hardly took notice of the devastation that had been inflicted on their home. Even the treasured *Hammerklavier*, whose sound had filled the Dyck home with wonderful music ever since Esther had learned to play, had not escaped the attack. Now its black and white keys lay scarred and silent, its strings broken, and its once gracious, dark brown case gaping with ragged holes made by the bandits' guns.

The girl's dresses, however, lay untouched, and as beautiful as before in the secret place where they had been hidden.

. . . . .

It was early April, just five months since Jacob Rempel had left, when word suddenly came that he was at the station. Hastily *Ältester* Dyck drove his *Droschka* to the station to bring him home. The children were at the gate, straining to catch the first glimpse of their Papa.

"There they come! There they come!" Little Anna was jumping up and down in the muddy driveway, and Heinz and Peter, perched on the top rail of the white wooden fence would have fallen off in their excitement had it not been for the steadying hands of Lisa and Tina. Jascha was on the fence too, straining to catch a glimpse of Papa.

They could see the horse trotting at a brisk pace as the *Droschka* turned off the street and into the Dyck driveway. Six children raced alongside.

As Jacob Rempel's feet touched the driveway, Anna flung herself against him sobbing.

"There, there my sweet," his hand trembled as he patted her head, his tender gaze sweeping over the rest of them.

"Are you staying home now?" Tina asked.

"Why were you gone so long?" Peter chimed in.

"Are the three years over already? Are they? Are they?"

Their excited questions spilled over in a jumbled welcome chorus. What an unexpected homecoming!

"Not so fast children," interrupted *Onkel* Dyck. "You can see your father is very tired and must rest. There will be time for talk later." And with that he took Jacob Rempel's arm and they disappeared through the big doors which *Tante* Dyck was holding open for them.

There was a moment of stunned silence at the abbreviated homecoming before the younger children ran off to play.

"What's wrong with Papa?" Jascha's face registered concern.

"He's tired," said Lisa matter-of-factly, hoping to still the fears welling up inside her.

"He's sick," retorted Tina. "Didn't you see how his hands trembled and how he leaned on *Onkel* Dyck when he walked?"

Lisa had seen it, but she was not about to admit it. There was no other reason that they would have let Papa come home early. This she knew for certain.

"Come on Tina, let's go help *Tante* Herta make supper." She turned abruptly on her heels towards the summer house.

The following two weeks were a blur for the Rempel children. The promised time for talking with Papa did not come. Instead, Papa lay isolated in the servant quarters of the Dyck house.

"He's got the typhus," is all Tante Dyck would say, shaking her head ominously. "We are all in danger. You must not go into the room!" But Tina caught glimpses of his wasting form as Mrs. Dyck slipped in and out with basins of cool water to ease his

52

burning fever. At first she had taken him some chicken broth too, but now it was just the water.

"Another glass of water *bitte*," Mrs. Dyck would call, and Tina would run and bring her the cool liquid to wet his fever-parched lips. She shuddered, hearing his delirious cries and moans.

*Tante* Herta, along with Agatha and Lisa, were having their own difficulties with the younger ones, who had grown impatient to be with Papa.

"Why don't you sing for us Heinza," they coaxed. "Come sit on the stool and sing all your favorite songs."

"No," replied Heinza firmly. "I want to sing *Hop, hop, hop*, on Papa's knee."

"Pretty soon Heinza. When he gets better. Now come on, be a good boy and sing."

But there was no persuading him, and they watched the usually cheerful lad of almost three set his jaw, and before Herta could stop him, bolt outside with his five-year-old brother Peter right behind him.

"You stay out of the mud puddles, you hear," called Herta after them in exasperation. But the boys did not answer.

# 8

# DEATH STRIKES AGAIN

Henry lifts the rocking horse he has been sanding and runs the tips of his fingers over the wooden surface. He sets it down again and takes up the fine sandpaper, resuming his painstaking work. His breath is laboured, but he is not aware of the chill that has settled in the garage. Outside the cold January wind is picking up.

In his mind he continues to study the photograph of his parents, willing himself to remember them, to feel some link with them, but their eyes look out at him, sadly it seems, still strangers. The woman is small, her body roundly curved, the man, tall and angular, is wearing a dark suit.

Ah, the suit. That is what Henry remembers. It is not much, but it is something. A tender, tentative link. It is all he has.

It is the day of Papa's funeral. April, 1918, as close as he can figure. Ironically, it's not even because of his father that he remembers it, but because of Peter, who cannot come to the funeral. Peter is still sick, alone in a darkened room at the Dycks.

. . . . .

Heinz and Peter were playing outside, *Tante* Herta's strict orders not to play in the mud long forgotten. Outside, in the fresh spring air, they could forget too that they still hadn't been able to sit on Papa's knee, and they could shut out the terrible groans coming from Papa's bedroom.

The afternoon passed quickly as the two brothers romped and tussled in the spring sunshine, happy to be free of the gloom that hung like a bad smell over the Dyck house. Theirs was a camaraderie not only borne of proximity of age, but also of shared hardship too deep for their young minds to fully comprehend. They found comfort in each other and depended on each other for the stability that had so suddenly disappeared from their young lives. Neither was aware of the special bond. It was one of the few givens they had learned to rely on.

The hollow in their stomachs reminded them that it would soon be supper time, and suddenly they were conscious of their mud-splattered condition.

"Quick, the rain barrel," said Peter, setting off on the run. Peter could easily reach in to swish the water over his face, splashing it over his hands and feet too, but Heinz had to stand on tip-toes to guiltily wash away his mud. They crept inside, their disobedience apparently unnoticed.

It was not until they both became dangerously ill several days later with their eyes swollen and infected and their bodies raging with fever, that their little secret was discovered. Upon further investigation, it was discovered that the water they had washed in had been contaminated by a rotting cat that a neighbourhood prankster had thrown into the rain barrel.

"Be sure your sins will find you out," admonished Wilhelm Dyck sternly. But the boys were in no mood for sermons.

For more than a week, they fought for their eyesight and their lives in a darkened room at the Dycks.

At last Heinz was declared well enough to be allowed outside again, but Peter's fever raged on.

In a nearby room, their father, Jacob Rempel, lost his battle with the terrible typhus. The long-promised reunion with his children was not to be.

. . . . .

A tremendous coughing spell wrenches Henry back to the chilly garage. He gasps as he sinks into one of the unpainted lawn chairs he has made. The little rocking horse for his grandson is nearly finished. He already imagines the boy riding it with carefree abandon. He is glad he did not listen to Katie and give him one of the other already finished toys. The boy will have this little pleasure, and that pleases Henry. Stubbornly he gets up and works on, disregarding his own pain. He is used to that.

. . . . .

Lisa, Tina, Jasch, Anna and Heinz followed as the casket was carried to the *Friedhof* behind the church. At the graveyard the lid was taken off for a final farewell as Scriptures were read and more prayers were said.

All little Heinz could think of as he stared at the sombre black suit in the casket was that his brother Peter was all alone in a dark room in the Dycks' big house. Someone should go to him! Rising panic churned in Heinz's throat, but in the silence around the graveside there was no one he could tell.

Then the final hymn was sung and the lid fastened. Slowly the casket was lowered into the ground. Several men took up shovels and began filling in the gaping hole, each shovelful of dirt thudding with finality on the coffin lid.

Suddenly, there were feet to Heinz's urgency, and without a backward look he bolted blindly from the churchyard, plunging down the street towards the Dycks' house, with an insane panic pounding in his chest.

"Peter! Peter!"

. . . . .

Henry rubs his eyes, scrutinizing the wooden horse, and then resumes sanding. Odd, he muses ruefully, that the only reason he remembers his own father's funeral is because of the dark suit and the concern it triggered for his brother Peter. Hard as he tries, he can't even remember feeling sad that his father had died. Maybe he did and has forgotten. Who can tell?

A violent coughing spell exhausts Henry, and he slumps into the lawn chair for another short rest.

. . . . .

*Ältester* Dyck cleared his throat. "As you all know, it is my obligation to see that the orphans in our community find a suitable home."

Thirteen-year-old Agatha Dyck tugged at her father's sleeve, and whispered,"Papa, they can live with us, just like before."

A stern look silenced her. "We know that these are difficult and uncertain times," he continued. "We will follow our usual practice of passing the children from home to home until someone can be found to keep them permanently."

There were other new mounds in the cemetery, also bearing

56

silent witness that needs had arisen before. He had confidence that once again the community would respond.

"Papa, please," Agatha urged, "at least the little ones." To her the Rempel children had become family over the past five months. She could not bear to think of being parted from them. Nor could she understand her father's reasons for not keeping them. She was not used to being denied her wishes, and now she pled.

"Not now, Agatha." Wilhelm Dyck's voice was firm.

"The eldest one can come work for us for now," spoke up a middle-aged man. "My wife has been sick and she could use the help with the little ones. We can't pay her, but we'll give her food and shelter."

Lisa, her head bent until now, lifted a fleeting glance in the man's direction and then continued to intently study the toe of her shoe.

Another man spoke up next. "We're too old to start up with little ones again, but we could use some help around the house and the garden too, couldn't we Muttie," he said affectionately to his white-haired wife beside him. "We will share our home with the second daughter, for now."

The woman caught Tina's eye and smiled her assent.

"You're a big, strong chap," said one man, laying a hand on Jascha's shoulder. "How old are you?"

"I'll be eight in July," replied young Jacob, not looking up.

"Only eight? My, you're a big boy. Can you drive a team of horses yet?"

"I can learn," said Jascha firmly.

"Well, it's settled then," said the man.

"Good," Willhem answered. "Now just the youngest three. You saw the youngest. He's the one who can run," he chuckled softly. "And one boy is still sick at our house. Then there's little Anna ."

There was an uncomfortable pause. She was a beautiful child of delicate build. At four and a half, she was not really big enough to be of significant help. If only someone could be found who wanted to adopt the little girl as their own, thought Wilhelm.

A shabbily clad man with a burly voice spoke up. "Well, if we were going to take one," he said grudgingly, "we would rather have had one of the older ones." He paused, hoping someone would trade one of the older girls for this little one.

When no one spoke up, he went on, "Really, the last thing we need right now is another baby." A nervous chuckle rippled through the crowd. Five children, the oldest no more than six, clustered around the man's wife, who was obviously pregnant with another child. "I guess we'll take the little one," he continued gruffly.

Wilhelm's heart sank. "She is rather small," he said, stalling, hoping someone else would speak up.

"Well, what's one more among so many anyway, eh mother?" the man jabbed his wife, grinning. His wife did not reply.

Anna tightened her hold on Tina's hand, biting her lip to keep from crying. She did not want to go away with anyone, especially not that man, but there was no one to say that to. Mama and Papa weren't here to say, "Don't cry Anna, you can come home with us where you belong."

Instead, she could hear *Onkel* Dyck taking a deep breath and saying, "Yes, all right then, you take her for now." But it wasn't all right. Nothing was all right. Her body trembled.

Wilhelm did not have the stomach for any more discussion. He would see about the two boys Peter and Heinz himself, later. For now, Peter needed to get well. It was obvious that his little brother Heinz was thoroughly attached to the boy. Maybe he could find a way to keep these two together. There was time.

Wilhelm looked over the group assembled in the cemetery. "Come," he said, "let us go back to the house of prayer for the *Trauermahl*. After we have eaten, you will please take the children you have spoken for. You will find their things in our summer house."

And with that, Wilhelm Dyck turned on his heels and strode briskly from the cemetery, his large frame casting even larger shadows in the late afternoon sun.

. . . . .

It was dark as Heinz and Peter lay in a bed in the big Dyck house that night. Peter, still hot and feverish, stared, eyes smarting into the darkness, numb with the finality of the hurried goodbyes. Strangers had taken them all away, Lisa, Tina, Jascha, and Anna, and he did not know where.

"Mama, Mama," the sobbing voice of his younger brother lying beside him echoed in the big room. "Where is Lischen, I want Lischen."

The plaintive voice of the little boy continued, but for five-year-old Peter there was no thought of answering, only the echoed question reverberating in the crushing emptiness of a dark night from which there seemed to be no waking.

"Agatha, do something." Justina Dyck shook her daughter from her sleep in the adjoining bedroom. "I can't get that boy to stop crying. He doesn't even seem to notice when I'm there. Maybe he will listen to you."

Agatha padded on bare feet into the boys' room. The little Rempel boy was weeping as though all the pain and disruption of the past six months had come unleashed all at once. His wrenching sobs shook his little body as though they would tear him apart.

Agatha climbed into the bed and gathered the weeping boy into her arms.

"Sh-shsh," she whispered, rocking him gently. "Sh-shsh."

The boy continued to sob, but Peter snuggled against her, silent, still burning with fever. She began to sing softly, as she often did, one of the many songs little Heinz knew by memory.

*"Kennst du wie viel Sternlein schauen...*

"Can you count the stars that brightly twinkle in the midnight sky?

"Can you count the clouds, so lightly o'er the meadows floating by?

"God the Lord, doth mark their number with his eyes that never slumber,

"He hath made them every one, He hath made them every one."

Agatha kept singing, her clear, childish voice bathing the room with warmth, soothing the sobbing boy. Finally, just the quivering little hiccups punctuated the tender lyrics. Beside her, Peter's even breathing told her that at least he was asleep.

# 9

# FLIGHT TO SAFETY

# SUMMER 1918

Henry can not remember any details of the months following his father's funeral. But he has heard and read enough to know that beyond the borders of his three-year-old innocence, anarchy and civil war was rocking a country already wrung dry by World War I.

The war effort had diverted and converted the nation's supplies and manpower to meet the military needs, absorbing men, horses, and machinery. The country's economy lay in shambles. Factories that had manufactured plows and pocket knives now made shell casings and artillery wagons. The transportation system no longer carried food supplies across the country. Instead it was the military's life-line.

Widespread shortages of food and fuel had resulted in ever increasing unrest, especially in the cities. The best horses had been confiscated by the military from the farming villages and estates, leaving many farmers unable to plant the crops upon which the country depended. And ever increasing demands of taxes or farm produce were leaving even the farming communities destitute.

Henry has even read of a rueful joke which became popular when farmers found their chickens strangled to death by the maruaders. The chickens, it was said, had committed suicide because they couldn't produce the number of eggs that the new regime demanded.

The strong anti-German sentiment caught the Mennonite

communities in midstride, adding additional trauma and suddenly making them enemies in what they had grown to think of as their *Vaterland*.

Their industrial and educational ties to Germany had been abruptly cut off at the beginning of the war, and laws had been passed prohibiting the use of the German language in public assembly, including schools, and in the press. More and more Russian teachers had been placed in the privately run Mennonite schools.

By the summer of 1918, the struggle between the Whites, the old guard czarist forces, and the revolutionary Bolsheviks was involving much of the country in bloody battles.

Workers' soviets, set up to govern the towns and villages, were bleeding the settlements with dictatorial and exploitative tactics, confiscating businesses and property and turning a blind eye to the marauding revolutionaries and anarchists. But the czarist forces were fighting back.

Millerovo, like hundreds of other Mennonite settlements, found itself caught in the middle of this political tug-of-war. The Bolshevik Red army would push back the White forces and would no sooner establish itself in the area when the White army would rally a counter attack and take control.

In between, bandits and anarchists plundered, ravaged, raped and killed, like unleashed demons, intoxicated by the promise of wealth and power.

. . . . .

Henry knows that during this time he must have been living with the Dycks, but has no personal recollection of this turbulent time.

It is only recently, since he has discovered Agatha Dyck Warkentin and her friend, whom he calls *Tante* Marichen, that he has been able to fill in some of the missing details of some of those lost years when he lived with the Dycks.

Now, as he works on Mathew's rocking horse, he lets his mind mull over each small detail Agatha, or Mrs. Warkentin, as he now calls her, has told him, holding it up against the blank screen of his memory to see if there is any recognition. Strange, he thinks to himself, how two years can so completely go missing, when there are such vivid memories immediately before and after.

He can not even remember the death and funeral of Martha Dyck, the invalid daughter of Wilhelm and Justina during this time, nor has he any recollection of the two eldest Dyck sisters being sent to the relative safety of the Halbstadt Girls' School in the Molotschna.

Only one brief incident has made an imprint on his memory at all, emblazoned on his young mind by the unexpected visit of a brother he has not seen since Papa's funeral. As close as he can figure out, it was July.

He cannot remember if Jascha has ridden to Millerovo, or if they have gone to visit him, but there is his brother, riding a beautiful, black, Shetland pony. He has gotten it for his eighth birthday from the people he lives with. Henry does not remember the name of the family, only that Jascha's eyes are shining with pleasure. He and Peter take turns riding Jascha's horse. He is aware of an uneasy, gnawing jealousy . . . to receive such a gift . . . . Even the Dycks do not give such gifts.

They ride and ride, all their loneliness forgotten in the joy of sharing the unexpected. And then it is over. No recollection of good-byes. Just one poignant snapshot, the last Henry has of his brother Jacob.

Only one further detail has he been able to glean about his brother over these many years. It is, ironically, that Jacob had sometimes been mistreated by the very people who gave him the Shetland pony. That is all.

. . . . .

The sound of guns shook the hot August night. There was a sound of horse's hooves beating on the Dycks' driveway, and then persistent knocking.

"Who is it?" Wilhelm Dyck opened the door cautiously.

"Brother Dyck, you and your family are in great danger," his friend Abram Fast panted. "The Bolsheviks are asking for you at the other end of the city. "Quick, run for your lives!" With that he swung back on his horse and was gone.

Wilhelm did not waste any time. Quickly he woke Justina, Willie, Agatha, Peter, and Heinz. They dressed in haste and crept quietly out the back door, running towards the back of the property, where they would find some shelter.

They could hear horses approaching, and just as they reached the far side of the mill, they could hear shouts as the riders came up the lane to their house.

"Wilhelm Dyck, come out. You're under arrest." Gun butts pounded against the door.

"This way," whispered Wilhelm, urging his little brood across the railway tracks behind the mill. "We'll hide in the corn field."

Their hearts pounded as they ran. They could hear the commotion around the house spill over into the rest of the yard as the buildings were searched. Breathlessly they crouched, hidden from view, among the tall corn stalks.

The village seemed to be overrun with Red army soldiers, and they could be heard shouting to each other. Gun shots punctuated the commotion.

"We can't stay here," whispered Wilhelm. "We must try to get away while it is still dark."

They ran, stumbling in the darkness, clawing their way through the corn stalks, then darting through a large stand of trees, and finally, crouching low to scurry across an open pasture.

"Papa, I can't . . . go any farther," panted Agatha, after they had run and stumbled in the dark for what seemed like a very long time.

"*Ja*, my child"—he was panting too—"we'll rest here a little."

They had just crossed the open field and now stopped to rest, hidden in a grove of bushes not far from a road.

"Riders!" Wilhelm Dyck whispered. They flattened themselves against the ground in the tall grass, hardly daring to breath as the pounding hoof beats approached and passed without slowing down.

"Bolsheviks!" breathed Justina.

"Are they after us, Papa?" Willie asked.

"Sh-sh," cautioned Wilhelm. "No talking! Come. We must hurry!" And with that Wilhelm scooped up little Heinz, carrying him as he ran. "Not much farther now," panted Wilhelm as they began making their way up the long incline of a hill. They were approaching the little village of Abramsfeld.

Wilhelm Dyck guided the group to the back door of a house he recognized. "I know the couple that lives here," he said, answering Justina's questioning look. "They are not of our people, but they are God-fearing. We'll be safe with them."

Looking back from where they had just come, they could see Millerovo in the distance. The sounds of the fighting still disrupted the night.

Wilhelm knocked softly. Then knocked again. The door opened a crack.

"It is I, Wilhelm Dyck, with my family," he whispered. "They are looking for us in Millerovo. They will soon be on our heels if they haven't been here already."

The door opened, and they were quickly ushered into the dark room. "No one has been here," their host whispered. "God has brought you to a safe place, you'll see."

They were taken into an adjoining room where the man pulled aside a bookshelf, revealing a low doorway. A secret door opened into a little, hidden room. There were straw mats on the floor. "For such a time as this," he said, motioning them to enter quickly.

"God be with you," the woman said.

"Thank you! Thank you!" whispered Justina.

They could hear the bookcase being moved back into place after the door had closed behind the couple.

How long they sat, shivering in spite of the warm night air, they could not tell. All was dark, but in the distance, they could hear the sounds of battle.

Gradually, the faint morning light began to probe the cracks around the secret doorway; then they could detect the sounds of the couple, going about their morning chores.

"Maybe they won't come," whispered Agatha hopefully.

"I'm hungry," groaned Willie.

"Sh-sh," cautioned Wilhelm. "We must be patient until our friends come and tell us it's safe to come out. Why don't we all try to get some rest like these two young chaps." He looked over at the two Rempel boys who were fast asleep on a straw mat.

"Faith as a little child," he murmured. He too must learn to trust more in the care of his Heavenly Father, as these young boys seemed to trust in him, an earthly guardian. Wearily, he lay down on a straw mat, dozing fitfully.

He had not slept long, when a sudden menacing shout had the little group instantly alert. More shouting accompanied loud knocking at the door of the house.

Time seemed to stop in the secret room. Not a sound could be heard there except for the occasional trembling breath.

They could hear the lady of the house answer the door, but could not make out the conversation.

A well-rehearsed plan now sprang into action. "Welcome to our home," said the lady of the house, smiling disarmingly into the stern faces of five Bolshevik soldiers. "What good timing. I was just going to go stir the soup simmering in the summer kitchen. Won't you come and try some?"

"Ah good," said the woman's husband, coming into view carrying a pail of milk. "Visitors. And welcome guests too. I heard my good wife invite you to a bowl of her delicious soup. Here, why don't I take those handsome horses and feed and water them while you eat," he said in flawless Russian. The horses stood, sides heaving and covered in lather.

The men looked at one another, momentarily taken aback. "Why not?" said one of them finally. The mood seemed to relax as they followed the woman into the little summer kitchen from where the soup's savory aroma was wafting, and before long they were eating heartily, laughing and joking, as though they had always intended a friendly, neighbourly visit.

When at last the soldiers, well fed and in jovial spirits, mounted their horses and rode away, they had not even thought to ask if the couple had seen the fleeing Dyck family. Little did they know that the very family whom they had been sent to capture was hidden only steps away from where they had sat, listening intently to the muffled sound of their voices.

The couple watched as the soldiers mounted their rested horses and galloped away, once more intent on their search for the man labelled "an enemy of the people" because of his wealth and his involvements with the church.

Inside the hidden room, that man was thanking God for once

more protecting him and his little brood.

"I think it is safe to come out now," said their host finally, sliding the bookcase aside and opening the door. Gratefully, Wilhelm, Justina, Agatha, Willie, Peter and Heinz, crept out of their hiding place.

It was not long before they too were eating hungrily from the same pot of soup which had fed the soldiers. As they ate they could hear the sounds of shooting intensify in the city below them. It was not until several hours later that the sounds of gunfire finally began to subside.

From their vantage point, the Dycks could barely make out what seemed to be the Bolshevik army beating a hasty retreat, with the Whites not far behind. Then all was quiet.

For several hours they watched and waited. Finally, when it was deemed safe, the Dycks' friends took them back to the Dyck home in Millerovo. There they learned that during the night the Bolsheviks had rounded up many people, herding them like cattle into box cars at the train station. But, providentially, before they were through, the White army had stormed the village and all but a few had managed to escape. Those who had not been so fortunate were either dead or even now being held prisoner by the retreating Bolshevik army.

All day Wilhelm struggled with the inevitable. Finally, late that evening he gathered his family around him. "We must prepare to leave now," said Wilhelm. "They will be back, and when they come they will surely be looking for me."

A plan was taking shape in Wilhelm Dyck's mind. He would take his family to stay with relatives in the Molotschna, where the German army, under the Brest-Litovsk Treaty, was offering some protection. And it would give him the opportunity to take the two Rempel boys to the Mennonite orphanage in Grossweide. It would be safer for them there, he decided, and the Harders were well known for the loving home they provided for many orphan children. The boys could be together there, at least until one or both were taken in. The four hundred kilometre trip to the Molotschna region should still be possible if they travelled with care.

Preparations were hastily made, and the next day no one

would have guessed that the subdued little group disguised as peasants making their way to the Millerovo train station was in fact one of the wealthiest Mennonite families in the region. Wilhelm and Justina, along with two of their children, Willie and Agatha, Oma and Opa Poetker, Justina's parents, and Peter and Heinz Rempel were joining others, who, because of the unrest, were also leaving their homes in search of safety elsewhere.

"Let's pretend we're just going to the Molotschna for a visit," said Agatha.

No one answered. It was a dream they all wanted to cling to, but deep inside the reality seemed far less promising. This farewell to their beautiful Millerovo home, to family and friends, might well be a final one. Only God knew what lay ahead.

. . . . .

The box car was crowded, heavy with the smell of sweaty bodies packed too tightly in the August heat, jostling its way south-westward towards safety and hope. Soldiers on leave and peasants in search of food, were among the perspiring passengers. The Dycks, dressed as they were in their peasant garb, were blending in with the other passengers, but hidden beneath their shabby clothing were bulging money belts and golden chains to which their expensive jewelry was fastened. One of the sacks which they guarded closely was full of money—their security for a new beginning elsewhere if the need should arise. They had taken as much as they dared without raising the suspicion of the people around them.

Now they sat, crowded together with other passengers like sardines in a can, on the wooden benches that had been hastily fashioned as seats along the walls. What little luggage they had brought was on the floor at their feet.

"Why couldn't we ride in a proper train car?" whined eight-year-old Willie, shrinking from a group of dirty Russian peasants next to him.

"Sh-sh-sh." Wilhelm hurriedly quieted his son. It would not do to be singled out as *Kulaks*, and he certainly did not want his identity discovered.

"Just be glad we have a place at all," he whispered in Russian. He had warned the children not to speak a single word of German in public. If anyone guessed who they were, the trip would surely end abruptly. He knew of others, who, like himself had been influential in their communities, and now were being rounded up like criminals, to be tortured, shot, or banished to Siberia. Many had been spirited away at night, not to be heard from again. Now they were after him.

. . . . .

The hours dragged on, with the train stopping at every station to take on even more passengers and only occasionally letting some off. It seemed that all of Russia was trying to get to the relative calm of the Ukraine.

There were further delays as they waited on a siding for a military train to pass. Four hours had passed, and according to Wilhelm's estimation they should be at least half-way there, even at this slow pace. Another few hours to Grünau, and then an hour or so south to Belgovka. From there word would be sent to Sparrau for the relatives to come and get them. The short trip to Grossweide to take Heinz and Peter to the orphanage would be made the next day. He would be relieved when that responsibility was finally off his shoulders. There was no question that the boys would be well cared for, he reminded himself. It was the right thing to do.

Justina, trying to keep her brood from becoming too restless, was just bringing out dried fruit and buns when suddenly, a violent explosion sounded above the chatter and clatter of the train, its tremors reverberating the length of the train. Brakes screeched and passengers and baggage flew forward. Children screamed out in shock and fear.

"What was that?"

"What's going on?"

People scrambled to collect themselves and their belongings, making sure that no one was seriously hurt. Faces craned to see out of the several openings that served as windows and through cracks in the walls of the box car, but no one could learn an explanation for what had just happened.

The minutes dragged by. No one came by to slide open the big door or to explain the delay.  Finally, the train shuddered and began to move, slowly at first, and then more quickly.

"We're going backwards," said Willie, stating the obvious.

"What is the meaning of this?" The questions bounced from person to person as the train continued its backwards journey.

Outside, hidden in the lengthening shadows of the trees beside the tracks, a group of men huddled on horseback, cursing as they watched the train's laborious retreat. The trestle bridge it was to have crossed, hung in tangled ruins.

"The vibration of the track must have set it off early," growled one of them.

"Batko, shall we shoot?" asked another.

"*Njet*," replied the leader, "let the *svolotchi* go." No need being stupid about this, Makhno thought. Why risk our necks in broad daylight. Besides, he grinned inwardly, the mission hadn't been a complete failure, even though the damned device had detonated before the train had gotten to it. At least the bridge was gone, and no supplies would be reaching the German swine in the Molotchna by this route. At least, not for a while.

He gave his horse a sharp kick in the flank. In his mind he was a young frightened peasant boy again, taking another beating from his cruel Mennonite employer. He had vowed that one day he would have his revenge. Eight years he had rotted behind bars in the Butyrki. And eight years he had nursed his growing rage. A year ago he had finally been set free, and already his name struck terror in the Mennonite households in the Molotschna. Let the cowards call in the German army to protect them, to fight and kill for them. He would show them that would not stop Makhno. He would have to be reckoned with!

The train continued backing up, as Makhno and his men, still undetected, disappeared like phantoms, into the trees. It was fifteen minutes before the passengers finally felt the train slowing to a stop.

"We're at a station," said someone who had been looking out through the little opening in the side of the car. There was more waiting, until at long last the door slid open.

"This train is being rerouted to the Kuban," a voice shouted in

Russian. "Anyone not wanting to go there can get off here and take the northbound train."

"But we don't want to go to the Kuban," muttered Willie.

"Well, we surely don't want to go north either," countered Agatha.

"Why can't we go back to Millerovo?" called out one of the passengers.

"What happened back there? Why can't we go on to the Molotschna?" another asked.

"The tracks have been blown out in front of us and behind us," was the reply. "There's no going ahead and no going back."

Confusion reigned as families quickly discussed what to do now. There was a flurry of activity.

When the train finally pulled out of the station, the Dycks were still on board with Heinz and Peter Rempel, and Oma and Opa Poetker. Their new destination was Alexanderfeld, a Mennonite settlement lying to the east of the Caucasus Mountains in the Kuban province. Two days by train would get them there, and then—Justina eyed her meagre food supply. They had not come prepared for this. And when they arrived, what then? She knew no one in Alexanderfeld. Wilhelm had been there once in his travels for the church, but they had no relatives there.

For a fleeting moment she longed for her own home in Millerova, not daring to think what might already be happening to it. Then she chided herself. At least they were all together. Their Heavenly Father had protected them and cared for them this far, He would see them through what lay ahead. She sincerely believed it.

# 10

# THE KUBAN 1918-1920

Henry has absolutely no recollection of living with the Dycks in the Kuban, but Agatha Dyck has told him some of their shared experiences there. She has told him of their deplorable accommodations in a common *Russekot*, a small peasant shack with a thatched roof and a dirt floor. And she has told him of the day that her father Wilhelm Dyck tried to buy a house from a lady who wanted desperately to sell. The agreement was made, but in the meantime money lost its value and the sackful of money became worthless. The Dyck family, along with Heinz and Peter Rempel, was now destitute.

Her father's response to the sudden turn of events still echoes in Agatha's ears: *"Der Herr hat's gegeben, Der Herr hat's genommen. Der Name des Herren sei gepriessen.* The Lord has given and the Lord has taken; the name of the Lord be praised."

The entire family had gone to work for the farmers in the village, and when even that had proven not to meet their needs, the gregarious Agatha had been delegated to go about selling their prized pieces of jewelry so they could buy food.

Only the beautiful satin dresses which they had brought along remained of their former refined life-style. These dresses they wore to the church on Sundays, much to the chagrin of some of the other Mennonite worshippers who saw them as a questionable show of wealth.

Throughout the Kuban there were many who like the Dycks, had been displaced. As recently as February, the entire Mennonite settlement of fifteen villages along the Caucasus had fled their homes, leaving everything to the pillaging, plundering

Tartar tribes of the surrounding hillsides. People drunk with the Bolshevik promises of restored lands and equality for all, even now were living in the Mennonite homes on land which the government had taken from them only seventeen years earlier to give to the Mennonite settlers.

If the Dycks had hoped for things to settle down in the Kuban, they were soon to discover that with the civil war raging no place was immune to the terror.

Even the Brest-Litovsk Treaty in the Ukraine was short-lived as Germany admitted defeat and signed the armistice which ended the War, in November, 1918. The German troops, which had been welcomed as heroes, protectors and brothers in the Mennonite homes and villages of the Ukraine withdrew, leaving a dangerous vacuum and memories of an alliance which the Reds would not soon forget.

The Molotschna region, which for a short period of time had seemed like a place of refuge, was now plunged into a period of unprecedented struggle as bands of revolutionaries, the worst among them led by the dreaded Nestor Makhno, ravaged, plundered, and killed as they fought the floundering White troops and, when it suited them, the Reds themselves.

Mennonite youths who had formed the *Selbstschutz*, with the help of the German army, having fought gallantly in the Molotschna had nevertheless been defeated and were now being hunted down. Even innocent people were slaughtered in vengeful retribution for their sons' alliances with the German army and for their armed resistance to the revolutionaries.

As the civil war continued, it was no longer just thieves and gunmen at the door. Now hunger and sickness stalked the land. It seemed that all of Russia was hungry, and dreaded diseases like typhus, cholera, syphilis, malaria, and even tuberculosis rode on the backs of soldiers and beggars alike, forcing a steady procession to the cemeteries.

It was not until the spring of 1920, over a year and a half since the Dycks, along with Heinz and Peter Rempel and the Poetkers, had found themselves in the Kuban, that they finally managed to get word to their relatives in the Molotschna about their whereabouts, asking for whatever help that could be given.

May came, and with it welcome visitors from the Molotschna. Wilhelm Dyck's brother and brother-in-law arrived with a *Droschka* and a team of horses.

"O Mama," cried Agatha, "can we all go back with them? Can we? Can we?"

Heinz, nearly five years old now, and Peter seven, watched wide-eyed as preparations were made for the journey to the Molotschna. They were excited. They and Oma and Opa Poetker were to be the lucky ones who would get to go for a special visit to Grossweide far away. Maybe they would visit Jascha, Anna, Tina, and Lisa there, reasoned Heinz. The rest of the Dyck family would have to wait until the next visit. There was not room for everyone on this trip, they had been told. Not even for Agatha.

"But Mama," Agatha cried when she was alone with her mother. "I don't want Heinz and Peter to go away. Please, please can't they stay with us." Being older, she knew that the young boys would not be coming back, and was voicing strong objections. "We can't let them go Mama, they are like family to us. Please let them stay with us. Please!" But the tears were of no avail.

"Now Agatha," Justina's voice was husky but firm. "You know they will be better off there. And besides, it won't be long and we will go there too. Then you can go and visit them often. You will see. Now hush your crying before they hear you and become upset."

# 11

# ABANDONED

# May 27, 1920

Another cough rips through Henry's chest, the pain searing his lung like a branding iron. He sits for a moment in the lawn chair, waiting, gasping, then slowly gets up and continues sanding. The exertion and the fine dust particles are not kind, aggravating an already infected lung. He doubles over, coughing again and again, retching, his face crimson, gulping for air.

"Henry!" There is alarm in Katie's voice. He looks up startled. He has not heard her come into the garage where he is working.

"I heard you coughing," she scolds. "You're sick, you've got to get out of the dust and lie down. Just leave that silly old horse alone."

He coughs again, unable to answer her, but it doesn't matter; there can be no giving up now. Mathew's birthday party is next week, and the horse has been promised. His grandson's childish trust is not to be broken, not now and hopefully not ever. This he feels strongly about, no matter what anybody says.

Katie sets down the cup of tea and plate of Arrowroot cookies she has brought for his mid-afternoon snack, watches for a minute, then goes back into the house shaking her head in disgust. He is a stubborn old man. Nothing she says is going to change anything.

A sinister memory . . . Henry pushes it away. He sits down in an unpainted lawn chair to have his snack. He has been through it all before. It doesn't bother him anymore he tells himself. The Dycks had good reasons for what they did. Two extra mouths to

feed when there was already so little food . . . the political insta-
bility . . . the promise of a good, stable home for both Henry and
his brother, a chance to keep them together maybe . . . he knows
all these things . . . has recited all of the reasons he has been able
to think of, to Katie and to himself over and over again, like the
refrain of a tired song, still . . . the questions burn. Didn't they
know how attached he and Peter were to them? How, inno-
cently they had taken for granted that the Dyck home was their
home too? And how lovingly they called them Mama and Papa?

Henry gives his shoulders a stretch. If he had been in their
place, he couldn't have done it. He is certain of it. Not after so
long, and definitely not like that.

Now why is he thinking of Betty? It wasn't the same. Not
even close. He and Katie did all they could, and in the end the
child was returned to her own home where she belonged. He
remembers it all clearly. It all worked out just like it was supposed to.

It was the first year he and Katie were married, and Katie's
Aunt Helen had become very sick after the birth of her tenth
child. The oldest was no more than thirteen, and little sister
Tina, only nine months old, kept taking away her baby sister's
bottle and drinking the milk herself. The baby was wasting
away, and Uncle Jake came to Henry and Katie in desperation.
Could they help?

Because they were living with Henry's adoptive parents,
they had to ask their permission to take in the little one. Permission was granted and Katie cared for the child for over a year as
though it were her own. Henry became attached to little Betty
too. She was like one of the family.

But when the baby's mother died a little more than a year
later, they gave the child to Katie's parents to raise not because
they wanted to, but because Katie's mother insisted. . . . Henry
gets up abruptly, takes a fresh piece of sandpaper and resumes
sanding more vigorously than before.

All right. He will admit it. One word from him and the child
would have stayed. But Katie was expecting their own child—
their first. He was not willing to risk Katie's health for anything
or anyone. She was already working far too hard, helping him

with the field work, the stooking and the threshing. He could not jeopardize her health, especially not now. He was already afraid of losing her. Many young husbands lost their wives as a result of childbirth. That he would not risk.

So the decision had gone unchallenged. Katie's mother would raise little Betty until she was old enough to return to her own father's home to be cared for by siblings.

Henry pauses to inspect his work. Yes, there was no question. It all worked out like it was supposed to. They'd had their own healthy baby boy, and Katie hadn't died, even though she was afraid she might with a birth so difficult. And Betty had been returned to her own family when she was three years old.

There are no hard feelings between them and Betty, Henry tells himself. He is pretty sure of that. She has always kept in touch with them, and to Henry and Katie she will always be special. He blows dust from the horse's neck.

He feels no such bond with the Dycks. An icy knot forms in the pit of his stomach. He pushes it away. He is not being fair. They had their reasons too. Katie often reminds him of it too. She's right. It shouldn't bother him.

But, the memory of it lingers, painfully real, even after all these years. He puts down the sandpaper, feeling the smooth surface of the little horse. Good, he thinks. Finally ready for a coat of paint.

The fumes permeate the garage as he opens the can and begins to paint with careful strokes. A rich, shiny, grey coat. Mathew's horse will be all he ever hoped for. . . .

Sometimes Henry imagines aloud what it would have been like growing up in the Dyck home. He and Peter together always. Mama and Papa Dyck, sister Agatha, brother Willie, and the others.

"My name would be Henry Dyck," he teases Katie, "How would you like that?" His mind plays with the possibilities. What might it have been like not to be Henry Rempel, or Henry Huebert, as he's known now.

"Well, that'd be it for me then, wouldn't it," she storms, finding not a shred of humour in the notion.

"What do you mean?" Henry asks, surprised by her vehemence.

"Who knows where you'd have ended up," she retorts, "somebody else's husband for sure."

"Or dead," he counters pensively.

"Don't talk stupid!" she snaps. It scares her to think about it. Not only does he torment himself with these silly thoughts about being somebody else, it's as though death has actually stalked him, still stalks him like the hungry neighbourhood cat stalks the sparrows flitting about the yard. She can't bear to think about any of it, and can't understand why he has to.

"It turned out just the way it was meant," she says with finality. "It was God's will, and you're stuck with me. So forget all that stuff about the Dycks!"

And he knows she's right. The fact is, he actually has forgotten almost everything about the Dycks and the two years he spent with them. His only recollections are of his father's funeral and his brother's visit on his Shetland pony. Almost everything else he knows he has had to learn from others, or figure out on his own. It is only since he has discovered Agatha Dyck Warkentin and *Tante Mariechen* in Winnipeg just last year, that he has been able to fill in some of the missing details of those lost years.

He goes over it all often as he works. How he first heard about Agatha from his young friends, Fred and Norma Bergen. Now widowed, Agatha was living in Winnipeg. He remembers how he and Katie took their motorhome all the way there, hoping to visit her. He goes over how he phoned Mrs. Warkentin, as he calls her, and how she nearly deafened him with her emotional outburst on the other end of the line.

"Heinz Rempel? Is it really Heinz Rempel?" she shouted in disbelief. "You are alive?" And then, how he heard her weeping softly at the other end of the phone.

He remembers how she insisted that they come and see her right away, and how much trouble they had finding their way through the meandering Winnipeg streets to Bredin Drive where she lives. He can still see them pulling up in front of the white, brick-fronted bungalow in a beautifully treed neighbourhood and seeing an elderly woman hurrying around the side of the house as quickly as her heavy frame would allow.

"Heinz Rempel! You haven't changed a bit," she puffs, grinning from ear to ear as they meet on the sidewalk.

Henry chuckles when he tells of it. The last time they saw each other he was five and she fourteen. It's been sixty-seven years and she says he hasn't changed a bit.

Katie tells the rest. "There they were," she says excitedly, "their arms around each other, hugging like old friends, and me standing there feelin' stupid."

"I introduced you," says Henry self-consciously, "and she welcomed you too."

"But I was nothing compared to her 'Heinz'," continues Katie, the pride in her voice belying her words. "Everything was Heinz this and Heinz that."

"Well," says Henry embarrassed by all the fuss, "that's only natural after all these years of wondering what happened to me and my brother."

It's reassuring to know he hasn't been the only one to wonder, thinks Henry. Agatha has told him how she cried and begged for her father not to send the Rempel boys away, and how she has never been able to forgive herself for letting it happen. All her life she has carried that guilt, never knowing if they lived or died because of what her family did.

"She didn't want her father to give us away you know," Henry says to Katie.

"I know Henry, I was there," says Katie.

All these years he has asked the nagging, painful question, "How could they do it?" And now Agatha's words run over the wound like a healing salve.

"I begged and cried for my father not to give you away. I loved you like my own brothers. Thank God, finally I know you are alive."

And Henry, who is too reserved to even touch his own wife in public, let alone allow any demonstration of affection, feels again the strength of her arms around him and his around her, absolving a guilt for which she, a fourteen-year-old, could not possibly be responsible.

From *Tante* Mariechen, Henry learns how he and his brother

were passed from home to home for a while, and how he stayed with *Tante* Mariechen for nearly four months. She has told him how, sitting on a stool, he would sing for her, *"Mariechen saß auf einem Stein,"* and many other songs which he knew, delighting her with his pure soprano voice.

He has no recollection of it, nor of the other things Mrs. Warkentin has told him of that time.

"It doesn't much surprise me, really," he says ruefully. "Even my own birth date got lost back there somewhere." May 27th, the day he claims as his birthday, is most likely the day he was brought to the Grossweide orphanage, as close as he's been able to figure out. And the year of his birth, he has been told, has arbitrarily been fixed as 1915. That's how little he or anybody really knows about who he is.

"Probably just a guess by the Harders," he tells Katie.

"Who knows," she teases, trying to lighten the mood, "you may be older than you think."

"Or younger," he counters moodily.

He has often wondered how he could have forgotten life with the Dycks so completely, but one memory is seared into his five-year-old mind like a branding iron. It is probably the one he has tried the hardest to erase and can't.

It is a beautiful, balmy Sunday, and the date, from what he has gathered, is probably May 27, 1920. He clearly remembers the visit that Papa Dyck has promised. And he clearly recalls how he and his brother are charged with the excitement of the anticipated visit to Grossweide.

Until recently, he has always believed that it was Wilhelm Dyck who actually brought them there, but Agatha firmly believes that it was an uncle who took them to the Grossweide orphanage. It matters little. In Henry's mind, it will always be Wilhelm Dyck who he holds responsible for the deception.

. . . . .

They had arrived at the Harders in Grossweide to find a large yard full of children, and not one house, but two. They were awed by the seeming opulence after the poverty they had experienced during the past two years in the Kuban.

It was not long before Heinz and Peter were swept along by

some of the boys Mr. Harder had introduced to them. They were anxious to see and try everything before the afternoon was over and they would have to leave with Papa Dyck.

They tried out the huge circular swing in the middle of the yard behind the houses, soaring and swooping to dizzying heights. They raced eagerly ahead of the Harder's eighteen-year-old son Johannes as he took a group of boys to the new orchard to eat a mind-boggling amount of May cherries and early mulberries—all their hungry stomachs could hold.

And then it was off to the old orchard with the other boys for a series of games in which they were joyously introduced to gnarled pirate look-outs, Bolshevik marauders, secret trails and wild-eyed stallions.

The afternoon wore thin as grey shadows began to slide long fingers beneath the trees, nudging Peter back to reality.

"Heinz," Peter's voice was edged with alarm. "We have to get back to the house. It's getting late, and Papa Dyck must be looking everywhere for us." They raced towards the main house, fearful of the stern reprisals they would receive for having forgotten the time.

As they passed the barn, they could see immediately that the *Droschka* in which they had come was not on the driveway. Surely Papa Dyck had not driven away without them, thought Heinz. What kind of punishment was that? They had not even heard him calling, nor had anyone been sent to fetch them when it was time to go.

An icy knot formed in the pit of Heinz's stomach. Mr. and Mrs. Harder were sitting alone on one of the benches on the verandah outside the main house. They did not seem angry, but Papa Dyck was nowhere to be seen.

"Where is Papa Dyck?" Peter's voice was tight with panic. "We did not hear him call."

Abram Harder cleared his throat uneasily. He got up as the boys rushed up the stairs and dropped to one knee in front of them.

"Peter . . . Heinz . . . " he said, groping for words. "Your . . . *Onkel* Dyck . . . " He took a deep breath.

The boys were mute with disbelief as the truth of what Mr.

Harder was about to say crashed in.

"Boys, *Onkel* Dyck has gone home. You will live with us from now on," he said gently. "This will be your home."

The boys stared at Mr. Harder in wide-eyed horror as the finality of the news sank in. There was not going to be any discussion. Papa Dyck had known all along that this was not just going to be a Sunday afternoon visit. He had planned right from the beginning, back in the Kuban, to send them away, just as he had sent Lisa, Tina, Jascha, and Anna away on that black day they had buried Papa—and they hadn't even suspected it! The boys stared, horrified, incredulous, fighting the torrent of pain and rejection that was threatening to swallow them up.

A blanket of icy white emotion, such as Heinz had never known, enveloped his gasping little body, threatening to crush the very breath out of him. They didn't want him—never had, never intended to be his and Peter's real Mama and Papa. No more brothers and sister either, first Lisa, Tina, Jascha and Anna, and now even Willie and Agatha . . . gone, everyone gone.

Heinz struggled with the suffocating emotion, and then the ice broke and from the depths of Heinz Rempel's being, a torrent of pain and rejection broke loose in great, rasping sobs, and tears streamed unbridled down the little boy's face.

Sarah Harder gently gathered the bitterly sobbing little Heinz into her arms, soothing him against the softness of her body. Abram Harder's outstretched arm circled Peter, drawing him close.

. . . . .

Henry sets the paint can on the table nearby. His hands are cold and trembling, but his face is set as always, not betraying his inner anguish.

*"Komm mien Kjind,"* he hears Mrs. Harder's gentle voice echoing through his inner storm just as clearly as he heard it on that terrible day.

"It will be all right. Everything will be all right." She rocks him, stroking his hair, pressing her cheek against his little face bathed in tears.

# 12

# A GROSSWEIDE WELCOME

By the end of May, 1920, the orphanage just outside the village of Grossweide in the Molotschna colony was in its fourteenth year of existence. It had been founded by a young couple, Abram and Sarah Harder, who had invested all they had in the creation of this family-style institution. It had been given legal status by the government and was well respected for its educational standards which equipped the children with academic as well as manual skills. Costs were met through the industry of everyone at the orphanage, and supplemented by donations from other Mennonite communities. The good work the Harders were doing for orphaned Mennonite children was known far and wide.

Visitors could not help but notice the motto which the Harders had placed over the main entrance of their home: *"My help comes from the Lord who created heaven and earth"*. The large letters EBENEZER meaning *"Hitherto has the Lord helped us"*, had been placed over the boys' dormitory entrance, bearing further testimony to the Harders' sense of dependence on and gratitude to God.

With the ravages of the civil war, the number of children at the orphanage had swollen from twenty-six to approximately fifty by May of 1920. A staff of seven, in addition to the Harders and their eighteen-year-old son, Johannes, helped with the care and education of the children. The Harders' eldest son, Abram, a minister and teacher, was already married and had a child of his own. He and his family lived in a neighbouring village. Bertha Harder, fifteen, and her sister Mariechen, eight, and Leenie, five, had to find their places among the orphan children, sharing their parents and answering to the nursemaids assigned to their particular age group. Annie, thirteen, was restricted in her activities because of a hydrocephalic condition.

It was not unusual to have new children coming and others leaving. Lately, however, with food shortages everywhere, it was growing less and less frequent that a younger child was leaving the orphanage to be adopted. Occasionally, one of the older ones was selected by a family to help with farm work or housework in exchange for food and lodging. The children could stay at the orphanage until they were eighteen, and then Abram Harder would help them find employment in the trade which they had learned in the large workshop at the orphanage.

Woodworking, blacksmithing, harnessmaking, tailoring, and basketweaving were some of the trades taught to the boys. Everything needed by the orphanage, such as rakes, hoes, machinery for field work, ladders, pruning shears, harnesses, farm wagons, and even toys, was made in that workshop.

The girls, on the other hand, were taught knitting, crocheting, quilting, sewing, cooking, weaving, and other domestic skills.

But on this day, in May, 1920, none of this mattered to the two Rempel boys as the Harders held and comforted them.

"Come," said Mrs. Harder in High German, taking the boys' hands. "It is nearly time for *Vesper*, and we need to get you washed up and settled in before everyone comes in."

They were on the verandah of the girls' dormitory. It was the building that housed the Harder family and contained the large dining room where everyone gathered for meals. But now Mrs. Harder took them briskly down the steps and along a well-worn path to the nearby newer, two-storey brick building.

"This is the boys' dormitory," she explained as they mounted several steps. She opened the door and they walked through a large entryway with rows of hooks for coats and hats, and into a large room. There were three rows of tables and chairs in the room, and here and there children were playing table games or sitting and reading.

"During the winter we have classes here," continued Mrs. Harder. "You will be able to attend classes this fall, Peter. As you can see, this is also used as a recreation room."

She led the way to one of the three long rows of tables and pulled out a drawer. "This will be your place, Heinz," she said. "You will keep your clothes, and anything else you want to store in this drawer. No one else is allowed to open your drawer, and you must not snoop in anyone else's."

"This one over here is yours, Peter," she said as she took several steps along another row. "Your drawer is with the middlers." She went to a large cupboard and selected a pair of shorts, a tunic, and a *Pojas,* for around the waist for both boys. Then she had them try on several pairs of shoes until the right size could be found.

"It's warm enough already to go barefoot outside," she smiled, "but shoes are worn for special occasions like Sunday, or for school." Peter and Heinz clutched their new clothes gratefully.

"Come along now, and I'll show you where you will wash up," she continued. "After that I'll take you to your rooms so you can get changed before supper." They followed her down a flight of stairs, past a boiler room and into a large washroom.

She went to one of the taps and ran warm water into a sink. Not since the Dycks' house in Millerova had the boys seen such luxury.

"Soon we'll be eating our meals in the summer kitchen outside, and then you will wash up at the tap outside," she said. "Don't worry," she added, noting their questioning looks, "the other boys will show you. For now just wash up here."

As the boys obediently washed their tear-stained faces, Mrs. Harder continued cheerily. "You have probably seen the outside toilets already. During the day you are to use them, but at night you may use this," and she opened a door to reveal a carry-out toilet.

The boys had been following her wordlessly, numb with shock, but taking in all the details she pointed out.

"Now," she continued gently, "we just have time to get your clothes changed and meet your nursemaids before it is time to eat." They followed meekly as she climbed the two flights of stairs from the basement to the second storey. On either side of the long hallway they could see rooms of various sizes.

As they passed one of the smaller rooms, Mrs. Harder said, "This is our son, Johannes's room. He is in charge of the fourteen to eighteen-year-old boys."

They followed Mrs. Harder down the hall to a somewhat larger room next door to where the older group of boys slept. Across the hall another door stood open. The room was larger than the one they had just seen.

"Peter, this will be your room. Here, see. Your bed will be this one." She patted a fluffy feather pillow covered with a beautifully embroidered pillow case. A brightly colored quilt covered the cot. Nine other cots stood just as invitingly in neat rows in the rest of the room. Just then a middle-aged woman stepped into the room.

"Nettie," said Mrs. Harder, "I would like you to meet your newest charge. This is Peter Rempel. He will soon be eight, so he will be in your group."

"Hello, Peter," she said smiling. "Or do they call you Petie?"

The boy did not answer, but kept staring at the floor.

"Peter is fine," said Mrs. Harder, throwing the woman a telling glance.

Nettie had already noticed the tear-reddened eyes and said tactfully, "I see you want to change before *Vesper*. I'll leave you now, but if you need anything Peter, I'm right next door. You may knock on my door anytime at all. I'd like to be your friend."

Peter's eyes followed Heinz as he was led out the door. Quickly he slipped to the doorway to be sure he could see into which room his brother would be taken. It was the one two doors down the hall.

Looking back, Heinz could see Peter watching. Without looking around Mrs. Harder said, "You better hurry and get changed, Peter. Heinz is going to be waiting for you outside your room before you know it."

Heinz's room was large. Thirteen cots stood in neat rows, just like in the other rooms they had seen. A large window was at the far end of the room. A door led from the large room into a small adjoining one. A young woman in her late teens came to the door. She smiled warmly at the small boy and before Mrs. Harder could say anything, she was kneeling with one arm around the five-year-old's shoulder.

"Everyone calls me *Tante* Greta," she said. There was a youthful lilt in her voice. "And what do people call a good-looking young man like you?"

The boy's eyelids fluttered self-consciously before he had the courage to look up into her warm eyes.

"My name is Heinrich Rempel," he said carefully, "but most people call me Heinz." He looked down, overcome with shyness.

"Well then, Heinz it is," she said with a squeeze.

It was not long before Heinz was dressed in the home's regulation shorts, with a tunic and belt overtop, just as he had seen all the other small and middler boys dressed. He had just done up the belt when Peter came into the room, dressed the same. *Tante* Nettie was a few steps behind. Just then a bell rang through the building.

"Suppertime. Better hurry," she said.

It only took a few seconds for them to run down the stairs, out the door, across a bit of the yard, and up the steps through the big double doors, into the large entryway of the girls' dormitory.

Heinz pressed close to Peter, afraid of losing him in the mass of identically dressed children. The girls, he noticed, were all dressed alike too, in long dark dresses and print aprons.

"What a lot of children," whispered Heinz to Peter as they followed the others through the spacious front hall and into a huge dining room.

"So there you are," said Mr. Harder pleasantly, coming through the crowd to where the boys were standing with their nursemaids. The other children had found their places at the long tables.

"I see you have met your nursemaids," Mr. Harder said gently. "I think you'll soon get used to things here." His hand swept the room in an arc, "All these children are your brothers and sisters now. We hope you'll be happy in our big family."

The nursemaids quickly propelled the boys to their places at the tables as Mr. Harder continued, "Now hear the Word of God."

Mr. Harder opened a well-worn Bible and read a short passage, then declared, "Let us pray."

The table grace was a familiar one, and the two Rempel boys joined in as everyone recited it together,

*"Komm Herr Jesu, sei unser Gast, und Segne was du uns bescheret hast. Amen."*

A din broke loose as soon as the grace was over, but Heinz sat with lowered eyes, swallowing hard to try to get rid of the lump tightening once again in his throat. He wanted to sit with his brother, not with all these strangers. He swallowed again. It would not do to cry here in front of all these people.

Heinz glanced at the food spread out on the table. He could not remember when he had seen so many fluffy white *Zwieback* at one time, or so many plates of *Platz* made from May cherries like those he had tasted in the orchard, and there was more milk than he had seen in a very long while. But somehow, he could not make the food go down. Throughout the meal he kept his eyes lowered, trying to escape the unabashed stares of the other boys at his table, purposefully pushing back the pain that threatened to disgrace him with public tears.

At last the meal was over. Everyone became quiet as Mr. Harder stood at his place at the table at the far end of the room. "Today we welcome Peter and Heinz Rempel into our Grossweide family. Some of you met them this afternoon. All of you are to make them feel welcome and help them get to know their way around. I know you will all do your best to help them feel at home." He paused, as if to let the admonition sink in. "Franz," he said quietly, "I would like you to remain behind with the two Rempel boys. The rest are excused."

As the other children stood and filed out of the dining room, Mr. Harder, Peter and ten-year-old Franz, also a middler, like Peter, came over to where Heinz sat alone.

"There is still a little time before you have to go to bed," said Mr. Harder. "Young Franz here is going to show you and your brother around outside. You have already been settled into the boys' dorm, *ja*?"

A nod from their dark heads confirmed that they had.

"Good. And I think you have seen the orchards too, and

tasted some of the fruit?" His eyes twinkled. "At least you won't starve, even though you did not eat much at supper." He put a kindly hand on Heinz's shoulder. "Now run along, and don't get into mischief, you hear?" He was only teasing, knowing full well that mischief was the farthest thing from the Rempel boys' minds.

"Come along then," said Franz, leading the way out of the dining room. Some of the younger children were already swinging merrily on the *Rundschaukel* in the yard, trying to squeeze as much as possible out of the remaining few minutes until the bedtime bell would ring for them.

"This," said Franz, as they came down the stairs of the girls' dorm to face the brick building directly behind the main house, "is the summer kitchen. It won't be long before we'll be eating all our meals here. Right now it's still just being used for games."

They stepped through the door and into a large room with tables and chairs stacked against one wall. Half the room was set up with kitchen cupboards and utensils, while in the other half a group of older boys were engrossed in a bowling game on the lanes they had built. Neither of the Rempel boys had seen the game before, but at the moment it did not spark any interest.

Heinz slipped his small hand into his brother's and held on tightly as together they followed Franz back outside. Another building ran parallel to the summer house.

"This is the workshop," continued Franz. "In the afternoon in winter, when classes are over, the older children learn a trade here. In the summertime we all have to help with the orchard and gardens, but some of the boys are assigned to the workshop then too. I have been learning wood working," he said with satisfaction, "and my friend Aaron is learning blacksmithing. Of course no one is working today because it's Sunday, but if you come by tomorrow, you'll see all the things we are taught to do here."

Inside, the boys could see many finished and unfinished articles hanging from hooks on the walls. There were rakes, hoes, ladders, pruning shears, harnesses, a child's wagon, and a larger wagon. At one end of the room hung large baskets, such as they had seen stacked up in the orchards. In one area, partitioned off from the rest, they could even see sewing machines.

From the workshop, the boys were led to a building which they immediately recognized as the *Schien*. Every Mennonite farm had a building where the farm implements and wagons were stored, along with grain and straw. Chickens scratched in the dirt floor in their pen in the corner.

"The big boys work in the fields outside the village," said Franz. "Sometimes us middlers get to help too."

Alongside the *Schien* was a shed, and from the grunting sounds coming from it the boys knew without being told that this was where the pigs were kept.

"I can hardly wait until butchering day," said Franz, rubbing his stomach. "Then we'll have *Schinkenfleisch*, *Reppschpää*, *Wurst*, and *Grüben* again, all we can eat."

The boys knew of the smoked ham, spare ribs, sausage and cracklings to which Franz referred. They had enjoyed all those wonderful things in Millerovo with the Dycks, but that seemed like a very long time ago.

"All we can eat?" asked Peter dubiously.

"Well, almost," backtracked Franz.

"I'm going to like that," said Peter thoughtfully. "How about you Heinz, won't that taste good?"

Heinz did not answer.

The next building was the barn. "Most of our cattle are in the common pasture during the summer time, and the horses too," continued Franz. "We just keep about ten milk cows here, along with the work horses, and the horse Papa Harder uses for pulling the *Droschka*."

The barn floor was swept clean and the smell of fresh hay pervaded the building. "The younger boys have to sweep the barn," said Franz, "that will be one of your jobs, Heinz. The girls do the milking. Guess who gets to do the smelly job," he wrinkled his nose.

"Us middlers?" asked Peter.

Franz nodded. "Lucky us, huh?"

They passed quickly down the center corridor of the cow barn, stepped through a doorway and found themselves in the section where the horses were kept. Now Heinz's eyes were alight with genuine interest. There were eight horses in the stalls and at the far end, in a stall by herself, a small dappled-grey mare caught Heinz's attention.

Franz noticed his interest in the animal. "Oh, that's Moschka," he said, going over to stroke the sleek animal. "She's the one Papa Harder usually takes when he goes on business to the villages."

The boys hung back shyly.

"It's all right. You can pet her. We're allowed," said Franz importantly.

The horse turned to nuzzle them as they came near.

"Here, let me give you a boost up so you can sit on her, Heinz." Before the boy knew it, he was mounted on Moschka's bare back. "Maybe Papa will let you ride her sometime. It's almost bedtime for you younger ones, so we can't take her out today."

Heinz looked down at his brother and Franz, and then across the tops of the stalls in the barn. What a wonderful place from which to see the world. This was even better than Jascha's little black Shetland pony. He could imagine himself outside, riding this beautiful little mare. It could take him anywhere. Anywhere in the world. Back to the Dycks—no! Not there! They had tricked him. The pain surged in once more. They did not want him. He could not ever go back there. Tears threatened. Where then? He thought with determination. Yes, he knew. He would ride and ride, until he found his Lischen, and Tina, and Jascha and Anna. He would ride and ride until finally, there they would be, Mama and Papa, waiting for him to come home, and everything would be just like it was supposed to be. Yes! That's where he and Moschka would go.

"Heinza," Peter was tugging at his leg, using his pet name. "Don't fall asleep sitting there. It's my turn."

The horse's coat felt warm and soft as he slid down the side of her belly to the floor. He walked to the front of the stall as Franz hoisted Peter up for his turn. He stroked the horse's neck and muzzle. "Moschka," he mouthed.

A bell sounded. "Oh, oh," exclaimed Franz. "Eight o'clock. That's your bedtime, Heinz. Us bigger boys," he gestured towards Peter, "can stay up until nine."

"That's all right," replied Peter, "I think I'll go in too," and with that the two Rempel boys dashed off towards the boys' dorm.

Only later, in the privacy of darkness, long after *Tante* Greta had listened to him recite his bedtime prayer and tucked him in, did five-year-old Heinz finally allow the tears to flow unchecked.

In another room, Peter lay awake on his own bed, too angry and hurt for tears or sleep, clenching his teeth against yet another upheaval in his young life.

And outside the safety of the brick wall surrounding the Grossweide orphanage, terror reigned in many parts of Russia as the civil war continued to rage. In the relentless turmoil of the time, the other four Rempel children were also finding themselves tossed hither and yon, on paths that were leading them farther and farther apart.

# 13

# A BIRTHDAY CELEBRATION

The long-awaited day has finally come. Mathew's birthday party is actually more of a belated Christmas and New Year's celebration for the Huebert family, but three-year-old Mathew has definitely been at centre stage today. It is becoming increasingly difficult to get the family together since all four of the Huebert children are married and have their own celebrations now, with in-laws to fit in. But Henry and Katie don't mind. They are glad to make the adjustments necessary just so they can have everyone together at one time. After all, what is Christmas, if it isn't a family get-together.

Henry's eyes are alight, watching his little grandson's raucous forays around the basement, first riding his rocking horse with all his might, and then clambering off and dragging it across the floor by its reins. His mother comes down the stairs, drying her hands on her slacks.

"Mathew, not so rough," she reprimands, "you're going to break it."

"Leave the boy alone Brenda," scolds Henry, "the horse can take it."

His daughter, the youngest of his four children, scoops her little niece, Elizabeth, out of the horse's path, deposits her in a safer place and plops herself heavily on the sofa beside her father. She is expecting her third child.

"We're going to call him Joshua, if it's a boy," she has told her Mom privately. Of such womanly matters Henry does not care to speak to his daughter, but Katie passes the information along to him.

Now Brenda watches her young son as he continues playing boisterously with his new toy. "I'm going to tan his little hide if he breaks that thing after all the work you've had making it," she says vehemently. "Mom told me how sick you've been."

"It's nothing," says Henry crisply, "you know how excitable your Mom is."

"You're spoiling him, Dad," scolds Brenda, not to be put off. "You know very well he would have been quite happy with any of those other things you've got in the garage."

"Mathew wasn't wishing for one of those 'other things'," says Henry quietly but firmly. "He was wishing for a rocking horse." There is no way he can even begin to explain what this little horse means to him, and why it's so important for Mathew to have it . . . maybe he can't even explain it to himself, come to think of it. Still, he can't understand why the family doesn't just leave it alone. If he wants to make Mathew a rocking horse, that's his business.

Besides, all this concern for his health is really beginning to annoy him. You'd think they had all discovered something new . . . him being sick . . . well, he's lived with poor health longer than most, and has learned long ago that it's useless to indulge in self-pity. Sure, he could give up and die. He's seen people do it . . . could have done it himself long ago, but not him . . . he's a fighter . . . has had to be to survive this long.

"Well, anyway," Brenda continues, pushing into his stubborn silence, "I'd feel a whole lot better if you had the doctor check out that cough. You know I worry about you."

There is nothing maudlin or sentimental about her. Henry likes that. She says it like it is, and she can take straight talk too. No need to get mushy. His three sons are like that too. Made of good tough fibre. Not that they don't have feelings, but he has to read them between the lines.

Brenda is the only one of his four children who doesn't live reasonably close by. It is a seven-hour drive to the northern Alberta town where her husband has found a good job as a civil engineer. Henry and Katie usually try to drive up in their truck and camper two or three times a year; and they phone."We're keeping Alberta Government Telephones going single-handed," he tells Brenda with a twinkle, when they speak of it.

Now he says testily, "Your Mom's been trying to get rid of me for two weeks."

"What are you talking about?" Brenda asks indignantly.

"If I go to the doctor they're just going to put me back into the hospital again, and you know what happened last time. I ended up sicker than if I'd stayed at home."

He is maddeningly serious about that, and Brenda is no nearer knowing if, finally, he will go to the doctor or not. He will only go if and when he is good and ready, she is sure of that. "Well you're sure not getting any better staying home, are you?" she retorts crisply.

Just then Mathew collides with Elizabeth and there is a vigorous wail. "I told you to watch where you're going, Mathew," says Brenda, giving him a firm smack. "Slow down!"

She picks up Elizabeth, whose feelings are more hurt than anything and dries her tears. Then, taking Elizabeth with her, she goes back upstairs to help the rest of the women-folk finish clean up from the big dinner.

Henry surveys the flutter of activity in the large basement room. There is a hockey game on TV, and Brenda's husband, Greg along with Henry's three sons and his teenage grandsons, Wally, Randy, David, Barry and Michael, are all slouched on chairs and cushions watching it.

Ten-year-old Katharine, Dennis's second oldest, is curled up in a chair reading, and Brenda's, eldest, four-and-a-half-year-old Michelle, is entertaining herself with toys, along with frequent trips to the candy dish.

The air in the room is close, and Henry coughs frequently. He is having difficulty breathing, but he feels a deep sense of satisfaction as he sits back to watch and rest. It is true, what Katie says—he has a family. Katie, the children, and the grandchildren, have been his life.

A loud, collective groan issues from the group in front of the T.V. "They're losing this one," says Rudy getting up in disgust. He grabs a few bonbons from the candy dish and nonchalantly passes the dish on before plunking himself back into an old armchair.

Henry's eyes take in his strapping son, dark-haired like his sister Brenda, both of them leaning more towards Katie's features. Wilmer and Dennis take after him more, in spite of their blonde hair.

"Game ain't over yet," pipes up Rudy's fourteen-year-old son, Barry. "Oilers c'n come from behind and blow the lights out for those Flames, no problem."

"Bets?" challenges his cousin Michael, the only one cheering for the Calgary Flames on this particular day. Henry's eyes flicker with amusement. He suspects that Michael's loyalties may have more to do with spicing up the afternoon that anything else, but his cousin takes the bait.

"You're on," replies Barry. "How much?"

"How much ya' got?"

Barry looks at him dumbfounded. There is a burst of laughter from the group.

"Hey, watch this." Randy silences them. He is at the edge of his chair. The announcer's voice is rising as he shouts above the mounting noise of the fans in the arena.

"Gretzky's got the puck . . . McDonald's taken out of the play by a hard hit from Semenko. Number 99's heading for the net, oh, a beautiful pass to Messier, back to Gretzky . . . he shoots. He scores!"

The room explodes in a volley of cheers.

"Who scored?" calls Marilyn from the top of the stairs.

"Number 99, who else?" shouts back Katharine over the din. "Oilers still behind by one."

Henry doesn't care much who wins. But he enjoys watching the game with his sons and grandchildren just to be a part of the good-natured teasing and camaraderie.

Wally passes him the candy dish, but he sets it down. He won't even allow himself the luxury of one lick. Not with his diabetes. He sticks to the diet resolutely, so he has to be satisfied just watching the others enjoying the sweets.

His eyes linger over the lively forms of the grandchildren before him. How different things are for them growing up than they were for him. Sometimes he envies them. Every one with a set of parents, and with whatever brothers or sisters they've been blessed, living in an atmosphere of safety, wanting for nothing. It's as though they don't even know what they've got because they've never been without it. He watches them and remembers what it was like to have nothing. To have no one. Living every day just trying to survive until the next.

It is those memories that have haunted him all his life, giving him a serious outlook on life even as a teen-ager, when he should have been happy and carefree like other teen-agers.

He remembers being a teen-ager. Katie remembers him too, and still teases him for his peculiar ways.

She shows people a picture of him, maybe seventeen or eighteen years old, the same age as Wilmer's Randy and Rudy's Barry are now. He is standing with a group of young people at the train station in Sedalia.

"I'm not on the picture," Katie points out self-consciously. "I'm sitting in the train, looking out the window at the people on this picture."

"We and some other families were moving north," she continues. "See, that's Henry. He was staying. The Hueberts came later."

"Why weren't you on the picture?" Henry asks, knowing full well what she will say.

"Me on the picture?" she asks incredulously. "I hate taking pictures! You know that."

"Obviously," he says, grinning. He remembers how one of the conductors asked him what he wanted when he tried to board the train, and how he told him it was a personal matter, and that he would be right back.

"I heard him talking to somebody," says Katie, and then he came walkin' down the aisle, right to where I sat. He shook my hand and said good-by. I didn't say a word, and he just turned around and left." She snickers. "It's a good thing he didn't know what I was thinking."

She has told Henry what she thought of him. It's an understatement to say that she wasn't impressed.

"That's your problem," he says firmly.

"Well, what was I supposed to think?" she asks defensively. "All I could think was: What does he want with me, a Mennonite

96

girl? I didn't want no Russian. Not me." She covers her mouth, giggling self-consciously. "I thought you were just Huebert's *hanjenomena Russejung*."

"Well, I was every bit as Mennonite as you," he says, "and no Russian," he adds emphatically. Such an insult he cannot let her live down.

She nods, but adds in her defense, "But you were adopted. I should've known I'd end up marrying an orphan," she continues. "Every time it was our turn to take care of the orphans that were bein' passed around our village, I'd beg and cry. I wanted to keep 'em all." She chuckles. "Guess I got my orphan."

Katie tells him how she remembers first seeing a group of Grossweide orphans. She could not have been more than five years old, and as close as they can figure out he must have been among them at the time.

"Sure, I remember," she says, her r's rolling. "We came from Sparrau to your village. And in you all came, like a bunch of little rabbits, one after another in a nice neat row, all dressed alike. You looked like a bunch of little Russians, dressed like that." She covers her mouth giggling.

"See," she continues, "there was no getting away from me." She loves to tell people how their lives have run parallel, right from both of them being born in Siberia, moving to neighbouring villages in the Molotschna, emigrating to Alberta and being neighbours again, first in Sedalia, and then in the Tofield/Ryley area.

"We were meant for each other, Henry," she teased.

And he believes it to be so too. She has been a loyal and devoted wife. A better one he could not have wished for. And he has always been able to count on her to speak her mind honestly. She can be trusted. That is more than he can say for most people.

He isn't much for saying how he feels though. He has tried to make it up to her in the gifts and cards he has bought her over the years. Why she bothers to save all the cards, he can't imagine, but if it pleases her, let her have the cards.

He cannot imagine life without Katie. Always there has been a gnawing fear that she too will be snatched away from him, like everyone else he has ever loved. Has she actually been with him for over fifty years? It doesn't seem near that long . . . and all this time, that terrible gnawing fear?

He is embarrassed when she reminds him how determined he was not to have children when they were first married. He knew that sometimes women died in childbirth, and he had decided that he would rather not have children than to risk Katie's life.

"That's ridiculous," she had said. "Women are made to have children." And that had been that.

Henry looks at the three strapping sons sprawled on the sofas and chairs: Wilmer, Rudy and Dennis. Each of them different in his own way, but all three tall and strong, a Rempel trait from what Henry can tell from the picture of his father, and from what he has seen of his Rempel uncles and aunts.

People used to stare questioningly from the diminutive form of father Huebert, to the big, strapping grandsons. The obvious incongruity pleases Henry. They're Rempels, even if they don't call themselves by that name.

He and Katie would have been quite happy with three children. They hadn't planned for a large family anyway.

"It's not fair to the wife," Henry insisted. Still, they had hoped for at least one girl. He can still remember how close Katie was to crying when he had come to visit her in the hospital after the birth of Dennis, their third son. "Henry," she whispered, "I just can't give you your little girl."

Henry watches as Brenda's daughter Michelle takes her turn on the rocking horse's leather saddle. The tail and mane swing with a rhythmic motion as she rocks.

Brenda has just come back downstairs, and is wheeling her son Mathew around in the new, red, wheelbarrow that his sister Michelle has gotten from Gramma and Grandpa. Their laughter drifts like music over the other sounds.

"Well, we got our girl," thinks Henry, watching his daughter. He can still remember Katie's reaction when she found out she was expecting again.

"What are people going to think," Katie had whispered in embarrassment, "an old woman like me expecting a baby?"

"Forty-one isn't that old, Katie," Henry had said, trying to console her. "Lots of women your age have babies." But she must have known how he really felt about women being seen "in that condition" at that age, and because she had felt so self-conscious about it all, Katie had not gone out much for most of the nine months.

Once the little dark-haired baby girl was born, however, there had been no more thought of apology or self-consciousness for either of them.

"She looks just like her Mom," people would say, and much to Henry's embarrassment Katie would cluck sympathetically. "She'd be better off takin' after her goodlookin' Dad."

Henry sighs. How enthusiastically he watched as Brenda began to take an interest in music, leaning against his knee as he played the guitar or the mandolin and sang to her, or watching as he sat practicing for the upcoming *Jugendverein Abend* at the church, fascinated as he blew into one of his harmonicas on a special contraption around his neck while he accompanied himself on the guitar.

It was for Brenda that they bought the little upright piano, now silent in the living room upstairs. How proudly he and Katie followed her progress in her piano lessons. Sometimes when she comes home she still plays for him from the hymn-book, the old songs he loves so much.

His breath catches. For him the music has stopped. That is a pain far greater than the stabbing in his lung. No more will he tell the plaintive tale of the lonely gypsy boy, or sing of the hope of a heavenly home. He is too winded to sing through a phrase, and his fingers tremble on the guitar strings. The harmonicas have been silent even longer. Sometimes he takes them out. He has one in almost every key. He fingers them, remembering, and then puts them gently back into their plush velvet cases.

It is an acute loss, like the death of a dear friend. But in his mind and heart the music has not stopped. Even now it is singing on, an echo of the hope, the consolation, the unfulfilled longing for home, no longer shared as he sings and plays. Now it is exclusively his, for him alone.

The music flows through his life with strength, from beyond his earliest recollections, its roots obviously embedded in his lost past, in a musical family from which he has obviously inherited his love and gift for music.

He has been told, by Rempel uncles and aunts, how his mother would sing constantly, teaching her children songs, including many from the *Glaubensstimme*, until they knew them by heart. And *Tante* Mariechen, whom he has found so recently in Winnipeg, has confirmed that even as a child of two and three years old, little Heinz could sing many songs in tune, entertaining the adults with whom he was staying.

It is one of the few tangible links with his past that he has fought to maintain throughout his life.

The words of one of his favorite songs echoes through his mind as he sits watching the activities around him. It is one he remembers singing at the church, at more than one *Jugendverein* program.

Into the tent where a gypsy boy lay,
Dying alone at the close of the day,
News of salvation we carried, said he,
Nobody ever has told it to me!

Did He so love me, a poor little boy?
Send unto me the good tidings of joy?
Need I not perish, My hand will He hold?
Nobody ever the story has told!

Bending we caught the last words of his breath,
Just as he entered the valley of death:
"God sent His Son!" "Whosoever," said He:
"Then I am sure that He sent Him for me!"

In some strange way, he seems to know the gypsy boy and his story. It strikes a chord somewhere deep within. . . .

Tell it again! Tell it again!
Salvation's story repeat o'er and o'er.
Till none can say of the children of men,
"Nobody ever has told me before."

Smiling, he said, as his last sigh he spent,
"I am so glad that for me He was sent!"
Whispered, while low sank the sun in the west,
"Lord, I believe, tell it now to the rest!"

The refrain repeats itself in his mind. "Tell it again! Tell it again! Salvation's story repeat o'er and o'er. . . . "

He can still remember the special meetings in Sedalia, when the minister spoke of this salvation, of having life eternal. A life where loved ones would be together forever, and where evil and sickness would have no place. Such a life, the minister had said, could be his. . . . Henry still remembers his resounding "yes" to such good news.

As he grows older, and his hopes of finding any of his "real" family fade, he finds himself counting more and more on that other meeting with those who have already gone before him. It is the one thing he can count on. Who knows, maybe they're all there already, waiting for him. Lately, it is this hope that makes the loneliness more bearable.

Still, it's amazing how things can turn up when you least expect them, he muses. Henry's gaze lingers on the ancient Kroeger clock ticking like an immortal echo on the west wall of the basement room. It is the same clock that ticked in his grandfather Rempel's home when his father was growing up in the Ukraine. The face is faded now, like the memories Henry carries, and the paint is cracked, but it, like the music, reassures him of the reality of his past and gives him hope for the future.

The clock has only recently found its way here "to its rightful heir," as his relatives like to say, since he is the only known living child of Jacob Rempel, the eldest son of Jacob Rempel, senior. The clock quietly affirms for Henry a continuity with an identity, a past that at times threatens to slip from his grasp. Now that it is here, it will continue to tick on in his children and grandchildren's homes, silently bearing witness to the Rempel name which might otherwise be forgotten.

It was a Rempel cousin who actually brought the clock to Henry, after the death of his own father, who was a younger brother to Henry's father. The clock has been in Canada since

101

1913, two years before Henry's own birth in some forgotten Siberian village.

Katie thinks the clock is too old-fashioned and faded to hang on the living room wall upstairs, so he has found a place for it on the basement wall. She is right of course. It has little apparent beauty left. Henry has tried to have the face restored, but because of the tiny cracks in the paint it is impossible to retrieve it's original detail and color. So it ticks, untouched, a faded ghost, reminding him, haunting him, reassuring him.

A pain grabs Henry's chest and he doubles over coughing violently.

"You O.K.?" Wilmer sits down beside him. The hockey game is between periods, and the spectators in the Huebert basement are drifting in different directions during the break.

"I'm fine," replies Henry, wiping his mouth with his dark checkered hankerchief.

"You're pretty quiet today. Are you sure you're not feeling sick?" presses Wilmer.

"I said I'm fine!" Henry says tersely. "A person can't even sneeze around here without everybody trying to pack you off to the hospital."

"That's no sneeze and you know it." Wilmer's voice has an edge. "You think we haven't heard you coughing and wheezing all afternoon?"

"I can take care of myself." Henry is not backing off. "Don't need everybody fussin' over me like a bunch of mother hens."

"Fine. Have it your way. But you're worrying Mom sick over you. You could at least get yourself to the doctor so she can stop worrying."

"I don't need no doctor." There is finality in Henry's voice, but Wilmer's words have cut deep. He does not want to hurt Katie or the kids, and he feels guilty. He will go.

He gets up to go to the bathroom. His diabetes dictates much of his life now: everything from frequent trips to the bathroom, to the needles, to when and what he eats. His lungs dictate the rest. He has given up his mill; he must live in well-ventilated surroundings; he sits on the aisle seat in church, and his lungs put him in the hospital. He doesn't like it, but he accepts it. It is either that or die, and he does not want to die.

There still might be a slim chance that somewhere his brother Peter and the other brothers and sisters may even now be alive, looking for him. He can't die without being sure. If there is even the slightest chance that any of them are alive, he must find them. It is a promise he made to himself many years ago. He will not be denied.

But, like the clock, it may be too late to retrieve any of them now. The one thing he has dreaded all his life is to die without knowing for sure whether or not any of them survived. Now there is an even greater dread: to learn too late that some of them did in fact survive, that he has grown old without finding them and that he may not get to see them after all.

They're probably long gone, he tells himself. I'm just about seventy-three. Lisa could be eighty-three and Peter seventy-six, with the others in between. Still, there might be a chance. If he's still alive, especially in the condition he's in, they could be too.

"They would have found you Dad," says Wilmer quietly when they talk of it. "If they were alive they would have looked for you until they found you."

"I don't know," Henry replies. If only he could be sure of that it would be easier to deal with. But what if they have simply forgotten him—or didn't care. If only he knew for sure.

He steps out of the bathroom. It is true what Katie says, he has a family. What more could he want, at his age especially. He is not five anymore, alone in the world and desperately in need of someone to belong to. He does belong. He has more than he could ever have hoped or dreamed.

# 14

# THE MOONWALKER

Five days had passed since the Rempel boys, Peter and Heinz, had been left at Grossweide. They had slipped into the predictable schedule and pattern of the home.

The wake-up bell rang at seven o'clock every morning, and by seven-thirty they were eating breakfast in the big dining room. Then it was morning chores. Franz had been right. Peter had been assigned to the group of middlers who had to muck out the cow barn, and Heinz and several other younger boys pushed big brooms, sweeping the barn clean.

It was June now, with school closed until October. Everyone was busy with the extra work that summer in the village of Grossweide brought with it. There was fruit to pick and preserve, gardens to hoe, cattle and fields to tend.

For Heinz and the other young children chores and duties were kept to a minimum, and much of their time was spent playing in the yard. Being five, and the youngest of the orphanage children, Heinz soon discovered a new playmate in the Harders' youngest daughter Leenie, also five.

At twelve-thirty the main meal of the day was served in the summer kitchen. After that was cleaned up it was back to work for most of the children, and naptime for the youngest group. Heinz waited eagerly for the end of nap-time because then, at last, he was allowed to join Peter and watch him at his work. All day he looked forward to those moments together.

A light supper was served at seven o'clock, and by eight o'clock the youngest children were washed and tucked into bed. Already Heinz knew the names of all thirteen boys that shared the upstairs room where he slept. But here, wrapped in the blanket of night, they were strangers, each hidden in his own cocoon of loneliness, poorly fortified against the tormentors that stalked the night hours.

It was the time of day that he most missed his family. During the day he could glance across the dining room tables to where his brother sat and spend those few moments with him while he watched him work, but in the blackness of night he was utterly alone, unable any longer to push aside the gnawing loneliness and the humiliating pain of being abandoned by the Dycks.

Each night stretched like a black chasm before the small Rempel boy, the sounds of the other children in the room only adding to his misery. If there was some semblance of normalcy during the daytime, the night became a place peopled with monsters, taunting and snarling, threatening to push Heinz from his lonely vigil on his narrow ledge of reality.

*Tante* Greta slept in the small adjoining room with her ear tuned to the night sounds. Heinz had seen her nightgowned figure move silently between the cots to where a boy had cried out in a dream, to shake him gently until he was free of the nightmare.

Tonight, as he lay staring out the window into the moonlit night, he was aware of movement in the bed next to his. Nicholai Friesen, Kolya for short, was pushing back the covers. Heinz could hear him sit up, swing his feet over the edge of his cot and stand on the floor.

Probably going to use the commode, thought Heinz, unconcerned. But the boy did not head in that direction, nor in the direction of *Tante* Greta's room. Instead he walked slowly towards the window at the far end of the room. It was propped open to allow fresh air in while they slept. Heinz stared in horror as the small boy pulled himself onto the window ledge.

By now a number of the boys were awake, straining to see what was going on. Abe, two beds over from Heinz, quickly slipped out of his bed and ran to *Tante* Greta's door. It was ajar and he went in. Heinz could see her nightgowned silhouette, hurrying towards the window just as Kolya clambered from his precarious perch onto a narrow ledge of roof outside. As they watched, horrified, he disappeared onto the roof and out of view. They listened, barely daring to breathe. Step . . . step . . . step. . . .

"What's he doing out there?" whispered Heinz, unable to bear the frozen silence any longer. "Why doesn't somebody stop him?" *Tante* Greta's finger flew to her lips. "Quiet," she breathed, "we must not wake him." They waited, tense and afraid, listening to his movements on the slippery, dew-wet tiled roof of the two-storey house. Step . . . step . . . step. . . .

The sounds were coming back towards the open window. And then he appeared, gliding along the narrow ledge outside the window. He bent down and slid through the narrow opening and walked sedately back to his bed next to Heinz's. Still oblivious to the staring eyes of the room full of children, he climbed in.

Heinz could not believe what he had just seen and lay staring wide-eyed into the night.

"He's a moonwalker," whispered Abe across the boy's bed after *Tante* Greta had tightly closed the window and gone back to bed. "If you wake a moonwalker when he's walking he could die," he whispered dramatically, "especially if he's walking on the roof. *Tante* Greta said so," he added importantly.

"She did?" said Heinz, amazed. Heinz stared at the now sleeping Kolya. "Does he do this a lot?" he whispered.

"I think it's only when the moon is full," replied Abe. "Sometimes he just walks through the dormitory. One time last winter he went outside in his bare feet and froze them."

"He doesn't look like a moonwalker," whispered Heinz. He didn't know what such a person should look like, but his friend Kolya, with his mischievous grin and playful pranks? Not Kolya.

"You can never tell," whispered Abe, yawning noisily, "but he doesn't scare me," and with that he rolled over and pulled the blanket up over his ears.

Heinz lay awake, waiting for the thumping in his chest to stop. Never before had he witnessed such a strange sight. What other secrets lurked behind the innocent faces of the boys with whom he played? He did not want to know their secrets, as he did not want them to know his. But somehow, in the darkness, no one's secrets were safe. He hugged his knees to his chest, letting himself drift, far away . . . until he was riding . . . riding on bareback with no bridle or reins, and the small grey horse was galloping . . . galloping towards a beautiful meadow.

Then, unexpectedly a gaping chasm appeared in the horse's path, widening even as they approached. There was no stopping. Heinz felt himself leaning forward as the little horse tensed her muscles and jumped. . . . They were floating . . . floating over the yawning pit. Just a little farther, and they would be across. The little mare was clawing frantically to gain a foothold on the far side. The dirt was crumbling and he could hear it falling in hollow thuds into the pit below. Thud . . . thud. . . .

He tried to scream, but no sound came out . . . and then he was falling, falling. . . .

"Peter!" His cry woke the children sleeping nearby.

"Do you want me to get *Tante* Greta?" Heinz recognized Kolya's voice in the cot beside him.

"No," said Heinz, stifling his sobs. He was too big for *Tante* Greta's night time consolation. That was for little boys and sissies, crybabies and bedwetters like Hans, whom some of the other children taunted when no adults were around. "Hans, Hans, wets his pants." He did not need anyone.

"Why do you cry all the time?" Kolya's voice probed.

"I'm not crying," replied Heinz resolutely wiping his eyes.

Kolya the moonwalker was silent once more, while outside the night sky grudgingly gave up its blackness as twilight crept over the horizon. Heinz lay on his bed, his shivering body gradually growing quiet in the gentle comfort of dawn's early light.

. . . . .

Henry's eyes travel over the sleeping forms of the three other men in his hospital ward. His own breathing is laboured and there is no escaping the pain that stabs his chest. He has been watching the silent beginning of another new day.

For as long as he can remember, he has been an early riser. There is something about those mysterious morning hours that fills him with a feeling of peace and hope he cannot explain.

Especially here in the hospital, during each seemingly endless, pain-filled night, he waits and waits for the morning. It is not that the pain is less, or his breathing easier during the daytime, only that he is not alone with it.

This is already his second week in the hospital, with doctors pressing and probing, studying him and frowning. An intravenous tube is taped to one arm, and oxygen tubes probe his nostrils. But he is not getting any better.

"If you were like other people," one doctor tells him, "we'd fix you up and have you out of here in no time. The trouble is," he continues, "your body does not seem to respond to the drugs the way most people's do."

So now they are experimenting with a new drug, flown in from the laboratory in Toronto at the cost of one hundred dollars a vial. It is not just that he has diabetes and pneumonia. They say he also has a very rare lung disease which is complicating everything.

Henry has always thought that his lung problems stem from a childhood case of tuberculosis, according to what he has been able to piece together from his past, but that has been categorically ruled out. The doctors tell him the name of the lung disease he has. It is such a difficult name to pronounce that they use an abbreviation. It is a disease, they say, that is found only in countries where malnourishment is common. To have it show up in an Alberta hospital is no small oddity.

No one has to tell Henry that they are fighting for his life.

"Nobody . . . dies from pain," he gasps, trying his best to comfort Katie and the children when they come to visit him. But he is grateful each time the nurse comes and the needle mercifully takes the edge off the flames in his chest. Only then can he catch a little sleep.

His appetite has been poor in spite of Katie's pleading and cajoling. He cannot bear to look at food, yet the doctors and nurses insist on continuing his regimented eating pattern because of his diabetes.

He is sure that they've got doctors from every department coming to see him. During the day they wheel him from floor to floor for tests ordered by the various doctors.

These include tests for his eyes, which, due to the diabetes, have gotten much worse lately. The eye doctor promises to operate on them as soon as he is well enough. But he is so weak and in so much pain that he can not even enjoy the prospect of improved eye-sight.

A nurse comes into the room and turns on the overhead light. "So how are we today?" she says cheerily as she replaces the bag on the intravenous stand and checks to make sure it is dripping at the right speed. "Another rough night?" she asks, giving him a scrutinizing look.

"About the usual," replies Henry, his eyelids fluttering self-consciously.

She pops an electronic thermometer into his mouth and takes the reading.

"Still up?" he asks, as though he doesn't know already. He feels himself burning with fever.

"Uh, huh," she replies casually, masking her concern.

Henry is familiar with the routine. She checks his pulse, takes some blood, and hands him the urinal.

"I'll be back in a minute," she says, smoothing his rumpled sheet.

"Thanks," he says, grateful more for the little kindnesses and the respect she shows for his dignity than for the fact that she will return.

By the time she comes back with the insulin and pain shots he has provided the specimen and is lying back on his pillow, exhausted and breathing hard.

The day passes like the rest, with Henry fighting for each shallow, excruciating breath of air, surrounded by a blur of doctors, nurses, tests, meal trays, and shots.

All day he looks forward to the evening, when there is a chance that visitors might come and distract him from the pain.

He is not to be disappointed. Today Marilyn has brought Katie to visit, and Rudy has met them at the hospital after work. Henry strains to keep up the conversation so that they will not go away so quickly.

"How were the roads?" he asks, looking at his daughter-in-law.

"Not too bad really," she replies, her words bursting out in a quick, clipped staccato. "A little icy in places. Snowploughs have gone and sanded them though." She smiles, her face a little tense, looking at Katie to corroborate her version of the road conditions.

It takes nearly an hour to drive from Tofield to the hospital in Edmonton when the roads are good. Today it hasn't taken that much more time. "It could be a lot worse."

"Marilyn's a real good driver," says Katie reassuringly. "I never worry when she's driving."

At least she knows she wouldn't need to worry, but she worries too much even when Henry's driving. "I'm such a bother," she continues, trying to make amends, "me not drivin'. Somebody always has to take me." She shakes her head. "If it wasn't for my terrific kids, I'd never get to see my Henry." She glances from Henry to Marilyn apologetically.

"I was coming anyway," Marilyn says with a short laugh. "You're no bother."

"I'd just die if I had to sit at home all the time wondering how he's doin'," Katie continues.

"No you wouldn't," says Henry, feeling responsible. "You could just forget about me and quit your worrying."

"Don't talk stupid!" She says angrily. She is close to tears.

He knows immediately that his words have not conveyed what he really means, and he hates himself for upsetting her. How can he possibly tell her how much it means to have her here? How can he let her know that he understands and appreciates her humiliation when she has to catch rides in order to come and see him, and her agony travelling over winter roads just to be with him. How can he explain how guilty he feels for causing her so much worry and trouble, and that he would even give up her visits if it would make it easier for her. He has never been good at telling her how he really feels.

He takes a sharp, painful breath. "Well," he says firmly, "it ain't no good for you to be comin' all this way all the time on these icy roads." A violent coughing spell doubles him over. He has been sitting up on his bed for the visit and now he fumbles with trembling hands to adjust the pillows behind him.

Rudy has been sitting quietly by, listening. Now he gets up from the chair. "Why don't you just lie down, Dad?" he says, helping him with the pillow. "You're wearing yourself out talking too much."

"I'm all right," says Henry weakly. But he does slide down under the covers, trembling with exhaustion.

"We'd better go and let Dad get some rest," says Marilyn, picking up her purse.

"No! Don't go," says Henry, still panting. "I have all night and all day to rest."

And so they stay a little longer, the tension gone, visiting between themselves, with Henry mostly listening, adding a comment now and again but comforted that he is not alone with his pain. He tries not to think of the endless hours of night ahead.

# 15

# GROSSWEIDE - SUMMER 1920

Throughout the summer of 1920, fierce battles continued to rage across Russia between the crippled White army and the Bolshevik revolutionaries. Anarchists like the notorious Makhno and his gang had aligned themselves for the moment with the revolutionary forces, so that they could plunder and terrorize villages under the guise of a noble political cause.

For the children in the Grossweide orphanage, life went on pretty much as usual; it was an island of tranquility in a country torn apart by revolution. Sometimes they could hear gunshots in the neighbouring villages, and occasionally even in their own. At such times a warning bell would ring and everyone would scurry for cover in the basement of the main house until the shooting stopped.

As Abram Harder travelled on business, he was discovering how unique the situation at the orphanage was. Everywhere he went he encountered the terrible after-effects of the continued unrest in the land. Little wonder that the financial support for the church-sponsored orphanage had been drastically lacking of late.

A grim reality was settling in. More and more the Harders and their orphans would have to rely on what they could grow and raise themselves. For now there was still enough food to feed the children, but the additional costs for clothing, staff, and the other expenses could no longer be met.

The home was also beginning to feel the increasing burden of the confiscation of livestock, machinery and farm produce by the local soviet. Until now the orphanage had been exempt from taxes, but now it was beginning to look as if that they would not even be allowed to keep enough to meet their own needs. Abram Harder's heart was heavy as the motto over the entrance to the main house caught his attention: "My help cometh from the Lord who created heaven and earth."

"Yes," thought Abram, "the God who watches over even a sparrow will help all these homeless ones whom He has entrusted to our care. We must trust Him!"

And so it was with renewed courage that Abram Harder left that afternoon to meet once again with the newly appointed Russian official in the village to ensure that the government would continue to licence and recognize the home. He was well aware that many of the Mennonite institutions had already been taken over by Russians, and the Mennonite workers banished.

"You have our word," the official reassured him, "your work with the orphans is well known. Your licence is not in danger!"

As the summer passed, Heinz and Peter began to feel at home at the Grossweide orphanage. There were Saturday afternoon ballgames to watch, with Peter and the other middlers challenging the visiting Sunday school children for the win; and when the weather was hot and the work was done, they went for a cool dip in the nearby creek.

Sometimes in the evening after he had gone to bed, Heinz would hear the haunting sounds of a mouth organ or someone singing to the strum of a guitar, the music wafting through the ceiling from the recreation room below as he and his young roommates drifted off to sleep.

The Sunday evenings, when visiting young people would come to the home with their musical instruments for a *Spielabend*, were special highlights for Heinz. The visitors, along with the youthful staff and the older group from the orphanage, would sing and make music unlike anything Heinz had ever heard. And even though the younger ones were not allowed in the recreation hall on these occasions, the music would drift through the house and up the stairs, filling him with hope and joy. Sometime, thought Heinz wistfully, I would like to play a musical instrument and sing like that.

Each day at the orphanage had its predictable shape, measured out by the seven o'clock rising bell to the bedtime bell, eight o'clock for the younger group and nine for the middlers and older group. But the lines of demarcation between the different age groups gradually diminished in the carefree camaraderie of summer days.

In the orchards and fruit gardens there was an ongoing harvest of fruits and berries: May cherries, mulberries, apricots, peaches, strawberries, raspberries, gooseberries, and more, before the summer was over. Everyone was involved in the picking, preserving and drying of the fruit that was not either sold or turned over to the government officials as tax. Heinz especially enjoyed the Sunday afternoon forays into the new orchard where, accompanied by one of the older staff, he and the other children could eat fruit until their bellies ached.

With summer came the hot weather needed for cutting and drying the hay for the next winter's feed for the animals, and for ripening the crops that had been planted in the land behind the orchards.

By early August the fields of melons, watermelons, cucumbers, and winter wheat were being harvested, and in the summer kitchen the older girls and women were boiling huge kettles of watermelon fruit to make syrup. No sugar had been available in the village for months because the sugar factories had been pressed into making bullets. The watermelon syrup was a most welcome change from the honey which they had been getting from the village bee hives.

With the help of the staff and the older boys and girls, the Harders had been able to harvest all the oats, barley, millet and wheat by the end of September, and what the village officials did not confiscate was carefully stored in the granary, alongside the machinery.

The last of the pumpkins had been sold too, and all the apples had been picked and stored in the vegetable cellar. The vegetables had been either canned or stored as well. Even the sunflowers had been harvested and roasted, and the last of the walnuts, hickory nuts, and hazel nuts had been picked from the ground.

For Heinz, who for more than a year had survived on a most

meagre fare in the Kuban with the Dycks, the abundance of the Grossweide harvest was nothing short of heaven itself.

Several days had been spent butchering chickens, a pig, and a heifer, and between errands the younger children had watched in amazement as jars of canned chicken and beef had emerged to fill the pantry shelves, and rings of smoked sausage, hams, bacon, *Reppschpa, Grüben,* and crocks of pure white lard had emerged from all the grease and gore. To their unpracticed eyes, it seemed that there was enough food to last a lifetime.

But even in the midst of Heinz's awe and gratitude for such abundance, wistful, homesick thoughts of his parents, whose faces were already fading into blurred images, and of his absent brother and sisters still often came unbidden, tugging hard at his firmly held emotions. And sometimes, in the privacy of night he allowed his loneliness a few moments free rein before checking them sharply.

He did have Peter, he reminded himself sternly, and even though he was often separated from him because of their different age groups, it was a comfort to know that they were together. Someday, when he was old enough, he promised himself, he would find the others too, and they would be a family again. Meanwhile, he did not speak of it. He dearly loved the Harders and this was home. He would not do or say anything to hurt them or to show ingratitude or disloyalty.

Sunday afternoons, when father Harder wasn't travelling, Heinz would see the Harders relaxing on the benches on the verandah outside the main house. Often one or more of the children could be seen with them. Sometimes there would be tears, sometimes laughter, sometimes quiet talking, and at other times silence. Heinz was well aware that with more than fifty children sharing one set of parents, each child's time with the parents was limited at best. So for him, as for some of the other more reserved children, it was enough just to know that mother and father Harder were there and available in case they needed them. Children living with the Harders seldom spoke of being taken into a "real" family. Especially those children who reached the age of eighteen and left to find employment elsewhere looked to Grossweide as home. Such was the love and loyalty to mother and father Harder and the Grossweide home.

Still, when visitors came looking for a child to take home with them, there was not one child in the long, neat row of children on display whose heart did not thump in hope and anticipation. "Maybe this time it will be me that is chosen."

. . . . .

Henry shifts uncomfortably on the hospital bed. He can still feel the sting of those rejections.

"I was never chosen, Katie," he says sadly when they talk of it. "Nobody wanted me." He fixes a questioning gaze on her face. "Why didn't nobody want me, Katie?"

She can only shake her head. It is something she can't understand either. Such a handsome, clever boy he must have been.

"Maybe God was savin' you for the Hueberts," she says, trying herself to believe it. But she knows, and he knows, that the Hueberts had their hearts set on a little girl.

It doesn't matter, Henry tells himself. Nothing Katie can ever say will take away the pain he still feels of being unwanted. That feeling has been deeply engraved.

In his mind, the Harder's warm welcome stands in stark contrast to the rejections, first by the Dycks, and then by those who came to the orphanage looking for a child to adopt. No one will ever know what it meant to him to be accepted by the Harders and to be treated as one of their own. It is the earliest memory he has of what it must mean to be part of a real family and he'll never forget it.

. . . . .

It was a hot Saturday summer afternoon. Breakfast was almost over and the day stretched before the children with tantalizing promise. Heinz could scarcely wait for the afternoon with its usual holiday spirit. It was a time to play in the orchards or to swing on the *Rundschaukel* in the yard. It was a time the children loved.

"You know your Saturday chores," Father Harder was saying. "I expect them to be done thoroughly by the time I return at noon."

Heinz knew what his group had to do. There were weeds to pull along the brick fence around the orphanage, and the yard

116

to clean up. Then there was the barn to sweep especially well, and paths to sweep clean too. To finish by noon, the thirteen younger boys would have to work hard. They had done it before.

He looked longingly after Moschka as she trotted briskly down the lane, pulling the *Droschka* with Papa Harder in it. Today there was to be an important meeting with government officials, and Heinz was not going along as he often did.

The work began with moderate enthusiasm, with Johann, Papa Harder's son, making sure that everyone was busy. Then he left with the older group to cut firewood in the forest at the other end of the village. As he left the young boys breathed a sigh of relief. If there was anything they feared it was Johann's volatile temper and his heavy hand. Papa was strict too, but he was not feared in the same way.

No sooner was Johann out of sight, when Dave leap-frogged over Isaac, his voice taunting, "Catch me, catch me if you can."

Isaac sprang after him, agile on his bare feet. They fell, rolling and laughing in the long grass.

Not far away the "swoosh, swoosh" of the scythe stopped. Thirteen-year-old Gerhard watched the tussling for a minute.

"Hey, you boys," he called out, "not so much playing and more working, you hear. You know what Father Harder said."

It was enough to send the boys tripping back to pulling the weeds and grass along the fence.

The sun was beginning to climb uncomfortably hot into the morning sky.

"I'm going for a drink of water," declared Franz. There was no need for a further invitation as thirteen boys trooped towards the tap on the outside wall of the big summer kitchen where they had been eating their meals all summer. From inside wafted the tantalizing Saturday smells of baking.

*"Zwieback,"* sighed Kolya, rubbing his stomach.

*"Perschkji,"* drooled Hans.

The thought of the warm, fresh double-decker white buns and the fruit-filled pastry set their mouths watering. It was really being baked for a special treat for Sunday, but today for *Abendbrot* they would get some too.

Distracted by the mouth-watering aromas and refreshed by the cool drink of water, all thought of work vanished and play began in earnest. Soon they were frolicking in the shade of the old orchard.

It was with alarm that the boys heard the lunch bell ring.

"Oh no," cried Heinz, "our work, it isn't finished."

"Maybe Papa Harder isn't back yet," said Isaac as they quickly climbed down from the branches and ran guiltily towards the summer kitchen for dinner.

But alas, one glance told them that Father Harder had returned. Heinz studied his face as he stood at the head of the table where the rest of the Harder family sat. Only the usual steady calm was evident. Guilt overwhelmed him. How would they make amends? Maybe, thought Heinz, Papa had not noticed the unfinished work and the boys could slip out quickly after the meal and finish it before he found out. But he remained ashamed and fearful, knowing that what they had done had been very wrong. Nothing could undo that now.

The meal of fried noodles and eggs passed with the usual clatter and chatter, the unfinished work all but forgotten. Then Papa Harder rose to dismiss them. "I would like to see the youngest group of boys," he said firmly. "The rest of you are excused."

His words fell like ice-cold water on the young boys. No trace of the bantering and laughter remained. Heinz watched, tight-lipped and grim as Papa approached their table.

In the three months he had been at Grossweide he had not seen Papa Harder discipline anyone, so he did not know what to expect, but even more painful than the fear of punishment was the knowledge that he had disappointed Papa Harder. Heinz's face registered none of this as they waited stoically for Papa Harder to speak.

"I see you boys have not done your duty." It was a statement of fact, spoken with a gentle sadness. Heinz sat, eyes lowered and ashamed. No one spoke, each aware that an apology now was not enough.

"What should we do about this?" asked Papa Harder.

Still no response. Only the sheepish faces of thirteen boys

caught playing instead of doing their assigned Saturday chores.

"You know your disobedience must be punished," said Papa Harder quietly.

There was another long, awkward silence, each boy aware only of his own fearful guilt, and only partially aware of the anguish being suffered by the gentle man upon whom it had fallen to deal with the disobedience.

"I think you better come with me," he said finally, his face now set in firm resolve.

One by one, they trooped after him, uncomfortably aware of the inquisitive eyes of some of the other children, as they crossed the yard and disappeared behind the barn where a large, three-sided woodshed stood. In front of the woodshed lay a long, sturdy log which had not been chopped up for firewood as yet. The boys hung back knowing full well what was about to happen. Papa Harder carried a leather strap in his hand.

"Who will be first?" he asked looking at them.

No one volunteered. It will be no easier putting it off, thought Heinz. Better to get it over with. He stepped forward resolutely.

"I'll be first," he said softly, bending over the log next to Papa Harder.

He did not see the look that passed over the man's face for Heinz was the youngest child at the orphanage and the newest arrival. Abram Harder had seen many children in the fourteen years since he and Sarah had begun taking in orphans. All of them were marked in some way by the upheavals that had robbed them of their own homes and families, and all of them held a tender spot in Abram Harder's heart. But with this boy it was different. Perhaps it was his uncharacteristic maturity, or the evidence of an inner strength or stubbornness that intrigued him; perhaps it was the sensitivity so fiercely controlled, or a certain spark, a tenacity for life. Whatever it was, the boy had won a special place with this man who was known to treat each child as he treated his own.

Then the strap came down, landing a smarting whack on the boy's behind. The thin summer shorts did nothing to cushion the blow. Heinz had known they wouldn't. He bit his lip, waiting for the next one, resolving not to cry.

The next one did not come. Instead he heard Papa Harder saying briskly, "Next."

Heinz straightened and stepped back as the next boy slid into his place at the end of the log. The others, he noticed, did not fare as well, especially the older boys in the group. For them the strap did not stop after once or even twice.

. . . . .

A flicker of a smile crosses Henry's face as he gazes into the semi-darkness of his hospital room, his breath coming in short laboured gasps. He remembers it vividly. It was the only spanking he ever got, and it was hardly even a spanking at that. But it is tucked away with the things he will never forget and never wants to forget. For him, his brief time with the Harders will always be remembered with great affection and loyalty. Even the spanking is remembered with great fondness.

When people talk about their growing-up experiences in their families and the discipline they have received, Katie encourages Henry to tell his story about the one spanking he got from Father Harder. And he loves to tell it. It is as though the story somehow validates his place as a full-fledged member of the Grossweide family.

And so he tells it, carefully, giving attention to all the small details, but showing little emotion. "From then on," he concludes, "we knew that when Father Harder said we were supposed to do something, he meant it." The grin, breaking out of his iron-clad features, tells volumes more than what he has allowed his words to tell.

# 16

# CAUGHT IN THE CROSS FIRE

For Heinz, the opening of school in October re-established the demarcation line between the "big ones" and the "little ones" at the orphanage. Even his brother Peter was in school. But the disappointment was softened as Papa Harder wisely gave Heinz more responsibility around the horses.

Often, when Papa Harder would prepare to go on short trips to neighbouring villages for meetings or to explore job openings for the children who would be coming of age soon, he would invite the young Rempel boy to accompany him. Right from the beginning, the sad, silent little boy had tugged at his heart. He noticed that a little light sprang to the boy's eyes when he was around the little grey mare that pulled the *Droschka*, so he had assigned Moschka's care to Heinz. As time went by, Papa Harder realized that his decision had been wise. Even though the boy was only five and a half, he was showing an intelligent sensitivity and firmness with the horse that was beyond his years, and when he held the reins the gloom seemed to lift from his face and an expectant look would fill his hazel eyes.

For Heinz, these trips were special times spent with the man he had grown to love and admire, and with a horse that was his closest friend. The visits to the various villages also provided him with an opportunity to begin a secret search for his brothers and sisters who, he was sure, were scattered across the southern Ukraine.

. . . . .

Abram Harder enjoyed watching the boy's interest in everything they passed. It made the familiar details take on a newness

Abram had begun to take for granted. The Mennonite villages which they visited lay in an orderly network across the various regions which the government, during the time of Catherine the Great and the later czars had allotted to them. They had been wooed to come from their overflowing villages in Prussia to breathe life into the desolate steppes of the Ukraine.

Nomadic peoples had been pushed back as the Mennonite villages sprang up. Beyond the villages, Russian peasants had also established villages. Now, in 1920, there was a sharp contrast between the once prosperous, orderly Mennonite villages, and the impoverished Russian settlements.

Until recently many of the Russian peasants had sought and found employment as cowherds in the Mennonite village pastures, as servants in Mennonite homes, or as farm labourers in the village farms, but now that was forbidden. Now there were peasants, some who couldn't even read or write, taking over the administration of Mennonite villages, helping the army requisition horses or food, or just demanding what taxes they wished to levy.

Mennonite villages were replicas of each other, many of them connected by tree-lined avenues which had been hand planted. Papa Harder told Heinz how barren the country-side had been before the village orchards and forests had been planted.

A main street ran down the length of each village, with a row of farmsteads fronting each side. The farms extended well back from the street, and each *Hof* had a house with an attached barn, a *Schien* for storing machinery, grain and straw, and several other buildings. Every farm, whether it was a full farm or a half farm, boasted a large vegetable garden and a fruit orchard. The communal pasture, forest, and the individual farmland all lay beyond the village proper.

About halfway up the street stood a church and behind it the cemetery, and on the other side of the street was the school, with a teacherage. Several properties along the street were considerably smaller than the rest, and housed the "landless" villagers, such as the storekeeper, or the village blacksmith, or those, who due to overcrowding or financial difficulties, could not get a farm.

Abram was familiar with the estates of some of the very wealthy Mennonite farmers and businessmen, who had outgrown the confines of the villages and lived some distance away. Many of these families, like the Dycks, had adopted the Russian language and culture, and had risen to places of prominence and prestige in government affairs.

There was, however, evidence of hardship everywhere, more pronounced in some places than in others. Pastures that should have been full of livestock were sadly depleted in number, having been confiscated by the government officials. Granaries that should have been bulging with this year's bountiful harvest were nearly empty for the same reason. Even the farmyards were strangely silent, as pigs, chickens, ducks, geese, and any other livestock had shrunk in numbers. Most of the horses, without which there could be no seeding or harvesting, had also been taken.

Here and there they could see the devastation left behind by the armies or by marauding bandits, and everywhere people feared for the future and for their lives.

Occasionally, they even went as far south as the port city of Berdjansk. It was in the city that the poverty and destitution were most evident. Abram Harder noted Heinz's horror, when he saw ragged, dirty, starving children roaming the streets, scavenging for food. They were the *bezprizornii*, with no one to care for them and nowhere to go. Some had run away from the state-run orphanages and now they lived in the streets, surviving any way they could.

Abram could see Heinz's relief when they could leave behind this place that smelled of death and disease and return to the clean, ordered security of his Grossweide home. Here at least, the war had not yet come. Here was safety for adults and orphans alike.

. . . . .

A nurse comes into the room with a needle.

"Is it time already?" Henry whispers, trying not to waken his room mates.

"It's been four-and-a-half hours since your last one," she replies. "Maybe you will be able to sleep now."

No sooner is she gone and he is on Moschka's back, riding . . . riding with no saddle and no bridle . . . riding across a meadow, and behind him the sound of guns, and riders pursuing him.

. . . . .

Heinz was outside playing when he heard the first shots. They were very near. Without waiting for the bell, he and the other small children dashed towards the house. Older children were running from the workshop, across the yard. As they ran the bell sounded.

"Hurry! Hurry!" Mother Harder called anxiously from the doorway. The last of the children and adults were finally accounted for, and together they huddled in the basement, cringing as each shot seemed to come closer and closer. One volley of gunfire was answered by another, and finally it seemed that it was directly overhead. The house shook with each explosion. The children could hear shouts and galloping hooves as horses and riders and artillery wagons thundered by.

Outside, the civil war had come to the quiet Mennonite village of Grossweide, the village trembled and prayed as the White and Red armies clashed in its streets.

Suddenly there was a loud thud. The orphanage house shook.

"I think we've been hit," whispered one of the boys.

They waited, barely breathing, expecting to hear banging at the doors and the splintering of wood as it was broken open, but the sounds did not come. Everyone had heard stories of the terrible things the Bolshevik soldiers did when they came to the Mennonite homes, and some people in the villages had been killed for refusing them entrance.

All that evening and into the night, Sarah Harder and her orphanage family huddled together as the fighting continued. Then gradually the sound of gunfire faded into the distance. They continued to wait in the eerie quiet that followed, wondering if it was safe to come out of hiding.

It was morning before Johannes Harder finally crept upstairs to look things over. With his father away on business, the responsibility of being the man about the house fell on him. He rather liked the feeling of power.

"All clear," he said importantly, coming back down the stairs. "They're all gone. It's safe to come out."

Eagerly everyone went to inspect the damage. No lives had been lost, thank God, but here and there, a chink in the meter-thick wall told them that the house had been hit more than once. Part of a shell was lodged in the door frame of the house.

"Shall I get some tools and take the shell out, Father?" asked Johannes when Papa Harder came home.

Abram Harder looked at the shell a long time, and then he said quietly, "It's not in the way, so we might as well leave it as a reminder."

So there it remained, an instrument of war and death, deeply imbedded in the thick wall of a home where no gun had ever been, a grim reminder of the realities of the revolution shaking the country.

Outside again, after a hearty breakfast, the younger boys continued to explore the Grossweide property for any further remnants of the battle they had been able to hear but not see. Empty shells lay scattered about, and these they eagerly gathered up to be used later for play.

"Hey, look what I've found," called twelve-year-old Corny excitedly. "I've got a live one!"

They gathered around to see the cartridge he held.

"Here's another one," called Franz. "I've got three of them already."

"I know how you can make them explode without hurting anything," boasted one of the older boys.

"You better not," warned Bennie.

"Show us, show us," chorused others.

So, out behind the buildings, in the privacy of the old orchard, the boy pounded a shell into the ground.

"Okay, everybody back," he warned importantly. He held a nail over it and began to tap on the nail with a hammer. The nail had barely punctured the metal shell, when it exploded with a huge thud. Dirt hurtled in all directions.

"Wow, where did you learn to do that?" someone asked.

"Here, let's do another one," cried Dave before the boy could answer.

"Stand back then," said the instigator of the game.

Again the process was repeated. The shell exploded amidst a volley of dirt.

"Ow, ow, ow!" Isaac was holding his face and jumping up and down, blood dripping from between his fingers.

"He's hit!" shouted Abe in a panic. "Let's get him to the house."

"Are we ever going to be in trouble now," groaned Bennie.

A piece of the shell's metal casing had imbedded itself near the boy's right eye, and could be seen protruding from the wound.

Guiltily they hurried to the house, knowing full well that there would be a firm punishment for the dangerous game they had played.

. . . . .

Henry has been dozing fitfully, with memories of Grossweide flitting through his consciousness. If anyone was punished, Henry can not remember. He knows that he, as an onlooker, was not. Most likely the older boys made a visit to the woodshed with Johannes or Papa Harder.

What he does remember clearly is that the young boy nearly lost his eyesight.

Henry lets his mind slip over other memories of Grossweide, etched vividly in his mind as though they happened only yesterday. Some, like the shelling and its aftermath, he does not like to remember. Some he has chosen to forget.

But there is one memory that is especially dear. He goes over it often, savouring it, reliving it, and cherishing it. It is one of the few happy childhood memories he has . . . a treasure from his past more dear than the Kroeger clock . . . and one that, like the Harders welcome, time cannot fade or destroy.

How often he has told Katie about it he cannot even begin to remember. Perhaps it is because it belongs to Grossweide, where his earliest memories of family begin and end, that it stands out so vividly in his mind; he can't say for sure.

# 17

# CHRISTMAS - 1920

It was December, and the ground was covered with a thick blanket of snow. Shorts had long ago been replaced by long trousers, and the front entry of both dorms was lined with warm coats, hats, mittens and galoshes.

Heinz had noticed a growing air of secrecy at the orphanage. The younger children, who had until now always had full access to every room and every corner of the orphanage, suddenly found themselves banished from the workshops and from certain rooms.

At first they were annoyed and irritated by the new restrictions. Then curiosity took over. What could be going on behind those closed doors, they asked.

"It's a secret," they were told. "You'll find out when the right time comes."

And so they had to wait, occupying themselves in their own small workroom, hammering and sawing on their own projects, trying to imagine what the secret might be.

Inside the main house, the sweet and spicy smells of baking began to waft with increasing frequency.

"No you can't have any more *Pfeffernüse*," said the cooks after Leenie and Heinz had come back for the third time to sample the spicy cookies. "They are for Christmas."

"Christmas?" thought Heinz. He could not remember celebrating Christmas before, but as the other children talked about it in excited voices, his own anticipation grew as well.

The days seemed to drag by. The staff and the older children seemed pre-occupied and the younger ones grew impatient with the waiting.

At last the day arrived. Everyone seemed to be hastily finishing something. The girls were finishing up the last of the polishing and the cleaning. The recreation room in Ebenezer was out of bounds except to the older children, who had been seen dragging in a huge evergreen tree cut just yesterday in the village forest.

By early afternoon, the three big cast-iron kettles in the basement of Ebenezer were steaming with water heated for the baths, and before long, thirteen little boys were taking turns being scrubbed down by their nursemaids. In the girls' dormitory, the procedure was being duplicated.

The older children were allowed to bathe themselves, but the supervisors made sure that they had done a good job.

"Done already, Franz?" said *Tante* Nettie. "Are you sure you washed behind your ears? They're not even wet."

"I was in a hurry," said Franz

"Better try again," said *Tante* Nettie.

And finally, all fifty-two children as well as the staff were bathed and dressed in their Sunday best, ready for a special Christmas Eve *Vesper*, rich with Christmas delicacies including *Pfeffernüse, Kringel, Hirschensaltz Kuchen,* and tiny meat buns called *Fleischperschkji.* Excitement reigned.

While the older children were clearing away the dishes from the meal, the younger ones eagerly rehearsed the *Weihnachtswunsch* which they each had memorized. Later they would say these verses for Mama and Papa Harder as their gift to them.

In the village of Grossweide, and in the Mennonite villages all over Russia, much the same was taking place. Everywhere families were preparing for the Christmas Eve service, whether it would be held in a church, a school, or in a recreation room, as was the case here at the orphanage. This service would officially begin the three-day Christmas celebration. A holiday spirit pervaded.

At last the time had come! Dressed in their best regulation outfits the children waited eagerly in the hall outside the recreation room. Heinz tried to imagine what was behind the closed doors. What was this "Christmas" that everyone was so excited about?

Suddenly the doors were thrown open. Heinz stared in amazement. The room had been mysteriously transformed! Not a lamp was lit, yet a warm glow filled the large room. Heinz's eyes were drawn to the source of the light at the far end of the room. The tiny flames of a hundred candles danced in the lush branches of a huge evergreen tree. And it seemed that a thousand shiny *Kugeln* were catching the reflection of the flames in their little round globes, filling the room with a rainbow of colour. As Heinz watched, wide-eyed, the *Weihnachtsbaum* began to revolve ever so slowly on its stand, shimmering and sparkling with light and color as it turned, and from somewhere in the mysterious depths of the stand, the wonderful sounds of *Der Christenbaum ist der Schönste Baum* floated forth.

All eyes were on the tree. A hush had fallen over the children as they looked, eyes shining, at the sight before them. "So this is Christmas!" thought Heinz. It was even more wonderful than he could ever have imagined.

Silently the children began to move through the candlelit room, taking their places in the chairs that now stood in neat, straight rows, ready for the Christmas Eve program. All the tables had been moved, and now lined the walls on every side.

Mama and Papa Harder and the staff watched, their faces beaming. Who could say where these homeless children would be tonight if they had not found a welcome here at Grossweide? To watch their eyes, alight with happiness, was thanks enough.

Then the pump organ was playing, and soon the room was filled with the sound of children's voices singing the Christmas carols which they had learned for this special night.

The program followed, including recitations, Christmas wishes recited by the younger ones, prayers, and more music, this time by a group of the staff playing guitars, violins and mouth organs.

Then they were reading a story. Heinz listened, enthralled. He could picture Mary and Joseph coming to Bethlehem and finding no room in the inn. He could see them settling down among the animals in the stable on a bed of sweet-smelling hay.

It was as if he were hearing it all for the first time.

What excitement there must have been in the stable when the baby Jesus was born, Heinz thought. How happy his father and mother must have felt, holding him in their arms. Heinz tenderly held the picture of it all in his mind: the happy little family, snug and secure in their stable home!

The baby Jesus was God's love gift to the world, Papa Harder was saying, given for all those who would receive him. Heinz could not imagine anyone not receiving such a gift. His own heart felt as though it would burst with love for the tiny *Christkind*.

And then the organ was playing once more, and they were singing *Ihr Kinderlein Kommet*, inviting children to come to the manger and see the wonderful Christ Child.

In the silence that followed, the tree, which had stood silently throughout the service, now began to revolve slowly once more, this time playing the familiar strains of *Stille Nacht*. Heinz sat watching and listening, unaware that around him the staff and children had begun to move the tables and chairs back into their places.

Silent Night, holy night,

All is calm, all is bright

'Round yon' virgin mother and child, Holy Infant so tender and mild,

Sleep in heavenly peace. . . .

"Come on Heinz," Abe was tugging at his shirt sleeve. "It's time to set up our plates for the *Weihnachtsmann*. Heinz jumped up. He had forgotten. Tonight, he had been told, the Santa Claus was coming. He must hurry and set up his plate to receive the gifts which this mysterious person would bring.

It did not take the children long to get into their beds and say their prayers that night, but it was more difficult than usual to get to sleep.

Outside, the snow was falling gently as one by one the children drifted off to dream of a place where wishes come true.

. . . . .

It was earlier than usual when Heinz awoke the next morning. He lay on his bed, listening for sounds from the other children, and wondering when it would be appropriate to get up. The feeling of excitement and anticipation was even greater this morning than it had been the evening before. What would the *Weihnachtsmann* have brought him, he wondered.

The floor was cold as he slid his feet out from under the warm covers and lowered them to the floor. A lamp was lit in *Tante* Greta's room, so it was probably all right to get up even though it was very early. Quietly he stole to his friend Abe's bed.

"Abe, are you awake?" He shook the boy's shoulder.

"Is it morning already?" whispered Abe, rubbing his eyes and peering at Heinz in the dark.

"I think so," replied Heinz. *"Tante* Greta's lamp is on." There were other boys stirring now, wide awake and shivering with cold and excitement.

"Let's go and see if the *Weihnachtsmann* has been here yet!" said Kolya. Quickly they dressed and dashed down the stairs and through the big doors of the recreation room.

The tree stood in all its glory, its candles burning, playing carols as it slowly turned. Several of the supervisors hung back in its shadows, obviously having gotten up early enough to light all the candles and set the atmosphere. They were not disappointed.

The boys rushed into the room, exclaiming as they ran, each one to his own place. There were squeals of delight, as their eyes took in the wonderful array of treats heaped high on their plates, and settled on the gifts underneath their own personal drawers.

Heinz hesitated in the doorway, his heart thumping with excitement and anticipation. Could he be dreaming? Never in all his life had he seen so many delicious treats all at once, nor so many wonderful new presents.

"Heinz, come see what you've got," shouted Abe.

Instantly, Heinz sprang to life, running to his place at the long table. It was true! His plate was full too, and oh, look at this . . . there, beneath the table, directly under his own drawer stood a brightly painted red wheelbarrow. Could it really be his?

Cautiously he checked with the boys on either side of him. Abe, to his right was exclaiming over a pair of ice skates, and

Kolya on the left was pulling around a shiny yellow wagon. Yes, the wheelbarrow must be his very own! He slid his hands over the handles, the smooth surface cool to his touch, and lifted gently. The wheel at the front rolled easily along the floor.

"It works!" he cried.

"Can I have a ride?" asked Abe, plopping himself into the wheelbarrow. Heinz looked around the room. The girls hadn't come in yet, so the room wasn't too crowded, and the supervisors seemed to be in a relaxed mood.

"Why not," grinned Heinz. Then they were off, racing around the tables and bumping into the other boys.

"I haven't looked to see what I have in my plate yet," said Heinz, when they came back.

"Everybody has the same," said Abe, popping a fig into his mouth.

Heinz turned his attention to the contents of his own plate. There was a shiny red apple from the barrel in the vegetable cellar. There were several walnuts and hazelnuts, harvested from their own orchard, and some dried fruit, roasted sunflower seeds, two bought figs and wonder of wonders, three store-bought candies, resplendent in their shiny wrappers.

Just then the girls rushed in from their dormitory, exclaiming in delight as they caught glimpses of the treasure-laden tables from the entryway where they were shedding their coats. They could not hang them up fast enough. Then they were in the room, laughing and chattering with joy over their new toys.

Heinz could see that they also had things made by the older children and staff. It was no longer a secret what had been going on behind those closed doors. He could see cradles, chairs and tables, and even handmade dolls making their appearance from underneath the long tables.

Heinz picked up one of the candies. He had never tasted a store-bought candy before. Carefully he unwrapped it, held it in his hand for a long moment, and then allowed himself one slow, luxurious lick. "Mmmm." It was as exquisite as he had imagined. Then, carefully, he wrapped up the candy and slipped it, along with the other two candies, into his drawer. He would allow himself one lick a day. That way he could make this moment last and last. The other treats he would ration too, starting later today with the apple.

The breakfast bell rang.

"Come now," urged *Tante* Greta, seeing that some of the children were reluctant to leave their play. "Your toys will be here waiting for you when we get home from church. We must hurry now so we won't be late."

Breakfast was soon over, and the children were once again bundled up and ready for the walk down the long village street to the church. Even the youngest group, who normally did not get to go to services, were on their way to the church for the special Christmas morning service.

The villagers were accustomed to seeing the front half of the church filled with children from the orphanage. The girls sat in the pews on the right side of the aisle, with the younger ones in front; the elderly women sat behind the children, and the rest of the women sat nearer the back. This arrangement repeated itself on the men's side of the church as well.

At the front, a choir of some twenty young people sat facing the congregation, with several of the leading men sitting in chairs in front of them. Because of the special occasion, the service included more choir and congregational songs than usual, all sung without accompaniment. And, as usual, there was time for Scripture reading, public prayers, and two messages. Everything took place in the High German language.

The service seemed long for the children, especially the sermons. In their minds they could see their new toys waiting for their eager play underneath their special place at the tables in the Ebenezer dormitory. As the service drew to a close, their stomachs reminded them of the wonderful Christmas dinner that had been promised.

At long last the service ended. In the silence that followed, the Grossweide family filed out of the church. As the children reached the village street, they broke into a run in anticipation of the special dinner awaiting them at the orphanage.

They were not disappointed. *Schinkenfleisch*, boiled potatoes, *Pflaumenmus, Zwieback,* and a variety of vegetables and pickles were passed up and down the tables as the children filled and refilled their plates.

When they were so full that they did not know where to put one more bite, plates of Christmas cookies were handed along the tables.

So this is Christmas! Heinz licked his fingers thoughtfully. In all his life he had not experienced anything like it. His happiness, like the food, seemed to know no limits.

. . . . .

Henry is only vaguely aware of the already familiar sounds of the night shift going off duty and the day shift coming on. In his mind he is back at Grossweide, remembering a Christmas too wonderful for words.

# 18

# A FRIEND'S VISIT

For Henry the days and weeks have been dragging on. February is almost over and this is already his sixth week in the hospital. He is convinced that he is no better than when he was admitted, in spite of the fact that the oxygen tubes have been taken away. Maybe he has forgotten just how ill he was when he first came in, but he doubts it. But by now he has grown restless, afraid, he tells Katie, that they will kill him before they cure him. He wants to go home. He badgers the doctors to let him go.

"It's just like last time," he complains to Katie when she comes to visit. "They're makin' me sicker." They both know what happened last time, when the doctor accidentally punctured his lung and it collapsed during a procedure to drain fluids from it. Now he is sure that if they would just give him the medicines he is taking in the hospital, he and Katie could get him back on his feet a lot sooner. They both understand how to regulate his insulin and his eating with new medicine. Here there always seem to be a lot of communication gaps that put too much time between a negative reaction he is experiencing and an appropriate action to balance things. He tries to tell them, but no one is listening.

Already he has gone into a coma twice because of the poor balance between the insulin and his food intake, but that only makes the doctors more stubborn about keeping him in the hospital. Even Katie, who is usually his staunchest ally because she can't stand being at home alone, says to him, "You're better off stayin' right here, Henry. Don't talk stupid about checkin' yourself out of the hospital."

If he didn't know better, he might think that there is a conspiracy to keep him here. He wouldn't really blame them. He's a lot of bother to everybody, especially to Katie when he's sick at home like he so often is.

He grimaces ruefully, groping weakly for the water glass on the stand beside his bed. He wets his parched lips sparingly.

If he were the doctor, he muses, he wouldn't check anybody out of the hospital in his shape either. But he's not just anybody. He's got problems that go back a long way, and it's obvious that the five or six different doctors who pop their heads in the door, asking how he is and prescribing all kinds of treatment and medicines, haven't been able to figure out how he ticks yet either. They tell him so themselves.

So where has it all gotten him? Six weeks of staring at the ceiling and four walls day and night, still coughing until he can't breathe, and the pain constantly tearing at his lungs. Good thing a person doesn't die from pain, he thinks, otherwise he'd be dead.

His children are worried. He can read it in their eyes and in their forced cheerfulness when they come to visit. Even Brenda has been out to see him, leaving right after work and driving seven-and-a-half hours just so she can visit him on Saturday and Sunday morning, and then driving all the way back home and going to work the next day. She wouldn't do that if they hadn't told her it was serious. He knows the doctors aren't telling him everything. They think he doesn't know.

He looks at the watch he keeps on his table, and adjusts his glasses so he can see the numbers better. Yes, just as he thought by the sounds in the hall. Afternoon visiting hours have begun already. He is not expecting anyone until after work later this evening.

His neighbours do not have visitors either. One is quietly watching the afternoon soaps on a little TV overhead, and another just lies, heavily sedated, and groans or sleeps. The young man that was in the other bed has gone home.

Sometimes there are bits of conversation, but each one, it seems, is preoccupied with his own immediate misery or, like Henry, is not given to much talking at the best of times. He can not even indulge in the distraction of reading. His eyes have gotten so bad that he can barely recognize familiar faces around him, let alone read. Besides, even if his eyes were better it would be too exhausting.

So the steady parade of nurses taking his temperature, giving him needles and pills, ventilating his lungs, and taking endless samples of blood and urine are, for the most part, a welcome diversion. Still, even with that, the days crawl by, and the nights seem endless.

Slowly, Henry pushes himself up on his elbow and maneuvers himself into a sitting position. He slides his feet over the edge of the bed until they touch the stool beside it. His feet, splotchy and scarred from being badly frozen way back when he was a child, are swollen to about twice their normal size, but he manages to slip his toes into his *Schlorre*. Then, trembling visibly, he grabs hold of the intravenous stand and propels it, along with his pajama-clad body, into the lavatory. If a nurse sees him he will be scolded for not ringing the bell for help, so he must hurry.

By the time he has gotten himself back into bed he is exhausted, and lying back, closes his eyes to catch his breath. It is not long before he is asleep.

Henry's young friend Norma Bergen is standing in the doorway, her eyes taking in the ash-grey face which even in sleep shows evidence of pain. Quietly, she tip-toes into the room and sits down in the chair beside the bed. She had driven in to the city to shop, and has decided to swing by the hospital before she heads back to Tofield. The news she had been getting from her friend Katie about Henry's condition does not sound good. He has them all worried.

His breathing is shallow and rasping, and there is a flush of fever on his face which does not hide the eerie grey pallor and the sunken cheeks. His hair is grey and thin, framing his once handsome features. There is a vulnerability about the six-foot frame now curled up in a childlike position, which is not evident when he is awake.

It shocks her to see him like this. There has always been a quiet, stony strength about him in spite of his poor health. To see him lying here, as helpless and vulnerable as a little child, does not fit that image.

He is not quite as old as her father, but old enough to share the very serious, black and white world he lives in. She remembers them, over the years, in conversation with each other, always in Low German, and Henry, speaking in his succinct, measured way, eyes lowered, and eyelids fluttering nervously, before he can bring himself to make eye contact.

Norma cannot remember ever hearing Henry raise his voice, or showing much emotion in his face. In this, the two men are opposites. But like her own father, he is a stubborn man of strong beliefs and firmly held convictions. He is not afraid, especially in his church, to speak out against change that he feels violates the principles upon which his beliefs are based, even at the risk of being shunned, ridiculed and misunderstood. Perhaps it is that, and their fierce loyalty to their Mennonite heritage, that has woven a firm friendship between them.

Not that they have agreed on everything. A rueful grin flickers across Norma's face. There are a number of things, primarily regarding the raising of children, which they have handled very differently over the years, much to hers' and her siblings' annoyance. Henry and Katie's children grew up in town, free to attend the movie theatre or go bowling at the town hang-out, and even go out on dates. Norma's father has always denounced such activities as sinful, categorically forbidding his own children to participate in any of them.

"But the Huebert kids get to go to movies and parties," Norma can remember arguing. "Their parents don't think it's sin."

"It's different vit dem," replies her father. His "r's" roll thickly and, like Katie, he still can't manage the "w" and the "th" sounds of this, his fourth-learned language. His answer to Norma's argument is simple: "Henry was an orphan and grew up different from the rest of us. He's got his own ideas on vat's right and wrong." And that is that.

If the two men have ever discussed these differences, Norma is not aware of it. What she does know is that over the years they seem to have treated each other with mutual respect and loyalty, able to somehow accept their differences.

But when Norma stops by these days, it is Katie who inquires after her father's health, telling her how much they miss him. Henry says little, but listens intently as she answers.

In some strange way, Norma feels that she and her husband and daughter have been drawn into the circle of friendship too. With her father living so far away now, and her mother long dead, Norma somehow finds comfort being with Henry and Katie. And perhaps, she wonders, with them missing her parents too, do they find comfort in her too? They don't say so in so many words, muses Norma, but when she hasn't called Katie for a while and finally does, it isn't unusual for Katie to lament mournfully, "I just said to Henry the other day, 'Norma's forgotten all about us old guys.' " And when she drops in unexpectedly, as she is in the habit of doing, Katie hurries to wherever Henry is, calling eagerly, "Henry, we have a visitor . . . Norma's here." And he drops whatever he is doing and goes to sit at the kitchen table where they visit.

"I'm keeping you from your work," Norma apologizes.

"What work?" he says briskly, "I'm just playin'. It's not work." He makes coffee while Katie and Norma visit, and then they all spend the next two or three hours talking. There seems to be no thought of returning to his carpentry project in the garage as long as she is there.

Norma remembers the day they talked about the fate of Henry's orphanage parents, after the Communist takeover. His love and loyalty for them permeates all he says.

"They died in Siberia, with nothing! Like criminals!" Norma can still hear the anguish in his voice.

"And for what? For giving up everything to make a home for kids like me." His lips close in a grim, thin line. More he cannot say. It is the most passionate outcry Norma has heard from him in all the time she has known him. A cry for the injustice done to someone other than himself. An injustice that nothing can appease or undo. That he too has fallen victim to that injustice is evident, but of that he does not speak.

Often they talk of Henry's search for his lost brothers and sisters, or about Norma's parents.

"Your Mom was a terrific friend. I sure miss her." Katie's

words echo in Norma's memory, jogging loose a story her father has told her about Henry.

It was the day her mother died . . . and Henry had come to her father and pressed two hundred dollars into his hand. "I thought you might be able to use some extra cash Jake, money for the casket maybe, or clothes for the children. It's a loan. Don't worry about payin' it back."

It's one of a very few times that she can remember her father accepting anything from anybody. Of course the "loan" was paid back, but the telling of it never fails to bring a tear to her father's eye.

Probably moved as much by the dignity with which the gift was given as by anything, muses Norma. Others around the town have similar stories about Henry, a stubborn, quiet, but generous man, who knows how to help out without making people feel small.

She watches now as Henry's eyes open and focus on her sitting beside his bed. He struggles to pull himself into a sitting position.

"Don't get up," she says, standing up and going to the end of the bed. "If you want to sit up, I can adjust your bed."

"No. Don't bother," he says, his chest heaving as he adjusts the pillow behind him. "It won't hurt me to sit for a while. Get tired of just lyin' down all the time." He sees her hesitate and motions to the chair.

"Sit! Sit!"

She goes back to the chair and sits down.

"You should have awakened me," he says, his eyelids fluttering self-consciously before he opens them again and looks at her.

"It's okay, Mr. Huebert," she says, "I haven't been here long. I thought you might need your rest."

"I got nothing to do but rest," he retorts. He looks down, his hazel eyes veiled once more behind the fluttering eyelids.

"So how are you doing, Mr. Huebert?" she asks.

There is a moment's silence, not unusual in her conversations with this man. "What's all this Mr. Huebert business?" he says finally, with his eyes averted. Norma looks at him, her brows furrowed questioningly. She has always addressed him this way, a younger person showing respect for an elder as she has been taught by her father's generation. Even Katie, only a few years younger than Norma's father, stubbornly addresses him as Mister—"to show respect".

"Just call me Henry," he says in a matter-of-fact voice.

Coming from anyone else, this would simply be a casual courtesy. But for this man it is an uncharacteristic break from his carefully guarded reserve and his pre-occupation with maintaining tradition.

Norma thinks back over the years she has shared in his and Katie's lives, visiting with them, listening to the recurring refrain of their search for Henry's lost home and family, hearing their concerns over changes that make them feel abandoned—strangers in the place they still call home.

And now, after all this time, this man has just opened the door to her in an unprecedented gesture. Before she can reply, Henry continues, purposefully avoiding any discussion on what he has just said.

"We're not sure which way it's going to go," he says evenly.

He sees her eyes grow serious. "The doctors tell me I'm a freak," he continues.

Norma waits, knowing full well that no doctor would tell him that, and wondering what he's really getting at.

"They say," he continues, realizing that his attempt to lighten things up hasn't worked this time, "that if I was like normal people, they'd have fixed me up and sent me home a long time ago."

Norma's face relaxes, "So you've got them scrambling, have you?" she says with a grin.

An answering grin plays at the corners of Henry's eyes. Good. The teasing is working. He hates everybody being so worried and serious all the time.

"Have they figured out what the problem is?" she presses.

"Well," he clears his throat, then continues, carefully measuring his words, "it started out with bronchial pneumonia, and it seems that now there's infection in the lungs that were sick already." He closes his eyes for an instant, takes a shallow breath and continues, "What they've found out is that I've got a rare lung disease. Only a few people in the world have it."

"At least they know what they're dealing with," Norma says hopefully.

"Maybe so," he says, "but every time they try me on a new medication, my diabetes acts up. It's a real mess. They even tried changin' my meals from seven times a day to three times. I told them I have to eat seven times a day." He pauses, and then continues bitterly. "Nobody listens."

She hears the discouragement in his voice. "You know a lot of people are praying for you," she says, trying to cheer him.

"Thanks," he says flatly. He understands what she means. He prays too. But ultimately, he believes that a person lives as long as it is God's will, and then he dies. He does not believe in pleading with heaven for extra time.

Besides, it is not the care of his Heavenly Father that he questions. God has seen him through seventy-two years. Already he has received more time than most in his situation, but the doctors and nurses, why can't they just listen to him for a change? After all, he does know his own body. . . . Has lived with it all these years. . . . Surely he has learned something about how it ticks! If he's not careful, he's never going to make it home! That is the thing that worries him.

The swish of a nurse's uniform announces her coming even before she is inside the door.

"Your antibiotics, Mr. Huebert, and a little something for the pain." Her voice is warm but professional.

The trembling hand reaches obediently to take the little white pill cup.

"See what I mean," he says drolly, "they're trying to kill me."

The nurse looks at him sharply.

"It's fine," he says hastily, noting her reaction. "You're just doing your job." How can she know that what she is giving him is only making him sicker. "We're all just following doctor's orders," he says. He accepts the glass of water from her and washes down the pills.

The nurse smiles fleetingly and is gone, leaving them in a pocket of silence.

"I'm their guinea pig," he says at last.

"What do you mean?" asks Norma.

"They're experimenting with a new drug." He repeats a name, too long for her to remember. "They get it straight out of the lab in Toronto. The doctors even have trouble pronouncing it, so they just call it by a nickname." He tells her the name with practiced accuracy. "Costs one hundred dollars a vial," he says, his eyelids fluttering nervously.

"Wow," grins Norma. "I'm impressed. They must really want to get you out of here bad!"

"Maybe," he counters, "but they're wasting their money. I'm not worth near that much."

Norma is about to protest, but Henry continues, tight-lipped and poker-faced, "What do they say the human body is worth? Ninety-eight cents, isn't it?"

Norma groans. So he is teasing after all, and she's been had. His wry humour keeps catching her off guard. It is a side of him not many people know.

"Well, you better make it worth their while then," she laughs. She is relieved. He can't be that sick, if he can still joke.

For Henry, the sound of her laughter is worth the excruciating effort it is taking not to let her see how much pain he is in, or how serious his condition is. The doctors have told him that in spite of the pills there will be no cure. His lungs are dying inside him, even as he sits on the bed visiting.

"Well," she says, standing up, "I've got to run."

Henry has been sitting up during the visit, and Norma knows that he is overtaxing himself. It is no use trying to get him to lie down. He probably considers it disrespectful or even indecent to lie down in a lady's company, muses Norma. So she will have to go.

She takes his hand in an unfamiliar gesture and squeezes it. "You're not allowed to give up," she says firmly. "I expect to see you out of here real soon, and that's an order!"

"We'll do our best," he replies soberly, returning the squeeze without looking at her. His eyes follow her as she turns and walks out of the room.

It is only when she is gone that he allows himself to slide

down from his sitting position, shakily adjusting the pillow under his head.

In many ways she reminds him of her father. A mind of her own, not afraid to strike her own path rather than follow the crowd. He likes that about her. He knows that in dogma and Christian principles, he is much closer to her father than to her. Why she bothers with two old people like himself and Katie, he cannot imagine. But her affection for them seems genuine, and they can talk to her.

Often when she comes to visit, she asks about Henry's past, and he finds himself telling her the details, while Katie fills in the parts he cannot talk about. Somehow, he doesn't mind. Maybe a few years ago, but not any more. He trusts her and what does he have to hide? Henry closes his eyes, Norma's parting words ringing in his ears. No, he is not ready to give up yet. Not on living and not on his dream to find his brothers and sisters, if they are still alive. Norma has even written to the Red Cross for him, inquiring about missing persons. But there, too, they've run into nothing but another dead end. Surely, somewhere, at least one of them must still be alive, praying and wondering what became of their little Heinza, just as he is wondering what became of them.

Wouldn't it be something if after all this time he found some of them? It's not just a pipe dream, he tells himself. With Russia's new policy of *glasnost*, people have been finding their loved ones. He has read of several who on a recent trips to Russia have been allowed to visit their old villages and have actually found living relatives.

No! He is not ready to give up yet. But first, he has to get out of here. Wouldn't Katie and the kids be surprised if one day he just got into his clothes and walked out on his own, doctor's orders or not. They hate it when he threatens to do it, but if the doctors won't let him go soon, he will.

# 19

# FAMINE AT GROSSWEIDE

"I don't know what we are going to do, Muttie." Abram Harder's usually happy face was lined with concern.

It was a mid-summer Saturday afternoon in 1921, and a hot, dry, breeze fanned the dry grass in the yard as the Harders sat across from each other on park benches on the verandah of the main house of the orphanage. In the yard, many of the children were at play, either on the sturdy equipment or under the shade of the big May tree. Their happy laughter surrounded the Harders like music. But Abram Harder was not listening to the music. He carried the weight of these children's well-being heavily on his heart.

Already by spring, the Grossweide orphanage had begun to succumb to the pressures which many families had been facing for several years. When Lenin and his supporters had first taken power, the unrest and the new policies had seemingly passed the orphanage by, but gradually they too had begun to feel the impact. Bit by bit their precious grain supply, along with much of their livestock had dwindled because of the ever-increasing demands by the new government for tax. The best horses had been taken by the army, and the little mare, Moschka, had been stolen by robbers late one April night.

Sarah Harder and the girls had churned every bit of cream that there was in order to try to meet the butter quota, but there was not enough. So the authorities had come to take the dairy cows, one by one, until now, there were just two left of the original herd of ten.

The chicken coop had fared in much the same way. Even

though they had given nearly every egg to meet the tax, it had still not been enough.

So in a matter of just a few months Grossweide had been plunged into a desperate situation. Sarah and the staff had been trying to make do with what little they did have. They especially depended on what had been left them of the fruit and garden produce. But virtually nothing had been canned or preserved for the coming winter.

So far the orphanage had been spared the burden of occupying soldiers, who thought nothing of commandeering homes and food and people, to be used or abused according to their whims. Other homes in Grossweide had not been so fortunate, being over-run, first by the Reds, and then the Whites, as the tug-o-war of power continued between the two forces.

Already in the spring, it had been only with a great, concerted effort that the people in the village of Grossweide had been able to prepare the land and plant what little grain they had left, using whatever resources they had, whether an old horse, a cow, or an ox. In this way, the orphanage too had been able to put in its meager crops.

And then the waiting had begun. They had waited and waited for the necessary rains to make the crops grow. But it seemed to Abram Harder that the rain, like the tears of the people, had wrung itself dry. Day after day the sky looked on in dry-eyed derision, as an entire nation already bled dry by war continued its suicidal struggle for power.

Even the garden and the orchards were suffering from the drought, in spite of the children's industry in carrying water to the thirsty trees and plants. In the fields, much of the grain had not even come up, and much of what had was drying up. It would be a miracle if they harvested anything, thought Abram.

Sarah watched the gloom on his face, reading his thoughts. "Listen to the children, Abram," she said, holding up a small, plump hand, as her eyes swept over the yard. "They laugh and play, without a care in the world. They are like sparrows in a nest. Innocent and safe." Her face broke into the radiant smile that endeared her to everyone who knew her.

*"Ach*, if only." Abram followed her gaze. "Yes," he said, "they

are like little sparrows, but a big, ugly cat is stalking them. They do not know how near the danger is." He paused thoughtfully. "And innocent, you say? Do you forget what we hear at night, when they cry out from some terrible dream, or call for parents long dead? Just look at them. Look at their faces."

"*Ja*, Abram. I know," Sarah sighed. "I especially remember the look on our little Heinz's face when he found out he had been left here. I thought the poor little one would never stop crying." She gestures to where Heinz was raucously swinging on the *Rundschaukel*. "But just look at him now."

"But that's just it," continued Abram, pulling anxiously on his neatly trimmed beard. "They think they're safe here with us, and give no thought to where the next meal will come from. Why should they? It is our duty as their parents to take care of them. But we can't do it anymore, Sarah. We cannot fill their bellies, nor can we protect them from the danger that is coming."

Sarah looked reassuringly into her husband's eyes. "There have been difficulties before, Abram. Our *Himmlischer Vater* has always seen us through."

"I know, *mein Schatz* but you know how things are. No grain for bread, no meat, and all our cows gone, except two. The children are not getting enough milk. And now the last good work horse has been taken. If God does, in fact, give us a harvest, how are we even going to get it in? That poor old *Schrug* we have left can't do the work any more. We can't go on like this, Sarah."

"None of our children has gone hungry yet, Abram, not even for a day."

"Yes," he nodded, "God has provided. But we must not be foolish. The writing is on the wall. The Reds have taken over everywhere: businesses, institutions, and factories. The Czarist armies are in disarray and floundering. We can not look to them to protect us. It is just a matter of time until they take over this home. Just think, Sarah. What will become of all these children when those godless Bolsheviks take over?"

"Sh-sh," Sarah hand flew to her lips. "You mustn't talk like that. It mustn't happen," she exclaimed. She could still see the crowded, unsanitary conditions and the gaunt, hungry faces of the children they had seen in one of the state-run orphanages they had visited while they had been on business two months ago in Berdjansk. The memory of all those dirty, emaciated children haunted her. There were seven such homes, she had been told, in that city alone. If only they had room for all those children at Grossweide, she had thought to herself.

The children on the streets had been in terrible shape too, scavenging like rats for a piece of food, whatever it might be. Maybe the homes served some purpose, she had conceded, if nothing else than to protect them from the evils of the streets. The sight of little ones lying nearly dead in the streets, too sick to care, haunted her still. No doubt they were dying in the orphanages too. That is what people said, but there at least they were safe from the prying eyes of the passing public.

How could the government possibly take over their beloved home and turn it into such a place? "They would surely die," she whispered. "No! A thousand times no! It must not happen."

"Yes," said Abram. "They will die, if not from hunger, then from disease because of the overcrowding and lack of proper care. Our Mennonite children are not used to the conditions that the Russian ones know."

They sat in silence, their hearts sending silent petitions to the only One who could help them in their increasingly desperate situation.

Abram dejectedly rubbed his thinning scalp with his hands. "If it would only just rain once."

"Abram, there must be a way out," said Sarah. "God always has a way."

"I can think of only one thing," he said quietly. "We have to try to get the children out of here before its too late."

"Send them away, Abram?" she gasped. It was not one of the answers she had looked for. "Where to?"

"I don't know Sarah . . . maybe Prischib . . . or, to people's homes. At least there they might have a chance."

"But people can't even feed their own children, and then to ask them to take in another child?"

"What hope is there if they stay here? As soon as the garden is finished, the food is gone. There is little extra to put aside for the winter. Certainly not enough for so many children. Besides, what if we somehow managed to carry on? It is only a matter of time before they take over. Then, who knows how they will treat the children. They are, after all, German. No, even if they have to go hungry, at least there is a greater chance that they will be well treated in Mennonite homes. Besides, the older ones can help out with the work. It's not as if they were just another mouth to feed."

Sarah's eyes swam as the realization of the inevitable hit home. "I can't bear to think of sending the children away," she whispered, dabbing her eyes with the corner of her Sunday apron.

"I know, my dear," Abram said sadly, "I know."

And so it began. One by one the children said their good-byes and drove off with Papa Harder in the *Droschka*, pulled now by the rheumy old *Schrug* whose only pace was slow. What lay ahead, they could not even imagine. Certainly nothing as wonderful as they had known these past years at their Grossweide home.

Papa Harder's admonition to each one was much the same: "You must understand that people everywhere have been suffering. They don't have much, but are willing to share what they have. Now be good, help as much as you can, so they're glad you came to them." Then, a firm handshake and a squeeze on the shoulder, and the orphan was gone. By October the number of children at the orphanage had greatly decreased.

. . . . .

Henry has often gone over those precious last months he spent in the Grossweide home, searching for any recollections that still remain. He can only imagine how desperate the situation was. What stands out are the two occasions when food aid came to Grossweide. That they already must have known a seriously limited diet is obvious, he reasons, because of the great importance they, the children, placed on the events.

. . . . .

"Heinz, Kolya." Abe was panting as he ran towards them in the old orchard. It was October. "Guess what we've got." He was eagerly waving a big, round, yellow object.

"What is it?" cried Kolya. "Something to eat?"

"Onions," panted Abe, coming to a stop. "Onions from Holland." He opened his hand to show them the firm, smooth vegetable, almost as big as his palm. Several bites had been taken out of it.

"Can I try it?" asked Kolya?

"How does it taste?" asked Heinz. His mouth watered, remembering the tangy taste of fresh-sliced onion on warm brown bread. It had always been one of his favourite Saturday suppers. Sometimes there had been *Ziltfleisch* with vinegar and sliced onions too. But not for a long time now had they eaten like that. Now it was mostly millet gruel. Sometimes that was all they had in a whole day.

"There's enough for everyone," laughed Abe. "Go to the house and get yours. There are bags of them."

They did not need another invitation, and dashed off to the house. Other children were coming out, taking big bites and crunching happily as though they were eating an apple. Quickly they got into line, and it was not long before they both had an onion too. Heinz slid his other hand over the slick golden skin of the onion. It was smooth as silk. Slowly, he opened his mouth and let his teeth sink into the crisp, juicy meat.

"Mmm," he said luxuriously.

. . . . .

Katie, Wilmer, and Myrna sit at Henry's bedside. He is propped up, his cheeks flushed with fever. "You haven't been eating properly, have you Henry," Katie's eyes are pinning him against the pillow. "You're starving yourself to death, and there's no need. You've got to start eating better."

"Takes a lot more than that to starve me," he says evenly. "Besides, I eat when I'm hungry."

"Is it the food?" asks Myrna.

"Well, it's not Mom's cooking, that's for sure," interjects Wilmer. "I've tasted the stuff."

Katie is not about to let it go. "It's good enough for all the other patients. They eat it."

"It's not the food," says Henry quietly. "I've had a lot worse, and have gotten by on a whole lot less." He pauses . . . his mind

150

tracing a scene he hasn't thought about for a long time . . . . "I've eaten whole onions raw," he says pensively, "back at the orphanage when there wasn't anything else."

"Ugh," replies Myrna, wrinkling her nose. "I'd have to be awful hungry before I'd eat a whole onion raw.

"It was a shipment sent from Holland," he continues slowly. "The onions were sweet—" there is a thoughtful pause—"well, I don't know if they really were," he says, the corners of his mouth softening, "but to us they were sweet. We ate them like apples."

How long they lasted he cannot remember. But when they were gone another food shipment came to them. This time from the newly formed Mennonite Central Committee in North America. He has read that its first attempt in 1921 to get a shipment through failed, but from what he can remember it was 1921 when Grossweide got the shipment of food from the MCC.

"That was after the Harders were taken away," Katie says.

"No. The Harders were still there," Henry says, "but the Communists had taken everything, and there wasn't much left to eat."

"How did you manage to stay alive?" asks Myrna.

"The MCC . . ," he hesitates and begins again, "we got some help. I can still quite vividly remember that they sent a lot of soda crackers. . . ."

His visitors sit quietly listening. It is not often that Henry gives anyone a glimpse into his past.

Henry is aware of what the silence means and goes on to explain in more detail. "It was an item that didn't need any preserving or much storage. They came intact, just like our soda crackers. They came twenty or twenty-one in a square package. They came in larger boxes, but they were packaged that way."

A flicker of a grin passes over his face, remembering. "We used to argue about it. We'd get one package for two kids, eh. We'd have to split it, and if there was twenty-one, then of course it was a little hard to split. Who would get the eleven and who would get the ten? We finally got smart enough and we divided the one in half. I can still remember that."

He pauses, wondering if his description conveys it all accurately. It's impossible, he decides, to tell it like it really was. Kids with hardly anything to eat, suddenly getting food sent to them from North America, a place they'd only heard about. It felt like Christmas. It still amazes him, the generosity and kindness of those North American Mennonites. No, he tells himself, it was God providing for them. For what reason he does not know. Others were not so fortunate. Now, if he is going to tell it, it's important to get all the details right.

"But they were not salty," he continues slowly. "They were sweet. They were different, but exactly this shape and pressed like that." He draws the shape on the table.

"They sent stuff that wasn't perishable. They sent quite a bit of rice, beans—" he pauses—"flour, some . . . "

"They had the canned milk," interjects Katie softly.

"Yes," agrees Henry.

"It was not milk," she continues.

"No," he echoes. "It was sweet."

"It was sweet like honey," Katie continues.

"Yes," he continues, their thoughts and words overlapping each other like a polyphonic text.

"It was highly condensed and sweetened," he presses on. "We used it as a spread."

"They spread it like honey," Katie's voice is barely audible as his continues.

"It was thick. It looked like mayonnaise, actually. It was an item that would not spoil. All those things were well thought out," he continues, "because there was no way of knowing when it would get there, and at what time of the year."

"Once the famine started in the village like that," he explains, "this home would be hardest hit, because nobody would have anything left to give to them. The food that came was distributed according to how many persons in the family. Not every home got help. The orphanage happened to get help the first, but they would only get the same amount as any other family."

Katie nods. It is a story she knows well by now, and in the knowing, it has become hers too. It is still a big part of who her Henry is today, and sharing in it makes her feel a little closer.

"We never had it so bad," she says softly. "We were hungry, but we weren't starving. Not like Henry."

. . . . .

By early November the Grossweide orphanage echoed with the ghostly footsteps and the absent laughter of those who had gone away. Even *Tante* Nettie and *Tante* Greta were no longer there.

Among the eighteen or so who were still left were Heinz and Peter Rempel, and of course the Harder children, Johannes, the boys' supervisor, Bertha, who still helped with the girls, Marichen, who helped look after her handicapped sister Annie, and six-year-old Leenie, Heinz's playmate.

The actual takeover, when it came in November of 1921, was swift and ruthless.

# 20

# GROSSWEIDE TAKEOVER

To Henry, it seems that it all just happened overnight. One day the Harder parents were there and things were going on very much as usual, and the next they were gone—banished to Siberia, he learned later, not having been allowed to take anything with them, not even a proper good-bye from those they left behind. All they owned they had put into the Grossweide orphanage. Now it all belonged to the state.

Being six years old at the time, Henry is sure he should have some recollection of how it all happened, but not a shred is left. All he has is a picture of the Harder family in front of their mud hut in Siberia, and the nightmare of memories of how things were afterwards. He can hardly bring himself to talk about it.

. . . . .

It was November of 1921 when a Mennonite turned Communist, a man called Boldt, arrived at Grossweide orphanage along with several wagon loads of Russian orphans, ragged, dirty, and some of them ill.

Fortunately, the Harders were spared from knowing how well-founded was their concern for the welfare of the Mennonite children under a Communist administrator. But for those children who had the misfortune of staying at Grossweide, life changed drastically and irrevocably overnight.

"Don't these kids believe in using water?" whispered Franz to Peter as they stood in a double line of children jostling their way to the breakfast table.

"Doesn't look like it," retorted Peter.

"Or smell like it either." Franz wrinkled up his nose.

"That wouldn't be German (hic) you little *sukin' syn* are talkin' there, would it now?" A sharp whack on Franz's back, accompanied the snarling, unsteady voice.

The boys wheeled around. A paunchy man who had seemingly come out of nowhere stood directly behind them.

"Yes, sir. It was," admitted Franz, shrinking back from the *samogon*-laden breath of the new administrator.

"So the boy tells the truth," sneered Boldt. How naive, he thought, or maybe just smart, since he could see he had been caught in the act. Boldt paused momentarily to savour his own wit, then turned a withering glare on the two boys.

"From now on no German. Is that clear?" His voice rose in pitch and volume, and the other children stood still, fearfully. "Did all you little *nemetskie gavnjoki* hear that?" He bellowed. "From now on," he paused dramatically, "you will speak Russian. This is Russia! Do you hear me?" Again he paused, enjoying his sense of power. "Any brat caught talking German will be punished like this." He brought down the stick on Franz's back with another whack that sent a visible jolt through the room. He struck him again, and again. "I don't ever want to hear any of that German garbage talk around here again. Ever!" He fastened a slit-eyed stare on Franz, and waited.

"No sir. I'm sorry, sir." Franz said in Russian. He was gulping to keep back the tears.

"Now get to the table, all of you," Boldt yelled. Quickly the children began to move towards the tables, and the two boys did the same.

At another table in the dining room Heinz and his friend Abe had witnessed the entire scene and exchanged knowing glances. At least they knew what to expect. Their own places had already been taken by some of the new children, so they sat at places still vacant.

They waited, unsure how to proceed. Always before, Papa Harder would read a passage of Scripture and would then stand and lead them as they all joined in the table grace. Only then they would eat. Boldt was leaning unsteadily against the head table, watching as the Russian children began to eat.

Well, thought Heinz, if no one is going to lead in the prayer, I will just pray silently where I am. He bowed his head and Abe, seeing it, followed suit.

"*K chortu van!*" Boldt's voice sliced through the room like a Spanish sword. "Now hear this you little Mennonite fanatics. If you want to thank somebody for the food, thank me. I'm the one that decides if you eat or don't eat. Religion is forbidden." He swayed unsteadily as he glared at them. "This is a Communist country now, and a Communist orphanage," he hiccuped loudly. "There will be no praying! You," he jabbed a finger in Heinz's direction. "You and your pious little friend there," he pointed at Abe, "get to the basement this instant!" As the two scrambled to leave the table, Boldt continued. "Let that be a lesson to the rest of you. If you pray, you don't eat. It's as simple as that." He glared at them menacingly, daring anyone else to bow their heads.

"Now eat!" he commanded.

The Mennonite children sat stunned. Never had they eaten a single meal without giving thanks to their Heavenly Father for it. Gradually, tentatively, the children began to eat, not daring to look into each other's eyes for their shame.

Boldt looked away. So much for the Harders' painstaking efforts to brainwash these little animals into being "good little Christians," he thought. Better for them to find out while they were young how the real world worked. Every man for himself. Survival of the fittest. To the devil with the next guy if you wanted to get to the top. When had God ever done anything for him? For anybody, for that matter?

Nobody had to tell him what it felt like to grow up alone in this world, to get by on your own wit, lying, stealing and cheating your way just to stay alive. Oh yes, he had been taken in by a Mennonite family when his own parents had died, taken in to work and slave for them. Cheap labour, nothing more. Treated no better than a common Russian peasant, until the night after the beating when he had finally run away. He pulled a little flask from his breast pocket and surreptitiously put it to his mouth. He drank greedily, then put it back in the pocket.

The basement was cold with the November chill as Heinz and Abe sat on the cement floor, their minds reluctantly hanging on to the image of the food, meager as it was, now being eaten in the dining room upstairs.

"What do you think of that?" Abe whispered in Russian. "He's a mean one isn't he, this new *zavedushchii*."

Heinz nodded. That was obvious. What troubled him more was the dilemma which they now faced. "He wants us to disobey what Mother and Father Harder taught us," he said quietly.

"I wonder how long a person could go without eating before he'd die," ventured Abe.

"Not too long, I expect," answered Heinz, "especially when we haven't been getting much as it is." He paused reflecting.

"We have to eat you know," countered Abe, "or we'll die." He looked at Heinz from his seven-year-old advantage, well aware that what he said went a long way with his six-year-old friend.

"Father and Mother Harder taught us to say grace before meals," said Heinz firmly, "and I plan to keep on doing that."

"Don't be dumb," retorted Abe. "We don't have a choice. Anyway, I think God will understand. He's not mean like Boldt is."

Heinz eyed him intently. "That's true," he said, an idea forming in his mind. "Maybe He wouldn't mind if we said our prayer on the way to the table with our eyes open, instead of at the table."

"You're a clever one, Rempel," Abe laughed. "I wish I would have thought of that." He jumped up and began dancing around to warm himself. Since the new administrator had come, it seemed as though the whole house was colder. Especially here, alone and hungry in the basement, it was very cold.

Heinz watched his friend thoughtfully. "And at night," he continued, "instead of kneeling beside our beds like we used to do, we'll say our prayers while we're lying down"—he paused—"on our stomachs." Yes, he thought, it would have to be on their stomachs. It would be disrespectful to lie on one's back while talking to God.

"That's a good idea," said Abe, still jumping up and down. "We'll tell the others."

"Just be careful where and when," cautioned Heinz, "the

157

walls might have ears."

"I know what you mean," replied Abe.

Time passed slowly. The boys tried to make themselves as comfortable as possible, trying not to think of their cozy cots upstairs. When sleep finally came, it was a welcome relief from the cold and hunger, and from the hard floor.

It was not until the next morning that the two boys were finally summoned to come back upstairs. Their bones ached from the cold, but they meekly walked to their places at the breakfast table. As they walked, they were silently saying their table grace and, as they had suspected, Boldt was none the wiser. He was watching as they sat down, but they made no move to bow their heads. They began to eat, just as the others were doing.

"Sure didn't take those little fanatics long to come around to my way of thinking," Boldt sneered to himself. "Amazing how a little hardship or hunger always flushes out the hypocrites. If only the Harders could see their precious little bastards now."

The rest of the Harder orphans had also been watching to see just how much of a power struggle would develop, some of them struggling with their own sense of guilt for having compromised what they had been taught. But there was no hint of bowing to pray. They watched with relief as the boys ate. Somehow, their own food had not tasted nearly as good, knowing the two would get nothing to eat.

It was not long before the secret trickled through the closely guarded Mennonite grapevine at the orphanage. God would most likely not mind, under the circumstances, if the table grace was said on the way to the table with eyes open, and the bedtime prayer at night, as they lay on their stomachs on their beds. Never again did Boldt punish another child for praying, and the Mennonite children could once again look each other in the eye and smile. They did not need to be ashamed. They had not disappointed Father and Mother Harder or God.

It was a round which Boldt thought he had won. Little did he know how badly he had underestimated the strength of loyalty to the Harders, or the child-like devotion of these little ones to the only Father they now had.

For Heinz, one miserable day blurred into the next, as 1921 gave way to 1922 at the Grossweide orphanage. The children's shocking introduction to the new *zavedushchii*, Mr. Boldt, was just a precursor of worse to come.

Meanwhile, in all of Russia, and in the south in particular, a famine of unprecedented proportions was following hard on the heels of civil war, pestilence and disease that had already taken their toll of human life. 1922 saw a second year of drought plunge "the bread basket" of Russia into another total crop failure. All the reserves of grain had long ago been depleted, and suddenly all manner of plant and animal life that until now had been considered inedible, was being used to sustain life. Many people died.

This situation would have been difficult enough for the Grossweide orphanage to handle, but it soon became apparent to all the children that the new administrator was drunk much of the time, and the more drunk he was, the more abusive and neglectful he became. His unpredictable angry outbursts, and harsh punishments became the order of the day, and no one knew what would ignite another explosion of rage.

Furthermore, none of the standards of cleanliness and order with which the Harders had operated the home were remotely adhered to. Bathing at regular and frequent intervals was a thing of the past, since no one thought to bring in and heat the water to do it. Washing before mealtime, or after a visit to the outhouse, was similarly neglected.

Load after load of Russian orphans were being brought in as the winter passed, until every available corner of the two dormitories was being used. With the new children, most of them louse-infested and ill, came disease and discomfort. Everyone seemed to be itching and scratching as the lice multiplied. For the Mennonite children, used to cleanliness and, until recently, nutritious food, the situation soon became intolerable. Not having had exposure to the conditions or the diseases that now surrounded them, they found they also did not have the resistance necessary to ward off the illnesses. It was not long before many of them lay gravely ill upon their cots.

Much of that winter has disappeared from Henry's memory,

probably because he was too ill to notice or comprehend what was going on around him.

But what was happening around him was the methodical destruction of his beloved home.

Heinz and about twelve other Mennonite children lay in one of the small bedrooms of the girls' dorm, too ill to notice.

It was April before anyone came to check on conditions at the Grossweide orphanage. When they did, Boldt was swiftly replaced, and the sickest children were loaded up in a *Leiterwagen* for the seventy-five *verst* trip to the sanatorium for sick children in the seaside city of Berdjansk.

# 21

# Berdjansk April, 1922

The fresh spring air caressed their faces as the children peered over the wagon's edge on their way south. Heinz and Peter Rempel, and their friends, Franz, Abe, and Kolya, were among the twelve seriously ill boys and girls who were being transferred from the Grossweide orphanage to Berdjansk to get well.

Thinking back, Henry cannot remember much about the details of their illnesses, except that they were coughing blood and apparently too sick to stay at Grossweide. The port city of Berdjansk was famous for its medicinal sea air and sea water.

Heinz lay propped against the hay in the wagon, unaware of his own sunken face, staring with big hazel eyes at the sights as they travelled southward towards Berdjansk.

The countryside was strangely quiet for this usually busy time of year. Many fields lay unattended, and what crops had been planted showed the effects of the dry weather. Few horses or other livestock grazed in the pastures, and on the farmyards there seemed to be none of the usual hustle and bustle of springtime. Here and there along the side of the road lay decomposing corpses, their bloated bellies and emaciated remains an odorous testimony to the plight of millions of people in the famine-stricken areas of Russia.

With the years of civil war depleting the supply of manpower and horses needed for farming operations, and with the shortage of farm machinery and grain due to the heavy demands made by the Communist officials, the villages in southern Russia and in the southern Volga basin had little to fall back on when the drought of 1921 and 1922 came. What little profits were still being made were nullified by the rampant inflation. Flour cost 10 million rubles for an 18 kg. bag, and 454 grams of butter was worth 300,000 rubles. To mail a letter cost 40,000 rubles. It was impossible to buy anything without a wheelbarrow full of money.

To keep starvation at bay, people resorted to eating anything they could get hold of. Crows, cats, dogs, mice, and cattle that had died from disease or starvation, all previously considered inedible, now found their way into the stomachs of those who were starving. Weeds, bark from trees, and even leather, were eaten.

The wagon passed a group of people with bloated bellies sitting beside the road, pulling up handfuls of grass and chewing on them.

Heinz shuddered. Never in all his travels with Father Harder had he seen anything like this, but during the past year he, too, had learned what hunger was, and the possibility of starvation and death had become very real, even to a seven-year-old. No longer could anyone be depended upon to provide regular and nourishing meals. It was up to each individual to look out for himself. He and the others had already learned this rule at Grossweide these past five months. Sometimes it was a fine line between life and death.

The wagon passed the body of a young man. Maybe only yesterday this one had breathed and lived just like he was doing, thought Heinz, hugging his legs close to himself, but since then he had crossed that narrow line and today he was dead. Heinz refused to look away. Death did not frighten him, but he was not going to cross that line if he could help it. He would fight.

The first day passed slowly, with several stops to rest and refresh the horses. The children drank thirstily from the streams as well, and scoured the nearby woods for edible plants and roots. Heinz and some of the others pulled bark from the trees and ate it. Then, back on the hay wagon, they slept, or just rested, too weak for anything else.

The road dipped up and down, taking them through hills and

valleys. When the hill was too steep, those who were strong enough to walk would have to get out to make the load easier for the horses, and when the wagon went downhill the horses speeded up.

The night was spent in the wagon and it was late afternoon of the second day by the time they came within sight of the city. Large ships, and ocean freighters could be seen moving slowly in and out of the docks. On the road ahead lay a long, steep hill that would take them down to the city nestled beside the Sea of Azov.

"Whoa." The driver pulled the horses to a stop.

"What's he doing now?" asked Kolya.

They watched, intrigued, as he fastened chains with steel sliders onto the wheels of the wagon.

"What's that for, driver?" asked Abe.

"They're special brakes," the man said amiably. "The hill is so steep and long that the horses can't hold the wagon if it starts going too fast."

At last they were ready for the long descent and they clattered their way to the bottom of the long incline. When they reached the bottom, the driver took off the brakes and they continued the last part of their journey into Berdjansk.

As they drove through the streets, ragged beggars of all ages called out to them, "Bread. A piece of bread. I have nothing to eat. Have mercy."

Their cries sent shivers through Heinz. How he longed for a piece of bread too. He imagined the mounds of *Zwieback* that the cooks used to bake every Saturday that first year at Grossweide. It had been a very long time since he had tasted anything half as good.

He noticed that many of the beggars were children no older than himself and some younger, all of them dirty, barefoot and clothed in rags. These were the *bezprizornii*, or homeless children he had heard about. He could see them being chased from the shops here and there. Apparently they knew how to help themselves.

The city was not completely unfamiliar to Heinz. He had travelled there several times with Father Harder on business, delivering some of the produce raised at Grossweide. Occasionally, freight from Berdjansk was delivered to the train station Nelgovka, and he would accompany Papa Harder there to pick it up. As the wagon rattled through the streets, Heinz watched intently, taking note of landmarks and the general layout of the city.

Finally, just before dark, the *Leiterwagen* turned from the street and stopped in front of a set of heavy wooden gates about four meters high. Heinz could not see through the gates because the boards were close together. A wall, also four meters high, ran on either side of the gate for some distance, and near the corner a smaller gate was set into the wall.

The driver got down and went to the side of the gate and pulled a chord. Somewhere inside a bell could be heard. They waited a few minutes, and then an official-looking man in uniform appeared and opened the gates.

"Good-evening," said the driver in Russian. "We come from the orphanage at Grossweide."

"Good-evening," the official replied. "I was notified that you were coming." He peered into the wagon.

"All sick," said the driver. He lowered his voice. "They have not been very well cared for these past months. Comrade Boldt has been relieved of his duties there and the new *zovedushchii* asks if you would kindly keep the sickest ones here until they recover."

"They are all orphans?" the official asked.

"Yes, orphans. I understand many of the children here are orphans too."

"*Da,*" he nodded, "but we like better to take children who have families. Sometimes they send food. There is little enough of that around, you know."

"I understand," said the driver. "You are to notify Grossweide orphanage just as soon as they are well enough to go back, and I'll come and take them off your hands right away. What do you think, a month or two breathing this good sea air and swimming in the waters of the Azov," he snapped his fingers, "and they'll be as good as new?"

"We shall see," the official answered evasively, looking once more at the assortment of children with heaving coughs and pale, thin, bodies.

"Come, come," he said, suddenly efficient. "Let's get these children settled into their quarters for the night. When did they last eat?"

"Well," the driver hesitated, "they did manage to find some vegetation here and there on the way . . . "

"A meal. When did they last have a meal?"

"Oh . . . yes of course . . , " the driver stammered, feeling suddenly quite inadequate, "I believe they were given something before we left . . . yes," he hesitated, stalling, "yes, I'm quite sure of it."

It was plain to see that it had been some time since the children had eaten, but the administrator was used to the lies.

"Well, I think there's still some soup left over from supper. Drive ahead and stop at the front door of the main building. Maybe you would care to join us?"

"Yes, sir. *Spasibo*, Thank you," said the driver eagerly. He too had not had anything to eat for more than two days.

The driver gave the horses a little tap with the reins and the wagon rolled through the gates. Heinz could hear them close behind them. Ahead, he could make out a large plain building. It had none of the grace or beauty of the Grossweide home. There was a functional, bleak look about it that was less than appealing, and beyond that there were several other shed-like buildings.

What he could see of the yard was that it was huge, with many trees around it, well back of the fence that surrounded it.

It was not far from the front gate to the front door of the main building, and the children climbed wearily from the wagon and were led through the front doors of the sanatorium. Only when the bowls of warm, leafy soup were put in front of them did their eyes show any sign of life.

Then the girls were told to go with the uniformed Russian woman to a nearby bunkhouse, and the boys followed the uniformed man who was assigned to them.

The sleeping quarters were large sheds, with two walls lined with bunks three tiers high standing side by side down the length of both walls. Another double row of bunks ran down the centre of the room.

"Look at this," whispered Kolya, "there must be at least fifty kids in just this one room."

"At least they've each got a bed," whispered Heinz, remembering the recent overcrowded sleeping conditions at Grossweide.

"This is where the younger boys sleep," said their supervisor quietly, trying not to awaken the children. "We have over two hundred children here altogether," he continued, as though reading their minds, "and more coming every day."

What he didn't tell them was that almost every day there were also children who left, having died from illness or malnourishment.

He pointed to a group of empty beds. "Those of you that are seven or younger can sleep over there. The older ones will come with me to the other boys' quarters.

Heinz watched as Peter and Franz and the other older boys left the room. In the morning, he decided, he would explore where Peter was. Right now all he wanted was to lie down and forget about the pain tearing at his chest. He coughed violently and wiped the red sputum on his shorts, the only item of clothing he wore. There was a dark, woolen army blanket on the straw tick on the bed, and Heinz needed no further invitation. The other Grossweide boys had also crawled exhausted into their bunks. It was not long before they were all fast asleep.

When the rising bell sounded harshly outside the door the next morning, Heinz was already awake. He had been lying on his bunk, listening for some time to the sounds of the other sleeping children. An air of lethargy pervaded as the children rolled out of bed. There was no need to get dressed, since they all still wore the shorts that they had worn the day before.

Heinz spotted Peter coming from his quarters and walked with him across the compound towards the building where they had eaten the night before.

"I hope there's a good breakfast," said Heinz, listening to the grumblings of his stomach.

"Me too," sighed Peter. "Us middlers all have been given

chores to do. If I don't get something to eat soon, I don't think I'll even be able to hold a broom, let alone sweep the dining room."

The supervisor met them at the front door. "Middlers go to your chores. The younger ones will follow me." And without a further word of explanation he marched briskly down the driveway and out through the small gate in the wall.

Heinz suspiciously looked after the man and then whispered to Peter. "I'm staying here with you."

"I don't think you better," said Peter. "One of the supervisors will see you and you'll get in trouble. Just stick close to Abe; you'll be okay."

"Where are they taking us?" Heinz asked.

"I'm not sure," said Peter, "but it can't be far if you're walking. Hurry up now, before they get out of sight."

Heinz ran on weak, wobbly legs, trying to catch up to the group already some distance down the street. He was coughing so much as he ran that he could hardly breathe.

At last he was beside Abe, who was at the back of the line and also having difficulty keeping up to the brisk pace. "Where do you think we're going?" panted Heinz.

"I can't imagine," gasped Abe.

They continued to walk for nearly a kilometer. The sound of the ocean becoming more and more distinct as they walked. Other water front sounds could also be heard clearly. A beautiful, sandy beach lay directly ahead of them as they turned a corner." Everybody into the water," one of the supervisors shouted.

Heinz and Abe watched as the other boys jumped into the water. It had been many months since they had gone swimming in the little creek that ran in the field adjoining the Grossweide orphanage. Now they shivered as they stepped into the chilly water.

"Last one in is a sissy," laughed Kolya as he splashed in ahead of them. They needed no further invitation. The cold water, their illness, and the hunger in their stomachs were temporarily forgotten as they splashed and swam in the water of the Sea of Azov.

The time passed all too quickly, and then they were summoned from the water and marched back to the Sanatorium. The sun shone overhead and by the time they were back their bodies and shorts were dry.

It was not until later that day, after a long nap in their quarters, that Heinz and his friends finally were able to sit down with Peter and the mass of other children to devour a bowl of soup made with an assortment of spring greens grown in the gardens around Berdjansk. The food was refreshing, as had been the cool water of the sea.

The days passed, with no particular routine or order of things except for the daily swim, with each group being taken down to the sea at different times of the day. To Heinz, it seemed that nobody really cared if they lived or died, just as long as they stayed off the street and out of everybody else's way.

Mealtimes could be anytime, or missed altogether. If a load of fruit or vegetables arrived, it was eaten immediately. If someone's family sent a care-package, it was divided as many ways as possible by the person who had gotten it.

This was not necessarily so much a gesture of generosity as of wisdom, recalls Henry, since all of it would probably have been taken away from the person if he or she had not been willing to share.

Gradually, the Grossweide children grew stronger, in spite of the meager food rations, no longer needing to spend most of their time sick in bed. But the coughing persisted.

Peter and Heinz were separated much of the time because of their ages, but anytime he could, Heinz would slip over to where Peter was working so he could be near him.

From the beginning, the Grossweide boys had noticed that there were many fish swimming in the waters where they themselves swam. "Why don't we catch some fish and take them to the sanatorium to fry?" they asked each other.

One day as they were swimming, Heinz and several of the boys managed to corner a fish.

"Hey," shouted the supervisor. "You, over there. You're here to swim, not to fish."

The boys hesitated. "We're hungry," shouted one of the boys angrily, "and there's food right under our noses. Why don't you let us catch the fish?"

Heinz could not believe his ears. To talk back to an elder was unheard of. He shivered, remembering how Boldt would have dealt with this.

"I think," said the supervisor, his voice taut and quiet, "that after you all stay in your room for the rest of the day without any food, you will think better than to question your superiors and the rules you have been asked to obey." He paused, looking about to see if the punishment had made an impact. "Now, everybody back to the sanatorium." A subdued group of boys followed him back to the building behind the high walls.

# 22

# SCAVENGERS IN BERDJANSK

Heinz, Abe, and Kolya sat in the branches of a walnut tree in the far corner of the sanatorium enclosure, holding *Schultebott*. It was well over a week since they had been brought to Berdjansk, and they had just returned from their early morning swim. It was time to take matters into their own hands. Since they had come, food had been extremely scarce, and in spite of the daily swims it was apparent that they were all still coughing and feverish.

Abe, the eldest of the three, was taking the lead. "How are we ever going to get well if we don't get more to eat?" he said.

"I'm hungry all the time," whined Kolya.

"We all are," replied Abe. "Complaining isn't going to help. We have to do something."

"Well," said Heinz, thoughtfully, "I've noticed that the supervisor doesn't do a head count before or after swimming. . . . "

"*Da*, and?" Abe prompted in Russian.

"And he might not miss one or two among so many, if they should happen to slip away for a while," said Heinz.

Abe's eyes glinted at the suggestion. "You mean away, like into the city, where there might be food?"

Heinz nodded. "Or maybe to go fishing after the supervisor and the rest of the boys are gone."

"That's a great idea!" exclaimed Abe.

"You'll never get away with it," said Kolya, scowling at them.

"For one thing, anyone can tell by just looking at these regulation shorts that we're wards of the state. If they see us in the streets, they'll turn us in to the authorities faster than you can turn around."

"We'll be careful not to get caught—or hide," countered Abe. "And we can still run."

"Sure we can," scorned Kolya, scrutinizing Abe's spindly, legs. "And if you should manage not to get yourself caught, just how did you plan to get back inside? Scale this four meter fence, I suppose?"

Abe looked at the fence, the light suddenly gone from his face. "I forgot about that," he said, eying the forbidding enclosure.

"I didn't," said Heinz clambering down from the tree. "Take off your shorts."

"What?" asked Kolya, looking at Heinz as though he were demented.

"Just do it," ordered Heinz quietly. Already he was standing beside the tree, stark naked, holding his sole piece of clothing in his hands. The other two followed suit, eying him questioningly as they handed him their shorts. Deftly, Heinz knotted Abe's shorts to his own, and Kolya's to Abe's.

"A rope?" exclaimed Abe. "Heinz, you're a genius."

"Of course we're going to need a lot more to make a rope long enough," he said.

"So you can make a rope," chuckled Kolya cynically. "If you're on the outside of the wall, and we're on the inside, can you imagine how many shorts it will take to make it long enough to reach from down here, over the wall, and all the way down the other side to you?" He burst out laughing. "You'll have half the kids in the sanatorium standing around naked, waiting for you to climb up." He doubled over, holding his sides laughing.

"And I'll bet not one of the supervisors would think a thing of it either." He danced around, convulsing with laughter. "Oh . . . oh . . . my side hurts." He gasped and coughed alternately, tears running down his cheeks.

"Oh, and don't forget," he continued, spitting on the grass, "when you get to the top of the wall, you can just climb right down the ladder, like this." He mimicked a climbing motion. "No problem. . . . "

"Kolya, get hold of yourself. Someone will hear," cautioned Abe, looking around anxiously to see if the noise had attracted any attention.

"No. Just think about it," laughed Kolya. "You can climb up the rope ladder as long as someone's holding on to it at the other end, but if you're coming from outside, as soon as you're at the top . . . there's no one to hold it tight, and plop . . . " he sprawled exhausted on the ground. "What is it, four meters? You might not break too many bones."

"We're not stupid," said Heinz, trying to silence him.

"Oh no?" said Kolya, sobering but still gasping. "Then how do you intend to use your rope ladder, may I ask?" He stood up shakily.

"Like this," said Heinz, and with one swift movement he was standing on top of Kolya's shoulders.

"Come on up Abe," Heinz said, motioning to his own shoulders.

Abe hesitated only a moment. Then clambered up the two boys until he stood on Heinz's shoulders. Kolya wobbled dangerously under the weight, grabbing the fence for support.

"I can nearly reach the top," called Abe, stretching as far as he dared.

"Hey, get down. You're too heavy," Kolya yelled. They clambered down. "You know, I think your idea might work," said Abe. "Maybe if we get two of the bigger, stronger boys at the bottom, and two of the tallest ones on top of that."

"And the top one can throw the rope over the wall so the person on the outside can climb back in," chimed in Heinz.

"Or someone on the inside could climb out that way," interrupted Kolya, not to be left out.

"Right," said Heinz, "then we can come and go, not just while we're swimming but anytime."

Kolya unknotted the shorts, feeling important for his good suggestion. "Why don't we try it right away then, just to see if it works," he said.

"Who can we trust not to squeal on us?" asked Heinz.

"Let's start with the kids from Grossweide," suggested Abe. "I don't trust the Russians kids to keep their mouths shut."

"But none of the girls, I hope," said Kolya, "not with us standing around in our birthday suits."

"Okay," agreed Heinz, "no girls, but if we bring back enough food we'll share with them."

"Do we have to?" whined Kolya, "I bet I could eat a horse all by myself, I'm so hungry."

Heinz gave him a dirty look.

"Oh, all right, we'll share, but no girls when we go over the wall."

"No girls," the two boys chorused.

It was not until later that day, and with utmost precautions not to attract any suspicion from the supervisors or the other children, that the Grossweide boys were finally together in the relative privacy of the shrubs and trees at the back of the sanatarium property. All had relinquished the only piece of clothing they owned in order to try to make the rope long enough to reach from the hands of the top person in the human ladder, over the top, and down far enough on the other side.

Abe explained the plan and demonstrated with Kolya and Heinz how to make the human ladder and drop the cloth rope over the wall.

"Be sure there is someone nearby when anyone is over the wall," Abe continued. "When the person wants to get back in they will give three knocks, like this," and he rapped once, waited a second and then rapped quickly twice more. "That's our secret code," he continued. "When you hear it, get everybody together quick and make the rope as fast as you can, so the people on the outside can get back in. Remember, the longer they have to wait out there, the more danger there is of someone getting caught."

"Can I go out first?" asked one of the boys.

"Heinz and I are going this time," replied Abe firmly. "Kolya is in charge of things here. All right. Everybody ready?" he asked. "Let's practice making the ladder first."

Quickly they chose four boys to make the ladder. It took a little experimenting before the rope was long enough so that

Heinz could stand on top of Abe's shoulders and unknot the last two shorts, which he and Abe would wear while they were outside.

Then the rope was lowered in response to their knocks and Heinz again climbed on Abe's shoulders and knotted the shorts to the end so that Abe could jump up and reach the end of it once Heinz was back inside.

They were all back inside the fence, after the trial run. "If we hurry," said Abe, "we can still go in search of food and get back before it's dark."

"You have to be back before dark," emphasized Peter to his brother Heinz. "You know what they say about people disappearing from the streets when they go out in the dark."

"Oh that's probably just a rumour," said Franz.

"Don't count on it," cautioned Peter. "And you boys be careful who sees you on the streets. They'll put you in jail if they catch you."

"I'd say we're in jail already," said Abe.

"I hear jail is a whole lot worse," insisted Peter.

"We'll be careful," Heinz said. "Don't worry. And when we get back"—he patted his stomach—"maybe a little food." The thought of food suddenly added urgency to his plan. "Come on Abe, let's go." He turned to the rest of the boys. "This time it's the real thing."

In no time the boys had stripped and Abe had knotted the shorts together, testing each knot to make sure it wouldn't come undone. "Good," he said, "now get into your places."

Peter and Franz planted themselves firmly not far from the fence, then Kolya climbed up, placing one foot on each of their shoulders. With a little help from the by-standers, David was up and standing on Kolya's shoulders.

"I'm next," said Abe. The ladder wobbled as he climbed up.

With him went the rope, which he gave to the boy at the top of the ladder. He pulled himself to the top of the fence, looked over to check if the coast was clear, and dropped it soundlessly over the fence.

"Now hold on tight," he cautioned from the other side. Gingerly he let himself down the outside, grabbing the knots on the rope with his hands and feet. He was still a good distance from the ground when the rope ran out, and he dropped the rest of the way. Then he could see Heinz clambering over the wall, and shinnying his way down the rope. He held up his arms, and as Heinz's feet came within reach, he guided them onto his shoulders. Above him, Heinz, standing on his tiptoes, untied two pairs of shorts and dropped them to the ground.

Heinz gave the rope one last yank and it disappeared up over the top of the wall, where the rest of the boys anxiously waited to get dressed again. Heinz quickly jumped down from Abe's shoulders, and the two boys put on their shorts and dashed into the safety of a thicket of shrubs nearby, breathing rapidly with excitement and fear.

According to plan, their first mission was to try to collect several nails, some string, worms and willows for fishing rods with which they would attempt to catch fish. Giddy with a sense of adventure and freedom, they set out, running a short distance and hiding, then running again and hiding again, always on the lookout for danger, as well as for the items which they sought.

"Abe, over here," called Heinz, in a stage whisper.

Quickly, Abe ran to see what Heinz was excited about. He was crouched beside a garden, pulling off onion greens and stuffing them in his mouth as fast as he could.

"Here, you have some," Heinz offered a handful to his friend.

"Oh, look," Abe nearly squealed with delight, "rhubarb too."

"Hurry," urged Heinz, "we can't sit in one spot all day eating. Someone's going to catch us stealing." Quickly he pulled a handful of rhubarb stalks, and ran to catch up to Abe, who had sprinted ahead.

"You think it's stealing if a hungry person just eats to stay alive?" gasped Abe, when they had found the shelter of another hiding place.

"You think it isn't?" asked Heinz. "I haven't heard that they've changed the laws lately."

Abe looked around nervously. "I didn't think of it as stealing." Heinz did not answer. In spite of his outward confidence, he couldn't help but wonder what Mama and Papa Harder would think of him and Abe, first disobeying their supervisors by sneaking out like this and then stealing from other people's gardens. He did not have time to contemplate the question, however. Abe was trying to get his attention.

"Here's a nail," whispered Abe excitedly, pointing to a place in the side of the old wooden building they were hiding behind. "It's almost worked itself out already, see." They took turns wiggling it, and pulling on it, and finally, when the tips of their fingers were nearly raw, it came out.

"That's one," said Heinz, bending it to make a hook.

It was nearly an hour before they had assembled all the items they needed for their first fishing expedition.

"Next time it'll be a lot faster now that we have our fishing tackle," said Heinz.

The boys were familiar with the waterfront where they always bathed, so they knew where to go for the best fishing. Before long they each had a worm dangling from a hook attached to a sturdy string at the end of a long willow, which they held over the water.

"Hurry up fishies," said Abe under his breath. "We don't have a whole lot of time." Both boys were aware of the lengthening shadows being cast by the late afternoon sun. With the interruptions to hide from passersby, it had taken them longer than they had anticipated to find the string and nails, to get the willows for the fishing rods, and finally to dig the worms. Now they were running out of time, and neither of them wanted to return empty-handed.

"We can't stay out much longer," Heinz voiced their concern.

Just then he saw Abe's line dancing. "You've got one," he said, his eyes wide with excitement. "Careful. Just coax him in. That string isn't too strong."

Abe was barely breathing, and biting his lip so hard he drew blood as he walked through the thigh-deep water towards shore.

"Keep it tight," coached Heinz, "just pull him in gently. Good. Good." He was so preoccupied watching Abe's catch that his own fish caught him by surprise.

In the next instant, a wave picked up both fish and landed them neatly on the shore. All the boys had to do was to hold onto the lines so the fish weren't washed back out to sea.

"It worked," laughed Abe with delight, "we've got ourselves some fish. Let's go."

They hid the fishing tackle under a big piece of driftwood and ran back towards the sanatorium, going by a different route than they had come and stopping now and again to pick up some treasured item such as more string, a match, and a handful of berries from a bush in someone's garden. They tried to avoid contact with people, and when someone appeared in their pathway unexpectedly they ran with hearts pounding and hid, waiting until it was safe to continue. By the time they reached the sanatorium enclosure, it was dusk.

Abe knocked once, waited, and then knocked twice more, then dashed into the thicket where Heinz was hiding with the fish. It seemed like an eternity before they saw the rope slide over the wall. They both ran to the wall and threw the fish over. They could hear the delighted exclamations of the boys on the other side. With their shorts tied together, Heinz climbed onto Abe's shoulders, secured their shorts to the end of the rope, and climbed up and over.

As soon as he disappeared over the top, Abe jumped up and grabbed the rope, pulling himself up hand over hand, his feet clawing for support against the fence. And then he was over, his feet finding Dave's shoulders. He clambered down with the agility of a monkey.

"Some of you guys make a small fire under the trees over there," said Heinz, as they put on their shorts. "We've only got one match, so make sure you get it going the first time."

"Do you think anybody is going to notice?" asked Kolya apprehensively. "What if we get caught?"

"That's the risk we have to take if we want to eat," said Heinz.

"Besides, it's a long way to the dormitories, and there are lots of trees and buildings in between," added Abe. "I haven't noticed that the supervisors come out here much anyway."

It wasn't long before a small fire was glowing and the aroma of frying fish was teasing the nostrils of the twelve hungry boys gathered around.

"Mm-m-m," sighed Kolya, when his small share was finally

handed to him, "a meal fit for a king."

"Heinz," said Dave, "you didn't save enough for you and Abe."

"It's enough," he replied. He broke off a tiny bite from the small piece of fish he had served himself, and placed it reverently on the tip of his tongue. After all, he and Abe had already snitched a few mouthfuls of vegetables and fruit when they were outside. It was only fair that the others should have the biggest portion.

There was silence as they ate. Each boy savouring every morsel, trying to make this delicious moment last. It was nearly dark and almost time for the bedtime bell to ring by the time they had licked each finger one last time and made sure there was no tell-tale trace of the fire left for prying eyes.

"Not one word of this now," reminded Abe. "Tomorrow I and Kolya will try to sneak away during the swimming. Expect us back around noon."

They dispersed at intervals, slipping away like phantoms through the trees in various directions to avoid rousing any suspicion. By the time the bell rang, there was no one left in the secret meeting place among the trees in the far corner of the property.

# 23

# CAUGHT

Henry watches two nurses come in. "Okay, Mr. Huebert," says the one, too cheerfully. "Time to go."

He has been expecting them. The doctor has explained everything. This morning they are going to wash out his lung. Henry has heard of washing a lot of things, but never has he heard of washing lungs before. He imagines his lungs coated somehow with the dust and debris of the mill after all those years of working around grains, some of them moldy.

Be easier if they could toss the lung in a dishpan, he thinks ruefully, like he does the dirty dishes after breakfast at home with Katie.

Somehow, the procedure that the doctor has explained does not sound at all simple, nor pleasant. He has been told that he can expect it to take a heavy toll on him, but the doctor thinks that at this point they have to subject him to this cleansing procedure so that his diseased lung will have a better chance of getting over this lingering infection.

There is of course no guarantee that it will work. Henry understands this, but he has signed the consent form anyway. He will try anything they suggest. It is his life he is fighting for.

. . . . .

For seven-year-old Heinz and his eight-year-old friend Abe, as well as for the other youngsters at the sanatorium in Berdjansk, it was a difficult choice to use prudence regarding the number of excursions that would be allowed outside the grounds; but the food that was brought back was soon considered an essential and important supplement to the very meager diet which they were getting.

The trips were made only when the pain of hunger became too intolerable. Only then could the risk of discovery and subsequent punishment be justified.

Various methods had already been explored. Abe and Kolya had slipped away several times during the swimming time and no one had noticed. Each time they had returned with at least one fish and a variety of spring greens stolen from gardens that were far enough from the sanatorium not to arouse suspicion. A rash of garden thefts in the vicinity might lead to too many questions and too many people being on the alert. Better to keep their activities well away from their home base, they had decided. In response to their coded knock, the rope had been lowered and they had climbed to safety over the wall. The vegetables and fish had preceded them, having been flung over the wall first, much to the delight of the boys waiting inside.

It was always a game of cat and mouse, however. The boys were constantly on the look-out for the "enemy", whether they be other children who might tell the supervisors, or the supervisors themselves. Always there was the fear of being discovered. Once outside, the danger intensified. Around every corner lurked the unknown that could lead to discovery and certain punishment. Many of the boys were only too glad to entrust the search for food to Abe and Heinz, not willing themselves to risk being caught and turned over to the police. For the older ones, it was more difficult to get away because of the chores which they were expected to do. A few, like Kolya, played out childish fantasies as they participated in the dangerous expeditions, thus unknowingly becoming a liability rather than an asset.

For Heinz and Abe, the risk they were taking, and the consequences of their actions should they be found out, kept them constantly alert and on guard. This was no game. It was a bid for survival, not just for themselves but for the other Grossweide children. Already they had been able to distribute some food to the girls, telling them only that they should say nothing of it to anyone.

It was not many weeks before the entire city of Berdjansk had become Abe and Heinz's backyard. They saw, but did not associate with the many other children that not only roamed but lived in the streets, also slipping in and out of view like so many phantoms, sometimes fighting over a treasured find but more often respecting each other's fiercely guarded turf.

No container or garbage receptacle was too dirty for the boys to examine for possible nourishment. Everywhere the possibility of finding something to eat existed.

Sometimes their forays took them past other high enclosures which street gossip said were other state-run orphanages. Word had it that they were little more than prisons, and one's chances of survival were better outside on the streets than behind the ominous walls.

At other times nearly the whole day was spent lurking around the busy train stations. Here, it was easy to disappear in the constantly moving mass of humanity, remaining undetected by people whose only concern was to reach their destinations. They too were in search of food, the boys discovered. Still, that did not stop the boys from making off with whatever they could pilfer from the unsuspecting and weary travellers. No ruble, accidentally dropped on the ground remained there for long and occasionally a kindhearted person would even press some money or food into outstretched hands.

The docks could also be depended upon to yield to the boys precious booty which they could take back and share with the others. There were many convenient hiding places from which the boys could watch activities such as the loading of grain. Workers squatted as two bags of grain, each weighing a *pud*, were placed on each shoulder. Then the workers would strain to stand and walk up a plank to take the load onto the ship. One plank took the workers into the ship and another took them back out. The lines or workers reminded Heinz of ants at work.

Sometimes the sailors, in a celebrative mood at having come ashore, would spot the hollow-eyed boys and toss them something to eat. It was a risk Abe and Heinz didn't mind taking.

Henry and Abe were returning from one such expedition not too long after the scheme for getting over the wall had been devised. They were relieved to see their knock answered by the appearance of the rope sliding down their side of the wall.

Heinz, being shorter than Abe, was the first one over, as usual. The look on the faces of the other boys as his head came within view told him that something was very wrong, and it only took him a second to spot the face of one of the supervisors, standing nearby, watching the well-oiled process. The look on his fleshy face was a mixture of intrigue, disbelief, and rage.

Abe's head appeared over the fence and one glance told him they'd been caught. We're in big trouble now, Abe's eyes said as he and Heinz looked at each other.

The supervisor had already confiscated the sack containing the food that they had tossed over the wall. Now his face darkened as he looked at the two culprits. "So the monkeys have found a way over the wall, have they? Whose idea is this?" he barked.

"Ours," said Heinz quietly, his eyes downcast. He nodded toward Abe.

"And the rest of you helped," the man growled. "That makes you all guilty. It looks like we're going to have to teach you all a lesson." He looked grimly from boy to boy, watching their reactions. Not one of them talked back or tried to lie his way out of the situation.

"Please sir," it was Heinz again. "It's not the other boys' fault. It was Abe's and my idea, and we were the ones on the streets outside."

"They can't think for themselves?" asked the supervisor angrily. Even if he wanted to turn a blind eye to the infraction, he couldn't. What if they tried it again, and the authorities discovered his charges scavenging in the streets of Berdjansk. His neck would be in a noose and his job on the line, sure as anything. He pursed his lips.

"All right, boy," he said to Heinz. "You talk brave trying to protect your little friends here. Let's see if you can take your punishment as brave as you talk." His eyes slid from Heinz to Abe, as though trying to decide on a suitable punishment.

"Let's see if a day in the cellar will help you remember the rules better from now on." He jabbed a chubby finger, punctuating his words as he continued, "And if any of you are ever caught again, you can be sure you won't get off so easy. Come

182

along now," he ordered.

Heinz and Abe followed as he marched them into an old building, down a set of stairs, through a door and into the basement. Ten centimeters of water covered the floor and it's dank, putrid smell assaulted them as they walked into the large room.

"Now let's see if the monkeys can climb out of here," he said dryly.

A quick inventory of their quarters revealed a large empty room. There was no place to sit down and no place to climb to escape the cold water.

Then they heard the door shut and a bolt being slid into place, locking them in the darkness, even though the sun was still shining outside.

Neither of them made a sound until the echo of the administrator's boots told them that it was safe to talk.

"He's gone," whispered Heinz.

"Did you get a chance to see if there was any way out of here?" whispered Abe, feeling his way along the wall.

"What good would it do?" said Heinz. "If we weren't here when he came for us, we'd be in even bigger trouble."

"The water's cold," said Abe, continuing his exploration around the walls of the room.

"There's no heat in the room either," said Heinz, groping his way around the opposite way from Abe. "I can't even find a ledge to climb up on," said Heinz finally.

"Me neither," said Abe.

The hours dragged by and their legs grew numb in the cold. The boys stayed within reach of each other, but tried to walk back and forth to keep warm and to keep up their spirits.

"I'm hungry. And I have to pee," said Abe finally.

"I have to do the other," said Heinz.

"Oh no!" exclaimed Abe.

"We'll use the far corner," suggested Heinz.

And so one corner of the water-filled room was designated as the outhouse, but the water in all the sloshing to and fro did not confine the wastes to the designated corner after all.

Time stood still as Abe and Heinz made a game of guessing what time it was. Each minute seemed like an eternity as they waited in the putrid water. Time stretched endlessly before them and behind them.

"How long do you think we've been down here already?" asked Abe.

"I'm not sure. It seems like days," answered Heinz. "I think it must be morning already."

"I'm so cold," said Abe.

"I can hardly stand up any more," answered Heinz, "but I can't sit down because the water's so cold.

"Just keep walking," said Abe.

. . . . .

Henry lies uncomfortably on the table while the doctor inserts the tubes through his nose and into his chest. He watches as the machine is turned on. He can feel the rush of water in his lung and feels like a drowning man gasping for air, his lungs gurgling with the water that is supposed to restore some measure of health to him.

Henry tells himself to trust the tube of oxygen that is pumping air into his other lung, but he is sure he is going to die. He fights the panic, forcing himself to concentrate on what he can see around him.

There is a jar beside him that is collecting the water that has just been pumped through his bad lung. The debris that has been flushed from his lung is floating in the jar.

He focuses on the grey bits swirling in the jar. He is aware that they are actual pieces of his own lung, part of him that was once alive but has died. His head swims.

. . . . .

"Heinz, say something." It is Abe's voice.

"I can't feel my legs anymore. I feel dizzy."

"Here," he feels hands groping for him in the darkness. "Lean on me. Can you try to walk some more?"

He feels himself propelled along by a gentle, unseen hand.

"That's it. Keep moving. It can't be much longer. Come on Heinz, you've got to try to stay awake. I can't hold you up much longer."

He doesn't want to fall asleep. If he does, he will surely drown. He tries mightily to hold on.

. . . . .

"Mr. Huebert. Can you hear me? Mr. Huebert." The voice is pushing in through his thoughts. He feels disoriented, trying to remember where he is.

"Mr. Huebert. How are you feeling?" The voice continues to drag him out of the fog. His eyes try to focus on where the voice is coming from.

He sees it is a nurse that is calling him. "It's over, Mr. Huebert. How are you feeling?"

What can he say? He feels like a drowning man who has been revived. Nothing else is important right now.

He gathers all his strength. "I'm fine," he whispers, his throat raw from the tubes.

"You're a strong man," says the nurse, patting his arm. "Now let's get you back to your room so you can rest."

. . . . .

The sound of footsteps on the stairs outside the basement door had Heinz and Abe suddenly alert. They could hear the bolt slide back. The door opened, and in spite of their eagerness, their legs felt like lead weights as they dragged themselves up the stairs. The brilliance of the late afternoon sun greeted them as they stepped outside. They had been standing in the watery basement without food for twenty-four hours.

"If I ever catch any of you trying anything like that again," the supervisor threatened, "you can be sure you will not get out of here so soon."

. . . . .

Yes, thinks Henry groggily, they should have thought of posting guards to warn them if anyone was coming. He drifts into an exhausted, fitful sleep as he is wheeled down the hospital corridor back to his room.

# 24

# A GRISLY DISCOVERY

Spring gave way to summer at the Berdjansk sanatorium. It was June, 1922 and still there were the daily swims in the sea, but they did nothing to relieve the constant ache of hunger in the bellies of the children at the home. So the cautious side-trips into the streets of the city in search of food continued, in spite of the supervisor's threats and the harsh treatment Abe and Heinz had received. Now, extra precautions were taken not to get caught, and guards were posted to keep a watch and signal if anyone was approaching.

With their growing familiarity with the city and their need to keep moving to new areas, Abe and Heinz kept expanding the radius of their territory. They had, like Peter Rabbit, visited some of the big vegetable gardens on the hillsides outside the city of Berdjansk.

Produce from some of these gardens was being sent to the sanatorium legitimately to be used in the watery cabbage soup that was the mainstay of their official diet, but what the boys were looking for was variety, and quantity.

Their explorations had also led them to several overgrown and neglected vineyards which had been the object of their latest ventures. The grapes which they had hoped to find were disappointingly sparse and, though edible, still not ripe. They would have to wait for another month or two before they would be ready. Meanwhile, the boys had discovered that hidden in the hills in the vineyards were caves, apparently used as wine cellars in better times.

On this particular day, Abe, Heinz, and Kolya had set out to explore several of them in hopes of discovering whatever edible treasures they might contain.

Cautiously they approached one of the caves, walking softly on their bare feet and ever alert. Even now there could be either man or beast lurking in its black recesses, watching the approach of the intruders.

They came to the opening and peered in.

"It's awfully dark," said Kolya. He hung back as Abe and Heinz stepped inside. Hesitantly, he followed as they edged past the circle of sunlight and into the darkness.

"Yoo-hoo," called Abe. "Anybody here?" His call echoed ominously through the cave.

"Sh-sh," cautioned Heinz. "If there's a rabbit hiding in here, we don't want to scare it away." He could almost taste the delicious meat they would fry over their fire in the corner of the sanatorium yard.

"I can't see a thing," whispered Abe.

"I have a few matches," replied Heinz, reaching into the pocket of his shorts. He lit one, and a little circle of light surrounded them.

"That's better," said Abe, looking around. "Wow, it looks like it goes back a ways," he said, starting off towards the blackness at the edge of the light.

"Take it slow," said Heinz, "you never know if there'll be a drop-off . . . "

"Or a bear," interjected Kolya.

They walked in silence for some distance, Heinz leading the way, shielding the match from the draft created by walking.

"Look, bones, lots of them," said Abe.

They had all seen them at once. There was something unusual and unexpected about the bones. They were not complete bones, as when an animal dies. Instead, they appeared to have been cleanly severed at predictable intervals, more like a butcher would do. There were too many to just happen to have gotten here on their own. But why a butcher shop out here? Unless it was illegal, maybe.

"Ouch," exclaimed Heinz, dropping what was left of the burning match. It flickered and went out.

"Hey, it's too dark." Kolya's voice was shrill with panic. He clawed the air, trying to grab hold of Abe's arm and not finding it.

Then there was the welcome scraping sound of another match being pulled over a rock, and the flame sprang to life.

"Good thing you had another one," said Abe, trying to hide his own panic.

"Grab a bunch of those bones and bring them out to the entrance where we can look at them better," said Heinz abruptly. "And hurry, this is my last match."

They each took as many as they could scoop up and headed back towards the opening as fast as they could. There was something sinister here, they were sure of it. No one voiced his thoughts.

The second match went out, leaving them surrounded by darkness, but up ahead they could see a dim circle of light which was the opening. Gingerly they walked towards it, carrying the white bones.

Heinz knelt on the cave floor as soon as they had dropped the bones and began piecing together the various lengths and shapes. It was obvious. These were not animal bones. There could be only one explanation, and it was making them all jittery.

"Maybe it isn't what you think," said Kolya, looking nervously from Heinz towards the cave opening.

"I'm not thinking anything," said Heinz firmly, "not until I make sure." He continued sorting through the bones, laying them out in an orderly way, and reconstructing them. Abe knelt down to help.

"I'll stand guard," said Kolya, edging towards the opening. "You never know who might turn up."

"Good idea," said Abe grimly.

It wasn't too long before the reassembled bones told their own story. Here was a human leg, an arm, and a hand. The three boys stared in horror. The stories of people disappearing from the streets of Berdjansk . . . this must be what was happening to them. A human butcher shop!

The boys looked about uneasily. Even now, the butchers

might be lurking in the shadows ready to pounce, or might be heading their way with another innocent victim, a sheep to the slaughter. What chance would three small boys have against whoever these people were?

"Let's go," said Abe, stepping outside the cave entrance. Heinz was right behind him.

"Coast is clear," said Kolya. They sprinted from the cave hurrying to seek cover in the overgrown vines nearby.

"What do you think," asked Kolya, shakily, "should we tell our supervisor what we found?"

"And end up back in that putrid basement for climbing over the wall?" replied Heinz. "Don't be stupid! Nobody's going to breathe a word of this to anyone. Agreed?"

"Agreed," echoed Abe and Kolya.

. . . . .

It's a good thing too, reflects Henry, lying in his hospital bed. Bad enough for the three of them to have to carry that gruesome memory around with them for the rest of their lives. No need to alarm the others who, like Kolya, had enough to deal with in their nightmares already.

Still, seeing it first hand like that, so young, well, it's left an impression. Hunger is a word he knows. He himself has experienced it: the bloated belly, the sunken eyes, the lethargy one feels. That experience has left it's own mark, but seeing it at its worst: the human bones, neatly sawed in ordered lengths, arranged on the ground in a cave: legs, arms, hands and feet, the meat scraped away and sold for a profit . . . that he wishes he did not have to remember.

Seven is too young to learn of Judases, who sacrifice their fellow human beings to feed their own greed.

Henry sits up in his bed, willing himself to think of something else. Oh yes, Kolya . . . the moonwalker. He remembers how a good idea backfired when a bunch of his friends tried to cure Kolya of his night-time demons. . . . Stuck his hand in a basin of water. . . . He can remember it vividly . . . how Kolya wet his bed . . . and how furious he was when he found out what they had done. It was an innocent mistake, Henry tells himself. How should they know what would happen?

His face grows serious . . . another boy with the same problem . . . not so lucky. . . . Climbed on the roof one night and fell to his death. . . . Death . . . the word reverberates in Henry's memories. . . . Sleeping or waking there just seems no getting away from it.

Henry waits out the early morning hours, listening for the six o'clock shift to come on duty. Then, laboriously, he gets up and goes to the bathroom.

By seven his breakfast tray is on the table beside him, and he bows his head for a moment, and slowly, methodically, begins to eat.

In the eight weeks that Henry has been in the hospital, his progress has been very slow. The cough has eased up some, however, and he is off the tubes. He forces himself to eat now just so they won't put him back on the intravenous, but most of the time, if he had it his way he'd rather not eat.

He believes the doctors have begun to listen a little more to him when he makes suggestions about when and how often he should eat, and the results have been better. Now, if they would just quit dickering with the medication, he tells himself, maybe he could get back on an even keel again. But just about the time he thinks they have one kind of medication licked, they change the amount or add something else and bang, he's flat on his back again. He is still on the expensive experimental drug. They seem to think that it and the lung-washing procedure are improving his lung.

He pushes the tray away and lies down exhausted, waiting for the doctor to come in and check on him. He has thought for days about what he will say, choosing his words with care as he always does when speaking English with someone who has education.

His lack of schooling has always rankled him. He can understand how he missed out going to school in Russia because of the Revolution, but in Canada, with the Hueberts, he was able to take only three years of education. Sure, in those three years he covered seven grades, but it's not the kind of education he has always dreamed of.

He does not blame his Huebert parents. They had their

reasons for deciding to help pay for their half-brother's and sister's educations. And Henry knows that it was his own choice to help on the farm when no one else was available. He can live with that, he tells himself.

Still, it rankles that he hasn't been able to study. Not even one year of Bible School. There is so much more to know and to learn. Now he has only what he can learn on his own from reading, talking to people, or watching television, and the dreams of becoming a doctor or a minister—long dead.

The doctor finally comes into the room, and before he has a chance to say anything, Henry clears his throat nervously, his eyelids fluttering.

"That fancy drug you've been giving me," he says slowly, "would it be possible to obtain it through my druggist in Tofield?" He looks at the doctor briefly, then lowers his gaze uncertainly. He knows the name of the drug, but will not risk mispronouncing it in front of the doctor.

The doctor looks at Henry, reading the question behind the question. Henry's impatience with being kept in the hospital for so long is no secret. He has been talking about going home almost since he was admitted.

"Nope." He replies casually, probing and pressing Henry's back and chest. "Not on the market yet. And at one hundred bucks a smack we're not allowed to move it around to pharmacies outside the hospital."

"Would it be possible for you to give me a certain amount of it then, and I could come back for more when it runs out?" Henry is grasping at straws. He knows it, but there must be a way. He will not stay here any longer. He will never get well here. He knows it. And Katie has been alone too long already. She cries a lot when she comes to visit, and he can see it's too hard on her. He has made up his mind. He is leaving, medicine or not.

The doctor grins. "You really want to get away from us, don't you?"

Henry is past joking. It is just like back when he was in the sanatorium at Berdjansk with promises and more promises that he would be able to go home when he was well. But they are not sending him home, just like then. It's high time for him to take matters into his own hands.

"I'm just lying here taking up space that should be occupied by somebody who needs it more," he says with forced calm, trying to use logic that the doctor will accept. "Just give me the required instructions. Katie and me are good at following instructions . . . "—he pauses—"have to be with the diabetes." He has often been far sicker than he is right now, and together they have nursed him back to health. If he had done as he felt, he would have demanded his clothes and marched out of here weeks ago; but if he has learned something over the years, it is to meet the enemy on neutral territory and try to plan strategies that will ensure survival.

The doctor sees the determination in Henry's eyes and is silent, arguing with his better judgment.

Henry interprets the silence as refusal, but is silent as well. He will not grovel or beg. That too is a thing of the past; he has learned there are other ways.

The doctor takes a deep breath. "I could get myself committed for discharging someone in your condition," he says with a short laugh. Still, he argues to himself, if he had to put money on anybody getting away with it, it would be this man. There is an inner strength, a twist of character that is impossible to explain. He has seen lots of people die with a lot less wrong with them than Henry, yet, time after time, this man has eluded death, and usually on his own terms too.

"All right Henry," he says finally. "I'll see if I can arrange for you to pick up the medication at the hospital pharmacy. I'm not promising anything, but I'll try."

"Thanks," says Henry simply. And then the doctor is gone.

Henry lies back on his pillow, his heart suddenly beating rapidly. He can not believe it. He is actually going home. Won't Katie be surprised when he springs it on her later. This is sure to be the last thing she expects.

# 25

# BROKEN PROMISES

"Heinz, they're sending me home," said Peter, his eyes shining. "Have they said anything to you yet?"

Heinz shook his head. "How many are they sending this time?"

"Quite a few," said Peter. "Almost everybody that's left, it seems."

Heinz, Peter and Abe had requested to be sent home with the first group from Grossweide when it had been shipped out in early August, but had been told that they were still not well enough and would have to wait.

"We'll send you back as soon as you're well," the supervisor said.

Now it was nearing the end of September and another group was going. Why hadn't he been included, wondered Heinz angrily. He was not going to risk being separated from the only brother he still had. What if someone took him away from Grossweide while Heinz was still in Berdjansk. There would be no way of finding out where he had gone. No! They could not do that! Either Peter had to stay here, or he would go back with him.

"When are you supposed to be going?" he asked.

"Today, I think," said Peter.

"I'm going too," said Heinz stubbornly. "Will you come with me to talk to the supervisor?"

"Sure," replied Peter. As much as he wanted Heinz to come back to Grossweide with him and the others, he had serious doubts that the supervisor would let him go. He eyed Heinz critically. His neck was badly swollen and he wasn't breathing right. The coughing hadn't eased up much either. He put his hand on his brother's thin shoulder as they walked towards the main building in search of Heinz's supervisor.

He was sitting at a table drinking a hot cup of tea when the boys walked into the room. Heinz got right to the point.

"I want to go back to Grossweide with Peter," he said slowly but firmly.

The supervisor looked at him with disinterest. "You will go when you are told you're ready," he said, turning his attention to his cup of tea.

Heinz stood waiting, trying to decide what to say. He was not used to standing up to his authorities, but this was urgent. His eyelids fluttered nervously as he gathered all his courage to look the man in the eye.

"Then let my brother Peter stay here until I'm allowed to go." He paused. "Please, sir." It wounded his dignity to beg and grovel, but the man seemed so distant.

Heinz's eyes shifted fleetingly to his brother's face. They had not discussed this option. What would he think of it? It was a great deal to ask of Peter.

Peter grinned. It was not the first time his little brother's resourcefulness had surprised him. Hopefully it wouldn't be too long before they could both go back. Somehow, even though Mama and Papa Harder were no longer there, Grossweide was still home. Anything would be better than staying here. Still, he decided, he would stay here a little while longer if it meant so much to his little brother.

"I can keep helping with the work, like I have been while I wait for Heinz to get well," urged Peter.

"We don't need any extra mouths to feed around here," said the supervisor, yawning. "Besides, we've got enough kids in here to sweep every street in Berdjansk every day, if we wanted them to, and more from where they came from." He paused significantly and went on to press home his point, "We don't want you, understand?"

Peter's face colored in humiliation. "Then let him come with me. It'll be one less mouth for you to feed."

The boy's sarcasm was not lost on the supervisor. He stood up. "Enough! The boy will be sent back when he's well. Now go." He motioned them impatiently towards the door.

Heinz was silent as they walked back into the yard and towards Peter's quarters.

"Come on pal," said ten-year-old Peter, "sooner than you think you'll get sent back too and we'll be together again, you'll see." He looked at the small boy. His usually cheerful, mischievous face was thoroughly dejected. "Don't forget," continued Peter, "your good friend Abe isn't being sent home either. At least he'll be here to keep you company."

Heinz nodded. How could he tell Peter that even though he and Abe spent a lot of time together and enjoyed each other's company, it wasn't the same as being with family. Not to be able to look across the compound and see his own brother going about his assigned chores, or know at night, when he lay awake with his loneliness for his absent parents and brothers and sisters, that at least Peter was nearby. He was all the family he had left. How could they take him away too? He swallowed hard, his throat tightening.

Peter's arms were around the small boy. "Heinza, please don't cry. I can't stand it either. I'm going to miss you too."

He buried his face in his brother's brown curly hair. "I'll wait for you at Grossweide. Promise."

"Peter, time to go. Hurry up." Kolya stood in the doorway of the barracks. "The wagon's waiting already."

Heinz turned away quickly, swiping at his tear-stained eyes, not wanting Kolya to see his shame. Kolya saw, but wisely slipped out the door, leaving the two Rempel brothers to their own pain.

In the days that followed, Heinz and Abe lay seriously ill on their bunks, both boys, feverish and gasping for air, too ill to go outside and join the activities of the other children. They had been sick before, but this was different. No matter how sick he was, Heinz could usually manage a grin or two, but since they had taken Peter away, Heinz had drawn into himself and Abe could not reach him. He seemed impervious to Abe's best efforts to draw out some semblance of the old, mischievous

Heinz he knew.

The mention of food had often before brought a spark of life to Heinz's eyes. They had had little enough to eat in the past few days, and what they'd had did not go down easily. Maybe if they could find some tasty morsel. . . .

"Heinz," said Abe, speaking with effort, "we've got to try to find something to eat. We'll never get well on the sauerkraut and sour tomatoes they're feeding us. We need fish . . . and air." He motioning to his constricted nose and throat.

Heinz just stared at the ceiling. All the other Grossweide children were gone now. There would be no more going over the wall in search of food; no more slipping away during the daily swim to scavenge for food in the streets. The human ladder had gone back to Grossweide, and the Russian children, he had concluded, could not be trusted. Each of them, he had noticed, knew only how to look out for himself, having little understanding about giving up something for the sake of the larger group. He would not put his life in their hands. The memories of the day and night in the watery basement were still too vividly etched in his mind.

"If you don't get hold of yourself, Heinz," continued Abe, "they're going to carry you out of here feet first, just like they did Sasha and Fritz, and the others."

They heard footsteps, and then the supervisor was walking down the aisle between the bunks towards them. The boys pretended to sleep.

"So what are you two doing, still lying around in bed?" he said loudly. "How are you going to get better in here? You should be outside."

Had someone told on them for missing the morning swim these past three days, they wondered. Then they would be punished for sure. Surely, thought Abe, they wouldn't be cruel enough to throw us back in the basement. Would they?

"Get up you two. Let's have a look at you." The boys sat up with effort, gasping for air. The supervisor noted their swollen glands. "Open your mouth," he said to Heinz. He could see the tell-tale yellowish-grey covering the tonsils and back of the throat, and he didn't need to be a doctor to suspect that he had a case of diphtheria on his hands.

"Now you," he said briskly to Abe. Just as he suspected. Not surprising since the two of them spent so much time together.

"Come along, both of you," he said, and marched ahead of them out the door and towards the main building. The two boys straggled weakly behind.

Before long, the two boys were sitting in a *Droschka*, riding through the streets of Berdjansk. Not until they stopped in front of the big, white city hospital building, did they have any idea where they were being taken.

"Is this place ever clean," whispered Heinz, as he and Abe followed the supervisor into the building. It even smelled clean. They stood waiting near the doorway, while their supervisor went and spoke to the nurse at the desk. She nodded, disappeared through a doorway at the end of the hall, and returned with a man whom she introduced as the doctor. It did not take the doctor long to examine the boys.

"They will need to stay in hospital for some time," he said to the supervisor. "We'll let you know when to come and get them."

And without a good-bye the supervisor was gone and a nurse was asking the boys to follow her.

They went down a hallway, through a set of double doors down another hallway, and turned into a small room. "This is your room," the nurse said. "Who wants the bed nearest the window?"

There were two real beds, with clean white sheets and pillows with pillow cases. Sunlight was streaming through the window at one end of the room. It was open, and the curtain waved gently in the warm breeze. The floor was polished to a gloss that reflected the furniture in the room. The boys stared, neither boy answering the nurse, thinking only that amidst such luxury, what did it matter who had which bed.

"How about you taking it?" asked the nurse, pointing to Heinz. She spoke a schooled Russian in a gentle voice that reminded Heinz of Mama Harder. "So this one nearest the door will be yours." She smiled at Abe. "But first, let's get you fellows cleaned up and into some pajamas." She led them to the bathroom across the hall.

"This is a quarantine ward," she said. "That means that what you have is catching, and you mustn't go past the double doors at the end of the hall or you could make the people in that part of the hospital even sicker."

The boys nodded, still overcome by their wonderful new surroundings. The nurse ran the bathwater and laid out the pajamas.

"Can you manage, or shall I help?" she asked.

Just like Grossweide, thought Heinz, overcome once more with homesickness. "We know how," he said.

She smiled and left them alone to luxuriate in the warm water. Finally, the last of the lather had been washed from their hair and bodies and they climbed into the clean pajamas. It had been nearly a year since they had worn anything but regulation shorts. The pajamas felt soft and warm against their bony bodies.

They padded across the hall to their room and climbed in between the clean white sheets.

Heinz closed his eyes. Everything smelled so good. The mattress was as soft as a cloud. Even the Harders hadn't had soft mattresses like these. Theirs had been straw-filled, but much softer than the ones at the sanatorium.

They had barely settled in, when steaming trays were placed in front of them. They lifted the covers and stared in disbelief.

"Can you believe this?" whispered Abe excitedly.

Heinz sat staring at his plate too. Could it be that all this was his to eat? He looked at Abe's plate. It was an exact duplicate of his own. More food in one plate than they sometimes got in two or three days, and all of it nice and soft so it was easy to swallow.

Abe was eating and drinking hungrily. "Well, don't just sit there and stare," he urged. "Eat up."

All Heinz wanted to do was to look at it, to make it last and last. Who knew when the next meal would come. Better not eat too fast . . . and save something for later.

He took the slice of soft white bread from the plate and slid it under his pillow. Then he began to eat, taking only a little at a time, savouring each mouthful. Abe was long finished when the aide came to collect the plates. She scooped up his tray and went to where Heinz was nibbling at his.

"That's okay if you can't finish everything," she said briskly, picking up the tray. Before he could find the courage to protest, she was gone.

Heinz stared after her in disbelief. "She took my food," he said angrily. "I was saving it!"

Abe laughed noisily, gasping for air. "Oh you silly. Is that what you were doing?" He stopped suddenly, seeing the look on his friend's face. "Don't you know that they bring food three times a day here?"

Heinz's feeling of horror melted into humiliation. He slid between the sheets and turned his face to the wall. What would Abe or the nurse think if they knew he had a piece of bread hidden under his pillow? They must not find out.

Twenty-one days passed quickly for the boys. Loving hands cared for them, brought them food in abundance, changed their bedding even when it wasn't dirty, and cleaned their room.

Gradually, their strength returned, and their bodies began to lose their skeletal appearance. The coughing had stopped and their throats were no longer swollen. To Heinz, it seemed that by some miracle he had landed in heaven, and he hoped that it would never end.

And then one day, at the end of October, the *zavedushchii* from Berdjansk was at the door of their room telling them to put on their regulation shorts and come with him.

"So this is it then," thought Heinz. "Just when we get settled in and start feeling at home, they send us away!"

He should have known that something so good couldn't last forever! Deep down he had known, but it had been nice pretending.

Heinz set his jaw. It was his own fault! If he'd thought about it at all, he told himself, he would have seen this coming. He and Abe had been getting well, and hadn't even noticed. They had been enjoying themselves too much. Well, there was one consolation, if they were being sent back to Grossweide he would be together with his brother Peter. Even if the place wasn't like it was with Mother and Father Harder, at least he would have

Peter. Another possibility nagged in Heinz's mind. What if they weren't being sent back to Grossweide? He had to make sure.

"So, we're well now," Heinz said to the man from Berdjansk. "Are we going to Grossweide now?"

"You ask too many questions," said the supervisor casually, as he opened the hospital door.

Abe and Heinz exchanged grim knowing glances. The man had no intention of returning them to Grossweide as promised.

"You promised that when we got well," said Heinz angrily, "you'd send us back to Grossweide. See for yourself. We're well now!"

"Well, we're not sending you back," said the man firmly. "It's not worth the trouble just for two. Now shut up and get in," he said, hoisting himself onto the wagon seat.

"We can't stay at the sanatorium," argued Abe. "That's only for sick kids."

"So, we have two boys with smart mouths. That's what a stay in the hospital does for you?" he added cynically.

"You can't keep us in Berdjansk," pressed Heinz. "You have to send us back like you said!"

"I don't have to do anything," answered the man curtly.

"Then we'll run away," replied Abe angrily. Heinz threw him a warning look, but it was too late.

"Oh, you will, will you?" replied the supervisor, scrutinizing the two boys in the seat beside him. He remembered the ingenious method they had devised to get over the fence, and the subsequent punishment he had administered. Yes. If they threatened it, they would probably try it.

"You talk pretty big for an eight-year old squirt, don't you?" he laughed. "We might just have to take that big talk down a few notches." He gave the horse a smart flick of the whip, and they were trotting briskly through the streets back to the sanatorium.

When they were finally alone in the trees behind the buildings, Heinz spoke.

"You idiot, Abe. Why did you have to blurt it out like that. Now he thinks that we're planning to run away."

Abe looked at him sheepishly. "I know. I shouldn't have said it out loud. But think about it. They're not planning to send us back and we can't stay here. Where does that leave us?"

"In one of the orphanages, I guess," said Heinz slowly.

"Wards of the communist government. We'll never get out, and you know what they say about those places."

"So we'll run away." This time it was Heinz who said it.

"What other choice have we got?" agreed Abe.

"We have to do it right away then," said Heinz, "before they move us someplace else or maybe split us up."

"If they do split us up," said Abe, "whoever gets out first will try to get to the other one and help get him out."

"Agreed," said Heinz. "We'll use our secret knock."

Two weeks passed, and each day Abe and Heinz kept on the look-out for an opportunity to escape. There was a sense of urgency about them. If they wanted to get out, it had to be before winter. Once there was snow on the ground, it would be impossible to travel in bare feet and a pair of summer shorts.

Already it was early November and they were having to break the thin layer of ice at the water's edge before they could plunge in for their bone-chilling daily swim.

But no opportunity had presented itself. It seemed that wherever they went, a supervisor was watching. Apparently they were not taking Abe's threat lightly.

And then suddenly one morning, before they had been able to execute their plan, Abe was gone. There had been no good-byes. No warning. Somehow, in spite of the fact that the boys were almost always together, the authorities had slipped him away without Heinz's knowledge.

"Where is Abe?" Heinz confronted one of the supervisors boldly.

"He's gone," he said simply.

Heinz's eyes widened. Gone? Like the other children who lay on their cots, too ill to swim or eat, and then one morning were gone? Gone, like Fritz and Sasha? Surely not Abe. He had gotten well.

The supervisor saw the horror flit over Heinz's face and hurried to reassure him, "You don't need to worry about him; he's fine. He's just not here any more."

"I want to see him," insisted Heinz.

"I told you, he's not here any more. You can't see him."

"Then take me to where he is."

The supervisor ignored him.

"You promised to send us back to Grossweide. Why can't we go?" demanded Heinz.

Still the man refused to enter into dialogue with the determined, angry boy, and simply turned his back on him.

Heinz's inner rage knew no bounds. The man had promised. Promised! One did not make promises and then break them. And as if the broken promise wasn't bad enough, now they had taken Abe away too. The prospects of somehow getting back to Grossweide and Peter were beginning to look very bleak. With seven orphanages in Berdjansk alone, how would he ever know to which one they had taken Abe. Together they could have run away to Grossweide, but all alone? He did not know if he could risk it.

Heinz turned dejectedly and walked to the back of the property. He climbed into the branches of the tree that had been the secret meeting place of so many *Schultebotte*, and buried his head in his hands. This was no time to cry, he told himself sternly. He had to think. There must still be a way out. But all his well-crafted ideas ended on the same discordant note. He was utterly alone. Locked behind high, unfriendly walls, maybe for the rest of his life, without a friend, without family, utterly and completely alone, with absolutely no way out. He wept bitterly.

All was silent, and then the sound of a woodpecker, tapping vigorously on a nearby tree broke through Heinz's anguish. At first he listened only half-heartedly, but the woodpecker's percussive beats continued, gradually pushing themselves into the young boy's awareness.

Heinz looked with renewed interest to where the bird was tapping tirelessly on the side of the tree. The tapping reminded him of the secret code he and Abe had devised for alerting the others of their desire to re-enter the compound. It was the same one he and Abe were going to use whenever one of them got to where the other one was.

"Whoever gets out first, will try to find the other and help him get out," Abe had said. It was the last thing they had promised each other. He would not give up. He would keep trying to find a way out, and all the while he would keep listening for that knock, from early to late. Even if he couldn't get out, maybe Abe would. No matter how long it took, he must not give up hope.

He felt better as he slid from the the tree's embrace and went to climb into his bunk. He was alone, a stranger surrounded by strangers sleeping in the cots which his Grossweide friends had left. Even Abe's bed already had a new boy sleeping in it. But even as he slept Heinz's ear was tuned for the music of the knock which must surely come.

It was only a few days later that Heinz was suddenly summoned early one morning, and told to get into a horse-drawn wagon. He watched the streets intently as they travelled, making a mental note of familiar landmarks, trying to decide which orphanage he was being taken to.

No need for Abe to look for him at the sanatorium now, thought Heinz. But how would he know? And if he should try and not receive an answer, which of the orphanages would he start with?

He gave the supervisor riding with him a side-long glance. What if he made a dash for it when the wagon stopped next, or even while it was moving. He tensed his muscles, waiting for an opportunity.

"I wouldn't try anything if I were you," the man said gruffly.

And then they were turning into the driveway of one of the seven Berdjansk orphanages, and the big gates were closing behind them. He was not going home, as promised. He was a prisoner, and not one of his family members or friends knew where he was.

# 26

# A DARING ESCAPE

Heinz lay on his bed listening to the even breathing of the boys around him. It was still dark outside the orphanage, but he was awake as he was every morning before sunrise.

Cautiously, he slid from his bunk, tiptoeing on bare feet through the narrow aisle between the beds towards the door. There was no need to dress. He, like the other boys, slept in his shorts and sleeveless tunic. One of the boys stirred. Heinz stopped, waiting. If anyone asked where he was going at this time of the morning, he would say he had to go to the outhouse. No need for them to know that he was going to sit on the verandah, as he had every morning since he had been brought here ten days ago.

So far his early morning vigils had gone undetected, and he wanted to keep it that way. It was his time alone, away from the unruly noise of the Russian children that surrounded him all day long. His time to think, to pray and to listen.

If there were a time of day that his friend Abe would be most likely to choose to come and try to get him out, Heinz reasoned, it would be early morning. Knowing Heinz's habit of getting up early and going outside to watch the sunrise, as well as the greatly reduced risk of getting caught at that time of day, Abe would most certainly come in the morning.

Heinz turned the doorknob and stepped outside onto the cold, wooden verandah floor. How much longer he could keep up this vigil he was not sure. Not only was there the risk of getting caught, but the nights were freezing cold and he had no jacket or footwear to keep him warm. Soon there would be snow, and then he would no longer be able to wait here.

He hugged his legs close to his body as he watched the night sky grudgingly give up its blackness. With each passing day, it took longer for the light to push away the last of the darkness. Gradually, mysteriously, the sky was changing colors, as though an unseen hand were painting in long, sweeping brush strokes. Heinz watched, enthralled. He loved the magic of his solitary morning vigils. As he watched he would try to anticipate the exact moment when the sun's golden eye would finally break over the horizon. Not that he could see the moment himself. The wall was too high, but he could tell by the colors in the sky.

Each morning as he sat, watching, listening, waiting, Heinz tried hard to hold the reins on his vacillating thoughts and emotions. Sometimes he felt his heart begin to race with excitement and hope as he imagined he heard the familiar signal he and Abe had arranged. At other times his spirits lagged, overcome by the hopelessness of ever getting out, or of ever finding his friend Abe, his brother Peter, or the rest of his family.

Heinz did not stir as a horse clip-clopped by on the street outside. The wagon it pulled rattled ominously through the morning silence, and then stopped. Heinz did not need to look through the knothole to recognize the already familiar sounds. He waited, knowing instinctively what to expect. There was a dull thud. Another dead body, thought Heinz, one more victim of starvation, collected like so much garbage and carted away with the others already piled on the cart.

By the time the business day started, thought Heinz casually, there would be no evidence of the death that stalked and littered the streets at night. A state of respectability would have been restored, like the respectability provided by the high walls that also locked from public view the plight of the hundreds of hungry, neglected children who, like himself, were without family and home. Who cared if they lived or died, as long as they didn't clutter up the streets and inconvenience others who were going about their own lives.

Heinz sighed. It was nearly time to sneak back inside. Another morning gone, winter one day closer and still no sign of

Abe. He was just getting up to go back into the orphanage when a faint sound caught his attention. He froze. Could it be? There is was again. Knock (pause), knock, knock. The signal! He hadn't imagined it! He glanced about, and seeing no one ran down the verandah steps and across the yard to the place from where the sound had come.

"Abe?" he whispered in disbelief.

"Heinz. Can you come out?"

Heinz's heart thumped wildly. "I don't think so," he whispered. "The gates are always locked." He had tried them often. They were always securely locked.

Now he ran to the big main gate, and tried the latch. Just as always. Locked tight.

He glanced over his shoulder. He had to hurry. Inside, people were beginning to move about. It would be just a matter of minutes until someone discovered them.

Heinz ran back to where he had heard the knock. "Abe, are you still there?"

"I'm here."

"There's a small gate at the corner of the wall. I'll try it." He could hear his friend's feet running along the outside of the fence in the direction he was going. The gates were always locked. He would have to think of a way to sneak out when someone went in or out during the day.

His hand was on the latch. He pressed gingerly. His eyes widened in surprised disbelief. The latch was moving. The gate was not locked! Of all the times for it to have been left unlocked! He looked around cautiously. No one was around.

In an instant he had pushed open the gate just enough to let himself slip through. He closed it soundlessly behind him. Heinz and Abe's faces registered amazement as their eyes met, and then, without a word, they turned and sped down the street towards freedom.

Questions flooded Heinz's mind as he ran. He wanted to ask Abe how he had managed to escape, how long he had been on the run already, and how he happened to knock on the wall of this particular orphanage at this particular time. But there was no time. Right now there was only one preoccupation, and that was not to get caught. This, he knew, was their one bid for freedom, and they had to get it right.

The months of scavenging in the streets had trained them in the fine art of eluding detection, and now as they ran they called on all the cunning they had learned, scrambling to hide in the darkness between buildings, or flattening themselves against recesses in the walls whenever someone approached, choosing the safest if not the fastest route to a free ticket out of Berdjansk.

At first the streets were relatively empty, and the boys were able to make good progress, but as more and more people appeared in the streets on their way to work or to the markets, the boys had to spend more and more time hiding. If only they could somehow ditch the tell-tale clothes, thought Heinz. If anything would give them away, it would be the regulation clothes. As long as they were wearing them, they could not simply blend in with the other ragged street children. But there was no time now to think of finding other clothes even if they were just rags. Heinz glanced around furtively. It seemed that official-looking men in uniform were everywhere. Probably by now word had gotten around that they were to be on the look-out for two runaway boys fitting their descriptions.

"Wait," whispered Heinz, as Abe moved to start running again. They crouched another few minutes under a set of wooden stairs, peering out at the passing feet. There was a lull, and Heinz stuck his head out. The coast was clear.

"Let's go," he said, and they were sprinting down the street again. They knew exactly where they were, and where they were headed. The months of prowling the streets of Berdjansk had prepared them for this moment. With every step they were getting closer and closer to their destination, the train station.

How often they had crouched in some hidden crevice, watching the trains come and go, watching the passengers and beggars, the train engineers and the ticket masters, until the routines were engraved in their minds like some predictable dance.

Now, even though they had not a *kopeck* to their name, they hoped soon to be on the eleven o'clock northbound train if everything worked according to their hastily constructed plan.

But first they had to get there without being caught.

Hours passed. The day was cold, and everyone on the streets seemed to be wearing warm coats and footwear. Even the *bezprizornii* had their feet wrapped in rags to keep out the cold. No snow had fallen, but there was a stiff November bite to the air. Abe and Heinz, running barefoot over the frozen ground, hardly noticed.

"It's not much farther," panted Abe, dropping down beside Heinz to crawl through the dry grass of an open area on his belly. They could hear the coughing and hissing of the steam engines in the train yards ahead.

It was early afternoon by the time the boys finally got to the station. "Oh no," wailed Abe, catching sight of the big clock on the station wall. "It's way past eleven. We've missed the train."

"Not for sure," replied Heinz. "You know how often they're late." Every available space on the platform outside the station seemed to be covered with a mass of humanity heaving at bundles and bags, calling out noisily, pushing and shoving.

The boys sleuthed about. Yes, the train had already left the station. They would have to wait until evening for the next northbound.

"Probably just as well," said Heinz, "be less chance of getting caught when it's dark."

Together, they dashed across the tracks and squeezed into an empty crate they had spotted. From their vantage point across the tracks, they could watch the activity on the station platform and monitor the incoming and outgoing trains. Even with a train in the station, if they lay flat on their stomachs, they could peer underneath the train and watch the feet coming and going.

"Might as well get some sleep," said Heinz, curling up in a corner of the crate. "It'll be hours before our train gets in."

Abe shook his head. "I think I'll go find us something to eat first. I didn't have much yesterday, and so far nothing today."

"Too risky," countered Heinz. "Better not chance getting yourself caught now if you can just hold on a little longer."

Abe groaned. "I wish we'd have known we'd have so much time. We could have got something on the way."

Heinz nodded. "Try not to think about it. We've gotten this

far. Just think, it won't be long and we'll be back home at Grossweide. Won't Peter be surprised?"

The boys curled up together, trying to keep warm. It was not long before Abe was fast asleep. "Must have been on the run most of the night," thought Heinz, wriggling uncomfortably on the hard floor of the box.

His mind drifted back to Grossweide. He imagined walking through the big front gate, down the tree-lined driveway. In the distance, behind the well-kept buildings the orchard trees, now bare of leaves, swayed their welcome. Smoke curled lazily from the chimneys of both dormitories as he and Abe walked up the steps. Once inside, they would soon spot the group of Mennonite children sitting at their desks, surrounded by the Russian orphans in the recreation room.

He imagined Peter looking up and seeing him standing in the doorway. There would be no thought of propriety; they would rush towards each other and shamelessly embrace. At long last they would be together, the two Rempel brothers, and together they would not stop looking until they found the others. Heinz shivered happily. It wouldn't be long now. They were on their way home.

The day passed with the boys sleeping and waking, and sleeping some more, checking regularly through the cracks and knotholes in the crate the activity on the station platform. It was dark when a shrill whistle sliced through the night air. "That'll be it," said Heinz, springing to his feet.

"We've got lots of time," said Abe. "There's a half-hour stopover before it heads out again."

"I know," answered Heinz. "We can't get on too early, or they might find us before the train pulls out, but if we wait too long we'll miss it." The waiting seemed endless.

Then a bell clanged through the crisp night air. Abe's body tensed. "Not yet," whispered Heinz. "It's fifteen minutes before the train leaves. We'll wait for the five-minute bell."

They waited on pins and needles, lying on their bellies beside the crate, watching the feet of passengers, some getting on and others getting off. They especially watched the steady stride of the shiny boots of the gendarmes as they marched back and forth on the platform. They must avoid being seen by them at all costs. Farther down the tracks they could see trunks being loaded and unloaded. Time seemed to crawl by.

The second bell sounded. "Five minutes 'till the train leaves," whispered Heinz. "Hurry."

The two boys scrambled to their feet and ran across the tracks, dodging between boxcars on the sidings until they came to a passenger car well back of where the conductor stood. They grabbed the bottom rung of a step that protruded on their side and swung themselves up. On the opposite side, in various places, last minute passengers were still being helped on by the uniformed train men.

"Stop!" The boys froze. Just a little way down from where they were, a guard was ordering someone to stop. "Show me your ticket," said the voice. The boys waited, crouched in the corner of the platform between cars.

"You can't get on," the voice continued angrily. "What do you think you're doing, trying to sneak on board without a ticket. Get lost!"

The boys could hear the answering volley of curses from the little street urchin darting away. With hearts pounding, they pulled open the heavy door and slipped into a dimly lit passenger car.

No sooner had they slid into the darkness under the seat, when they heard a guard show someone into the seats above them. Judging by the boots they could see it was a Russian family. Just like one of the kids to go poking around under the seats for something, thought Heinz.

They flattened themselves against the wall as luggage was pushed under the seats. Electric lights cast eerie shadows in the car, but their beam did not reach the dark corner under the seat where the boys were hiding.

The minutes ticked by slowly while the boys lay in silence, waiting for the train to begin to move. Above them the seat creaked as the Russian family settled in, shifting to find a comfortable position for the night's journey northward.

Probably headed for Moscow, thought Heinz. His own destination was much nearer. Nelgovka would be the first station out of Berdjansk. If everything went as planned, they would be getting off there. From there it was an eighteen verst walk to Grossweide and home. His heart pounded.

Suddenly a bell clanged and there was a jerk. The floor beneath them began to move. Outside they could hear the engine building up steam. Heinz felt Abe's hand reach over and give his shoulder a squeeze. They were on their way. Go faster, faster, cheered Heinz inwardly as the train laboriously gathered speed. They had to get out of the city before the conductor came to collect the tickets, otherwise they might be found out and thrown off.

Breathlessly, the two boys waited, trying to imagine the train's progress through the city. With every minute that ticked by, they breathed easier. All they needed was for the train to be well out of Berdjansk before they were discovered. From his hours of watching the movement at the train station, Heinz knew that stowaways were unceremoniously thrown off the train at the first opportunity.

The door at the far end of the car opened, and with it a blast of noise, cold air and soot from the train's smokestacks. "Tickets please. Show your tickets please." Heinz could hear the man's feet step, stop, and step again as he moved down the aisle checking tickets. The man carried a lantern, and as he moved down the aisle collecting tickets Heinz could see the light bob as he checked under each seat for stowaways.

Now he held his breath as the man came nearer. Timing would be everything. If the train was well out of Berdjansk when he and Abe were discovered, the conductor's only recourse would be to throw them out at the first station. According to his calculations, that should bring them to Nelgovka, just where they wanted to get off. But they needed to be discovered, otherwise they might end up in Moscow.

Heinz held his breath. The train could not be much out of Berdjansk.

"Tickets please." The man's feet were nearly beside Heinz's face as he took the tickets from the man sitting above him. The lantern light was bobbing, and then its glare flooded Heinz's face.

Towering above the boys was the conductor, his uniform as crisp as his manner, right from his high, shiny, black boots to his wide trousers tucked into the boots, the black blouse worn over his trousers and belted at the waist, and the fur hat on top of his head. A silver braid and shoulder strap identified him as the head conductor. The man emitted a volley of crude curses.

"What the devil do you two think you're doing?" the conductor asked angrily. "You can't travel if you don't have tickets! You know that!"

Heinz felt himself being dragged bodily from underneath the seat. Abe scrambled out after him. He stood with head bowed and eyes lowered.

The conductor glared at them. It was the same with all the beggars and stowaways he had to deal with. The story was always the same. No money. No food. Trying to get somewhere to find food. He did not wait for an explanation. Too bad the train was out of the station already or he'd throw the boys out on the spot. Now he'd have to wait until the first stop. Maybe that was even better, he thought smugly. Teach these *gavnjoki* a good lesson, being thrown off in the middle of a cold night in the middle of nowhere.

"Sit over there," he said, gesturing impatiently toward an empty seat in a compartment a few rows back. The boys hurried to the seats indicated, avoiding the eyes of the two occupants sitting opposite them.

"Now see that you stay put until I come for you!" the conductor ordered. The boys nodded agreeably, and then the man pulled open the door through which they had come and went through the next door into the next passenger car.

Abe and Heinz glanced at each other, allowing their eyes to meet momentarily. There was just the glimmer of a twinkle before they lowered them again. The plan was working.

Across from them, two Russian men in warm wool suit jackets sat staring unabashedly at the two boys. They were used to seeing children begging in the streets, but to see them out barefoot in this weather in nothing more than a pair of summer shorts and a sleeveless tunic, and travelling, was an added curiosity. Strangely, the boys did not beg, and the men did not offer anything.

Heinz and Abe sat in the dimly lit, unheated car, very much awake in spite of the lateness of the hour. Theirs was the veiled alertness of street urchins grown cunning and wise through constantly having to outwit the enemy, be it hunger, sickness, cold, supervisors, other thieving children, or policemen. They felt the curious stares of the people around them, but their stoic faces did not betray the fact that they noticed.

Only one thing was important now. Getting to Grossweide. The hunger and the cold they would deal with later. The stares were immaterial.

Hours went by, and around them people were dozing. Then they felt the train begin to slow.

"Our stop, I believe," whispered Abe with a grin.

Just then the conductor came bustling through the door. "This is where you two get off," he said briskly. Grabbing each boy by the scruff of the neck, he propelled them towards the door. He needn't have worried. There was not going to be any resistance from either boy.

Before the train had come to a complete stop, the boys were pushed from the platform between the cars. A brisk breeze rushed to meet them as they leaped into the darkness. And then the train was pulling away.

The boys found themselves on a little wooden platform beside a station marked "Nelgovka".

"This is it," said Heinz, shivering.

"Nobody around at this time of night," observed Abe. He tried the latch on the door. It was locked. "Maybe we should go as far as the town," suggested Abe.

"Nelgovka's at least four kilometers west of here," said Heinz, "no point trying to travel at night. Too dark to see anything." He looked around for a sheltered spot.

"How about here," Abe was crawling under the platform. They slept fitfully, curled up like kittens, conserving what warmth their thin bodies could generate.

The sky was just beginning to lose it's blackness when Heinz shook Abe. "Come on," he said, "we're going to get something to eat."

The mention of food was enough to have Abe wide awake and wriggling his way out from their hiding place under the station platform. From here it was Heinz's territory. Abe, faint with hunger and cold, was content just to stumble along letting Heinz lead the way. An hour later, when they finally arrived in the small Russian village of Nelgovka, the sun was up and people were moving about in the streets.

"Don't worry," said Heinz, sensing Abe's skittishness whenever they approached someone, "these people won't hurt us or turn us in to the authorities. Papa Harder says they're shrewd in their business dealings, but they're decent and friendly. Just leave the talking to me."

He walked down the street with confidence towards the building he recognized as the town office where Papa Harder had sometimes gone on business.

The town administrator, or *zavedushchii*, was at his desk when the two small boys walked in the door. He looked up casually and then continued with his work. The boys waited awkwardly.

"Please, honored sir," said Heinz slowly in his most proper Russian, keeping his eyes lowered. "We are very hungry." He was trying very hard to stop the chattering of his teeth that had begun soon after they stepped into the warm room. He had not realized how cold he was.

"When did you eat last?" asked the man abruptly.

"Not since the day before yesterday," said Heinz. He glanced at Abe, standing unsteadily beside him. "Longer than that for him," he added, giving Abe a nod. Abe, he noticed, was having just as much trouble staying on his feet in the warm room as he was. He too was shaking violently.

The man snapped his fingers, and from somewhere in another room an errand boy of about thirteen emerged. "Nikolai, see if you can find someone who can give these two something to eat," he said. The boy grabbed his coat and was out the door.

"You can sit over there while you wait," the village administrator motioned towards a bench near the door. He watched as they went over and sat down on the bench.

Everyday it seemed there were more beggars. They seemed to be getting younger and younger. Usually he simply sent them

214

away, but there was something about the small, dark-haired one. He reminded him of someone, he could not remember whom.

He bent his head to his work once more, but glanced up occasionally to study the two on the bench. Not Russian, he decided, although the boy had spoken Russian as well as any Russian child. But these two looked like Germans to him. He tried to remember if he had ever seen a German beggar before. Usually the Germans lived much better than their Russian neighbours, and when hard times came did not have to resort to begging. They were known to help each other too in hard times. He respected them for that. His face wrinkled in a smirk. Better to watch them in business dealings though. They knew how to talk down the price, and before you knew it they had themselves a good bargain.

The door opened, and instantly the boys were alert. The man at the desk stood up and greeted the two men who had entered. "Good of you to come," he said amiably. "We have two boys here who need a little warm food in their stomachs. Haven't eaten since the day before yesterday."

"These men will take you home and give you something to eat," said the administrator as the boys stood, waiting expectantly.

Food! Abe and Heinz's eyes met briefly.

Eagerly, they followed the men out the door and down the street. The town was not laid out like the Mennonite village where Heinz had lived, with each yard fronting the street running down the center of the village.

Instead, houses seemed to be scattered randomly, here and there, in no particular plan. It was not long before his host was taking him in a different direction from where Abe was being taken. He watched as long as he could, so that he would be able to find him if the need should arise.

Heinz did not have far to walk before he found himself sitting in a simple Russian cottage, watching hungrily as a slice of rich brown bread, a bowl of millet porridge, and a glass of milk was set before him. It was the first bread he had tasted since he had left the hospital over a month ago. And before that he couldn't remember when he'd had bread last.

He was aware of the eyes of the elderly couple on him as he sat at the table. That this food was by far the most valuable thing that this family had, he did not doubt for a moment. And they had given it generously and without grudging.

Instinct urged him to gulp down the food, but he held himself tightly in check, silently repeating the table grace he had learned from Mama and Papa Harder, and then deliberately eating slowly, savouring every morsel. It would be a very long, cold walk to Grossweide, and there would be no more food before they got there. Too soon the food had disappeared, and he got up to leave.

"Where are you off to now?" asked the Russian man.

"Grossweide," replied Heinz.

The couple looked at each other.

"On foot?" asked the grandmotherly woman, looking at the boy's bare feet and thinly clad body. Her heart went out to him, but she had nothing left to give him.

"It's a long way," said the man.

"Eighteen verst," replied Heinz confidently. "My friend and I can get there." Of that he was absolutely sure. Hadn't they come this far?

"Ready then?" said the man, putting on his jacket.

Heinz stood up. "*Spasibo*, thank you," he said, his eyelids fluttering nervously. For a brief moment, he looked into the warm, motherly face of the old woman and then, as he turned to go, Heinz felt the woman hastily press a thick slice of bread into his hand.

"*Spasibo*," he murmured again, his eyes lowered. And then they were outside, he and the old man, walking into the November wind back to the town office.

Abe had just been brought back to the town office when Heinz and the old man walked in. Abe noticed immediately the bread clutched in Heinz's hand, but said nothing. They would be sharing it. That he knew for sure.

"So," said the administrator, "what are we to do with you now?"

"Well," replied Heinz, "I know where I am, and I know where

we're going."

"And where might that be?" asked the man, amused at the boy's obvious determination.

"Grossweide," answered Heinz simply.

"How is it you know the place?" asked Abe's host.

"We come from there," volunteered Abe.

"It's a long way from here. How will you find your way?" pressed the administrator.

"I know it well," said Heinz. "I used to travel with Papa Harder."

So that's it, thought the administrator. He had seen the *mal'chik* before. This was one of Harder's orphans, the little shaver who drove the horse when Harder came on business. Heinz, wasn't it? How was it that the boy was now trying to get back to Grossweide, he wondered. Didn't he know that the Harders were no longer there. Rumour had it that a lot had changed since they had left. Obviously the boy didn't know. But one look at the boy's determined face told him that there was no point trying to dissuade him from going there.

"Good luck then," said the man.

It was mid morning when the boys stepped out of the Nelgovka town office and headed northwest for Grossweide and home. The day continued cold, near freezing, and the clouds hung ominously low. Hurrying over the hard ground on bare feet, the boys hoped the weather would hold until they were home.

Home! Visions of Grossweide, its warm orderly life with Mama and Papa Harder filled Heinz's mind as he walked. It would never be the same with the new Russian administrator, he kept telling himself, but at least Boldt was gone and Peter would be there. It was the place he had grown to love as home. It was the only home he had now, and it wouldn't be long until he would finally be back. Anticipation surged in his chest, shortening the distance with surprising speed.

# 27

# THE RETURN HOME

Henry walks out of the hospital into the crisp March air, his step unsteady, but his resolve firm. He is finally going home. Katie is waiting there. His daughter-in-law, Myrna, has come to pick him up and take him home. She is carrying his small suitcase, keeping a sharp eye out for him as he walks to the passenger's side of the car parked at the hospital entrance. He is already breathing hard from the exertion.

"You okay, Dad?" Her crisp cheerful voice belies the concern she feels. The doctors have made it very clear that he is not well, but is determined to go home. They don't know Dad, she thinks, as she takes a firm hold of his arm and helps him climb into the car. It's a miracle they've been able to keep him here as long as they have, and no surprise to any of the family that he has convinced the doctors to let him go home, even though he is far from recovered.

"There now," she says brightly, "we'll have you home in no time." She is used to being around sick people, having worked for many years as a nursing aid.

"How's Mom?" he asks once he is settled and they are driving away from the hospital.

"Oh," a little laugh catches in Myrna's throat, "she's just so excited you're coming home. She's been fussing since you called yesterday."

"She fusses too much," he says wryly. He is afraid she will overdo it and make herself sick. Still, it gives him a warm feeling to hear it.

"Aw well, you can't blame her." Myrna throws him an impish

grin. "You'd be fussing too if it was her coming home after more than six weeks in the hospital."

He hasn't thought of it that way, but she has a point worth remembering. Soon enough he will be tired and embarrassed over all the fussing Katie is bound to do.

They drive in silence, the city disappearing behind them as they turn off the freeway and onto the highway. Henry feasts his eyes on the familiar countryside as they drive by. Where has the winter gone, with all its snow and ice. It's hard to believe that he has actually missed the last of winter, and that spring is almost upon them. There is still a little snow in the ditches and the trees show no signs of life, but the fields are nearly bare from the sun's warm rays.

It will be nearly two months until the garden will need to be worked. By then he will be able to do it, he is quite sure. He feels better already, just being away from the hospital and the city. The familiar landmarks reassure him as they drive by. He is as good as home already. This is his territory. The hospital already seems like just another nightmare, over and done with now, its four drab walls a thing of the past.

The hour long drive is punctuated by snatches of conversation, but most of the time Henry just sits resting, revelling in the feel of the tires rushing over the pavement and the welcome scenery floating by.

A song spins through his mind, accompanied by the soundless rhythm of the power poles flicking by. The song is one that goes a long way back—to when he cannot remember. It is a buoyant song, expressing a joyful anticipation of a home where loved ones will be united and pain and suffering will be unknown.

The words flow through his mind, together with the lilting melody, like the jubilant little stream in the ditch beside them, celebrating its freedom from winter's icy grip.

*Meine Heimat is dort in der Höh*
*Wo mann nichts weis von Trübsal und Weh*
*Wo die heil'ge, unzählbare Schar*
*Jubelnd preiset das Lamm immerdar.*

*Viel Geliebte sind dort in der Höh,*
*Wo ich sie einst verklärt wiederseh,*
*Und dann bleiben wir immer vereint*
*Dort, wo ewig die Sonne uns scheint.*

*In der Höh, In der Höh*
*Meine Heimat ist dort in her Höh. . . .*

The song seems to carry him along, speeding him on his homeward way. He has had this feeling before . . . the feeling that nothing in all the world could be sweeter, more wonderful than what he's doing right now . . . going home. . . .

. . . . .

It was dusk as Heinz and Abe, blue with cold, stumbled into the driveway of the orphanage on the outskirts of the village of Grossweide.

"Something's different," panted Abe.

The boys stopped in their tracks, their eyes sweeping the yard. There were children here and there, dressed like themselves, in nothing more than summer shorts, with no shoes on, outside, in spite of the cold weather. But there was something else.

"The trees," said Heinz. "What's happened to all the trees?"

Hardly a tree was left in the entire yard, and in the back of the property where the two orchards had grown there was not a tree to be seen.

"Do you see Peter anywhere?" asked Abe.

"Not yet," said Heinz.

The boys dashed around the yard looking closely at the groups of children huddled here and there. Peter was not among them.

"Some of the trees in the old orchard were a hundred years old," panted Heinz as they ran.

"And all that work to get the new orchard going," replied Abe, matching his stride. "Who would do such a thing?"

Heinz did not reply. The damage was incomprehensible, the years and years of labour, all for nothing, and the baskets and baskets of fruit that could have fed them for years to come were gone forever.

"Let's try the dormitory," said Heinz, speaking in Russian as he always did. He turned and together they ran towards the boys' dormitory. The word EBENEZER still hung over the door. "Hitherto has the Lord helped us." That was what the Harders had said the Hebrew word meant. It's true, thought Heinz. Here he was, home at last. Who would have thought it possible just two days ago?

He ran up the steps and pressed the latch. The door would not open.

"Let me try." Abe rattled and pushed at the door.

"Hey," called Abe to one of the children nearby. "Why is the door locked?"

"We don't use that building," answered the boy in Russian.

"You don't use this building?" Heinz echoed. "Why not?"

If there were less children than when the Harders ran the home he could understand it, but judging by the number of barefoot, hungry-looking children loitering around the yard in nothing but a pair of shorts, there were a lot more.

"No heat. No furniture," the boy said cryptically.

"What happened?" Abe asked.

The boy shrugged, scratching his head lethargically. "Last winter, that drunken *svolotch*, Boldt, didn't bother getting fuel for the stoves. Water pipes froze and burst." He eyed Abe and Heinz, sizing them up as non-Russian intruders. He turned to go.

"And the furniture?" pressed Abe.

The boy motioned to the other dormitory. "Firewood."

"Like the trees?" asked Heinz.

The boy nodded.

"While Boldt was here?" asked Abe.

The boy nodded again.

"But that would have been while we were here yet," said Heinz. "Why didn't we know about it?"

"Too sick maybe," replied Abe.

A picture was forming in the boys' minds of the senseless destruction that must have been taking place even while they were still in the orphanage, too ill to be aware of it. When the new housefather had replaced Boldt, the damage had already been done, but they had been spirited away and had not known of it. Now they stared in horror and disbelief at what the boy had told them.

"Where do they keep everybody?" asked Heinz.

"In that hole," sniffed the boy, wiping his runny nose with the back of his hand and pointing to what had been the girls' dormitory.

"Come on," urged Heinz, "maybe Peter's in there."

A foul smell greeted them as they opened the door to what used to be the girls' dormitory, the dining room and Harders' living quarters.

"Phew," Abe held his nose, but it was warmer inside and the boys were glad they were finally out of the cold. Everywhere they looked there were hollow-eyed children, some with big bellies and many of them scratching and itching, or swiping sporadically at runny noses. There were children of all ages, from toddlers to teens.

"Can you believe the mess?" said Heinz under his breath. They pushed their way through the double doors and into the dining room. A huge pile of straw covered the floor. Here and there children sprawled sleeping, or just lay listlessly staring at the ceiling.

"Looks like everybody sleeps in the same room, boys and girls mixed," whispered Abe aghast as they stepped over the bodies, looking for Peter. Whatever would the Harders say if they saw this, he thought.

They went through the kitchen. It was unusually quiet for the number of children that must be fed here daily. "Wonder when they eat," said Abe. Nothing seemed to be cooking on the stove, but probably they had eaten already. If so, why was there no evidence of the clean-up that was usually done after a meal?

"Maybe he's downstairs," said Heinz, still searching for his brother.

Together they went down the basement stairs. This was where the laundry and girls' washroom facilities had been before. As they came to the bottom of the stairs, they could see in

222

the dim light of a lamp that one of the three cast iron cauldrons used for heating wash water was steaming.

"Look, hot bath water," said Abe. "Maybe somebody is going to make all those kids upstairs take a bath."

"Good thing too," said Heinz. "They smell like they haven't had one in months."

"Hey, what are you two doing down here? Supper's over."

A young man's quarrelsome voice surprised them. They looked in the direction of the voice. An older boy and a girl were lying together in a dimly lit corner of the room on a clump of rags. The boys turned away, embarrassed, and started for the stairs.

"You're new," said the girl in a conciliatory tone. "Go ahead and grab one of those tin cups and get yourselves some soup."

"And then scram," ordered the boy.

The boys hesitated.

"Soup? Where is the soup?" asked Abe.

"In the cauldron," said the girl impatiently.

They each took a cup from the table beside the steaming cauldron and looked into the pot dubiously. It did not look like soup. There was nothing in it except a small piece of bone at the bottom. They dipped their cups into the liquid and lifted them to their lips.

"Ugh," sputtered Abe. "Salt. This isn't soup."

"Better drink up," said the girl, "that's all you get around here."

The two boys gulped down the salty water.

"Now scram," she ordered.

The boys ran up the stairs. "I've got to get a drink of water," said Heinz, making a dash for the kitchen, where he had noticed a pail of drinking water. They both drank thirstily.

"Who are you?" A man's voice behind them startled them, and they wheeled around, ready to run.

The man grinned at them. "Don't worry. I won't hurt you."

The boys watched him warily. Who was he, and what did he intend to do to them? By his uniform, they concluded that he must be some kind of official.

The man continued. "I'm the *zavedushchii* here. Who are you and what are you doing here?" He was certain that these two German boys had not been assigned to his care. The last of the Mennonite children had been sent out shortly after they had returned from Berdjansk. He had been assured that was the last of them.

"This is our home," volunteered Heinz, his eyes lowered. "We got sick and were sent to Berdjansk. Now we've come back." He paused. "I'm looking for my brother, Peter Rempel. He came back from Berdjansk two months ago.

The man eyed the boys critically. The story made sense. But how was it that these two hadn't been sent back with the others. And how had they come to be here now? Perhaps it was better not to know everything, he concluded. The boys certainly seemed to know what they were about, and like the others they had come back in better shape than the children in his care, but with none of the resistance and resiliency that the Russian kids seemed to have. Products of the soft life, these fair-skinned Mennonites, he thought to himself. As soon as he had discovered how vulnerable they were, he had shipped them out. Probably would have died if he hadn't. Now there were two more. Already all the possible places to send them were over-crowded beyond every reasonable limit. What was he to do with them?

"Well," the man said thoughtfully, "you two can't survive in there," he nodded towards the door leading to the dining room. "You better come with me." He led them to one of the small rooms that had been one of the nursemaid's quarters when Harders had been there, complete with a bed and a straw mattress.

"Where did you send Peter?" asked Heinz, as the man was about to leave the room.

"Probably to Prischib," he said, "I couldn't say for sure."

There was an orphanage there which Heinz had heard about. "Can you send us there?" asked the boy.

"*Njet*," the administrator shook his head. "They're full up. Can't squeeze in another one."

When he had left them, Heinz went over and sat on the bed

to think. He was not giving up. "We're going to have to make a run for Prischib," he said firmly.

"Do you know how to get there?" asked Abe.

Heinz shook his head. "Never been there."

"Well then," said Abe, "we'll have to find out how to get there first."

Heinz nodded. They would begin scouting around tomorrow morning. They had to hurry if they wanted to beat the winter snows.

In the privacy of the little room the two boys knelt beside the bed to say their German prayers, and climbed into bed exhausted. Had it only been yesterday, thought Heinz, that they had hidden on the train out of Berdjansk, and just this morning that they had eaten that last piece of bread given to him by the kind old Russian grandmother? It didn't matter now. This wasn't the home he had imagined. It was all a bad dream. Maybe in the morning he would wake up and everything would be as it should be.

# 28

# GROSSWEIDE'S
# FINAL FAREWELL

Heinz stood at the window, gloomily watching the snow pile up outside. During the night, as the temperature dropped, it had begun to snow. Now Heinz and Abe would have to wait until spring before they could make a break for Prischib to catch up with Peter. The seven-and-a-half-year-old boy sighed in resignation and turned from the window.

There was no routine anymore at the Grossweide orphanage, the boys soon discovered, except for the cup of salt-water soup which they were given three times a day, and the frequent trips to the drinking water pail to try to quench their salt-induced thirst.

Beyond the orphanage walls, the famine still raged. There was little food available to be bought, and survival depended largely on the ingenuity of each person. In the orphanage the last of the bones from a horse that had died and had already been eaten were simmering in the bottom of the cauldron, and every day water and a kilogram of salt were added. Even as the children weakened from lack of food, the salty soup kept them going back to drink from the water pail. Their bellies became distended, but they hung on to life.

With the onset of below freezing temperatures and snow, the scantily clad, two hundred and ten children were forced to stay inside. Formerly used as the girls' dormitory, the building was intended for not more than thirty, including staff. Now, children filled every available bit of floor space of every room in the house, mostly just lying listlessly in the straw, many too weak for exercise or play.

Four pair of boots stood beside the door in the front entry-way. The children in the orphanage had to take turns wearing these if they wanted to go to the outhouse, or go outside to escape the squalor of the house. Some, like Abe and Heinz, ran in bare feet, shorts and sleeveless tunics through the snow to the outhouse and back. Others, too lazy to make the effort simply added to the frozen, odorous, yellow mound beside the front steps.

For Abe and Heinz, the days soon became unbearably boring. "Let's go skating," said Heinz one day not long after they had returned. He was holding two pairs of skates which he had found hanging in the blacksmith shop. His body glowed red from the cold. It was early December.

"By now the ice on the creek should be strong enough to hold us," he went on. "What do you say, Abe?" The skates were simple, a blade attached to a metal platform, with straps to go around any winter footwear that a child would be wearing.

Abe laughed. "Are you crazy? We can't just walk out the door with two pairs of boots and go skating, and we don't have any jackets."

"We don't need boots," said Heinz. "We can tie the skates onto our bare feet just as well as onto boots or shoes. The blades will keep our feet off the ice. And we won't stay out too long, just a few minutes at a time."

"You think it'll work?" Abe's eyes sparkled for the first time since they had come back to Grossweide.

"Won't know unless we try," said Heinz, grinning slowly. "We'll have to make some soles first though."

"What are we waiting for?" asked Abe.

The boys dashed outside through the snow to the now un-used workshop and hastily cut soles the size of their feet from some heavy paper which they found. Their teeth chattered from the cold.

"We better go back to the house and warm up before we go skating," suggested Abe, rubbing his body vigorously.

Reluctantly Heinz agreed, but it was not long before the two boys were back outside, running as fast as they could go towards the nearby creek. There they put the paper soles on the metal frames and strapped the skates to their bare feet.

In a few minutes, they were on the ice, gliding and swooping, like birds let out of their cage. The air nipped sharply at their ears, noses, toes, and fingers, but time seemed to stand still in the exhilaration of the carefree minutes ticking by. Back and forth they skated over the frozen surface, purposefully ignoring their tingling bodies, playing tag, trying to skate backwards, and falling down in the trying, then getting up and trying again. Each second and each minute burst with their joyous, childish celebration.

"Heinz," Abe's voice suddenly sounded with alarm. "Your feet look funny."

Heinz looked down. Large, white blotches covered both feet. Now that he thought about it, he couldn't feel his feet at all, or his fingers. He patted his cheeks. Even his cheeks had no feeling. He knew what that meant. He looked at Abe's feet. "Yours do too." Abe looked at his own feet and gasped.

Together they ran back to the house and into their small room, stamping their feet, rubbing their faces, hands and bodies to try to get life to return. Pain shot through them as circulation gradually returned.

In the days that followed, ugly cracks appeared, and large oozing sores erupted on their feet where they had been frostbitten.

"From now on," said Heinz already planning for the next skating expedition, "we'll make sure we only go for five minutes at a time."

Their feet did not have time to heal properly before they had gone skating several more times. Each time, their feet, hands and cheeks showed the effects of the freezing cold, but to Abe and Heinz, the pain was a small price to pay for the five minutes of sheer heaven that the skates gave them.

But each day their strength seeped away as they continued to subsist on nothing more than the salty soup. Gradually, their bodies succumbed once more to the lice and diseases being bred in the overcrowded, filthy orphanage. By the middle of December there was no more strength for the courageous forays outside. Now they too lay listlessly on their beds, like many of the others, with gaunt faces and distended bellies. They were too weak and ill to care about anything.

The supervisor, meanwhile, had spoken to the village administrator, Cornelius Martens, asking him to try to find someone to take in the two boys. Nothing had come of it. Everyone was struggling to put food on the table for their own families, and after nearly two years of famine conditions no one had anything extra to share. Besides, Christmas was nearly upon them, and families busy with preparations for the upcoming holy days did not have time to worry about two sick, homeless strangers.

When the supervisor noted the boys' dangerous decline, he urgently contacted Cornelius Martens once more, telling him that the two Mennonite boys were seriously ill and that unless someone could be found to take them they would certainly die.

Heinz and Abe knew that the search was on for someone to take them. "Nobody wants a sick orphan," said Heinz, more to himself than to Abe. Somehow they had to get well. He set about trying to convince the supervisor that he was well enough to leave.

It was December 20, 1922. Heinz was standing at his window, watching a man walk down the driveway towards the orphanage. Cornelius Martens was coming to get him. Excitement welled up in his throat. He would soon be leaving.

In the weeks since he had come back to Grossweide, only to find Peter gone and the home utterly devastated, a dream had begun to take shape in Heinz's mind. Always before he had dreamed of finding Peter and together searching for the other brothers and sisters and making a life together once more. Now, that dream was beginning to fade. They were all getting older year after year and would probably soon be establishing families of their own. Who was to say where any of them were, even Peter, who had supposedly been taken to Prischib. By the time he got there, when the snow was finally gone, Peter would probably be gone too. And then what?

The supervisor's suggestion that someone might be found to take in Heinz and Abe had struck a new and welcome chord in

Heinz's heart. Imagine, having a real home again, with a mother and father, and brothers and sisters. Heinz's mind reeled as he tried to curb his excitement. The supervisor had said only that Mr. Martens was going to try to find him a home. No promises, he had told him. Heinz had overheard the conversation himself.

"The boy can stay with us while we look for someone to take him," Mr. Martens had said. There was no guarantee that they would be able to find him a home. That had been clear from the conversation. Only that they would try. It was enough to send Heinz's hopes galloping, heedless of all caution. He didn't care. It felt good to be able to dream and imagine, to have something to look forward to.

Heinz heard the steps outside his door. Except for those wonderful few minutes in the little Russian cottage in Nelgovka, he couldn't even remember being in someone's home. Now Mr. Martens was coming to take him to his home.

"Abe," Heinz whispered bending over the feverish boy in the bed near the window, "Abe, I'm going now."

Abe looked at him listlessly. "Abe, you have to try to get well, do you hear? Mr. Martens said he'll come and get you as soon as you can walk out of here." He paused, and then continued severely, "You give up now, Abe, and I'll never talk to you again!"

Their eyes locked, and a glimmer of a twinkle crept into Abe's lifeless eyes. Heinz grinned back. "Good!"

He turned abruptly and was at the door when it opened. The administrator and Cornelius Martens were waiting for him.

"Better put on a pair of boots," said the supervisor when they got to the front door. "It's quite a long walk. Hey you," he motioned to one of the boys watching, "you go along and bring his boots and clothes back." The boy scurried to put on a pair of boots too, glad for an opportunity to get out.

"No jackets?" asked Martens, eyeing the thin shorts and tunics that the boys wore.

The administrator shook his head. "Not a one."

"Well," said Martens in Russian to the boys, "we'll walk fast." The day seemed gloriously warm to Heinz as he trotted beside the man, oblivious to his own heaving chest as he panted and gasped for air. He could hear Micha's footsteps behind him. It was the first time since he had come back to Grossweide that he had worn the treasured boots. They made his feet feel warm, and the snow crunched a happy rhythm as each step brought him closer and closer to the Martens home.

Cornelius Martens looked straight ahead as he strode briskly through the snow. A frown wrinkled his face. The young boy was sicker than he had expected, and with his starved, hollow-eyed look and big stomach, he was not a pretty sight. Who would want him? It was next to impossible any more to find a home for a healthy child, especially a boy. People seemed to want baby girls. What if no one would take him? The thought tormented him. With six of his own and ten additional orphans living with them already, he could not possibly think of adding one more. He must find a home for this lad. A fervent prayer went up as he walked.

"Oh God, You, who sees even the little sparrow fall, who numbers the hair on our heads, and numbers our days, see this homeless, half-starved, sick little boy and have mercy on him." They had walked for about ten minutes, when Cornelius Martens turned and walked through the gate towards his own front door. He turned to look at Heinz. The happy, expectant look haunted him.

"Son," he said gently, "this is just going to be a temporary home until we can take you to a more permanent one. But as long as you are with us, we want you to feel at home."

Heinz was suddenly overcome with timidity as the door opened.

"Come in. Come in out of the cold." Mrs. Martens urged the two inadequately clad boys into the room and hurried to close the door behind them.

Children of every age, with freshly scrubbed faces and warm, clean clothes, stared at the boys from every direction. The boys stood as though glued to each other, their heads bowed and their eyes lowered.

"You may leave your boots at the door," said Mr. Martens.

The boys, relieved to have something to do, quickly removed their boots.

231

"Sarah," said Mr. Martens to one of the older girls, "take these young chaps to the kitchen and give them something to eat. Annie, see if some of Bennie's clothes will fit the little one. We have to send what he is wearing back to the orphanage with the other one." He spoke a high-class Russian that seemed to match his dignified, self-assured manner.

The children scattered as Mrs. Martens ushered the two boys into the spacious kitchen. With each waif brought to her home, of first importance was to find something to eat. She and her family considered themselves among the fortunate ones. So far they had not gone hungry in spite of the shortage of many items. Somehow, they had been able to coax vegetables out of the dry ground, and there had been the fruit from the trees and bushes which they had carefully nurtured. Bread and meat were scarce of course, but it was a fact that because her husband had been allowed to continue as the town administrator, they had been spared some of the indignities and confiscations which others had endured. Cornelius was no stranger to the new government officials, and had won their trust and respect.

"To whom much is given," Mrs. Martens often quoted, "much shall be required." And so it was their practice to share what they had with beggar and orphan alike.

She glanced at the two boys now, noticing the small one hesitate a moment before his bowl of milk and porridge. Then he bowed his head. They ate as though it was the first food that they had seen in a long time. Their bodies were little more than skin and bones, but their bellies protruded like small watermelons in front of them.

She was glad she had heeded her husbands advice not to give the boys anything heavy. It was obvious that these children hadn't had any solid food in weeks. She shuddered to think what conditions must be like at the orphanage. By the time the two boys had finished eating, a fresh change of clothing was lying on the bed in an adjoining bedroom, and a round metal tub stood waiting.

"Come Heinz," she said gently, "you need to get out of your clothes so we can send them back with your little friend." She put her hand on his skinny shoulder and directed him into the bedroom. As soon as Heinz had slipped them off, she gathered up the two little articles and took them out of the room. Heinz stuck his toe into the warm water and then stepped in, lowering his body into the tub. He closed his eyes, the warmth of the water enveloping his tiny frame and soothing the sores on his feet.

Outside, the little Russian boy trudged down the street back towards the orphanage, tightly grasping the precious pair of boots and the shorts and tunic still warm from Heinz's body. His belly was full for the first time since before he could remember, and the vision of the cozy home, the warm clothing and the friendly faces surrounding Heinz still clung to him. For a few luxurious moments he allowed himself to imagine what it might be like to be Heinz, welcomed into the comforts of such a home, to be surrounded by such kindness.

And then abruptly, he pursed his lips and stared ahead of him into the falling snow, concentrating on the swirl of the snowflakes as they fell.

Heinz wished he could stay in the warm water all day, but gradually the water began to cool and he set about the task of scrubbing himself clean enough for Mrs. Martens' inspection. Soon dark soapy froth was clinging to the sides of the tub, and the water had turned a satisfying grey. He scrubbed his head especially hard, using something Mrs. Martens had given him, trying to rid himself of the lice that crawled there. What would Mrs. Martens think if he infested her whole family with the dreadful pests?

"Good. Good," crooned Mrs. Martens, as she inspected his head and ears. Then, as he stood wrapped in a towel, she began combing his hair with a very fine-toothed comb.

"Now," she said, when she was finished, "you can get dressed and see how our Bennie's clothes fit you." Her face crinkled in a smile. "They are going to be a little big, I know that already. He's not that much older than you, but you're rather small for your age."

Heinz did not know what to say in reply, but set about quietly getting dressed. The shirt hung loosely over his thin shoulders and the pant legs had to be rolled up. A *Pojas* was found to tie around his waist to hold up the pants. Even a pair of shoes and socks were found. Heinz felt like a prince. It had been more than a year since he had been so well dressed. He had all but forgotten how fine it felt.

Hesitantly he followed Mrs. Martens out of the bedroom to meet the rest of the family, his face showing none of the mixture of emotions surging through him as he went. Here at last was a family he could be part of, at least temporarily. It pleased him immensely. Still, they were strangers. How did they really feel about having him here? How long would he be staying? He must not allow himself to forget that this was to be temporary. No one had promised he would be staying.

What the Martens family saw, apart from his sickly, physical appearance, were the marks that Heinz's months as a scavenger of the streets had left on him. At seven and a half, the boy was polite but wary, a youngster, somehow self-possessed beyond his years, yet strangely hidden by some protective wall around him. Cornelius Martens scrutinized him intently. It will take nothing short of a miracle to find this boy a home, Cornelius thought ruefully.

# 29

# A HOME FOR HEINZ

Cornelius Martens paced the floor while his wife stirred the porridge for breakfast. He was going over in his mind all the people who might possibly be able to provide a home for a small boy in as poor shape as Heinz Rempel. Hardly a good candidate to help with the field work next spring, he thought ruefully.

Everyone he thought of he had already asked. No one could take the boy. All day yesterday he had gone from place to place, and from village to village, but no home could be found for the boy. Already it was the twenty-second of December, and everyone was pre-occupied with trying to get ready for Christmas. After two years of drought, Christmas in the Mennonite villages would be a meager affair. No one wanted to concern themselves with one more gift, one more Sunday outfit to prepare, or one more mouth to feed.

"I don't know what to do, Katharina," he said quietly. "I thought that by the time he was well enough to leave the orphanage I'd have found someone to take him. I didn't expect him this soon."

"As sick as he is, he should be in bed," she said, shaking her head. "The way he coughs, I just hope it isn't T.B. We could be sorry we brought him into the house if he spreads that around."

Cornelius shook his head. "I wouldn't be surprised if he has pneumonia. You should see them, Katharina, running outside in this weather, barefoot, with no coats or hats, not just to the outhouse. The supervisor said Heinz and his friend even went skating barefoot."

"No." Katharina looked horrified. "Why would they do

that?"

"It's a terrible mess there," continued Cornelius. "You wouldn't believe your eyes. The children live like animals in a barn, cramped into one building with no proper food. I don't think I could survive in there either. Who knows, maybe I'd go skating in bare feet too, just to get out once in a while."

Katharina shook her head, her mind at once trying to grasp the details of the situation at the orphanage and trying to push the information away. It was incomprehensible that the new government would take over the orphanage just to let it come to this.

"The boy's friend, he is still there?" she asked, taking the spoon out of the pot and laying it on the shelf above the stove.

"Abe?" Her husband nodded gravely. "I would have brought him too, but he couldn't get out of bed. It doesn't look good with him. Besides, I don't even have a place for this one," he nodded in the direction of the bedroom that Heinz had shared with some of the other boys.

"What about your sister in Alexanderthal?" asked Katharina, wiping her hands on her apron.

"Lena?" He shook his head. "She's already got her hands full with the six half-brothers and sisters they took in last year."

"But they're all nearly grown up already," pressed Katharina. "It's not the same as having a small one of your own."

"But she talked of adopting a baby, not a seven-and-a-half-year-old," said Cornelius. "Besides, they're struggling to put food on the table too."

"Just ask her Cornelius. She can always say no."

Sitting at the head of the table a few minutes later with Katharina, their sixteen children and Heinz Rempel, Cornelius made the decision. The weather was holding, no storm brewed, and Christmas Eve was only two days away. If he wanted to find a place for the small, half-starved boy, it would have to be today. He would go to Alexanderthal and implore his sister and her husband to take the boy. There was no other way.

As soon as the meal was over, he went out to saddle up the horse for the trip. The village of Alexanderthal lay about fourteen verst southwest of Grossweide. There was no way to notify his sister that he was coming. He would have to take his chances that the family would be home. With Christmas so near, they would probably be busy with preparations. He was depending on that. If this mission failed, he did not know what he would do. He prayed as he rode down the snow-covered roads.

It was an hour and a half later that he slowed his horse and guided her into the yard in Alexanderthal, just as his brother-in-law was coming across the yard with his horse and sleigh. I wonder where he's off to, thought Cornelius.

Heinrich cantered up beside him. "*Goondach*, my brother," said Cornelius in low German, getting down to shake Heinrich's hands. "It looks like I nearly missed you."

"We weren't expecting you," said Heinrich, looking questioningly at the horse and rider. This was not an ordinary visit. He could feel it. "You haven't come with bad news I hope." The man was in his mid-forties, greying around the temples, his diminutive form and gentle manner making him appear older.

"No," replied Martens, "I'm here on business. And you? Where are you off to?"

Heinrich grinned slowly. "We're about to become parents."

Martens looked at him startled. He had seen Lena not that long ago. He did not think she was expecting. Then the light dawned.

"You're not thinking of taking in a child, are you?" Cornelius asked incredulously. What if he were too late. How could this be happening?

His brother-in-law looked at him questioningly. "I thought you of all people would be pleased. You know how much your sister has always wanted a little girl."

Cornelius nodded, stunned by the sudden turn of events.

Heinrich continued. "We're just on our way to Steinbach to pick her up. She's the youngest of seven small children whose parents have both died in the past two months."

The two men looked at each other.

"You said you came on business," said Heinrich, seeing that his news had upset Cornelius.

"You won't believe this," said Martens, "I came here today, desperately hoping to persuade you and Lena to take in a seven-year-old boy. He's half-starved and sickly. He's left over from the Harder orphans. Didn't get out with the others for some reason. He doesn't have a chance of making it if he stays in the orphanage. We've got him at our house for now."

"*Oba uk*," exclaimed Heinrich regretfully. "You're too late. If only you had come a few days ago." He paused. "Then maybe . . . but now?" He shrugged his shoulders helplessly. "Everything is arranged. Even the older children are excited about a baby girl. They're expecting us in Steinbach this morning."

Martens was tempted to say no more and return the way he had come, but the image of the young boy with big eyes and a big stomach would not give him any peace.

"If I can't find a home for this boy," he said slowly, "he will have to go back to Grossweide. He will die there."

The seriousness of the dilemma weighed like a heavy blanket of snow on the two men. "Why don't you come inside," said Heinrich finally, after an awkward pause. "We'll talk it over with Lena."

Gravely they went into the house. Lena had been watching from the window and knew by their expressions that there was some kind of trouble. Maybe her brother had brought news of a death in the family. These days it was not uncommon. She braced herself for the worst as she sat down with the men in the *Grootestov*.

"He wants us to take in a little boy Lena," began Heinrich uneasily, "seven years old, sickly, and half-starved. He's left over from the Harders' orphans."

"But we've decided to take the little Friesen girl," she said firmly.

"I'm sorry Lena," said Cornelius. " I wouldn't have come if I would have known you had your heart set on that little girl. I just didn't know who else would take him, and then Katharina suggested you. We'd keep him ourselves, but we've taken in ten already and just can't find any more room."

"No," said Lena emphatically. "You can't take in any more. It's too hard on Katharina already. This boy," she hesitated, "what's he like?"

"To tell you the truth, Lena," said Cornelius reluctantly,

"when I first laid eyes on him, he looked just a little *vekomna Russejung*, filthy, full of sores and lice, and half starved to death. But I brought him home yesterday, and he turns out to be a nice boy, polite, but a little shy. He's got spunk too. I'm told he goes skating in bare feet."

"He goes skating in bare feet?" asked Lena incredulously. What kind of boy must this be, she wondered?

Lena looked from Heinrich to her brother. How could this be happening? Just when the sleigh was already hitched and waiting for them to go and pick up the baby girl they had prepared for, to have Cornelius present them with such a dilemma.

It was almost as though they had no choice. How could they selfishly insist on the little girl, whom others would also want, and turn their backs on a boy whom no one wanted, who would die if he didn't find a home.

Was this God's way of speaking to them, she wondered, telling them to take the little boy? A great sadness welled up inside her. First the disappointment of reaching her forties without being able to bear any children, and now to have to give up her dreams for the little girl. She got up to go to the kitchen.

"He has my name," said Heinrich softly. "They call him Heinz."

"What will the other children say?" she said, standing in the doorway with her back to Heinrich.

"They will understand," he said.

They could not see the tears spill from her eyes, but Heinrich saw her hastily wiping them with the corner of her apron. "We don't have to take the boy if the girl means that much to you, Lena," he said standing up and going to her.

She struggled to gain her composure. "I know," she said, blowing her nose vigorously in the apron, "but they will be able to find a home for the baby girl. The boy, nobody will want."

As Cornelius Martens swung into his saddle and began the ride back towards Grossweide, he could not help but feel a little guilty for being the one to shatter his sister's dreams. There seemed to be no end to the contradictions and dilemmas these days. At least there was one consolation: the boy would have a good home, and for that he was glad.

# 30

# A MEMORABLE CHRISTMAS

Heinz could barely contain his excitement. Since Mr. Martens had come back to Grossweide and told him that a home had been found for him, he had thought of little else. He would say good-bye to all the lonely days and nights of feeling utterly alone in the world. Once more, he would be able to say *Mama*, and *Papa*, and there would be a special place that he could call home.

Who were these people, he wondered, who would give a home to someone they hadn't even seen? Already he felt a rush of love and gratitude towards them. He pursed his lips in a determined resolve. He would make sure that they would never have to regret this decision.

Mr. Martens had said that there were no other young children in the family, but Heinz didn't care. He would look for Peter and the others, and maybe his new parents would take them in too. Meanwhile, the couple's six half-brothers and sisters in their teens and early twenties, were living with them. These would be Heinz's aunts and uncles. A ready-made family, thought Heinz. Surely, in all the world, no child was as fortunate as he.

Morning finally came, and with it the good-byes to the Martens family. Heinz sat in the sleigh beside Cornelius Martens, his face sober and silent.

The man was silent too as they traveled. He hoped that his sister would be able to love this boy. What if she took one look at his skinny, bloated body, and sent him back. No, he said to himself, she would never be able to do that, no matter how she felt. She would keep the lad.

He sighed, trying to reassure himself. Lena's heart had been set on a baby girl, and now he was bringing her a street urchin, half grown, scarred by the hardships he had already endured. Still, he wouldn't be at all surprised if with proper nourishment and care the boy would turn into a fine looking boy after all, and even though he was small for his seven-and-a-half years, he showed the intelligence and maturity of someone much older. Heinrich might just find him to be a good little worker when he got a little meat on his bones.

Inside the Huebert household an uneasy air reigned. As expected, the older children had been disappointed to hear of the change of plans. They had looked forward to the prospects of a little girl to pamper and spoil, but a wretched seven-year-old boy? Their skepticism was firmly restrained, however, knowing that the decision was finally not theirs to make. After all, they too had been taken in by their brother and sister-in-law. They did not want to begrudge someone else this kindness.

They heard the approach of the sleigh and watched curiously as Lena Huebert opened the door.

All the way to Alexanderthal, Heinz had said it over and over again to himself. I am going home. I am really going home. And now, finally he was there. It was something he had hardly dared to dream of, and now it was coming true.

He watched the door open, and in a flash Heinz was down from the sleigh. His legs felt numb as he walked with Mr. Martens towards the couple waiting in the doorway.

The boy that Heinrich and Lena Huebert saw coming towards them was little more than a skeleton, the ill-fitting clothes unable to conceal the thin arms and legs, and the enlarged stomach. They could see open sores on his hands and cheeks, and he walked towards them with eyes lowered. His hair was dark brown and curly. Lena wanted to laugh and cry. In some ways, he looked to her like a little old man, this boy who was to be her son.

"Heinz, this is Heinrich and Lena Huebert, your new parents," said Cornelius Martens. The couple hesitated, unsure how to approach the boy, not wishing to frighten him.

Heinz raised his hazel eyes and looked into Lena's face. Then, suddenly, his arms were around her waist and he was hugging her with all the energy he could muster.

Tears filled her eyes as she looked across the boy to her husband. Heinrich nodded, smiling.

For several moments Heinz clung to her. His happiness knew no bounds. This was his mother. Not just for today, or for this year, but for always and always. He wanted to hold her so tight that no one would ever be able to take her away from him.

"Come inside," she said gently in Low German, "we must return the borrowed clothes to *Onkel* Martens." They went inside, past the curious stares of the other foster children, and into a bedroom where she showed him an everyday pair of trousers and shirt that she herself had borrowed for him just that day from a neighbour.

"Soon you will have clothes of your own," she continued in Low German. She helped him out of Bennie Martens' clothes. "*Onkel* Martens tells me that you have been asking about a brother," she continued, trying to make it easier for the lad to talk to her.

There was a flicker in his eyes as he looked up at her. "Has Mr. Martens found him?" he asked in Russian.

Lena looked at him in surprise. "You don't speak German?"

He shook his head. "I used to," he said in Russian, "but after the Communists took over, we weren't allowed to speak German." He looked at her intently. "Do you know if they found my brother?" he asked again, as she helped him into the borrowed clothes.

"Heinrich," she said in exasperation to her husband, who had been standing in the bedroom doorway watching, "can you make out what this boy is saying? I can't even talk to my own son." She knew only a little Russian. Her husband had the contacts with the Russian people, and knew the language much better. Even the other children knew Russian. They had learned it in school. Suddenly she felt left behind.

"He says the Communists didn't allow them to speak German at the orphanage," said Heinrich. "And he wants to know if we have word of his brother." He turned to Heinz and said in Russian, "You understand Low German, don't you?"

The boy nodded, answering in Russian, "I understand, but I think I have forgotten how to speak it."

"That's okay," said Heinrich, "the more you hear it, the more you'll remember. You can talk any language you want here." He looked over at Lena and said in Low German, "It won't take long and he'll be talking *Plautdietsch* like a true Mennonite again, you'll see."

"As for your brother"—he switched to Russian—"When Mother and I heard that you are looking for your brother, we asked Mr. Martens to help find him, so he can come and live with us too. They say he left Prischib not long after he got there and nobody knows where he went. Mother and I are going to keep looking for him."

Heinz lowered his gaze, hiding his excitement. "Oh, *Spasibo*, I mean *Dangscheen*. I will help look too."

Heinrich and Lena smiled. Their difficult decision was going to turn out to be the right one, after all. Now Lena turned to thirteen-year-old Martha, the youngest of their six foster children, who had been hovering near the door, watching. "Why don't you show Heinz around his new home and introduce him to the rest of his new uncles and aunts."

The boy followed obediently, having already overheard the whispered comments coming from the next room.

"Look how *älendich enn vemukat* the boy looks."

"Nothing more than a *vekomna Russejung!* Whatever possessed Lena and Heinrich to take in such a child?"

In the months on his own, Heinz had developed a keen ear, and an even keener sense of observation. It did not take him long now to notice that the foster children resented his half-starved appearance and his Russian speech, and that they were generally not overjoyed at his coming.

He noted it only as a fact, telling him to tread carefully and to be on guard and warning him not to venture too far beyond the invisible borders of his own safe territory. It was the way he had survived in alien territory after the Russian orphans had come to Grossweide and also in the Berdjansk sanatorium, and it was the way he had survived on the streets. He knew for certain that his position with his new parents was secure, and beyond that nothing mattered, he told himself.

It did nothing to diminish the overwhelming joy he felt at having finally come home and, if anything, it only intensified his fierce resolve to make sure the Hueberts would not be sorry they had taken him in as their son.

The rest of the day went by in a blur of activities. It was easy for Heinz to slip away unnoticed and sit alone on a window ledge, watching the people coming and going on the street outside. It seemed that the whole village was bustling to and fro.

"Do you know what day this is?" Father Huebert asked him the next morning.

"Yes, I know," he had answered eagerly, "it's December 24th." How could he not know? It was the day after the most important day of his life, December 23rd, the day he had come to the Huebert home.

"But do you know what we celebrate on this day?" Father Huebert pressed.

Heinz thought very hard for a moment. What could there be to celebrate that was more important than his finally coming home. Apparently Father Huebert had something else in mind. His mind scrambled for the right answer.

A memory flashed through his mind of a winter's evening a long time ago it seemed, that first year with the Harders. He remembered the doors to the recreation room being flung open to reveal a shimmering tree playing Christmas carols. There had been songs and poems, and the story of a special family, the baby Jesus born to Mary and Joseph . . . and yes, the next morning . . . presents and all sorts of wonderful things to eat. He could not remember the date, but that must be the answer Father Huebert was looking for.

A hint of a smile crept over his face as he looked shyly at his new father. "It is Christmas Eve," he said, "the day the Christ child came down from heaven to make his home with his new parents, Mary and Joseph."

"Where did you learn that?" asked Heinrich.

"From the Harders, when they were still at Grossweide," said Heinz, looking down at his feet.

"They have taught you well," said Heinrich, "and it is good

that you haven't forgotten." It came to him as a shock, suddenly realizing that for Heinz there would have been no religious celebrations while he was in the care of the Communist-run orphanages. What was happening to his beloved Fatherland, if children weren't allowed to celebrate Christmas anymore?

All that day the Huebert household was bustling with activity. With mounting excitement Heinz watched all the polishing, cleaning and cooking that was going on.

It was mid afternoon. Father Huebert had just left the room with Gerhard to go through the hallway from the kitchen to the adjoining barn to do the chores early.

Mother Huebert stood at the front door with her coat and boots on. "Heinz," she said, "I have to go to the neighbours to see if I can borrow some Sunday clothes for you to wear to the Christmas Eve program tonight."

"Can I come with you?" asked Heinz, fighting with the knot of panic squeezing his chest. What if she left and never came back . . . like all the others. . . .

"You don't have a coat, Heinz," she said, "and I won't be long." She gave him a little hug and was gone.

Quietly Heinz slipped into the corner bedroom where Mother Huebert had taken him just yesterday to change his clothes. He climbed onto the wide window ledge. He scraped a circle of ice from the window pane and pressed his nose against the window. He watched intently, catching comforting glimpses of his new mother going from door to door up and down the street, borrowing clothes for him.

Excitement surged through him. Everywhere he looked, people were busy preparing for the Christmas festivities, and tonight, he would be a part of it all, dressed in a fine outfit that his own new mother was at this very moment finding for him!

Finally she was back, her plump cheeks rosy from the cold. In her arms she carried the borrowed clothes for Heinz. Heinz clambered from his perch and ran to meet her.

Just then the iron door between the house and the hallway to the barn clanged shut as Heinrich Huebert and Gerhard came in from their evening chores.

"Supper," called sixteen-year-old Susie from the big iron

stove in the kitchen.

Soon everyone was seated at their assigned places at the big wooden table. Heinz still felt like pinching himself to make sure he wasn't dreaming. There seemed to be so much of everything here. So many clothes, so much heat in the house, so much food on the table, so much washing, so much German, and so much reading the Bible and praying. And on top of it all, it was Christmas Eve! He felt as though he would burst with happiness and excitement.

Father Huebert led in the table grace, and soon everyone was eating and talking. Heinz ate slowly, letting each bite roll deliciously on his tongue. Nothing had tasted so good in a very long time. The girls were already clearing the table by the time Heinz had finished the last drop of milk, and had licked the last crumb of bread from his plate.

"Time to get scrubbed up, Heinz," Mother Huebert said, as she dipped water into a round metal tub from a pot heating on the stove. "You get to go first today, because you're the smallest."

There was no time to luxuriate in the pleasant warmth of the water. Others needed their turns too. Soon Heinz was out and dried, standing on the braided rug on the kitchen floor, dressing in his new clothes. Heinz ran his fingertips along the coarse fabric of the woolen pants. So many different outfits in the past few days. It didn't matter that all of them had been too big. He felt better dressed than he had ever been.

He wiggled his toes in the shoes. He had all but forgotten what shoes felt like. From his perspective on the streets of Berdjansk, only the wealthy had shoes. And now he, Heinz Rempel, had shoes too. Granted, his were borrowed, but Mother Huebert had said he would soon have a pair of his very own. At least he would not need to be ashamed of himself when he went to the church this evening.

He went back to the *Akj Stow* and curled up on the window ledge once more, eagerly imagining what it would be like at the service in the church. At Grossweide he had been too young to go to the services. Only very rarely had he, along with the other younger children, been allowed to go to the village church, and never to a Christmas Eve program at the church. Now he was older, and the son of Heinrich and Lena Huebert. He could go wherever they took him, and they were taking him to his very first Christmas Eve service in a church.

People were already going to the church, as Heinz watched. He looked around anxiously to see if Mother and Father Huebert and the older children were ready yet. He did not want to be late and miss anything. It was all he could do not to dash across the street to join the others who were going into the church.

Finally, everyone was ready in hats, coats and boots for the short walk across the street to the Alexanderthal Mennonite Brethren church. Snow flakes were gently falling as they crunched their way through the snow and up the church steps.

Once inside, they took off their boots and hung their coats on hooks at the back of the church. The building reminded Heinz of the church in Grossweide, with two rows of benches down each side and an aisle in the middle. The pews were already filling up, with the men sitting on the left, and the women on the right. Everyone was in their Sunday best. At the back stood a big, pot-bellied stove, and in the front on a raised platform was the pulpit. Behind the pulpit sat several men on fancy wooden chairs, and behind them, to Heinz's delight, was a choir.

Near the right wall, at the front of the church, stood a huge evergreen tree covered with decorations. It was alight with candles, and an angel hovered at the very top. Underneath the tree, Heinz noticed, were presents and many brown paper bags.

Father Huebert walked with Heinz to the row second from the front, and propelled him towards the end of a bench of other small boys squirming with excitement.

"That's the Huebert's *Russejung*," one boy whispered derisively.

"Look at his big belly," said another. "He's *gauns vemukat*. He looks awful."

Heinz steeled himself against the stares and whispers, concentrating on the angel at the top of the tree. "Behold, I bring you good tidings of great joy which shall be to all people, for unto you this day is born in the city of David, a Saviour, which is Christ the King."

Heinz nearly jumped as he realized that he was remembering the German words that had imprinted themselves in his mind on the only other Christmas Eve he had ever celebrated.

He did not know how he could possibly contain more of the "great joy" the angels had announced. Any moment now, he was sure that his chest would explode with too much of it.

Then the choir began to sing, and it was as though the angel had been joined by an angel chorus singing "Glory to God in the highest, and on earth peace, and goodwill towards men."

Nearly two hours passed. The choir and the Sunday School children alternately sang, children stood at the front and nervously recited their recitations, Scriptures were read and prayers were said, and everyone joined in singing the familiar German carols that Heinz loved.

Now the children were all going to the front, and as they passed by one of the adults standing in front, the candles they were holding were lit. A simple triangular structure had been brought out from behind the tree, and the children were taking their places on it. The last one stepped into his place. A living Christmas tree alight with candles had taken shape before Heinz's very eyes. The children's faces glowed in the soft light. Softly they began to sing, "*Stille Nacht, Heilige Nacht, alles Schläft, einsam wacht. . . .* "

Heinz sat alone on the bench, overcome with the joy and the wonder of this holy night, silent tears trickling down his frost-scarred cheeks. The last note of the song died away, and the hush that had fallen over the congregation gave way to restless movement as the children filed back to their seats.

Heinz, suddenly aware of the moistness of his cheeks, quickly wiped them with the back of his hand. The program was over, he was sure of that, but no one moved to go. Something else seemed to be about to take place. Young people, including his six new uncles and aunts, were coming to the front of the church, making their way towards the tree in the corner.

He watched as one by one each of the children was given a wrapped present from under the tree. By the comments of the children nearby, he concluded that these gifts were from their Sunday School teachers. Some received bookmarks, with a

Scripture verse printed in ornate letters on it. A yellow tassel hung from the top of each bookmark. Others were receiving wall mottoes, also beautifully decorated and engraved with a Scripture verse. Heinz, not having had a Sunday School teacher, had to be content to share in their joy vicariously. He had not expected anything anyway.

Then he felt a tap on his shoulder. He turned to see who it was. "This is for you," said the young man, handing him one of the paper bags he had seen under the tree.

"For me?" asked a surprised Heinz, forgetting to speak German.

The boy nodded and continued handing bags to the other children as well. He did not hear Heinz's dumbfounded "*Dangsheen*."

Carefully Heinz opened the bag to look inside. Treats of all kinds stared up at him. He could see peanuts, walnuts, and hazelnuts. His mouth began to water. There were store-bought candies in shiny wrappers too, just like at Grossweide. Peeking out from underneath the treasure of nuts and candies, was a shiny red apple. Heinz looked around, his eyes bright with excitement. Every child had a bag such as this.

He clutched the bag close as he followed his new parents out of the church a few moments later. He must not drop it. When they got home he wanted to share it with his parents.

The family sat in the *Grootestow* for about half an hour, feasting on the goodies from the bags. Each of the young people had also received one. Eagerly they relived the highlights of the evening. Finally Father Huebert stood up. "It's time for bed," he said, stretching sleepily.

The older children stood up, laughing and talking, self-conscious that maybe they were too old for the traditional Christmas Eve ritual in which they were about to take part. Heinz watched them go towards the cupboard where the good dishes were displayed, but he did not follow. Instead he got up and went towards the corner room which he had been told he would be sharing with his new parents.

"Little boys that set up their plates on Christmas Eve," said Mother Huebert, "just might find in the morning that the *Nätklos* has brought them something."

Heinz turned to look at her questioningly, and seeing the twinkle in her eye also went to the cupboard and took out a plate. So he was to be included too. His heart skipped a beat. He remembered setting up his plate one other time, that first Christmas at Grossweide. Such treasures he had received! He almost felt guilty remembering. Carefully, he carried his plate to the kitchen and set it at his place on the table as the others were doing.

The night seemed long, as Heinz stared into its blackness. He did not sleep much for the excitement pulsing through his veins. So much had happened, so fast. And now there was to be even more. He could not even begin to imagine what treasures he might find in his plate in the morning.

He was awake very early, but did not get up until he could see that dusk was creeping across the night sky. Then he was out of bed, tiptoeing across the floor grown cold as the embers of the fire had burned down in the big brick stove in the middle of the house. He hurried into the kitchen. In the semi-darkness he could see that the plates on the table were full, and beside each plate lay a gift. He ran to his place. There on the floor beside his place stood a shiny new, wagon. His very first store-bought gift. It glistened in the dim morning light. Eagerly, he picked up the smooth red handle and pulled the wagon across the floor. The wooden tires rolled effortlessly and with hardly a sound across the wooden floor.

Then he was back at his plate, ready to sample the tantalizing treats that were piled high. Then he saw it. What was this? Another present? There, lying on top of the goodies in the plate like a crowning jewel, was a shiny new harmonica. His delight knew no bounds. Now he would be able to make music like the older children at the orphanage.

Gently, he picked it up and held it to his lips. It was cool to his touch. He could not try it out yet. The parents might still be sleeping.

"Go ahead, try it." It was Father Huebert's voice behind him. "It's nearly time for the others to be getting up anyway."

Without turning around, Heinz took a breath and blew

gently into the openings. A timorous sound fluttered to life, growing stronger as Heinz got the feel for how much air to blow through it. Slowly, he slid the instrument along his lips. The sounds went high and then low, depending on which way he moved the instrument. He experimented for a few minutes, revelling in the variety of sound and pitches that he could make, and then, tentatively, a melody began to emerge.

"Listen to him," said Heinrich to his wife, now standing beside him, "the boy has talent."

# 31

# PREPARATIONS FOR ANOTHER JOURNEY

It is April, and Henry has been home from the hospital for more than a month now. He is able to get up for short periods of time and can even walk outside to the corner of the street and back. Everyday he pushes himself to walk just a little farther, before his shortness of breath and the pain in his lungs make him turn around and go home. Soon, he hopes to go as far as the post office, which is nearly three blocks away.

Getting the mail and doing the grocery shopping has always been his job, along with taking care of the bills and the banking. Katie has been doing what she can since he has been sick, but the cheques and bills she will not touch.

"I don't know nothing about that stuff," she says adamantly, so one of the children comes by and looks after them for her." You should learn to do this yourself," they chide her. "What would you do if Dad was suddenly gone?"

She shudders. That is something she doesn't want to think about. The fact is she doesn't know what she would do. She's never even learned to drive a car, and Henry has always looked after the money matters. She won't even buy a dress without his approval. Secretly, she has always taken for granted that she will die first. She simply wouldn't be able to manage without her Henry!

"The kids will look after you," says Henry now, as they sit at the kitchen table, as they sometimes do, talking about these things. "It's all looked after in the will."

"I know, Henry," she replies softly, "you've always looked after me real good."

Maybe too good, she thinks guiltily. "You're so much better at things than me," she says gloomily. "I'm just no good."

Henry looks at her sharply. Does she really believe that, or is she being dramatic to try to get him to reassure her? "Why did you ever pick me anyway, Henry?" she continues accusingly. "You could have had any other girl for miles around—smart and pretty, and you had to go and pick me."

"What do you think Katie?" he replies flatly, "I married you because I loved you."

She laughs ruefully. "You hardly knew me."

"I didn't marry nobody else," he says firmly.

She still wonders what Henry, the envy of every girl in the community, ever saw in her, Katie Ewert, a shy *plautdietsche Mejal*, and *Kirchlijch* yet . . . she didn't understand it then, and she still can't make any sense of it—especially with Henry being such a strong Mennonite Brethren, just like his Huebert parents. It occurs to her now that his real parents were *Kirchlijch* too, like her. . . .

"Maybe you were just lookin' for your mother," she declares pointedly.

She sees his face turn stony and knows immediately that she has hurt him. She would do anything to take back her words, but it is too late.

Henry is silent. He can't understand why she hasn't got the message yet, that it was her and only her he ever wanted. If she hasn't caught on yet, or can't accept how he feels about her after all the carefully chosen presents and cards he has given her over the years and from the way he has treated her, he may just as well quit trying to convince her. He shakes his head in exasperation.

"I know you love me Henry," she says trying to make amends, "but I want to go first."

Henry looks at her sharply. So this is what the conversation is all about then: who's going to die first?

"It'd never work," he says quietly. "You know I'd never manage with all these pills and the meals for the diabetes without you." Surely she has noticed how forgetful he has become since his last stint in the hospital. He looks at her intently. "I've got to go first, Katie," he says firmly.

When he puts it like that, she is almost willing. It is almost as though she is hearing the voice of God . . . and then she imagines herself alone in the house, day in and day out, having to look after everything by herself and never having Henry near again. She shakes her head.

"If you die, Henry," her voice is little more than a whisper and her body is quivering, "I'll die too!"

They sit for a few minutes, overwhelmed by the pain of a grief they can only imagine, trying to prepare themselves for what will inevitably come. So often, death has been so close, yet each time, they feel so totally unprepared to face it.

"Please, dear God," Katie prays, "not this time. Give us a little more time together." And here they are, two old crocks, sitting across from each other at the kitchen table once more with nothing better to talk about than dying. Katie gets up abruptly, gathering the dishes. "Just look at us," she snorts, "sittin' here sad, while the sun's shining in the window on another day that our *Groota Gott* has given us."

Henry gets up, too, and carries his dishes to the sink.

"You go rest, Henry." She shoos him away from the sink. "I've got lots of time to do these few dishes. You've been up too long already. Just go lie down now."

Reluctantly, he turns and shuffles into the bathroom, and a few minutes later he is propped up against his pillow in his bed reading *Die Mennonitische Rundschau*.

Katie has not finished the dishes when she hears him call from the bedroom.

"Listen to this Katie!" There is a lilt to his voice that she has not heard in a long time. She stands in the bedroom door, wiping her wet hands on her apron.

"Tour to the USSR, July 11 to August 1," he reads in German. "Leningrad, Moscow, Karaganda, Zaporozhye, and other destinations in Southern Ukraine."

Katie looks at him, pretending ignorance. "So what," she says curtly. "There's been tours to Russia for years." She turns to leave the room, hoping to have discouraged any hare-brained notion he might be toying with.

"Southern Ukraine," Henry repeats pensively. "That's the Molotschna, Katie, where both of us are from. They're letting people into the out of the way places like the Molotschna now." For years he has dreamed of going back there in search of his missing brothers and sisters, but always the area was closed to foreigners. Now he has a chance to go. He looks up at Katie.

"So who wants to go there anymore anyway," she says tersely. "There's nothing left there. It was almost all wrecked already by the time you left in '26. By now, for sure there's nothing left." But she knows it is not so much the place that he is thinking about. He is tormenting himself with this new possibility of trying to find his missing *Geschwister*. And what if he goes and finds no one, she asks herself? It will kill him for sure, that's what. And she will not allow it!

"I'd like to go, Katie," he says firmly.

"The shape you're in?" she snorts.

"We wouldn't be leaving today or tomorrow," he replies dryly. "The way I've been improving, I can easy make it by July."

She sinks heavily into the chair by the bed. "You're way too sick," she says wearily, "and I don't want to see it." She is suddenly homesick for a place she knows can't possibly still exist. Sparrau, the little Mennonite village in the Molotschna where she lived until she was nine. When her family left in 1925 the village was still intact, but with all that has happened over the years, including the collectivization, what could possibly be left?

She has heard that most of the Mennonites who didn't leave Russia in time were shipped off to some remote corner of Siberia, or to a prison or labour camp. There would be nobody left in Sparrau even if the place could still be recognized, and for Henry it can only mean another disappointment. She cannot let that happen again!

But as the weeks pass, she can't help thinking about the advertisement of the tour. What if one of Henry's brothers or sisters still live in that area and because of her they never find each other. It would be her fault. That she can not live with.

Recently too, there have been stories of people going to Russia and finding long-lost relatives. It is what hundreds of people like Henry, who have lost family members during that terrible revolution, have dreamed of all their lives. Henry's hopes and dreams cannot be denied. He has to try.

So when she sees Henry writing for their passports and writing for more information about the trip—"Just in case we decide to go," he tells her—she does not say anything to stop him.

The ad has caught the attention of some of their friends too, and several have already decided to go. By May, Henry and Katie are caught up with the plans and preparations to go to Russia. Some of the children are less enthusiastic, worrying about Henry's fragile health and the problems of his diabetes diet and insulin shots, to say nothing of the complications if he should become very ill on a trip like that.

Henry has been pushing himself to walk farther every day in preparation for the trip. He talks of the places they will try to see and of preparations they are making, but rarely does he speak of the hope, throbbing like a newly discovered song, in his heaving chest. He is trying to downplay the possibility of discovering one of his siblings, telling himself that it would have to be a miracle for it to happen. But the song keeps reverberating in his heart, filling him with determination not to miss this opportunity, no matter what.

In the breast pocket of the jacket he will wear he has a Rempel genealogy, as close as he and Norma have been able to figure out, with approximate dates of the births and deaths wherever possible. Not at all accurate, he realizes. Even his own birth-date—May 27, 1915—is somebody's guess, but these lists he hopes to leave with people who might be able to help him locate his family.

He has already discovered over his many years of searching that there are numerous lines of Rempels. And what he knows of his own family tree is really too sketchy to be of much help. Still . . . he has to try, even though he tells himself not to expect anything. He keeps reminding himself and others that just because others have found loved ones does not guarantee that he will find anyone. He can hardly allow himself even the slightest hope lest it be dashed again, but in spite of everything he says, his heart is full of anticipation.

By early July, they are ready. Henry's suitcase is bulging with medication for his lungs, needles and insulin for the diabetes, tablets Myrna has gotten for them to put into the drinking water to make it safe, and medicine for diarrhea.

"They're going to take one look at the needles and drugs in my suitcase and turn me back," says Henry, half seriously. He and Katie have also taken great care in trying to pack gifts for people they will be seeing.

"They'll probably never let us in with this stuff," frets Katie fearfully. "If they find us tryin' to smuggle all this in, they'll send us to jail for sure."

"We're not going to smuggle anything," says Henry. "If they ask us what's in our suitcases we'll just tell them the truth. And if they look for themselves, which is what they'll probably do, they'll probably take it for themselves."

"What if they check their books Henry," worries Katie, "and find out that your Huebert parents smuggled you out when you were a boy?"

Henry has been thinking about that too. There are many who, like him, left the country illegally. Many have not dared to go back for fear of reprisal. It is a chance he is willing to take.

"Their books must have been in pretty bad shape back then, not to notice the change in the passport application," he says, "so I doubt if they could trace it now." He grins impishly. "Besides, what would they want with somebody as old and sick as I am?" Then his face becomes serious. "I'm no good to them anymore. They want them young and strong."

Katie is not so readily consoled. She is more afraid than she lets on. It is a fear grown out of her own encounters as a child with a Communist government that sends people scurrying for their lives across oceans to strange countries where people don't speak your language, to start over with nothing but a railway debt.

She and Henry share that distrust. The memories are still far too vivid to be denied. But in spite of everything, when July 11th

257

arrives Henry and Katie are on the airplane as it soars above the clouds, taking them back to the country they haven't called home in over sixty years.

. . . . .

For two years, Heinz had been living in the Huebert home. There was a normalcy and stability to his life such as he had never before experienced. Heinz continued to go by his real name, Heinz Rempel, because as a run-away from a state institution there could be no legal adoption papers for him. The Hueberts could not risk applying to adopt Heinz because in all probability the authorities would come and take him back. What more loyal and useful citizen than those whose young, pliable minds could be molded to the wishes and needs of the state? Already, there were rumors about the government's intended uses for the thousands of orphan children in its institutions.

"Better just leave things as they are," Father Huebert decided.

To Heinz's great delight, he was sent to school in January of 1923, less than a month after he had been taken in by the Hueberts. His hungry mind devoured the lessons that were taught, and it was not long before he had caught up and passed the children who had begun the school year the September before. In his mind, he was already planning for the future. He would study hard and either become a doctor or a minister. Either way, he would serve God and man, if God would allow him. It was a secret hope, tucked away, but very much alive.

One day blended into the next in the happy routines of family life with Mother and Father Huebert and the six newly acquired uncles and aunts, who had by now accepted the young boy. A highlight for Heinz was the Sunday evenings when the family gathered in the *Grootestow* with their violins, guitars, mandolins and harmonica, to sing and play. It did not take Heinz long to master the small harmonica he had received for Christmas, and if the song was in the right key he could play along with the rest.

When he showed interest in the guitar, his *Tante* Susie showed him how to play the basic chords on her guitar, first in one key, and then another. This, too, proved easy for Heinz, and the family took delight in asking the young boy to accompany himself on the guitar and sing for them in his clear soprano voice. It did not take long before the boy could play every instrument in the house.

Meanwhile, the Hueberts had been trying to find Heinz's brother, Peter, hoping to take him in as well, but no trace of him could be found anywhere. After his return from Berdjansk to Grossweide, they discovered, he had been taken to the orphanage in Prischib, but had left from there on his own and no one knew what had become of him.

They did learn however, much to Heinz's relief, that his good friend Abe had been taken out of the Grossweide orphanage not long after Heinz had left, and had also found a home.

The Hueberts' search also led them to Heinz's two eldest sisters. Lisa, they learned, had been adopted into a family of thirteen, and Tina was working for her room and board for another family. A visit was being arranged. Heinz thought of little else.

There was an urgency to Heinrich and Lena Huebert's search for Heinz's siblings. A plan was beginning to take shape in their minds that might mean leaving behind all hope of seeing friends and relatives again.

With the government beginning to implement a long-range economic plan, things were going much better. There was bread on the table once more, and they did not have to rely on the MCC care packages any more. But the effects of a communist state on the personal and religious life of individuals was being felt. A great migration out of the country was building up steam.

How long would the government allow such an exodus before closing the doors to the outside world, they wondered? And how safe was Heinz Rempel with them? A ward of the state and a run-away: they did not have any legal claim on him. How sure could they be that one day a government official might not come to the door and take Heinz away? They might even be punished for harbouring a run-away. Cornelius had explained the risks to them before they had agreed to take him.

Gradually, Heinrich and Lena's hopes became set on Canada, a sprawling land similar to Russia, their friends wrote. The government was welcoming immigrants, encouraging them to help open Canada's vast western regions, and even allowing people to travel across the continent via railway on a gentleman's agreement to pay later. Land was bountiful and cheap, and it was still possible to live there by one's convictions and beliefs.

And so it was decided. They applied for passports for themselves, their step-brothers and step-sisters living with them, and for young Heinrich Rempel.

As they waited for their passports, they began to sell all they owned, including their home. It was sold on the condition that they would be able to live in the house until their passports were cleared to leave the country.

Finally everything was ready. There was money enough for the passage on the ship, and finally the passports came. Everyone had been cleared to leave except Heinz.

"According to our records," the rejection letter said, "Heinrich Rempel is a ward of the state, and as such will not be permitted to leave the country."

"So, it will be good-bye again, after all," thought Heinz. It had seemed too good to be true. He should have known it wouldn't last. Nothing ever did. As soon as he thought he had someone to love, they were snatched away. How could it be that he had not expected it this time? Stoically, he began trying to prepare himself for the inevitable. The Hueberts would leave without him, and he would have to go back to live like a prisoner in the state orphanage.

"What are we to do, *Muttie*?" asked Heinrich Huebert of his wife, when they were alone.

"We can't go without him," said Lena firmly. She had grown to dearly love the spunky little ten year old with his unruly brown, curly hair and his brooding hazel eyes. As his emaciated body had filled out, he had become a handsome lad, strong of body and an obedient, willing child, eager to help with the chores and the farmwork, or even in the house.

"I was thinking the same thing," said Heinrich with a sigh. All his dreams for a new beginning in that land of promise and freedom called Canada suddenly seemed at an abrupt end. Who would have thought that an innocent act of kindness would determine his entire future in such a drastic way. And if they stayed? What would become of them here under the increasing pressure of a state that persecuted the rich and the religious?

"We can't stay, either," said Heinrich seriously.

"What choice do we have?" asked Lena.

They discussed their choices, and finally, after much soul-searching, they decided that they would wait a year, and then apply once more, this time, doing the unthinkable: falsifying the document so that the authorities would think it was their own son, Heinrich Huebert, and not the orphan Heinrich Rempel, for whom they requested a passport.

"What if they check their records?" asked Lena fearfully. "They will know right away that we're not telling the truth."

"We can only hope and pray that it gets past them somehow," said Heinrich, knowing full well that should the deception be discovered, they could be shot on the spot or at the very least be sent to prison as others had been.

What had begun as a routine preparation for a move to a new country, if such a major move could ever be called routine, had suddenly escalated into a dangerous life-and-death gamble. But first they would have to wait a year, and they had already sold everything.

Quickly, arrangements were made with the people who had bought their *Wirtschaft* to let them continue to live for one year in the *Sommastow*, a small separate shed with kitchen facilities. The eldest children were hired out to work for room and board at neighbouring farms. Even Heinz stopped going to school to work in the fields, to help pay for the costs of an additional year in Russia.

The search for Heinz's brother, Peter Rempel, intensified over the year that passed between the two passport applications.

"If we can get one out, we might as well try for two," said Heinrich. But all their looking and inquiring was to no avail. Nor could the older brother Jacob, or the youngest sister Anna be found.

But the long-awaited visit with Heinz's two oldest sisters was finally arranged, and it was a very shy but excited eleven-year-

261

old boy who met Lisa and Tina, when they finally came.

· · · · ·

Henry remembers that visit vividly.

· · · · ·

It was a warm, emotional reunion. The eight years of separation had seen his sisters grow out of the lithe youthfulness Heinz remembered into tall, husky women in their early twenties. He was not prepared for the change in size and appearance.

And for their part, the sisters were shocked to see their baby brother, just three when they were separated, so mature and independent for his eleven years.

There was not a great deal of time to visit, and then it was time for their final good-byes.

"When you get to Canada," Lisa said, "you be sure to look up Oma and Opa Rempel." And Heinz, without any idea of the vastness of the country, and the virtual impossibility of such a task, promised that he would.

Both Lisa and Tina promised to write, and as they parted, Heinz tucked the carefully written addresses into the safety of his pocket.

Never again would they have to lose track of each other. From now on, even though they lived an ocean away, they would keep in touch, and maybe one day, they would visit again.

· · · · ·

That good-bye was the last he ever heard of them, he muses as he watches the clouds below the airplane. Not one of his letters was ever answered. Henry has often wondered why. It is possible that they got lost, he tells himself, or that the sisters moved. But then why didn't they try to contact him through Mennonite papers like the *Rundschau*, where many contacts with relatives were renewed.

Although he tells himself there must be some good reason, he cannot help but feel that maybe they just didn't care. He was, after all, much younger than they and going off to a distant country. If only they would have answered at least one letter.

Still, the fact that not a single letter was answered suggests to him that there might have been a good reason, that perhaps they were spirited away from the addresses he was given. It is a hope

262

he clings to. The alternative is that they simply didn't care, and that feeling of rejection he can not deal with. He has since been told that one of his sisters married a Thielman, and the other a Wall. Which Wall family he has not been able to find out. But he has tracked down the Thielman family, whose son is to have married the Rempel girl. They tell him that they have long ago lost touch with him too. They don't know what happened to the couple either.

Henry tries to imagine what they might look like at eighty-five and eighty-three. He sighs. It would be a miracle if they were still alive, especially if for some reason they ended up in Siberia somewhere, like so many other Mennonites who stayed.

He has read that by 1927, just one year after the Hueberts took him out of Russia, the government imposed severe restrictions on emigration. And if they are in Siberia, he will not find them even now. He tells himself that he is being silly even hoping, but no matter how sternly he talks to himself, he can not let go of that tiny refrain of hope that repeats itself endlessly in his ears.

. . . . .

It was 1926 when the second application was finally made for the passport. This time Heinz was registered as Heinrich Huebert, and the passport was granted without any questions.

The Hueberts breathed a sigh of relief. "Their records must be a mess," said Father Huebert as he looked at Heinz's passport. "That can be the only reason they didn't catch the change." Still, there was no guarantee that someone might not still stumble on the first application and notice the falsification. They would not be safe until they were safely outside the Russian borders. They would continue to pray for success as the final hurdles to freedom were crossed.

At last the day of departure arrived. The train chugged out of Moscow and headed west towards the freedom.

"There's the border!" exclaimed Heinz.

The others craned their necks to look at the big gate that marked the border up ahead. The Communist star stared menacingly down at them. Once beyond it, no one could stop them and send him back, but now joy was mixed with fear. Heinz's body tensed, as he waited, fully alert now, as he had learned to learned to be on the Berdjansk streets, poised and ready for the worst.

Suddenly brakes screeched and steam hissed, as passengers and baggage were flung forward. They could feel the cars jolting to a stop. Heinrich and Lena looked at each other, fear staring from their eyes.

"Why are they stopping the train?" asked Martha.

"Quiet!" Heinrich's voice was tense. "You are to remember not to speak unless you are spoken to if someone comes by. Do you hear?" He had gone over everything before they had boarded the train. People had reported surprise searches before, and any mistakes now could cost him and his family their lives.

Heinrich's eyes sought out Heinz's. "And remember, this is Heinrich Huebert," he whispered. "Now act natural."

It was hard to act natural with their hearts beating wildly and guiltily in their chest. At this very moment, a man in uniform might be making his way to their car to inform them that the deception had been discovered. They did not want to think what the consequences might be. They had heard too many grisly stories of others who for less reason than this, had lost their lives.

The seconds ticked by, then the minutes. Several cars up they could see a family being roughly removed from the train and their baggage with them.

"I wonder why they put them off?" whispered Martha. A stern look from Lena silenced her.

It seemed forever that Heinz sat perfectly still, like a bird being stalked by a cat, watching, waiting. One thing was becoming very clear. Mother and Father Huebert were risking their lives to get him out of a country where he, Heinz Rempel, a run-away ward of the state, would never really be free. They had called him Heinrich Huebert on the application, and that's what it said on his passport too. No matter what happened, from now on he would call himself Heinrich Huebert. That was the least he could do to show his gratitude.

The guard was making his way down the aisle, checking passports, searching passengers to see if they were trying to take any money or valuables out of the country, and cross-checking his list for names of people wanted by the police.

"Your passports," he ordered.

Heinrich produced the passports for himself and Lena, his six half-brothers and sisters, and Heinz. They watched and waited, trembling and silent as his eyes scanned the documents. Then he handed them back briskly and moved on to the next seat without a search.

Not a word was spoken as the guard finished his search and passport check and moved into the next car. The Hueberts waited. They were still on Russian ground. Anything could still happen to interrupt their escape.

Then, slowly, Heinz could feel the train car begin to move as the engine ahead hissed and sputtered, building up steam. The cat was not going to pounce. He watched, his eyes hungrily gobbling up the distance to the gate. And then they were on the other side.

"*Gott sei dank!*" whispered Mother Huebert fervently, tears of relief trickling down her cheeks. She squeezed her young Heinz to herself. They were safe at last, free to be the family she had always longed for, on their way to Canada, a country of freedom and hope.

# 32

# RUSSIA REVISITED

The plane touches down in Amsterdam, and there is a brief stopover before the tour group is finally on board a Russian aircraft, flying towards Leningrad.

Henry is immediately aware, as are the other passengers, that they have stepped from a modern, well-maintained aircraft to a somewhat antiquated model. There are minor inconveniences because of the lack of amenities, but everyone is in good spirits and ready to make whatever adjustments that will be needed.

The hotel they check into is modest by Western standards, with shared washrooms, but the beds are clean. Henry walks around the room, surreptitiously checking behind pictures, underneath the lamp shades, and behind the bed.

Katie sees him. "Don't be silly, Henry," she scolds, trying to calm her own suspicions. "What do they care about us old folks."

"Can't be too careful," he says quietly in Low German. He has reason enough not to trust these people, after what they put him through as a kid, he tells himself, not to mention all he's read and heard. Besides, it doesn't hurt to be on guard. Somehow, just being back in Russia brings back the need to watch over his shoulder, to be on the look-out. He doesn't want any surprises—not the kind they dish out here.

The next morning his distrust of his Russian hosts is further piqued when the Russian tour guide tells the group that their itinerary has been changed. There is no explanation, only that the Russian authorities have rescheduled the tour.

"Just what you could expect," says Henry under his breath,

"they can't even keep their word on a simple thing like a tour schedule."

The change inconveniences several people who have made written contacts with relatives, arranging to meet them in a certain place at a certain time. Now there is no way to let them know of the change, and the meetings will not take place.

The tour takes the group from Leningrad to Alma Ata, and then to Karaganda. Not until Saturday evening in Karaganda is Henry finally able to make his first inquiries about possible contacts with Rempels.

Word travels quickly, and before long he and Katie are sitting in a tiny apartment surrounded by a variety of men who either have the Rempel name or Rempel connections. They have left their wives and children at home to make room for others.

Henry studies each face, looking for a glimmer of recognition. He is sure that even after all this time, he would know if they were family. No one looks familiar.

Several of them are able to speak a little German, and Henry remembers enough Russian to be able to communicate quite well. Eagerly, they trace Henry's family tree and their own, hoping to make a connection somewhere.

There is not a person in the room who does not know, first-hand, the bitterness of families torn apart by revolution, war or religious persecution. They too are looking for lost relatives. Many of them are so starved for kin-folk that anyone coming from abroad speaking of a Mennonite past such as they have had are welcomed with open arms, almost as though they were relatives.

Hope sparks and fans the conversations and questions, until the room is humming with a polyphony of male voices, patiently, but persistently, unravelling family lines. Finally, the conversations begin to flag and draw to a close. It is becoming painfully evident that Henry is no nearer finding out anything about his own relatives than he was at the beginning. For each of the men, the same conclusion echoes through the room. None of them has found a relative tonight either.

Disappointment is played down as good-byes are said, and the firm handshakes seal them in a brotherhood of mutual pain and understanding that needs no discussion.

"*Da svidanija,* brother Rempel," they say to Henry. "May God give you success in your search."

Back in their hotel room, Katie watches Henry pace the floor. "It's just the beginning of the trip," she says hopefully, "you'll have lots more chances to ask around." But deep down she is seriously wondering if maybe they shouldn't have come. What if he really does not find out anything. She can not bear to think of it.

"Come to bed, Henry," she implores. "You need your rest so you don't get sick again. Tomorrow's another day."

Henry climbs into bed and lies quietly until finally, he hears Katie's even breathing. The evening has left him with a mix of emotions. There is disappointment, yes, deep disappointment that not one person in that room, crowded with Rempel men, was even a distant relative. But there is something else. It surprises him . . . the bond they all shared as they spoke of their lost loved ones, and of the tragedies in their lives. For those brief hours he was not alone with his sense of loss and his grief; instead, he found himself surrounded by people who under-stood, and shared it. The strange sense of belonging lingers warmly as he finally drifts off to sleep.

In the morning he is up early, and goes out to the street for a breath of fresh air before breakfast. He sees cars lined up along the street across from the hotel, and walks over to satisfy his curiosity. The drivers eagerly explain that they are there to take anyone to church who would like to go. There are several churches to choose from.

Henry hurries back into the hotel to pass on the news to the other tour group members. Most of them have roots in either the *Kirchliche,* General Conference Mennonite Church, as Katie does, or in the Mennonite Brethren Church, as he does, and are eager to experience a Sunday morning church service in Russia.

After breakfast, Henry and Katie, along with Katie's cousin and her husband, are driven to the Mennonite Brethren church in Karaganda. Henry explains to the driver that he is searching for brothers and sisters, and when they arrive at the church the driver helps arrange for Henry to be given an opportunity to address the congregation.

Henry is shaking visibly as he stands behind the pulpit, facing a congregation of at least four hundred people. He is not a total stranger to pulpits. In years past, he has stood behind the pulpit of his small home church in various capacities: to lead the Scripture reading and prayer, to serve as the moderator of the congregation, and even occasionally to preach. He has learned to speak with a quiet poise and dignity, despite the involuntary trembling, and as he begins to speak his voice is calm and steady.

"I greet you, fellow brothers and sisters," he says slowly in Russian, "as a brother in Christ." He pauses, the impact of what he has just said reaching into the deep crevices of his own being. For a moment, he has an overwhelming feeling that they are perhaps a more real part of him than the phantom birth family he seeks. Still the search is not to be denied.

He tells them that he and the other visitors are from Canada, and that they bring with them greetings from a minister friend who just a few years ago delivered a sermon to them from this same pulpit. The people nod in appreciation for being remembered by the Canadian minister. They are always glad for visitors and the insights and encouragements that they bring, but with their own dearth of trained ministers, they are especially grateful for anyone who can come and preach to them.

Briefly, Henry tells them of his life-long search for brothers and sisters separated from him in the days of the Russian Revolution. There is compassion in their eyes as they listen. It is a refrain heard over and over again here among many of these people whose roots take them back to Mennonite villages whose people were scattered into the wind in the early part of the century. Many of them have been searching too, and they listen eagerly, hoping that Henry or Katie might be one of their own lost ones come home. The information, Henry knows, is sketchy, but he hopes it is enough to jog a memory or trigger a recognition.

Henry goes back to his seat and the service goes on for another two hours. The church vibrates with the hearty, full-throated singing, and a hush falls as one after another rise for spontaneous, fervent prayers. The sermon follows, its inspiration more from the fervor with which it is delivered than from its content. Finally the service is over.

Several people come up to Henry and talk to him, taking an interest in his story and in his search, but no one comes forward with any information about his relatives.

He and Katie are taken to the apartment of a Mr. and Mrs. Boldt for a hospitable noon meal. They are received as friends, even though they have never met before, and are introduced to the entire family. Henry smiles inwardly over the irony of being invited to dinner at the Boldts in Russia. His last encounter with that name was the cruel and drunken *zavedushchii* who replaced the Harders at Grossweide. He will not insult this generous family by asking if there is any connection.

They talk excitedly of the plans of a married son who is hoping to emigrate to Germany soon. Once there, he will try to help bring his parents over too. It is an all-encompassing dream, to finally be able to leave this repressive country and to live out their final years in freedom. They will not be allowed to take anything but the barest essentials with them, but they do not care. What are material things compared to their freedom?

There are photographs and handshakes, and then Henry and Katie are taken back to the hotel.

Monday is spent touring the city of Karaganda. Dutifully, Henry snaps picture after picture; after all, the kids have bought him this nice, easy-to-use camera so he can record the trip. They will want to see all the places where he and Katie have been. He himself doesn't need pictures to remind him.

Later that day the group is invited to the General Conference Church for supper. Once more Henry is given time to ask for help in finding his brothers and sisters. Supper is over when one of Katie's friends comes bustling over to where the Hueberts are talking to several who have come to unravel possible family connections.

"There is a lady over there," she says excitedly, "who says she remembers you and your brother from the Grossweide orphanage."

Henry's eyes light up. "I want to talk to her. Did you get her name?"

"She gave me her name and address," Katie's friend states, handing Henry a scrap of paper. The name does not ring a bell.

He is just wrapping up the conversation with the other people he has been talking to. Nothing has come of their intense discussion. There apparently are no family links here. They bid lingering farewells, loathe to admit one more disappointment in their mutual search for relatives.

Henry gets up to go talk to the woman his wife's friend has pointed out.

"Everybody on the bus." The call stops him in his tracks. He is out of time. Well, he looks at the paper in his hand, he can write to her later. It would have been good to reminisce about Grossweide, but he doubts if it would have led him to his brother anyway. The woman would have been gone from Grossweide before either he or Peter would have left. He tries not to let his disappointment with the results of his search so far show.

But Katie is not fooled. "Maybe when we get to the Molotschna," she says when they are back on the bus. "Lookin' for them in the cities is like lookin' for a needle in a haystack."

"Lookin' any place is," says Henry tersely.

The next morning the tour guide tells them they are going to visit Tashkent, a stop not planned for on the itinerary. Kiev is visited in the same way. Henry is getting impatient to get to the Molotschna. All these other places are interesting, but he has not come primarily to see the sights of Russia; he is here so he can go back to what used to be home, to try to pick up the missing pieces of who he was when he was still Henry Rempel.

His patience is stretched as taut as a violin string in the days that follow.

At long last they are able to go back to their pre-arranged schedule. The tour takes them through Frunze and then finally they are heading south to Zaporozhye.

"It's about time they stopped taking us on a detour and let us see what we came for," says Henry coldly.

But in Zaprozhye they are thrown another curve.

"The tour bus will not take you to the Molotschna to see the villages," they are told.

There is a unanimous exclamation of dissatisfaction from the tourists.

The guide continues, "If you wish to go on your own, you will be allowed to hire your own bus. There is a list of villages that are open to foreigners. Your driver will need to adhere strictly to the restrictions."

So, thinks Henry, first they tell you that the entire tour is included in the package deal, and once you get there they start tacking on expenses. This shouldn't surprise him, he supposes, but it reinforces his distrust of the way things are done in this country. He can easily see that these people need all the foreign dollars they can get, seeing that the economy is in shambles. Everywhere you look, there are old, run-down buildings, and from what he has seen even the people who consider them-selves middle class live in cramped apartments very close to the poverty line. Even with both husband and wife working, most people he has met cannot afford either a house or a car . . . but to steal so blatantly from the tourists? Well, it is certainly in keeping with what he has always thought this kind of govern-ment was like. Lately, with all the talk about *perestroika*, he had dared to hope things were different, but obviously nothing has changed.

A bus is hired, and a list is issued by the Intourist showing which villages they are permitted to visit. The list shows the Russian names of the villages, as well as their original Mennon-ite names.

The driver holds up the list, ready to read. Henry and Katie hold their breath. Will they get to see what they have come all this way for, or will this be the final disappointment?

"Schönsee, Sparrau. . . . "

"Sparrau." Katie says triumphantly, with a sigh of relief. "We're goin' to Sparrau, Henry."

"Sh-sh, just listen," he whispers. The list continues.

"Konteniousfeld, Gnadenfeld, Waldheim, Grossweide. . . . "

"Grossweide, Henry!" Katie is ecstatic. "He said Grossweide!"

Henry's heart is pounding, but he says nothing.

Several of the tour members are not so fortunate, however.

They have come all this way, only to find that their villages are among those once again forbidden. All share their deep disappointment, a little guilty for the rush of joy they are experiencing that their own village is on the list.

They are barely settled on the bus before they are skimming through the outskirts of Zaporozhye. Nearly too late, they discover that this section of the city used to be the village of Schönsee, the former home of several people on the bus.

Craning frantically to look back, they can see the Mennonite built factories and flour mills that the tour guide points out, still standing after all these years. There is no time given to get out and walk through the streets to try to identify people's homes, or to try to find the old church cemetery where relatives are buried.

They drive a little further, heading southeast. The countryside seems strangely desolate and neglected. So much good farmland going to waste, thinks Henry. What farm machinery he can see is sadly outdated and inadequate. There is a brief stop in Waldheim, and then the bus continues south.

The next stop is Gnadenfeld, the centre of municipal government (the *volost*) for the Mennonite villages in the eastern half of the large Molotschna settlement, Henry remembers. It was larger than the surrounding villages, and had three streets instead of just the one. Now they are told that they will only be able to drive along two of the streets because the recent rains have made the other street impassable. Henry notices that even in the larger, once progressive villages like this one, there is no electricity, no plumbing, and none of the streets are paved.

Next the tour takes them through Konteniousfeld, where because of landmarks described to them by earlier visitors, several people are able to identify where their homes once stood.

Henry recognizes the trades school building where his Uncle George went. He can recall going there often from where he lived in Alexanderthal to take him supplies sent by his Huebert parents. He also clearly remembers coming with Father and Mother Huebert to Konteniousfeld to visit Huebert relatives on several occasions.

The *Mädchenschule*, or girls' high school, is still where he remembers it, and is one of the few buildings still standing. What these buildings are used for now, no one seems to know.

Again, inquiries affirm that no one who is connected to anyone who used to live there is left in the village.

"The village of Sparrau up ahead," says the guide.

The bus stops. Katie has been straining to look out the window, trying to catch a glimpse of the village. She is not prepared for the desolation that was once her beloved home. She begins to cry.

"Come on Katie, let's get out and take a look," urges Henry gently.

"I don't want to get off," she sniffles, shaking her head vigorously. "There's nothing left."

Henry persuades her to at least have a look, since they've come this far. They get off the bus and walk around. None of the familiar landmarks remain. All the original, beautifully kept brick homes and yards have been replaced by little shacks, their yards overgrown and unkempt. Katie is not even sure exactly where her own home would have stood. So much has changed in the more than sixty years since she lived here.

"I thought with brick walls this thick," she says angrily holding her hand a meter apart, "they'd never be able to break everything down."

They look for the cemetery, and are able to find several old stones, but they are so weathered that none of the names can be read. After inquiring around, they discover that there is not a single descendent of the Mennonites who used to live here.

"What's happened to everybody?" Katie asks sullenly.

"You know what happened to them," says Henry. "Either they got out, like your family did, or they were shipped off to the forests or salt mines someplace in Siberia,"—he takes a sharp breath—"or killed."

He can hardly bear the thought of that ruthless, bloody time. His own experiences are nothing compared to what others had to go through. He has heard from others and read about what happened in those final years of the revolution, and then in Stalin's purge later.

"They used to call all this," says Katie, her arm sweeping in a wide arc, "the bread basket of Russia." She looks derisively at the bleakness and the poverty. "Now look at it!"

"They didn't want us Mennonites," says Henry, echoing her sarcasm, "so now they buy their wheat from Canada."

There is some small justice in the world after all, he thinks morbidly. Today, so many years later, when hardly anyone even remembers the Mennonites who turned these desolate steppes into thriving, prosperous farming villages, the scene is still one of desolation. It is, thinks Henry, as though the land still remembers, and mourns.

Once more they are travelling, now headed towards Grossweide along a bumpy road. Henry sits at the edge of his seat, trying to catch a glimpse of something familiar. So many memories are flooding in just now. He can see exactly how it was. But none of the homes that he remembers along the street remain. Instead the place is dotted with poor little shacks randomly scattered about, it seems, and put together like the houses in the other villages with what seems to be an odd assortment of any materials that the occupants have been able to collect.

He is the only one who has any reason for visiting Grossweide, so he instructs the driver to continue just past the outskirts of the village to where he believes the Grossweide orphanage must have stood. He is not sure just where the edge of the old village would have been.

Then he sees the creek. He remembers that it used to run just outside the Grossweide property. "Stop here," he tells the driver. There is the little bend in the creek where they used to skate. His heart skips a beat. An old Russian peasant is fishing in the creek, and Henry goes up to him. He is the first person they have seen in the entire village.

"Hello, how are you?" Henry says in Russian.

The man looks at him curiously, but responds pleasantly.

"Do you know where there used to be an orphanage close to here?" Henry asks.

The man says he cannot recall there being one.

Henry thanks him and goes back to the bus. He is trying to

recall the exact position of the buildings in relation to that little creek. Carefully he goes over it in his mind. It has not occurred to him that nothing at all would remain to give him a sure sense of just where things were.

"I think the buildings would have been right over there," he says pointing. There is nothing there as far as he can tell, except an office building that now stands on what could well have been part of the orphanage property.

Katie is right behind him as he leads the way towards where the buildings once stood. The others, caught up in this orphan boy's past, follow eagerly.

"That's not one of our buildings," he says, dismissing the intruding office building. Someone goes to knock at the door, but there is no response. They can't even ask anyone.

"The big, two-storey boys' dormitory would have stood right over here," he says, "close as I can tell, and the girls' dormitory, where the Harder parents lived, would be right there next to it." They look for anything, even a piece of old foundation, but nothing remains of the two elegant buildings. Is this the place, or isn't it? Henry thinks so, but there is really no way of being sure, and he likes to be sure.

"Out back there, if this is the place," he points out," was a big walnut tree." Henry can't even find the stump. "We had a big circular swing; we spent a lot of time playin' on it in the yard."

"A *Rundschokel*," offers Katie.

Henry nearly stumbles over some broken rocks that look like a pile of rubble, and a memory jogs loose.

"This could be where the old cistern was," he says, hiding his excitement at having found some tangible evidence. "We used to get our running water from here. So then the two houses must have been about over there."

Photographs are taken of Henry at the cistern. And more photographs of Henry and Katie next to the office building, which is now the nearest landmark to what was once the Grossweide orphanage.

"Back there, close to the girls' dormitory," Henry continues, "was the *Sommakjäatj*." The others nod, chatting and reminiscing about the summer kitchens where the cooking was traditionally done during the summer months. "It was bigger than what a lot of the regular homes had," Henry continues with a cough. "And in winter we'd use it as a bowling alley." His face does not betray the warmth he is feeling as he remembers.

They follow him as he walks farther back into the property. "Of course, every *Wirtschaft* had a *Schien*," he says, pointing out where theirs likely would have stood.

"The barn was probably over here," he points again. The Harders always kept lots of horses and cows. We were pretty self-sufficient, he says, feeling a  surge of pride and ownership about the way the place used to be. "Raised pigs, chickens, geese, you name it." He pauses, clearing his throat self-consciously, enjoying the interest that everyone is taking.

"The barn wasn't connected to the house?" someone asks.

"No." He gives a little cough. "No, in that way it wasn't set up like the other *Wirtschafte*."

"Tell them about the woodshed," prompts Katie eagerly. He looks at her, annoyed, but realizes that it's too late to silence her now. He does not want this to get too personal. "It was back there, behind the barn," he says, slightly embarrassed.

"The only spanking Henry ever got," she explains unabashedly.

The others are gathering nearer, hoping to hear more of this man's story. It has been coming out in snatches now and then, as Katie prods him into telling it.

"It wasn't a spanking really." His eyes flutter nervously.

"Go on tell us," someone urges. He takes a deep breath. "With so many kids livin' at the orphanage," he begins hesitantly, "there was a lot of work. It was a Saturday morning, and Father Harder had given us our chores to do." He pauses, making sure he gets all the details right. "I was in the younger group. We were supposed to clean the yard, pull weeds, stuff like that." His audience is attentive and waiting, and he continues self-consciously.

"Father Harder had to leave on business, but before he went he said, 'When I get home at noon, I want all the chores done.' Well, you know how little boys are. No sooner had he left, and us boys started playin'. There were two big orchards out back

277

there," he says, gesturing towards the far back of the property, "not a stick of it is left anymore as you can see. Wrecked when the Communists took over." There is pain in his voice.

"That's another story," he says hurriedly. "Anyway us kids were allowed to play in what we called the old orchard. Well, before we knew it, it was dinner time, and we run in, hoping that Father Harder wasn't back yet." He grins, "But he was, and after the meal he says, 'I want to see the younger group of boys.' We wondered what's going to happen next. He says to us, 'I see you haven't done your duty. What shall we do about this?' That's when he takes us out here to the woodshed. There's a big log that hasn't been cut up yet, and he says, 'Who's going to be first?' Well, I figure it won't be no easier putting it off, so I lay myself over the log and wait. The strap comes down just once. The others didn't fair so well, as I recall."

The others in the tour group have been listening intently, watching Henry's ashen, stony face as he tells the story, and when he stops speaking there is a moment's hush. They respect and understand his need for measured understatement and restraint. They too are carried by emotions that must be firmly held in check.

The details of his story are different from their own, but there is a common theme as they have stopped in one village after another. Each person has come, in some small way, to reclaim a part of themselves—a part left behind, lost in the chaos that was their childhood—to deal with a part of their lives which they cannot share. It seems fitting that they look in the crumbling cemeteries, the broken cisterns, the overgrown, empty expanses of Russian grass among the tattered shacks and along the rutted village streets. In some strange way they see themselves reflected in the destruction and desolation, but if they are aware of it, it is something of which they do not speak.

Too soon, it is time to drive on to the next village. Henry is not on the bus long, before he realizes that he has not even thought to take a picture of the one landmark he is sure of: the creek. He cannot forgive himself that he was there, and in the rush and excitement did not even get a picture. There will be no next time either. He knows that for sure now. He will not be back.

The tour continues for several more days, each day bringing Henry closer to the thing he dreads most. Another dead end. He is incredulous. Is it really possible that he has come all this way without gaining even a shred of information about his Rempel family or about the lost little orphan boy that was Henry Rempel?

The closest he has come is the lady who knew him and Peter at the orphanage, and he missed the chance of talking to her. Still, the tour isn't quite over. There is still time. He clings tenaciously to that shred of hope.

It is the afternoon of their second last day. The Intourist leader stands in front of them. "I've been instructed to inform you," he says coldly, "that you are to get your things together. You will be leaving for the airport in an hour. You are flying to Amsterdam tonight."The announcement creates a great deal of havoc.

"What about the last day of the tour?" Henry asks. "What's happened?" Others echo the question but get no answer.

"The hotel in Amsterdam isn't expecting us until tomorrow night," says Henry, hoping to stall for time.

The leader shrugs. "All I know is the orders I've been given."

"Will our money be refunded?" asks another visitor.

"I couldn't say," says the leader.

An hour later they are packed up and ready to go home. Henry's hopes of finding anybody are abruptly dashed. The return flight to Canada is uneventful. Henry and Katie talk and talk, the events of the past three weeks parading endlessly through their minds, trying to avoid the subject that is uppermost in both their minds. The trip is over and Henry is no closer to finding any of his brothers or sisters than he was before.

The sight of their neat, white bungalow back in Tofield is reassuring and comforting. Not only are they relieved to be home safely, but back in the modest luxury of their middle-class home in an orderly Alberta town surrounded on all sides by lush crops just beginning to head out: the contrast to what they have just seen and experienced strikes them as jarringly discordant.

Their friends come by to welcome them back, and Henry brings out the thick album of pictures he has taken and carefully explains each face and each place. He remembers it all.

Sometimes they spend the evening watching the video of the trip, which one of the group has sent them.

But when Norma drops in to ask Henry about his search, he only shrugs and says little.

"He's hurting," explains Katie when they are alone in the kitchen. "He had his heart set on finding somebody, but he didn't even learn a single thing. I can't stand to see him hurt so bad."

In the days that follow Henry escapes once more to his workshop in the garage, pouring himself into the items he is making for his grandchildren and for the MCC relief sale that will be held next year.

As he works, his mind plays and replays his most recent search for his missing brothers and sisters, his ears keenly tuned to every conversation he has had with people who might either be his relatives or know about them. He has to make sure that he has not missed any important details.

Time is running out for him. He feels it. And his promise to himself to be re-united with members of his real family is beginning to take on a hollow sound.

He is tempted to give it up. Reason tells him that would be the smart thing to do. But how can he, when he knows that it's possible to live only kilometers apart from someone you've been looking for and not even know it. If it could happen once, it could happen again. It haunts him. What if he was that close to one of them on his recent trip to Russia . . . there's no way of knowing. . . .

His hand moves absently over the wood of the wishing well he has nearly completed.

In his mind he is eleven again, living on a homestead in Saskatchewan. . . . Everyone calls him Henry Huebert now, instead of Heinz Rempel. . . .

Henry pauses, holding a small nail against the shingle on the roof of the wishing well. It's possible that the name change has been part of the problem all along, but it's something he had to do. He wouldn't do it any different, even knowing how close he and his sister Anna came to missing each other altogether.

An ache tightens his throat. If only they had found each other sooner. . . .

# 33

# A REUNION

It was 1926, and for the Huebert family the start in their adopted country of Canada was a difficult one. Their trip ended in Saskatchewan, where they were taken in by people from the Turnhill Mennonite Brethren Church. From there, arrangements were made for them to move to Herbert for the winter months until more permanent arrangements could be made.

By the following spring, Heinrich had been able to rent a farm in Sedalia, Alberta. He moved his family there, and began in earnest trying to put down roots for himself and his family.

Meanwhile, Henry had not forgotten his promise to his sisters, Tina and Lisa, to try to locate their Rempel grandparents who had emigrated to Canada in 1913. But Canada, he had already discovered, was a vast and sprawling land. Where would one begin to look? The only vehicles for communication open to him were word of mouth and the two German papers that came to the Huebert household: *Der Bote*, and *Die Mennonitische Rundschau*.

"Henry, listen to this," said Heinrich Huebert one day as he was reading one of the papers. "There is a letter here from someone called Anna Rempel. She is looking for her brothers and sisters." He read the letter aloud. It said that the girl was now living with her grandparents Jacob and Katherina Rempel.

Young Henry's eyes shone as he listened. "It's her!" he said, unable to hide the excitement in his voice. "It's got to be our Anna! Those are my grandparents she's living with! What does it say the address is?"

His father read out the address. "That's not ten kilometers

from where we were living just last winter," he said in amazement.

"That's how close we were, and didn't know about each other?" Henry's face registered his shock. "I'm going to write her a letter, just to make sure," he said, trying to rein in his wildly galloping emotions. The last time they had seen each other was in 1919, the day of their father's funeral, in the cemetery in Millerova, Russia. Now, eight years later, the dream he'd so desperately clung to was beginning to be realized. They would be together again—Heinz and his real family. His hope of finding the others was renewed. If he could find her, he would find the others too. He was sure of it.

And sure enough, her letter had confirmed it. She was his own sister, Anna Rempel, whose mother, Maria, had died on a train in 1917 enroute to the Molotschna from Siberia, and whose father, Jacob had died the following year. Henry's joy knew no bounds.

But being eleven, and living in Alberta, he couldn't just rush over to see her. In fact, it was three years before he had both the money and the opportunity to visit her in person. Three years of writing to each other, of looking forward to that long-awaited reunion. Three years of knowing he was no longer alone in the world.

Finally everything was arranged. He would come to Main Centre, Saskatchewan for her baptism. Mr. Ed Bauer was planning to drive his Model T to Saskatchewan on business anyway, and Henry had arranged to catch a ride with him.

In Henry's pocket was enough money to help pay for the gas. It all worked out perfectly, too, except that they had arrived too late for the lake-side service. People at the church had directed him to his grandparents farm, and that is where he and Anna finally met. The year was 1930, and he was fifteen years old.

Henry taps the nails into the shingles, brooding. He will never forget that meeting. He had not known what to expect. He could remember from the brief reunion with his eldest two sisters, Lisa and Tina, just before leaving Russia, that they were tall, robust, and big-boned.

Of Anna, he had no earlier recollection, so it had come as

quite a surprise to meet her, a tiny, fragile slip of a girl, just seventeen years old, so unlike her sisters.

What a glorious three weeks they'd had, he and Anna, getting re-acquainted, retracing their steps after the painful separation, sharing and arguing over the fragments of details that they had each garnered about theirs and their siblings' pasts.

The corners of Henry's eyes wrinkle in a grin. Yes, they even argued about their real ages; about whether Anna or Peter was the older one. Not that it matters much either way, muses Henry.

Together they wondered aloud why the letters Henry had written to Lisa and Tina since arriving in Canada had gone unanswered. Anna's own search had been just as fruitless until now. But theirs was a beginning, and it seemed that a world of possibility and promise lay at their feet.

Henry often thinks back to that happy time. It was a celebration of being family at last. The painful experiences carefully understated in the joy of this long-awaited meeting.

For Henry, it was nothing less than a homecoming. And then it was time to go. Henry takes a long deep breath.

Saying good-bye was difficult. "Stay with us Heinz," Anna begged.

And he would have liked nothing better, but after all the Hueberts had risked for him, he couldn't even begin to think of doing it.

"Maybe if I'd known . . . " he stops himself firmly. "No, not even then," he tells himself, "there's no way I could ever have left the Hueberts—not after savin' my life like they did, and risking theirs. It would take somebody pretty ungrateful to turn their back on them after that."

He has gone over it many times. It was a decision he must live with. It was the right thing to do. Besides, who was to know that in less than a year his Anna would be dead, and he would be going back to take his final leave of his newly found sister.

Henry has since learned that life for his orphaned sister had been a nightmare of mistreatment and abuse until she could escape to live with her newly found Rempel grandparents. Maybe he should have guessed how fragile her health was. Anyway, he tells himself, he will always have those three weeks they spent together.

. . . . .

It had rained, and the country roads were almost impassable. Once again Henry had been able to catch a ride to Saskatchewan, this time for his sister's funeral. They were still thirty kilometers from the church in Main Center when they got badly stuck. No amount of pushing and rocking the vehicle could budge it.

"We'll never make it," thought Henry, trying hard to swallow the panic creeping into his chest.

Fortunately, they were able to find a telephone at a nearby farmer's house and phone ahead, asking the minister to delay the service until they could get there.

A team of horses pulled the car through a three-kilometer valley of mud, and finally, mud-splattered and exhausted, they made it to the church. The hearse, also having had trouble on the roads, had gotten there just before them.

. . . . .

And so Henry had been there to see Anna buried, along with his short-lived joy of having finally found a member of his real family. Henry shifts uncomfortably, trying to straighten the kink in his back from all the bending he's been doing.

It is too painful to dwell on the ironies of his badly timed and ill-fated reunion with his sister, the only sibling he has ever found since coming to Canada sixty-two years ago. If only they could have found each other sooner, when they lived so close to each other in Saskatchewan. . . . Still, it was better than what happened with his brother Peter. He still remembers how thrilled he was to get word that Peter had been located. But by then he was fifteen years old, and couldn't be brought out of Russia. And then he was lost again.

Finding Anna has given him hope to keep trying, because who can tell when or where he might catch another glimmer of his childhood dream to be family again. And even if there is never another reunion, at least he has his memories and the three wonderful weeks when he and Anna knew a little of what it might have meant to belong to their real family. He has that much, and no one can take that away from him.

# 34

# ONE! ONE! ONE!

"What's the matter with you, Henry," says Katie, eying his erratic movements as he dresses.

"Nothin's wrong with me," he replies firmly, trying to ignore the strange sensation in the left side of his body. Somehow, it seems that movements that are usually automatic have to be carefully thought out this morning. Myrna will be here right after breakfast to take him to the city for his eye checkup, and he is disgusted with his body for choosing this morning to act up on him. Already they have had to put off the appointment several times because he has been so slow getting back on his feet after the bout of the flu just a week after getting back from the trip to Russia.

His left leg doesn't seem to want to keep up, as he goes about his morning routine of checking his sugar level and giving himself his insulin shot. He walks unsteadily to the kitchen for breakfast. Fortunately, Katie is already in the kitchen, bustling about, and does not see him steady himself on the hallway wall. There, six more steps and he will be in his chair.

"Henry, you're walking funny. What's the matter with you?" There is alarm in Katie's voice. This is exactly what he does not want. She is already upset enough by the prospect of the eye operation, even though he has explained that thousands of people have them, and there's nothing to it.

"It's nothing Katie. My leg just feels like it's gone to sleep."

"Prob'ly slept on it funny," she says, sitting down heavily.

They bow their heads as Henry asks God for His blessing for the day and gives thanks for the food.

Breakfast is eaten in silence. Katie notices that Henry is having difficulty with the simplest tasks, and his coffee cup shakes more than usual. She hovers over him.

"You're not eating again, Henry," she clucks. "You better have a another piece of toast."

A puddle of coffee moistens the tablecloth as he sets his cup down, and she hurries to get the dishcloth from the kitchen sink. "You're shaking bad this morning, Henry," she says. "What's the matter with you? Aren't you feeling good?"

A train rumbles by two blocks away, its whistle piercing the morning stillness.

"Quit your fussing," grumbles Henry, pushing back his empty cereal bowl.

He takes the big German Bible from the little corner table for their morning reading. Ever since he's had to fuss with the insulin and eat right on time they've done their readings after breakfast.

Fortunately, the script is large enough, and the text familiar enough for him to still be able to read it. Beyond this, his reading has stopped because his eyes are so bad. "Psalm 68," he says, "A Psalm of David. A song." Then, carefully, sometimes pausing to squint at a word, he begins to read.

> " . . . Sing to God, sing praises to His name;
> Cast up a highway for Him who rides through the deserts,
> Whose name is the Lord, and exult before Him.
> A father of the fatherless and a judge for the widows,
> Is God in His holy habitation.
> God makes a home for the lonely;
> He leads out the prisoners into prosperity,
> Only the rebellious dwell in a parched land. . . . ."
> Psalm 68:4-6

The words ring with familiarity and conviction. Henry hears the voice of a simple shepherd king, in the words of this ancient song. It is his song too.

About half-way through the Psalm, Henry stops reading. His movements are slow as he puts away the Bible. Katie bustles about clearing up the breakfast dishes.

They have just finished cleaning up the kitchen when Myrna is at the door to take her father-in-law for his ten o'clock appointment. She notices his left leg dragging as he coaxes it one step at a time towards the door, and doesn't like the ashen color of his face.

"Are you feeling okay, Dad?" She takes his arm to help steady him.

"I'm fine," he says, brushing by her to walk on his own. He is embarrassed by all this commotion. It's bad enough to have to be chauffeured around, without having them fussing over his health too. He would rather just be driving himself to his appointment. Everybody fusses too much. The doctor says he's not allowed to drive, but he drives the five blocks to church and can see well enough. Any driving required beyond that, Katie and the children gang up on him and won't allow him to do it.

He is quiet as they drive to Edmonton, choosing instead to lean his head against the headrest with his eyes closed. The strange feeling is not going away. If anything, it is getting worse. He feels woozy.

By the time they are at the hospital entrance where Myrna wants to let him out, he cannot get out of the car by himself. He cannot make his body obey his commands.

Myrna tries to help him, but he is like a rag doll and she eases him back into the car and runs into the hospital.

"Get a wheelchair down here," Myrna calls to the girl at the information desk, "and hurry!" She runs back out to the car.

"Dad, what's going on?" she asks, thoroughly alarmed.

"I don't feel too good," mumbles Henry thickly.

An orderly appears with a wheelchair and they help Henry into it.

"Are you feeling dizzy, or what?" Myrna asks as they wheel him through the doors. He does not respond.

"We're just here for an appointment with his eye specialist," says Myrna to the orderly, "and now I don't know what's happening. He wasn't acting right all the way here."

A doctor is hastily summoned. He takes one look at Henry and orders him taken to intensive care immediately.

"What do you think it is, doctor?" asks Myrna, hurrying to

keep up as they head for an elevator.

"I'm not sure," he replies, "could be a stroke, or a heart attack. We'll be able to check it out when we get him up to the ward." The doctor keeps checking Henry's pulse and his heart rate as they ride up the elevator.

"Dad," Myrna bends over him. "Dad, can you hear me?" Still there is no response. He is slumped in the wheelchair, but his eyes are open. He does not seem to be in pain.

Myrna is asked to stay in the waiting room just outside the room where Henry is taken. She paces, praying for God to take charge of whatever's going on in there. By now, she tells herself, she should be used to these emergencies with her father-in-law, but no matter what, she's never ready for them.

Inside the intensive care unit Henry is laid on a bed and hooked up to monitors. His vital signs are taken. It looks as though he is having a stroke.

He has been there only a few minutes when, without warning, the EEG goes flat. The room is suddenly in chaos.

"One! One! One!" The urgent call goes out over the hospital's public address system. Feet and hands fly.

Henry is unaware of the commotion around him. He feels himself propelled effortlessly, as though he were on a moving sidewalk floating towards a light. He is in a beautiful place such as he has never imagined. He knows a joy and a peace beyond description. It is as though all his life he has been longing and searching for this place. There is no loneliness, no desolation here.

Gradually, the motion stops. He is outside the gates. He cannot see through them, but he knows what is beyond. A lifetime of longing wells up in his throat. He is going home at last! He waits in breathless anticipation for the man at the gate to open it.

"Why don't you open the gate?" asks Henry impatiently. There is nothing else that he wants anymore, only to go through.

"I cannot open the gate just yet," is the gentle reply. "You will have to wait a little longer."

Henry looks at him in astonishment and disbelief. He is so very near. And now he is not being allowed to go in? A lifetime of searching, of going back to a lost and broken past, flashes before his eyes. Here, within reach is all the wholeness, and the home he has ever hoped and longed for, and he is being turned away? Rejected again?

And then, just as suddenly as he has come, he feels himself going back along the smooth, bright path, through the beautiful meadow. . . .

. . . . .

"Stand back," the doctor orders. "Now!"

A second jolt of electricity surges through Henry's body. Tentatively, the needle on the monitor begins to flutter, gradually gaining strength. There is a collective sigh of relief in the room.

"Henry. Henry." The doctor says urgently. "Can you hear?"

And then Henry is back, groping through the fog of unconsciousness towards the voice that is calling him back. His eyes flutter, and he is able to make out the faint lines of a face.

"Welcome back," smiles the doctor, relieved. "We lost you for a minute there. How do you feel?"

Henry struggles to speak, but his tongue feels thick and uncooperative. There are no words to express how he feels.

The doctor sees him struggle. "Don't exert yourself," he commands. "We can talk later. I just want you to squeeze my hand when you feel me squeeze you."

Henry nods. That he can do.

He feels the doctor squeeze his right hand and squeezes back feebly. He does not feel the doctor's pressure on his left hand. The doctor continues his probing and testing. He is more convinced than ever that Henry has suffered a slight stroke. But he cannot find an explanation for why his heart stopped.

The doctor pats his arm. "You rest now Henry. You're going to be fine."

# 35

# HOME FOR CHRISTMAS

Several weeks go by and Henry's life seems to hang in the balance. Several times, the doctor calls the family to tell them that his condition has turned very grave and that they should come. Then he rallies, and he is talking about going home again.

His left side is still weak, but he is working to regain the use of his left hand and leg. There are days he even feels well enough to have a therapist come in and work with him.

"When can I go home?" he asks the doctor.

"Oh," the doctor chuckles. "It's going to be a while yet."

September has been slipping by, and for Henry's liking, his progress is much too slow. Now, to complicate matters, he seems to have developed some kind of black-outs that send the doctors and nurses scurrying, and bring his entire family, grim-faced and worried, to the hospital.

Today is one of those days, and Henry is doing his level best to calm all their fears and put a stop to all the fretting.

Katie is sitting in a chair nearest him close to tears, and Genevieve, his daughter-in-law, is beside her. Dennis, her husband, is sitting at the foot of the bed, shifting uncomfortably in the chair. It doesn't seem to help telling them that he's fine and that they should be at work instead of fussing over him.

A young doctor walks purposefully into the room. "How are you feeling, Mr. Huebert?" giving him a critical once-over.

"I'm fine," replies Henry, "but I can't seem to convince anybody."

"Well," answers the doctor, taking his pulse, "you gave us all a pretty good scare again last night."

Henry chuckles. "Maybe I did, I can't remember, but I feel fine now." He pauses, his eyelids fluttering, "I want you to send me home."

The doctor looks at him, trying to pick up on the joke, but realizes he is serious.

Henry continues. "Katie and I are real good at looking after things," he says to the doctor. He is not on the lung ward this time, and the doctor is new. It's going to take a little doing to get him to come around to his way of thinking, but he is a patient man. Has to be.

The doctor shakes his head. "You're a sick man, Mr. Huebert."

His three visitors have been sitting quietly listening to the exchange. Now Dennis throws his vote with the doctor.

"You just listen to your doctor," he says firmly. "He'll know when you're well enough to go home."

Katie puts a trembling hand on Henry's arm. "You know I want you home Henry," she says softly, "but you don't look so good. Do like the doctor says."

He can see that he is badly outnumbered. The worst of it is, he can't even remember the black-out, or whatever it is that happened during the night to scare everybody half to death. The truth is he doesn't feel very well, and is trembling and tired, but then he is used to not feeling well. Apparently they all must think he's dying. How else would you explain all the kids here again all at one time, when they should be at work. Usually, they work it out so they take turns, and they come after work. It seems like everybody around here knows about his heart stopping on him when he first came in, and it's got the doctors and nurses kind of jumpy.

Now, because of his black-out last night, the kids have been notified again, and some of them have been here all day and are out in the waiting room, and Dennis and Genevieve have just arrived.

"I'd like to meet with the family in a few minutes," the doctor says to Katie, Dennis and Genevieve. "We can meet in the little room down near the lounge area," he declares. And then he is gone.

Fred and Norma Bergen step off the hospital elevator and

walk down the hall and through the doors to the ward where Henry has recently been transferred. It is mid-afternoon, and they are not expecting Henry to have any visitors, so have decided to stop in for a little while.

They see Wilmer and Myrna, and Rudy and Marilyn sitting in the waiting area. "Is something wrong?" asks Norma, trying to swallow her alarm. "What are you all doing out here?" Her words tumble out on top of each other before she has time to think about what she really wants to ask. All she can think about is that it's the middle of the afternoon, when Wilmer and Rudy are usually at work. And they aren't in the room visiting their father. There are no tears. They don't look as though someone has just died.

"Just taking a break," says Wilmer amiably. "We've been with Dad most of the day. Dennis and Genevieve just got here a little while ago, so they're with Dad right now. Mom's in there too."

"How is he?" asks Norma.

Wilmer shakes his head. "We're not sure. He gave everybody another scare last night, and they called the family. Brenda and Greg are driving out too."

"Maybe we should come back another time," Norma suggests to Fred, who has been standing quietly beside her.

"No," responds Wilmer before Fred can answer. "He'd want to see you. Mom too. Just go on in. We're just waiting for the doctor. He said he wanted to meet with us."

"You're sure?" asks Fred.

"Yeh. Go on."

They go down the hall but hesitate outside the open door, not knowing what to expect. If the family has been called, the man must be dying.

They walk into the room. There is a certain incongruity in the scene before them. Katie is obviously upset, and Dennis and Genevieve look serious as they sit at Henry's bedside. Henry, however, his face ashen grey and his body trembling, is sitting up in his bed, his splotchy feet crossed in front of him, visiting.

Katie turns to look at the visitors and begins to weep quietly. Norma goes to her, puts her arms around her and they hold each other.

Fred makes the rounds, shaking hands with everyone else, and hellos are said.

"I didn't expect to find you sitting up in bed," says Norma, giving Henry's hand a squeeze.

"Last night nobody was sure he'd even be here today," says Genevieve before he can answer. "We're lucky to have him." Her eyes are suddenly wet and shiny.

"I don't die that easy," Henry says, trying to lighten the mood.

They talk for a few minutes about the strange occurrences of the night before, and of Henry's unusual hospital stay during the past few weeks, but no one has given them any details or explanations.

Dennis gets up. "We're supposed to meet with the doctor," he says, moving towards the door, "maybe he'll tell us more. You go ahead and visit. We'll be back a little later."

They have no sooner left, than the doctor is poking his head around the door. "Are you family?" he asks, looking at Fred and Norma. "I'd like to meet with the family for a few minutes."

Fred and Norma both open their mouths to explain that they are just friends visiting.

"Yes, they're family," interrupts Henry quietly. Fred and Norma look at him, startled. His eyelids flutter momentarily, "But the ones you want are already out there waiting for you."

The words echo in the poignant silence after the doctor leaves the room, and Fred and Norma's eyes meet Henry's.

In all the time they have known him, there has never been a word or gesture to tell them how he feels towards them, just a tightly guarded silence, which slowly, painfully has broken up over time, in the shared fragments of his past as they visit with him, and in his tenacious presence whenever they drop in.

They are overcome now, with the force of the softly spoken words coming from a man who has never used the word "family" lightly.

Henry is fully aware of what he has just said. Lately he has begun to feel that family is sometimes more than blood-relatives. He feels richer for having discovered it, and glad that he has finally been able to tell Fred and Norma how much they mean to him. But he cannot risk having them get sentimental on him.

"How do you like that," says Henry, with a grin, "now they even tell you when they're going to be talking about you behind your back." The comment has the desired effect

His visitors chuckle. "It doesn't matter," says Norma, "No matter what they say, you're going to get well and go home before they think you're ready."

. . . . .

And by Christmas time, Henry does just that. He is home before the doctors think he should be. Christmas is a quiet affair, with Henry and Katie going over for just a few hours to Rudy and Marilyn's, where everyone has gathered.

"We didn't even put up no tree," Katie complains when Norma phones her. "But it doesn't pay for just us two." It's the first time that none of the festivities has taken place at their house, and she is a little sad.

"Oh well," she confides to others, "at least I have my Henry home. Maybe next Christmas he'll feel good enough so we can have the family home for Christmas like we usually do." She sighs. "I'm no good no more either," she lowers her voice in confession, "the girls do most of the work you know."

It is late January when Fred and Norma, along with Norma's father, who has been with them since Christmas, are invited for a Sunday afternoon visit. Several of Henry and Katie's elderly friends have dropped by during the course of the afternoon. They shake their heads to find Henry doing as well as he is after his "close call".

Katie has laid out the *Vesper* in the dining room that is used only on very special occasions. A hand-embroidered table cloth, edged in crocheted lace, graces the table, and the table is set with her best Sunday dishes.

She has baked *Zwieback* and has taken the last of her *Hirschenzalts Kuchen* from the freezer for the lunch. Several kinds of homemade jams and pickles, plus cheese round out the repast. Her hands shake as she pours the coffee in the kitchen. Norma carries the cups to the dining room.

Henry sits at the foot of the table beside Katie. Norma's father has been given the honored place at the head. He is the one who is asked to say the grace, and his prayer includes thanksgiving for Henry's improving health.

The food is passed and conversation flows easily, coming around finally, to Henry's most recent illness and his four-month hospital stay. He has regained almost full use of his left side, he tells them.

Katie is looking at him significantly. He ignores her, talking about how unsure the doctors were at first, whether or not he was actually having a stroke, and still not being completely sure what it was, since there wasn't the usual reaction.

He talks about how, once they had him in the hospital, his lungs had flared up again and he ended up with pneumonia.

"Of course," he concludes, "I'm an odd case anyway. My lungs got wrecked way back in the Revolution. If I'd had proper care then, they could have cured it, but I was never treated for the disease. They thought I had T.B."

"Henry," Katie cannot contain herself any longer, "tell them what happened when you first got to the hospital."

Everyone is listening.

"There's not much to tell," mutters Henry, visibly embarrassed. "Pass the cookies around, will you Fred," he continues. "You haven't had any yet."

"There is too," she says, not to be denied. She turns to Norma, sitting just around the corner from her. "He died," she says dramatically.

Norma looks from Katie to Henry. "He what?" she asks incredulously.

"Tell them, Henry," Katie urges.

"You can tell them," he says.

She shakes her head in disgust, then takes a deep breath.

"Henry was supposed to get his eyes checked," she begins self-consciously, "so Myrna picked him up and drove him. He's not supposed to drive, you know. His eyes are terrible." She shakes her head and takes another breath.

"I could tell already before they left, something was wrong. He wasn't acting right." She pauses, throwing Henry a furtive glance. "He was having trouble with his walking. By the time they got to the hospital, he was doing real bad. They got him to lie down, and then all of a sudden his heart stopped." Tears spring to her eyes.

"You tell them, Henry," she whispers, wiping her eyes with the corner of her apron.

"Well," he says reluctantly, "I don't remember nothing about that, except all of a sudden I was moving, like on a conveyor, or a sidewalk, smooth like, towards a bright light." He hesitates, looking dubiously at the guests around the table. "It happens to a lot of people," he says, trying to close the subject.

"Tell them what you saw Henry," Katie urges, her voice quivering with emotion.

"It was a beautiful place, peaceful," he clears his throat nervously, "and then I was at a big gate."

Everyone has stopped eating, and is listening incredulously. This is something you read about, but it doesn't happen to anyone you know.

"I thought I was going to go in," he continues softly, "but the man at the gate wouldn't open it. I said to him, 'Why don't you open the gate?' And he said he couldn't let me in yet. I had to wait a little while longer." He pauses again, catching his breath, but showing no emotion. "And then I felt myself coming back, and the doctors and nurses were working on me."

He stops. There is absolute, stunned silence in the room.

"That's it," he says with finality, picking up his china coffee cup. His hands are trembling.

"They didn't want my Henry," Katie speaks so quietly she is almost whispering. "Why do you think they didn't want to let him in?"

"It wasn't time yet, that's all," declares Henry firmly. And then to Katie under his breath, "It's nothing."

"Well, I want him," she says. "I'm glad you came back to me, Henry." Again the tears moisten her eyes, and she dabs them with her apron.

Henry's bravado does not fool Norma. Somewhere behind that stone wall of reserve is a well of emotion waiting to come out. After a pause, Norma asks, "How did you feel when the man wouldn't let you in?"

Henry looks at her intently for a moment, then looks away.

297

"Like anybody would feel I guess, when he's not allowed to go home," he says off-handedly. His voice betrays nothing of the anguish he is feeling, but the poignant words reverberate through the stunned silence.

"How about some coffee, Jake?" says Henry, trying to break the uncomfortable silence. "Katie . . ."

Katie pushes back her chair. "I'm getting it."

"Don't get up," says Norma, "I'll get it."

She goes into the kitchen.Dusk is settling over the town as she stands for a moment at the kitchen window, watching the snow swirl in phantom patterns as a car drives by. She can hear the conversation in the next room return to a comfortable ebb and flow, like the snow outside.

In her mind's eye, Norma sees a little boy alone, running, struggling and searching his whole life for that elusive home to which he, Henry Rempel, really belongs. She sees him outside the gate, only a breath away from finally having his life-long dream come true. His real mother and father, along with his sister Anna, and who knows which of the others, wait for him just beyond the gate, and he is turned away. . . .

As Norma comes back into the room his words echo in her ears like the plaintive tones of a sad, unfinished melody. Now Katie is speaking. The sadness is gone, and her voice has a cheerful ring to it.

"Henry says we're going to Paraguay, or maybe Germany next summer." Katie looks at him for affirmation.

"God willing and we live," he affirms, with the slightest hint of a smile. He hears the music of hope in her words. It is a song they share—have always shared.

"A lot of Mennonites are coming out of Russia," explains Katie. "He's hoping to find somebody yet."

Henry's eyes travel over the faces of his friends around the table. For an orphan, he has surely been blessed. He has not always realized it, but he is part of a very large, very real family. Still, there is a little lost boy somewhere inside, whose promise to himself to track down his brothers and sisters cannot be denied. The truth is he is still hoping to find somebody. He takes a deep breath.

probably long gone." He pauses. "But I guess it can't hurt trying."

# EPILOGUE

---

"Through all eternity to Thee
A joyful song I'll raise;
For O, eternity's too short
To utter all Thy praise."

Joseph Addison

On November 8, 1989, the gatekeeper opened the gate for Henry Rempel Huebert, and welcomed him home. His search through the broken fragments of his past for a part of himself, for lost family members and for the real meaning of family and home is finally over.

Perhaps it is significant that Henry's search ended only one day after the date that marks the beginning of the Russian Revolution; an event in history that would change forever the lives of thousands and thousands of people and leave in its wake scores of orphaned children like Henry Rempel.

Henry died as he lived, thinking of his family. His last moments were spent working on a deacon's bench that was to be a Christmas present for his first great-grandchild.

In honour of Henry's life-long concern for homeless children, the family designated the Gwynne Children's Home as the recipient of memorial gifts.

Henry Rempel Huebert's life was a song of hope and despair, of joy and sorrow, and ultimately, of triumph in the face of death under whose shadow he had lived.

His song lives on in the many wooden articles he made, in the example of his firm faith in God, in the songs he sang and in the understated but detailed story he shared.

# GLOSSARY

Words are indicated as follows:
High German (H.G.), Low German (L.G.) and Russian (R.).

Abendbrot (H.G.) - evening meal
Ach mein (H.G.) - Oh dear
Ach, min Kjint (L.G.) - Oh my child
Ältester (H.G.) - elder, leading minister
Akjstow (L.G.) - corner room
Alendich (L.G.) - sickly, miserable

Bezprizornii -(R.) - the wild children; homeless orphans living on city streets
Bitte (H.G.) - please
Burzhuazii (R.) - bourgeois or capitalists
Bruder (H.G.) - brother

Christkind (H.G.) - Christ child

Dangscheen (L.G.) - thank-you
Da svidanja (R.) - until we meet again
Der Christbaum ist der schönste Baum (H.G.) - literally, the Christ tree is the most beautiful tree.
*Die Mennonitische Rundschau* (H.G.) - a Mennonite magazine, literally "The Mennonite Look-about"
Droschka (R.) - a four-wheeled wagon used by the Mennonites, often very light, almost a platform on wheels with springs.

Elendig (H.G.) - sickly

Faspa (L.G.) - late afternoon lunch
Fleischperschji (H.G.) - a small bun filled with ground beef
Friedhof (H.G.) - cemetery

Gauns vemukat (L.G.) - completely emaciated
Gavnjok (R.) - little turd
Geschwister (H.G.) - siblings, brothers and sisters
Glasnost (R.) - openness, transparency
*Glaubensstimme* (H.G.) - a hymnbook used among the early Mennonites
Grootestow (L.G.) - living room; literally, big room
Grosser Gott (H.G.) - great God

Grossestube (H.G.) - great room; living room; literally large room
Gottlose (H.G.) - Godless
Gott sei dank (H.G.) - thank God; God be praised.
Grüben (H.G.) - cracklings
Goondach (L.G.) - good-day
Gutentag (H.G.) - good-day


Hammerklavier (H.G.) - piano
Hanjenomena Russejung (L.G.) - adopted Russian boy
Himmlischer Vater (H.G.) - Heavenly Father
Hirschensaltz Kuchen (H.G.) - a soft, traditional peppermint cookie
Hof (H.G.) - yard
Hop, hop, hop, hop, hop, Pferdchen lauf galopp - (H.G.) a nursery rhyme song
    meaning "Hurry little horse, take me out into the world so I can follow my dreams"


Ihr Kinderlein kommet (H.G.) - O come little children


Jetzt kommen sie. Wollen wir alles schnell weg schaffen. (H.G.) They're coming now.
    Let's hurry and hide everything.
Jungendverein Abend (H.G.) - youth evening in church


Kchortu van (R.) - to the devil with you (plural)
Kirchlich (H.G.) - term used for the General Conference Mennonites with whom the
    M.B.'s had some differences in Russia
Kjinja (L.G.) - children
Kjinjamäatje (L.G.) - babysitter; literally, children's girl.
Kjleena Kjnirps (L.G.) - pip-squeak
Komm mien Kjind (L.G.) - come my child
Komm Herr Jesu sei unser Gast und segne was du us bescheret hast (H.G.) - Come
    Lord Jesus be our guest and let this food to us be blest. (A common table grace)
Kopjek (R.) - a great many of the small coins
Kopjeka (R.) - singular for the small coin equal to 1/1000 of a ruble.
Kopjeki (R.) - a few small coins each equal to 1/100 of a ruble
Kringel (H.G.) - a fancy, twisted bun
Kugeln (H.G.) - colorful balls used for decorating the Christmas tree
Kulak (R.) - a rich or middle class farmer who was alleged to be exploiting his workers;
    it literally means "fist"


Ladawoage (L.G.) - farm wagon with ladders added to increase load capacity
Leiterwagen (H.G.) - farm wagon with ladders added to increase load capacity


Mädchenschule (H.G.) - junior high school for girls
Mal' chik (R.) - little boy
Mariechen sasz auf einem Stein (H.G.) - Mary sat on a stone
Meddach (L.G.) - noon meal
Mein Schatz (H.G.) - my sweetheart; literally, my treasure


Nätklos (L.G.) - Santa Claus
Nemetskie burzhuazija (R.) - German capitalists. When the German-speaking people
    first came, they were referred to as nemetskie (people who speak gibberish)

Nemetskie gavnjoki (R.) - gibberish-speaking turds
Njet (R.) - no

Oba uk (L.G.) - an exclamation, like "Oh no."
Onkel (H.G. & L.G.) - term of respect used for an older man, also meaning uncle or Mr.

Perestroika (R.) - progress
Perschkji (R.) - a term borrowed from the Russian and used to refer to meat or fruit-filled pastry.
Pfeffernuese (H.G.) - peppernuts, a traditional Mennonite Christmas cookie
Pflaumenmus (H.G.) - a fruit soup made with plums and often other fruit
Plautdietsche Menist (L.G.) - a Low German Mennonite (low class is implied)
Platz (H.G.) - a dough base topped with fruit
Plautz (L.G.) - a dough base topped with fruit
Pojas (R.) - belt
Prips (L.G.) - postum, sometimes made from roasted barley
Provodnik (R.) - attendant
Pud (R.) - a measure of weight 18 kg. or 40 lbs.

Reppspa (L.G., H.G) - deep-fried spare ribs
Rundschaukel (H.G.) - circular swing
Rundschokel (L.G.) - circular swing
Russejung (L.G.) - Russian boy
Russekot (L.G.) - Russian shack

Samogon (R.) - homebrew
Samovar (R.) - a metal urn with an internal tube for heating water in making tea
Schien (L.G.) - machine shed
Schinkenfleisch (H.G.) - ham
Schlorre (L.G.) - footwear, often a wooden platform with leather across the top of the foot to keep them on
Schrug (L.G.) - a horse of poor quality
Schultebott (L.G.) - a village assembly or discussion
Schups (L.G.) - hair worn in a bun
Selbstschutz (H.G.) - self-defence, local militia raised by the Mennonites during the civil war
Singe (L.G.) - sing
Sommerstube (H.G.) - summer kitchen, often a separate shed or shack
Spielabend (H.G.) - an evening of music-making
Spasibo (R.) - thank-you
Stille Nacht (H.G.) - Silent night
Stille Nacht, Heilige Nacht, alles schläft, einsam wacht (H.G.) - Silent night, holy night, all is calm, all is bright
Sukin' syn (R.) - son-of-a-bitch
Svolotchi (R.) - swine

Tante (H.G.) - a term of respect for an older woman, also aunt or Mrs.
Tante Mariechen (H.G.) - Aunt Mary
Toom aundenkje (L.G.) - as a keepsake
Trauermahl (H.G.) - a fellowship luncheon after a funeral

303

Tweeback (L.G.) - a double-decker white bun; literally, two-bake

Vaterland (H.G.) - fatherland
Vekomna Russe Jung (L.G.) - literally, a bedraggled Russian street urchin
Vemukat (L.G.) - emaciated
Verscht (L.G.) - Russian measure of distance; 1,0668 km or .663 miles
Verst (H.G.) - Russian measure of distance; 1.0668 km or .663 miles
Vesper (H.G.) - late afternoon coffee or tea time
Vorhaus (H.G.) - front entry

Weihnachtsbaum (H.G.) - Christmas tree
Weihnachtsmann (H.G.) - Santa Claus
Weihnachtswunsch (H.G.) -a short recitation; literally, Christmas wish
Willkommen (H.G.) - welcome
Wirtschaft (H.G.) - property with buildings
Wollen wir schnell alles weg schaffen (H.G.) - Let's hurry and hide everything
Wurst (H.G.) - farmer sausage

Zentralschule (H.G.) - high school
Zhid  (R.) - Jew, used as a racist slur
Ziltfleisch (H.G.) - head cheese
Zwieback (H.G.) - double-decker white buns
Zavedushchii (R.) -  an administrator